HARD TIDE

BLACKSTONE HOUSE
BOOK 2

ELISE NOBLE

Published by Undercover Publishing Limited

v3

ISBN: 978-1-912888-61-0

Edited by Nikki Mentges, NAM Editorial

Cover design by Elise Noble

www.undercover-publishing.com

www.elise-noble.com

Time and tide wait for no man.

CHAPTER 1
ARI

"Get your hand off my thigh."

"Nobody has to know."

Seriously, he thought *that* was my concern? I'd heard on the grapevine that Dale Jankowski, my boss, had wandering hands and a wandering cock too, but until now, I'd never experienced the "pleasure" for myself. Probably because I'd made sure to wear pants every day and avoided smiling, small talk, and make-up. Boring low ponytail, flat shoes, clothes in fifty shades of beige—that was me.

I'd also heard that some women liked his attention—Jankowski might have been in his early fifties, but he kept in shape, and as the boss of the Twilight Agency, he was quite the catch. His third wife had certainly thought so when she married him two months ago. Not one but six hotel residents had complained about the noise coming from the honeymoon suite, or so I'd been told.

"I'm not interested."

His right hand stayed in place, and he used his left to sweep the bangs away from my eyes. A chill ran up my spine. During the daytime, Jankowski lorded over his peons, slightly obnoxious but tolerable. In the five months I'd been working at Twilight, I'd grown used to his demanding management style and learned to live with it, but this was the first time I'd visited his office late in the evening. I'd only meant to drop off a report, but he'd asked me to sit down and talk him through the details, and I could hardly decline. He did pay my salary, after all. So I'd done as requested, and I was certain he hadn't listened to a word I'd said. No, his mind had been on other things. When I'd asked if he had any questions, he'd risen from his fancy leather swivel chair, walked around his desk, and perched a butt cheek on the polished walnut.

"You fascinate me, Arizona. Such a pretty face, and a great ass too, yet you keep it hidden under those dowdy clothes."

"I need to go home." I waved toward the file I'd just dropped onto his desk and pushed my chair back, freeing myself from his touch. "If you need more information, it's all in the report."

"Ah, yes, home to your daughter. Everybody warned me not to hire a single mother for this job, but I saw something in you that they didn't."

The chill turned to full-on ice.

"Really? And what was that?"

He leaned in close, so close that his lips brushed my ear. "Desperation."

I slapped him before I could stop myself, and I would've knocked his teeth out too, if he hadn't swung me around and slammed me backward onto his desk. Blunt pain radiated through my head as I tried to gather my thoughts.

"Now, now," he chided. "I like a girl with fight in her, but there's a time and a place."

"Get your filthy hands off me!"

"So demanding. You need to learn to negotiate, Arizona. When somebody else holds all the cards, there has to be a little give and take."

"Let me guess—I give, and you take."

"Coulson was right. You *are* a smart girl."

Morty Coulson had been my old boss, right until his forty-a-day habit caught up with him. He'd wheezed his denial for years, and by the time I finally convinced him to see a doctor, it was too late. Coulson Investigations was no more, and I'd been forced to take a new job. Twilight was the second-biggest investigations agency in Las Vegas, with a fancy office building downtown and a client list that included half of the big casinos. But the glossy brochures and slick sales patter hid a culture of filth.

Why hadn't I quit? Because jobs for a twenty-seven-year-old recently qualified private investigator with an eight-year-old daughter weren't easy to come by, especially when that investigator had breasts. And I had rent to pay. Out of the two job offers I'd received, only Jankowski paid enough to cover the bills.

And it wasn't just the cash; it was the reputation. People *aspired* to work here. Mostly men, I realised that now. Jankowski had probably hired me because he was running out of secretaries to molest.

But I refused to be his next piece of ass. If I let him take advantage of me now, the sleaziness would never stop, and no job was worth sacrificing my dignity over. Even scrubbing the private rooms at Sin City's seediest strip joint would be a better option.

So when he tried to unbutton my shirt, I gave him one last chance.

"Stop."

"Make me, sweetheart."

His eyes bulged when my knee connected with his groin, and he let out a satisfying *oof*.

"Coulson also taught me how to defend myself, pervert."

"You... You're..."

"And don't bother to fire me because I quit."

Jankowski collapsed to the floor, alternately groaning and

spewing curses as I scrabbled around for the purse I'd dropped when he grabbed me.

"You stupid little bitch! You'll never work in this town again, you hear me? Never!"

"And you'll never father children."

I marched out with my head held high as he retched behind me, and it wasn't until I reached the sidewalk outside that the reality of what had just happened hit me. And the horror. I had six hundred dollars in the bank, I'd lost my job, and I'd alienated one of the most powerful men in Las Vegas.

Fuck.

Fast forward a month, and during that time, I'd used up most of my overdraft and called every investigations firm in Clark County. Every. Single. One.

And I had to concede that Jankowski had kept his word— I'd been blackballed by ninety-five percent of them. None of the remaining five percent were hiring, although Blackwood —the biggest—had at least promised to keep ahold of my résumé and call if there was an opening. Fat chance. Nobody ever quit a job at Blackwood.

I'd even tried a few law firms, although thanks to the rumours spread by my ex—Haven's father—they didn't care for me either. When you messed with a senior partner from Mathison, Howard and Suker, his former peers tended to give you a wide berth.

Well, he should have paid his child support.

And also not embezzled funds from his clients.

In the past week, I'd spread the net wider, hunting for a temporary job to tide me over until I could fight my way back into my chosen field. The manager at Lonnie's Pizza had offered me a trial as a waitress, but I'd been let go three hours into my first shift after slapping a guy's hand away when he pinched my ass. Honestly, was it too much to ask to not be sexually assaulted at work? And how was I supposed to know the guy was the manager's brother?

Yesterday morning, I'd been turned down for a cleaning job at a strip joint because I was overqualified. Over-freaking-qualified. The manager said I'd just leave when I got a better offer, which was true, but sponging cum stains out of velvet banquettes was hardly a job for life, was it? As I walked out the door, he'd complimented my ass and offered me a job as a dancer. I'd carried on walking.

"How did the job hunting go today?" Nana asked as I closed the door behind me.

Truthfully? I was wondering whether pole dancing would be a feasible option.

"It could have gone better."

"Nobody called? How many of those flyers did you hand out?"

"Around two hundred so far."

At the end of April, temperatures in Vegas were already touching the nineties. Sweat dripped down my back, and our AC was out. Again.

"I gave fifty to Darlene Reacher. She knows everyone, and she promised to pass them around."

Yesterday, I'd had a thousand flyers printed. Black ink on pink paper, the colour scheme chosen partly because I was female but mostly because it was the cheapest option. The fuchsia paper wasn't a bestseller, the guy in the print shop told me. I could have it for half price.

An hour later, I'd walked out with an empty wallet. Call it hope, call it stupidity, but I couldn't give up on a career I'd worked so hard to succeed at. Not yet. Gaining my full PI licence had taken five years and ten thousand hours of investigative work.

DANNER INVESTIGATIONS
Experienced female investigator available
Licensed in Nevada, California, and Arizona
Undercover work a speciality
Good rates

So far, my phone had remained silent, and the only email had come from a guy who wanted me to find out the truth about Roswell. For free.

Maybe I shouldn't have put my gender on there? But Morty Coulson had always told me to be proud of who I was, and besides, spurned wives looking for help to nail their wayward husbands' balls to the wall sometimes felt more comfortable talking to another woman. And with my reputation trashed, the only way I was able to take work from pricks like Jankowski was to offer something they couldn't: two X-chromosomes. But still the phone was dead.

Nana had tried to stay positive since I confessed what I'd done, and she even congratulated me for standing up for myself, but I could tell she was worried. The wrinkles around her eyes had gotten deeper, and she'd been cleaning constantly. Our one-bedroom apartment in East Las Vegas was tiny, but every inch was spotless. If she polished any harder, she'd wear right through the floor. On the good days, she preferred to sit in her favourite chair and knit, but the same half-made sweater had been sitting on the arm for weeks.

"Thank Darlene for me, okay? Tomorrow, I'm gonna hand out more flyers and start looking for another waitressing job."

"Will that pay enough?"

No, but if I worked extra shifts and cut down on everything but the absolute essentials, we'd be able to survive for a few more months. I conjured up a smile.

"We'll manage. I'll just have to hustle for tips."

"Back when you worked at Parlette's, the customers used to love you."

Perhaps "love" was too strong a word for it. Some of the regulars at the fancy French restaurant in Summerlin had liked me enough to screw me, one in particular. Maxwell Suker had eaten at Parlette's every Tuesday. Eighteen-year-old me had been flattered by the attention, blinded by the charms of a platinum credit card, and too dumb to realise that Tuesday was the evening his wife always went for a massage with her sister.

Never again. Never again would I be that stupid.

Thankfully, Parlette's had closed down after the owner had a run-in with the IRS, so I couldn't get tempted to repeat... Well, I couldn't call it the biggest error of my life because I'd ended up with Haven, but at the time, I'd been so scared. Only Nana had kept me sane through those early years of motherhood, and how had I repaid her? By losing our main source of income.

"I'll find a job." Somehow. "But it won't be at a place like Parlette's."

"Someday, you'll meet a good man."

"You don't really believe that." Her marriage to Grandpa had been far from rosy. I'd witnessed the arguments firsthand as I grew up. But despite men clearly being more trouble than they were worth, she was determined I shouldn't quit looking. "And besides, I don't have time to date at the moment."

"What about Kenneth from the grocery store? He always asks how you are."

"He's the cashier. That's literally part of his job."

"But he smiles so nicely when he says it."

"He's paid to do that as well."

"Nobody should have to go through life alone."

I saw an opportunity and seized it. "I'm not alone—I have

you and Haven. Now, what do you want for dinner? Pasta? Is Haven still refusing to eat anything but cupcakes?"

Cartoons had a lot to answer for. Haven's favourite character ran a bakery, and unless her food came bite-size and topped with frosting, she was on a hunger strike. Yesterday, Nana had baked dinner rolls into cupcake liners and piped squeezy cheese onto them in desperation.

"Today, I baked beetroot into the bread rolls and topped them with hummus."

I'd be lost without Nana. She spent her days running around after Haven instead of relaxing in what should have been her retirement, and although she assured me that she wouldn't have it any other way, guilt still ate at me. For years, my goal had been to earn enough money to send her on the trip to Paris she'd always dreamed of, but now I just wanted to stay above the breadline.

Or, in Haven-speak, the cupcakeline.

"Do you want me to take a turn at making her meals tomorrow?"

Nana patted me on the arm in that comforting way of hers. *Everything will be okay.* She'd been telling me that since I moved in with her—or rather, got dumped with her by my mom—when I was two years younger than my daughter was now.

"Ari, the two of us are just fine. Right now, finding a job is more important than you making dinner."

Yes, it was. I *had* to find work, and quickly.

CHAPTER 2
ARI

"Do you want fries and onion rings with that?" I asked.

"Sure do, darlin'. How's about givin' me your number too?"

Uh, no. And not only because the guy smelled like an ashtray and hadn't brushed his teeth this decade, but because the pale dent on his finger said he usually wore a wedding ring. And since my only two cases in the past eight weeks had both involved cheating spouses, I had no desire to add to Las Vegas's infidelity problem. Not to mention the fact that I'd sworn off men forever.

"Sorry, I'm already taken." When he leaned in closer, I resisted the urge to tell him what I really thought. Last week when I'd done precisely that to a man, the asshole had thrown a ketchup dispenser at me, and then I'd gotten a lecture from my boss on how the customer was always right. "Cheese and bacon on your burger?"

"Nobody needs to know."

What was it with these pricks? Had Clark Public Utilities started putting something in the water? *Smile, Ari. You need the tips.*

"About the cheese and bacon? No, sir. I'll keep very quiet regarding that."

I backed away before he could make any more inappropriate suggestions and glanced at the clock above the jukebox. Seven p.m. Five hours until my shift ended, and approximately five minutes before I lost the will to live.

But at least I had a job. It paid minimum wage, but I usually doubled that in tips, and I'd picked up a few regulars who always sat in my section. If I managed to steer clear of lecherous slimeballs, I might even make enough to pay for Haven's field trip next week. Oh, who was I kidding—she'd go to the petting zoo with the rest of the class even if I had to walk to work for a month instead of taking the bus. The exercise was good for my health. And at least my new boss let me take home all the leftovers I could eat.

I had to stay positive.

But sometimes, in the early hours of the morning when Haven was asleep, I'd shed a quiet tear for what I'd lost and what I'd never had. When I was my daughter's age, I'd longed to be an actress, a famous one with all the wealth and sparkles that came along with the job. After I'd played the wicked queen in a school production of *Snow White* at the grand old age of twelve, Nana had taken me to an audition at one of the big hotels on the Strip to get a head start on my dream, but in reality, I'd been given an early lesson in disappointment. I'd never told a soul, but I overheard the casting lady telling her assistant that I was "too chubby for the main role, not chubby enough to play the sidekick," and after I finished crying, I'd decided that Hollywood wasn't for me.

Teenage Ari had gone on a diet, then tempered her ambitions to getting a college degree and a job in one of those glass-and-steel offices with the fancy coffee machine and a ping-pong table in the break area. Guess what? I hadn't managed that either.

I'd come close, though. At eighteen, I'd been enrolled in community college and studying business administration when I'd had the misfortune to meet Maxwell Suker. Nana had still been working then, we'd had a small but nice apartment in Lone Mountain, and on the weekends, I used to go rollerblading and hang out with my friends.

Then the condom broke.

Pregnancy had been terrifying, and as my bump began to show, my friends distanced themselves. But no matter what happened, I'd vowed to love my baby, planned or not. Not like my mother had done with me. I'd been an inconvenience, a burden, at least until she dropped me off with my grandparents for the day and never came back.

Three years ago, I'd grown curious and tracked her down. Did she feel guilty for abandoning me? Had she found herself in an impossible situation and felt unable to cope? Far from it. Our brief conversation still came back to haunt me every time I had a black moment.

"Yes?" she'd asked when she opened the door of her Florida condo. The place was tidy, modern, and mortgaged to the hilt.

I'd waited a moment for recognition to dawn, but there was nothing.

"Whatever you're selling, we don't want any."

"It's me, Arizona. Your daughter?"

She'd looked me up and down. "Oh. I see you finally lost the puppy fat."

Puppy fat? Yes, I'd been overweight as a child, but was that really all she had to say?

"Grandma enrolled me in ballet lessons. And I ran track in high school."

"That'll be your father's genes." Her lip curled in distaste. "He was a runner."

She wasn't lying—when Morty had grudgingly helped me to track down the man named on my birth certificate, we'd found him in the Washington State Penitentiary, serving forty-six years for drug trafficking and attempted murder. Fortunately, the undercover DEA agent he'd shot had survived. Thirty cops had chased Jackson Danner on foot through the backstreets of Seattle for almost half an hour before a police dog grabbed him by the ankle.

A runner.

No wonder Nana had never wanted to talk about him.

"Well, I guess you had that much in common," I told my mom.

She glanced at her watch. "Did you want something in particular? I don't have any money to give you."

That was why she thought I'd come? Money? I took in our surroundings—the manicured grounds, the shimmering pool, the polished floor and chandelier in the hallway behind her—and realised how much importance my mother placed on material things. Then there was her appearance. The designer clothes, the expensive haircut, the face covered in make-up despite the fact she was at home. None of it could be cheap to maintain, and all of it took precedence over her own flesh and blood.

So I walked away.

"No, I don't want anything in particular," I called over my shoulder. "I hope you have the life you deserve."

She'd shouted after me, but I hadn't stopped. Visiting had been a mistake, and one I wouldn't repeat.

At least my father had shown remorse for his wrongdoings, according to the trial transcript, anyway. My mom would choke on an apology. Secretly, I thought there'd been a mix-up at the hospital when she was born—how else could a lady as sweet as Nana have ended up with such a cold-hearted bitch for a daughter?

That was one mystery I'd never solve.

In the kitchen at the Big Bite Diner, the cook took a long pull on his beer and held out a hand for Mr. Tooth Decay's order. I handed the slip over just as my phone rang. *Unknown number.* Where was the boss? He hated us taking personal calls, but when I checked over my shoulder, he was behind the counter, flirting with a bottle blonde who probably charged by the hour. No other customers were waiting to be served.

"How long for the food?" I asked.

"Five minutes."

The cook wouldn't tell tales—he was a man of few words—so I slipped into the staff bathroom and locked the door. I was due a break anyway.

"Ari Danner speaking."

Please, don't let it be the landlord. The rent was only two days late, and I'd have enough cash to pay it by tomorrow.

"Are you the detective?" The caller was a woman, middle-aged at a guess. Local accent. She tried to hide the exhaustion in her voice, but there was a hint of raggedness around the edges. "Somebody passed me your flyer."

Could this be a client? I'd almost given up hope.

"Yes! I mean, that's me."

"It says you do undercover work."

"I do."

"We'd be interested in making an appointment to meet with you."

"We?"

"My boss."

"And who's your boss?"

"Is this level of detail really necessary?"

Tired, but pushy. A harried executive assistant with a degree of seniority?

"A name? Yes, it is."

"He told me to keep everything confidential."

"I can't meet with him if I don't know who he is."

"I'll give you the address."

"What's the meeting about?"

"He'll explain that when he sees you. Can you make nine a.m. tomorrow?"

She spoke with a prim entitlement that said she was used to getting her own way. Or, at least, her boss's. Who was he? With an address, I could find out, but I still wanted her to tell me. One of Morty Coulson's many snippets of wisdom echoed in my head. *If you let a client push you around at the beginning, they'll push you to the edge of your sanity.*

"I can make nine thirty." After I'd taken Haven to school. "But I'm gonna need a name first."

Silence.

Silence that stretched for so long that I worried I'd gone too far and she'd hung up.

But finally, she spoke.

"Digby Rennick." She read out an address downtown, repeating it twice as I scribbled on my order pad. "Nine thirty. I'll meet you in the lobby."

"Okay, I'll be there."

Digby Rennick? Unusual name. It only took me a minute to find his profile online, featured on several business websites. Digby St. John Rennick was a math genius who graduated from Harvard at the age of nineteen. He'd shot to fame after he collected a million bucks for solving a hideously complex mathematical problem called Baxter's Last Theorem, and then he'd gone on to start the world's fastest-growing gambling empire. Based in Las Vegas with a second office in Antigua, AnyBet LV, Inc. ran online gambling sites in those jurisdictions where it was legal, plus a network of sports betting lounges across the United States.

An old video showed teenage Rennick in college, bumbling his way through an acceptance speech after he won a mathematics award. Now, it seemed, he eschewed public appearances in favour of carefully staged magazine interviews and the occasional photoshoot.

Hammering from outside made the bathroom door shake.

"Ari, what're you doing in there?" my boss yelled. "Better not be drugs."

Shit. I quickly flushed the toilet. "Just coming."

He was waiting with a scowl when I hurried into the kitchen. Had his girlfriend gone off with a client?

"I pay you to wait tables, not to wipe your ass. The guy at table four wants more coffee."

"Sorry."

"And some kid dropped a milkshake on the floor."

Terrific. "I'll clear that up right away."

"And smile, Ari. Nobody likes a sourpuss."

Even the worst undercover job in the world was better than cleaning sticky milkshake off a grimy floor. The last time I'd been down there on my hands and knees, I'd found a dead cockroach under the table, and I swear a mouse ran across the kitchen counter last week.

Whatever Rennick wanted me to do tomorrow, I'd do it.

CHAPTER 3
ARI

AnyBet LV's global headquarters was a twelve-storey glass-and-steel monolith that towered over the AnyBet sports betting lounge next door. Inside, the marble-floored lobby was a study in cream and grey with low leather chairs clustered around a slate coffee table that held a neat stack of lifestyle magazines. Five bucks said none of them had ever been opened. The only splash of colour came from the huge vase of purple orchids on the oversized reception desk, and even the brunette seated behind it wore beige lipstick with French-tipped nails to go with her cream shift dress.

"May I help you?"

I'd worn a pantsuit, but I still felt woefully underdressed. "I'm here to meet... Actually, I don't know what her name is, but she works for Digby Rennick."

"We all work for Mr. Rennick."

"I meant, she's his assistant."

"Which one? He has two assistants, and neither of them mentioned an appointment this morning."

"She definitely said nine thirty."

Was I wasting my time here? The receptionist glared, and

we were about to get into a game of *who blinks first* when the elevator dinged behind me.

"Ms. Danner?"

"Yes?"

Was this the lady I was here to meet?

She studied me, assessing, while I did the same to her, although I liked to think I wasn't quite so obvious about my inspection. She was younger than I'd guessed, couldn't have been older than me, but she exuded a gravitas beyond her years. Twenty-five going on forty. She was probably two inches shorter than my five feet seven, but her high-heeled pumps meant she looked down on me. Finally, she nodded as if to say "you'll do" and held out one limp hand.

"Lila Margot."

Was Margot her surname? Or a middle name? "Arizona Danner."

"You're early."

Only by ten minutes, and wasn't being a little early a good thing? "Would you like me to go away and come back again?"

A pause, as if she was actually considering my slightly sarcastic offer.

"No, it's fine. We should go upstairs."

"To meet Mr. Rennick?"

"Yes."

She waved me toward the elevator and stood in silence as it ascended. Reflected in the mirrored wall, her face gave nothing away. This whole place was weird. Lila could have been the receptionist's twin—she wore the same low ponytail, the same snooty expression, and the same neutral colour palette, except her dress was grey instead of cream.

We emerged on the eleventh floor in a small anteroom, and I used the term "small" relatively since it was still bigger than my entire apartment. And emptier. Two grey desks faced each other on either side of imposing double doors. Did they lead to Rennick's office? Each desk held a monitor, a mouse, and a keyboard, and the larger one had a mug of coffee on a square of slate. No steam. It had been there for a while. A small tree stood in an oversized grey bowl in one corner, its twisted branches crowned with pom-poms of tiny green leaves. Some kind of giant bonsai? As with the lobby, there was only one hint of colour, this time from a clock mounted over the double doors, a cerise disc with zigzag hands and no numbers.

"Take a seat." Lila waved at a single metal chair beside the left-hand desk. "Your appointment isn't actually until ten, but you'll need to sign a non-disclosure agreement first."

NDAs were common in my line of work, but the setup still made me uncomfortable. Morty had taught me how to evaluate any situation, but I struggled to get a read on Lila, and her boss was still mostly a mystery. A reclusive multimillionaire obsessed with numbers was as far as I'd got. Digby Rennick didn't seem to have a family or any hobbies.

"Can you tell me *anything* about the job before I sign my life away?"

I'd intended it as a joke, but Lila didn't crack a smile. In a previous existence, she'd probably been a gargoyle.

"Please read the document through, initial each page, and then sign on the dotted line."

Part of me wanted to walk away, but my overdraft wouldn't let me. Plus there was my damn curiosity. Nosiness was as much a part of me as blood or skin, a blessing and a curse, Morty used to say. I *needed* to know why Rennick had summoned me here.

I signed.

Lila's mouth twitched at the corners, which seemed to be about as close to congeniality as she got.

"Thank you."

I nodded toward the double doors. "Should I go through now?"

"Mr. Rennick hates being rushed almost as much as he hates tardiness. Three minutes."

The zigzag hand swept around the giant clock with agonising slowness. *Tick, tick, tick.*

"Can you at least tell me why I'm here?"

Lila focused on her computer screen. "I'm afraid not."

Wouldn't or couldn't? From the way she avoided my gaze, I was inclined to believe it was the latter.

"You don't know, do you? Rennick hasn't told you why he wants to see me."

"That's *Mr.* Rennick."

Whatever. "I'm right, aren't I?"

Lila nibbled her bottom lip, leaving a smear of nude iridescent lipstick on perfectly white teeth. Nervous?

"I was instructed to find a private investigator with certain attributes."

"Which were?"

A long pause. Lila was fond of silence, wasn't she? Up in this ivory tower, we were insulated from the outside world, no music, no voices, no rumble of traffic. The only sound came from the damn clock ticking away, a countdown on my sanity.

"The investigator needed to be female."

Interesting. But there was more—she'd said attributes, plural.

"And?"

"In her twenties."

"And?"

"Uh… She had to look good in a bikini."

What? "I'm sorry?"

The lock on the double doors clicked, and Lila let out the breath she'd been holding. "You can go through now."

"Wait a freaking minute! Why does he want me to wear a bikini?"

"You need to go in." For the first time, Lila's voice held a hint of panic. "Please? And keep your voice down. He doesn't like noise."

Was this guy a fruitcake? Silence, secrecy, and swimsuits? What did he want me to do? Go undercover at a beauty pageant? Or a strip club?

Lila was halfway out of her chair, arms outstretched. What did she plan to do? Wrestle me into the inner sanctum? Entertaining as that might be, I didn't want to get escorted out by security. I'd had that pleasure enough times in my life already.

"I'm going, okay? But if I don't come out in twenty minutes, call the cops."

Again, no smile. At least I'd told Nana exactly where I was going and who I was meeting today, because I didn't trust Lila one bit. What kind of woman sat in a fancy prison cell each day, catering to the whims of a lunatic? No wonder we'd stopped on the eleventh floor—Rennick's elevator clearly didn't go all the way to the top.

I pushed on one dark-grey door, and it swung open on well-oiled hinges. Wow. This was…interesting.

CHAPTER 4
ARI

Inside, Rennick's lair was split in half. The left-hand side followed the same theme as downstairs, decor-wise—bland, beige, mostly empty—with a desk at the far end and a glass table surrounded by four squat stools in the middle. But the windows had been covered up, and the entire wall was decorated with handwritten letters and numbers. Mathematical graffiti. Some weird take on modern art? I thought so at first, but then I spotted the marker pens on Rennick's desk. No, he really did use the wall as a giant whiteboard.

The right-hand side of the room still had its windows. And it also had a zen garden. Fine gravel covered a sunken floor, with three rocks at one end and a fountain burbling away in a pool at the other. Digby Rennick stood in the middle, barefoot as he raked the stones.

"Uh, hi?"

He glanced up as if my presence were somehow a surprise, then aimed a remote at the doors. *Click.* I was trapped.

"Ms. Danner. Thank you for coming."

Rennick's biography said he was forty-four, but he looked

younger than me, tall and slender with the muscle tone of a desk jockey and curly brown hair two months past needing a cut. The gravel *shoosh*ed as he raked it into a complex pattern of swirls. *Shoosh, shoosh, shoosh.* Now I knew where Lila had gotten her penchant for long silences. Did this guy not understand that time was money? Probably not, since he had oodles of cash and his time was therefore more valuable than mine.

"Do you know how difficult it was to find the perfect rocks for this garden?" he asked.

Rocks were rocks, surely? "No?"

"A visit to Kyoto and consultation with two zen masters, plus I read the *Sakuteiki* in the original Japanese."

"The *Sakuteiki*?"

"The first known manual of Japanese gardening. My gravel was imported from Canada. Please, sit."

He waved toward his desk, and I hesitated because there was only one seat there—his grey leather swivel chair.

"Where?"

"The garden was designed to be viewed from a seated position behind my desk." He waited while I gingerly took a seat. "What do you think?"

"Very..." Boring? Grey? Dry? Stony? Freaking hell, what was I meant to say? "Very inspiring."

Rennick nodded, satisfied, and stepped out of the pit, tracking dusty footprints across the cavernous room as he headed for the meeting table. I rose and followed. Could we get to the point now? Because at this rate, I'd be late picking Haven up from school.

"Why did you ask me to come here, Mr. Rennick?"

I could've learned Japanese in the time it took him to reply.

"I have a problem."

No shit, Sherlock. "What kind of problem?"

"Somebody's cheating the system."

"The system? What system?"

"Are you familiar with the World Surf Tour?"

Huh? What did that have to do with anything? I might have caught a few minutes of it on TV as I channel-hopped—fools with a death wish risking shark attacks and serious injury as they careened down mountains of water protected only by their enormous egos.

"It's a surfing contest, right?"

"It's *the* surfing contest. Fifteen events, nine countries, forty-eight contestants—twenty-four men, twenty-four women—and a million bucks to the winner of each category. AnyBet is this year's headline sponsor."

"Congratulations?"

"My company prides itself on giving our clients the best odds, the best service, and the best betting experience. Our algorithms work in real time to protect our margins, but also to ensure that gamblers win big when it's deserved. We don't cheat because we don't need to. But somebody's cheating us."

A surfer? "And you want me to find out who?"

"We know who. We just need you to prove it. If word got out that AnyBet had not only accepted bets on a rigged event, but also that the event was one with our name splashed all over it, our reputation would suffer. Rivals are waiting to exploit any chink in our armour."

"You're gonna have to start at the beginning. Who's cheating, and how do you know it?"

"You signed the NDA?"

"Yes, I did."

Rennick fished the remote out of his pocket again, and a screen whirred down from the ceiling.

"Meet Zach Torres." A picture of a blond guy appeared, the subject shirtless as he surfed toward a crowd on the beach. "Last year, he finished the tour in third place, and the year before, he came second. We first began to suspect a problem halfway through that season."

"Why? What happened?"

"Torres was on fire. He won four events running, but during the seventh contest, the WST Teahupo'o Pro in Tahiti, we began to pick up on strange betting patterns. How familiar are you with the running of a sportsbook, Ms. Danner?"

"Honestly? I'd never thought about it before today."

"AnyBet makes its money in two ways. Firstly, through our lounges. Clients pay a premium for the experience, and food and drink sales are extremely profitable. Secondly, we offer gambling via our online sites. We actually have seventeen different brands under the AnyBet umbrella, tailored to local markets, but they all run the same software. And that's where we picked up the problem."

"Go on."

"Margins are thin in sports betting. We rely on volume. Let's say there are ten horses in a race, some more likely to win than others. Bet a dollar on the favourite, and you might get two dollars back if it wins. Bet a dollar on an outsider, and if the other contenders fall by the final fence, you'd get a lot more. But the odds are always adjusted so that if you bet proportionally on every horse in the race, we'll still win over time. Only four or five cents on every dollar, maybe six if we shade the lines, but we always win, and those cents add up."

"So how can Torres cheat?"

"Because if somebody knows for certain that one of those horses isn't going to win, it unbalances our calculations, and we lose."

Okay, that made sense. "And Torres knows he's not going to win, so he can, what? Bet on everybody else?"

"Exactly. And he's trying to be clever about it. The bets on the other competitors were spread across multiple accounts covering all of our brands, but when viewed together, there was a large anomaly. I was watching the numbers, and when

I saw the feed from the WST, I knew he'd throw the contest before he fell on the last run."

"It couldn't have been a coincidence?"

"I don't believe in coincidences. I believe in statistics and cold, hard data."

"How much money are we talking here? How much did you lose?"

"On that particular event? Fifty thousand dollars. Same on the next. On the third contest where Torres crashed out, eighty thousand. And last week at the J-Bay Open, we lost one hundred thousand dollars. Torres is getting bolder. And richer."

"You couldn't just… I don't know, not take the bets?"

"The clue is in the name—*Any*Bet. Any time, any place, any size. Our biggest marketing promise is that we never restrict a wager, unlike many of our competitors. Our proprietary software recalculates the odds in microseconds and ensures we make a consistent profit. We can adjust for late withdrawals, injuries, and social media stirs. The one thing we can't factor in is cheats. But we *can* identify them."

"Has this happened before?"

A long pause. "Once, several years ago. With a tennis player."

"What happened to him?"

"Her. She retired through injury, but not before she cost us over a million dollars."

"Is that a large percentage of your profit?"

Rennick's eyes narrowed. "This isn't about profit; it's about the principle. I don't like being taken for a ride, Ms. Danner."

My own math skills might have been basic compared to Rennick's, but they weren't lacking entirely.

"You said you make four to six cents on a dollar. Assuming Zach Torres works with a similar margin to yours, someone would have to bet two million bucks to make a one-hundred-thousand-dollar profit. Does Torres have that amount of cash?"

Rennick smiled for the first time. "No, he doesn't. The investigative team has concluded he must be working with a partner."

"Can you trace the bets?"

"When a client opens an account with us, we validate that the address exists, but when we began digging further, we found that although the addresses on the suspect accounts are all legitimate, the names used don't match the residents. The funds are deposited from a variety of e-wallets."

"You don't ask for ID?"

"We do, but firstly, passports don't show addresses. And secondly, around two years ago, we had an issue with an employee behaving inappropriately. A software engineer. We had to let him go, but unfortunately, the IS administrator didn't revoke his remote access fast enough, and he replaced several thousand ID scans with pictures of his genitals."

"Nice."

"When we threatened legal action, he denied it, of course, but we were able to verify that the photos were him."

"Dare I ask how?"

"He'd sent similar pictures to several of his female colleagues. Ultimately, we decided that the lawsuit had the potential to turn into a PR disaster, so we didn't continue down that path."

And brushed it under the carpet, no doubt. Wow.

"So all the ID documents are gone?"

"Not all of them. We salvaged eighty-two percent of the records, including three of the IDs in question—those belonged to a young woman working as a nurse in Florida who told us gambling is a sin, a retiree from California who claimed he didn't own a computer or even a smartphone, and a college student who died in a car crash in Massachusetts."

Rennick sighed. "The funds in question are deposited from a variety of e-wallets."

"And you can't trace those either?"

"No. But interestingly, this isn't the first time Torres's name has been connected with illegal activity."

"Really? What else did he do?"

"Have you heard of the Blackstone House affair? It happened eight years ago."

Eight years ago, I'd been too busy freaking out about motherhood to keep up with the news.

"Sorry, I haven't."

"A woman died in his home."

"And he was involved in her death?"

"Another man was convicted of the murder, but there were rumours of a cover-up. If Torres was involved in one serious crime, it's not too much of a stretch to imagine him taking part in another. He also spent time in jail for vehicular theft when he was younger."

"So what do you want me to do? Investigate Torres and his network? I've had experience with financial crimes, and if you provide me with details of the transactions, I could look for a pattern and—"

"No, no, no. That side of the investigation is already in hand. We've been pursuing various methods of electronic surveillance, but we haven't unearthed any suspicious communications." Translation: they'd hacked Torres's email and probably bribed an employee at the phone company. Maybe checked out his bank account too. "So we have to consider whether the arrangements are being made in person. Which means we need someone who can go undercover and get close to Zach Torres."

Ah, shit. Now I understood where the bikini came in.

"And you want me to be that person?"

"We need an investigator who won't look out of place in

the surf crowd, and nobody at the Twilight Agency appears to have the right attributes."

Twilight? Double shit.

"The Twilight Agency is working on this case too?"

"We keep them on retainer."

I nearly walked out right then. Many times over the next several months, I'd come to wish I'd done exactly that. But I was desperate, okay? Desperate for rent money, and also determined to cling onto the job I'd once loved so much.

"Does Torres live in Las Vegas? I mean, there isn't exactly much surf here."

"He lives in Santa Cruz."

"So you want me to…?"

"Travel to California? Yes. Lila informs me that you're licensed there."

Indeed I was. Morty had insisted upon it. Since Clark County butted up against the California and Arizona borders and the licensing requirements were less rigorous in those two states than in Nevada, it had made sense to obtain the additional credentials in case a project spilled over state lines. But Santa Cruz was five hundred miles away, and I had a daughter.

"That'd get awful expensive. You haven't considered hiring somebody from the West Coast instead?"

"Lila found me two girls. The first used a twenty-year-old photo on her website, and the second must've put on eighty pounds since her promo shots were taken. But you… How many cases have you solved in the past?"

"As in an actual number?"

"I'm a numbers man."

"For the first six months, I was learning the ropes, and I cleared my first solo case at the age of twenty. For the next six years, I probably averaged one a month. Tricky problems like murders usually take more legwork than, say, ferreting out a dishonest employee."

"So, seventy-two cases?"

"Something like that. Plus all the usual surveillance and background checks and things that weren't actual cases as such."

"And that makes you twenty-six?"

"Twenty-seven."

"You haven't solved anything in the last year?"

"My partner died, and I took a new job that didn't work out." Had Jankowski told him I'd worked at Twilight? Clearly not, or I wouldn't be here. "Now I'm starting out on my own."

"Died?" Rennick shook his head. "Inconvenient. I could have hired him to assist."

Inconvenient? The man had the empathy of a razor blade. But if Rennick was seeking additional help, did that mean Twilight's investigation wasn't going so well?

"It was a difficult time."

"When can you start?"

"I haven't said yet that I'll take the job."

"Why wouldn't you?"

Why wouldn't I? Because my whole life was in Nevada—Haven, Nana, our crappy apartment. And I didn't even own a bikini. Why? Because I didn't much like water. Okay, I hated it. Ever since I fell into a lake as a child and nearly drowned, I'd kept my feet firmly on dry land. Plus I'd have to report to Jankowski, and I'd rather crawl over a mountain of shattered glass than speak to that prick again.

But on the other hand, I really, really needed money, and Rennick had plenty of it. Investigative work paid a hell of a lot more than waitressing, plus the odds of a disgruntled customer throwing a bottle of sauce at me were considerably lower. And if I broke a case for one of Las Vegas's wealthiest businessmen, that could lead to more clients, not to mention the satisfaction I'd get from succeeding where Jankowski had failed.

"You're talking about long-term surveillance. That's time consuming."

"And you have a heavy workload right now?"

"No, but—"

"You don't think you're up to it? Posing as a surfer chick?"

"Of course I am. Ocean's my middle name."

"Are you being flippant?"

"No, my middle name really is Ocean. My father was a sailor."

According to the court paperwork, his yacht had been seized after he was convicted. The cops found almost three million dollars' worth of drugs stashed on board. And as for "Arizona," that had been my mother's idea—according to Nana, she had a weird obsession with Stevie Nicks, who was born in Phoenix.

For a moment, Rennick's mask softened. "My father was English. He named me after the village he grew up in."

Was English? "I'm sorry for your loss."

"It was a long time ago. What are your rates?"

"Fifty bucks an hour, plus expenses."

Not quite bargain basement, but halfway down the stairs.

"Forty," Rennick countered. I opened my mouth to object, but he held up a hand. "Hear me out. If the case gets wrapped up by the end of this year's tour, I'll pay a fifty percent bonus."

Sixty bucks an hour? Even when I worked for Morty Coulson, I'd never made that much. Jankowski had charged me out at a hundred and twenty, but I only saw a fraction of that amount. A bonus would pay for the horse-riding lessons Haven had always wanted to take, and I could treat Nana too.

"How long is the tour?"

"Eight or nine months total. Possibly ten—it all depends on when the swell's right for the big-wave contests. They're the finale. The competitors are just coming off their mid-season break, so there are five or six months left to go."

Five or six months?

Ouch.

But I couldn't afford to pass this job up, even though I'd be separated from my family for longer than ever before.

"I'd need to stay in California the whole time? The expenses would be substantial."

"You'll be based in California, but you'll need to follow the tour as necessary. Send Lila the contract, and I'll sign it."

"I'm not sure my licence allows me to operate overseas."

Actually, I *was* sure; it didn't.

"Are you intending to get caught?"

"Well, no, but—"

"Lila will also give you the files we have so far and provide administrative support. We'll need regular progress reports by email, every other day at least."

Digby Rennick might have been whiter than white when it came to his customers, but with that little exchange, he'd revealed that behind the scenes, his moral code was shadowed with shades of grey. I found that oddly comforting. At least he wasn't trying to hide his true nature. And if I could email the reports, then I wouldn't need to speak to my pig of an ex-boss.

"Twice a week. Otherwise I'll spend too much time writing and not enough time doing."

"Twice a week, plus immediate notification of any important developments."

"Agreed."

This could be the most lucrative case of my life, and one that had the potential to get my stalled career back on track. But it also promised to be the most challenging. I'd be on my own, my only backup an executive assistant who looked at me as if I were something to scrape off her shoe and a man whose testicles were intimately acquainted with my knee. And that was only half of the problem. I glanced up at Zach

Torres, still frozen mid-wave. How the hell was I meant to get anywhere near him?

"Lila will show you out."

Rennick rose gracefully and padded back to his zen garden, our conversation over.

I'd lost my freaking mind.

CHAPTER 5
ARI

S*o, this is Zach Torres.*

On my first day in California, I watched from a spot on the cliff as he paddled out to sea on a surfboard, flat on his stomach. Fog hung low over the water, and at times I had to squint to see him, but his lime-green shortie wetsuit was a beacon in the otherwise grey sea.

A week had passed since my meeting with Digby Rennick, a week spent researching my target, studying surfing jargon, brainstorming possible cover stories, and studying maps of Santa Cruz. Oh, and getting my car fixed. It still made a weird knocking noise whenever I turned left, but at least the temperature gauge wasn't jammed in the red anymore.

When I left Rennick's office, I'd assumed that my biggest challenge would be tracking Torres down and then spying on him without being caught, but now I was reconsidering. Why? Because Zach Torres seemed to love attention. He positively basked in it. Last night, he'd announced his plans for this morning on Instagram and invited the whole damn world to join him at Pleasure Point. Around half of them had taken him up on the offer, despite it being seven a.m. and cloudy. Hundreds of people packed the sidewalk along the edge of the cliffs, the sliver of beach below, and various rocky outcrops in between. Dozens of surfboards bobbed on the waves while jet skis waited to the side. A drone buzzed around our heads, and there was even a helicopter in the distance. The Zach Torres circus was in town, and I was a pesky fly on the wall of the tent—barely noticeable but potentially annoying at some point in the future.

Torres stopped paddling and sat up on his board, one leg dangling into the water on each side. Didn't he realise there were sharks around here? The drone zoomed in for a close-up, and he waved.

The purple-haired girl standing next to me, the one who'd squeezed over to give me space to watch, sighed. "He's so rad."

"Do you mean Zach Torres?"

"Who else? I mean, Kai Kealoha's cool too, but Zach has this…*this* magic." She leaned forward as Torres caught the wave and stood up. "Look at that drop."

Torres carved back and forth across the water, defying gravity as the wave carried him to the shore. Spectators whooped and hollered, and a girl in a bikini rollerbladed past, handing out tins of ZT-branded surf wax. The purple-haired girl grabbed one and kissed it.

"You're a big fan, huh?"

"Since I was fifteen." She didn't look much older now. "I mean, he's the best surfer in the world, and he's right here on my doorstep. Well, almost. I mean, I had to drive for ninety minutes, but Santa Cruz is closer than Hawaii."

"Isn't he ranked the third-best surfer in the world at the moment?"

Oops, wrong thing to say. Her mouth set in a thin line, and she put her hands on her hips.

"So you know how Google works, huh? Congratulations. Now try using your eyes instead. How many other surfers have that flair? That connection to the ocean? He always finds the right waves."

I could accept that Google didn't tell the whole story. From what I'd seen, Torres either won in spectacular style or wiped out with equal drama. Which fit with Rennick's throwing-the-contests theory.

"I don't actually know much about surfing," I told the girl clutching the tin of wax.

She gave me a once-over. "Figures. Your shirt says 'Beach Bum,' but your complexion says you don't get out much."

Was it that obvious? Honestly? Yeah, of course it was, but I'd always found it easier to analyse other people than myself.

"You come to the beach a lot?"

"Every chance I get. Which isn't often enough, seeing as —" The girl ducked behind me as the drone came closer. "Oh, shit."

"What's wrong?"

"My boss'll kill me if he sees me here. I told him I had period pains. Can you tell me when it's gone?"

"Uh, sure."

"I'm Erin, by the way."

The drone circled, and I shifted left to block her from view. "I'm Ari. Where will they broadcast this footage?"

"YouTube, Zach's website, the sponsor's website, social media. Maybe the local news if it's a slow day. And my boss's son spends most of his time watching TV in the break room, so…"

"The drone is circling away now. Where do you work?"

"In a grocery store. Someone has to sell the big-tech crowd their organic carrots and wheatgrass smoothies."

"I thought they were all about the avocado toast?"

"This month, they're eating asparagus with poached quail eggs and microgreens. Hey, Kai's joining the line-up."

Kai Kealoha was one of Torres's buddies and a fellow pro on the World Surf Tour. The two of them hung out with a third guy, Tyler Peralta, but I hadn't seen him in the water today. Erin probably knew where he was, but I didn't want to ask. After all, I was meant to be clueless about surfing in general and Zach Torres in particular.

But as Erin *oohed* and *aahed* at the next person to catch a wave, I did spot Maya Torres on the beach below, speaking to a guy holding a clipboard. Torres's younger sister worked as his personal assistant, according to an article I'd read. Torres had credited his support team with being instrumental in his success—Maya; Kai; Tyler, who shaped his surfboards; the Sal's Army safety crew; his trainer, Chuku; and his many sponsors. Special thanks had gone to Zed Nelson, promoter and head honcho of the World Surf Tour. No mention of a girlfriend or other family, and his parents had both passed away. I'd found little information on his mother, but his father had also been a surfer before he famously drowned a stone's throw along the coast from here.

Torres had vanished from the surfing circuit after that, just abandoned his upcoming contests and disappeared. Occasionally, he'd been mentioned as a footnote in a surfing article: *Whatever happened to Zach Torres? How tragic that a promising junior career was cut short.*

Over four years had passed before he popped up again, this time in Virginia as a player in the Blackstone House mystery. The cops had cleared him, but conspiracy theories still abounded—had the wrong man gone to jail for the murder?

Another year, and Torres had exploded back into the surfing world. Quite literally—he'd blasted out of a barrel wave on the cover of *Surf Style* magazine, bare-chested, flicking back his hair as he grinned at the camera. Two more years of gruelling contests later, he'd qualified for the World Surf Tour, and now here I was—standing on a cliff, clutching a small tin of wax with his photo on it.

I'd had worse jobs—searching through a guy's garbage at

three a.m. for evidence of infidelity was no fun, let me tell you —but I'd also had better jobs. Sure, my bills were taken care of for the next couple of months at least, and I no longer had to serve fries to perverts, but I missed my family already. Saying goodbye to Haven had been the hardest thing. When I worked for Morty, I'd occasionally gone away for a night or two, a week max—he took the longer jobs because he didn't have a family of his own—but now I'd be in Santa Cruz for what seemed like an eternity. In an ideal world, I'd return home for visits, but with a sixteen-hour round trip and a deadline, the chances seemed slim. Haven was on summer break. Not only was I missing out on precious time with her, but I also felt guilty that Nana wouldn't get any rest. Taking care of an energetic eight-year-old was a full-time job.

Plus I still had no idea how I'd get close enough to Torres to carry out meaningful surveillance.

My research told me he didn't do the groupie thing, not anymore—although he was often spotted chatting with the girls who followed him around—and he seemed to spend most of his time in the water. Yesterday evening, I'd scouted out his home in Seagrass Point, and surfing clearly paid better than PI work because he lived in an architect-designed masterpiece overlooking the ocean in a small enclave to the north of Santa Cruz. If I worked three lifetimes and didn't eat, buy clothes, or go out—ever—I might be able to afford the secondary suite over the garage. *Modern Living* magazine had done a feature on the property last year, and the inside was as stunning as the outside.

Erin squealed in my ear as Torres caught another wave and leapt up on his board, arms stretched out to balance himself. There was something strangely hypnotic about watching him carve his way across the water. I'd brought a camera with me, a DSLR with a zoom lens, and I snapped a photo or two. Nothing unusual about that—half the people watching were filming Torres on their phones. Okay, yes, I was meant to be keeping a record of the people he talked to, not Torres himself, but there was no harm in practising, right?

And Torres sure didn't have a problem with being on camera. After he'd glided to shore and picked up his board, he shook the water out of his hair in a move that he must have rehearsed, then flashed a grin at a female reporter waving at him from the high-tide mark. Erin sighed, and I had to admit that—objectively speaking—Zach Torres was hot. Sex on a surfboard. A real— Urgh. Thankfully, he derailed that totally inappropriate train of thought by spitting onto the sand.

"Gross," I muttered.

"It was probably a nurdle," Erin told me. "The sea around here is full of them."

"A what?"

"They're, like, little plastic pellets. A bunch of containers fell off a ship last year, and now the nurdles are everywhere."

"I've never heard of them."

"Tell me you've never spent time on the beach without telling me you've never spent time on the beach." She rolled her eyes. "Nurdles are a big problem for wildlife. Sea creatures eat them and get sick."

"Can't somebody clean them up?"

"Who? The plastic companies don't care, and there are billions of nurdles out there. *Trillions.* I volunteered on a count last year—damn, it was boring—and we found thousands on one small stretch of sand alone. Cleaning them up would take *forever.*"

"You just sat on the beach and counted nurdles?"

"Yup."

Boring or not, it gave me an idea... "How did you get involved with that?"

"There's a website where you sign up. OMG! Zach's taking off his wetsuit. Can I borrow your camera?"

"Huh?"

When I didn't answer fast enough, Erin grabbed it and zoomed in. "Wow, this lens is *great*. You can see, like, every detail of his abs."

True. I'd lived on ramen for three months to afford that lens, but over the years, it had repaid me with interest.

"Uh, the drone's coming back."

"Who cares? This is so totally worth getting fired."

Okay, maybe there was one small plus point to this job—I was getting paid, and paid well, to watch *Glamour* magazine's Bachelor of the Month. But damn, I missed my daughter.

CHAPTER 6
ARI

Monday 11 July

- *07:12 Kai Kealoha arrived at Torres property.*

Haven's Rest. The Torres home was called Haven's Rest. Every time I saw the nameplate screwed to the front wall, I felt a pang of homesickness.

- *07:26 ZT and KK loaded surfboards into ZT's pickup and left property.*
- *07:32 ZT and KK arrived at Seagrass Beach.*
- *07:59 Tyler Peralta arrived at Seagrass Beach.*
- *08:25 - 11:49 Various unidentified women dropped by to speak with ZT. Appeared to be fans. Ref photos SP32 - SP38.*
- *12:18 ZT returned home alone.*
- *12:26 Chuku Haruna arrived and went running with ZT.*

The trainer was a tall Black man with the physique of a long-distance runner. But he was tough too. I'd seen him do fifty push-ups on the lawn beside Zach and barely break a sweat.

- *13:12 ZT and CH arrived back at Torres property.*
- *13:47 CH left property.*
- *13:57 ZT left property with Maya Torres. Visited grocery store.*
- *14:29 ZT returned home with MT. Three unidentified females noted outside property, one holding a "We love you, Zach" sign. ZT waved but did not converse. Ref photo SP39.*

At first, I'd considered joining the girls. Being a surf groupie would have given me the perfect excuse to loiter near Torres for hours. But potentially, I might have to keep up the surveillance for the remainder of the surf season. Holding a "Zach, you're the best" sign for that long would not only tip me from superfan into deranged stalker territory, but it would also destroy the single ounce of self-respect I had left. And I very much wanted to keep that.

- *14:35 Brunette female arrived at Torres property. Identified as Sharon Sansom, freelance journalist. Ref photo SP40.*
- *15:08 Middle-aged female left property. Did not see her arrival. Drove away in white Toyota Corolla with license plate 3HCF521. Ref photo SP41.*
- *16:24 Sharon Sansom left Torres property.*
- *16:32 ZT observed swimming laps in pool for approx 20 mins.*
- *16:47 Package delivered by UPS. Truck license plate 6KYD947.*
- *16:59 MT observed speaking on phone while pacing backyard.*

And she'd looked upset. Bad news? When Zach came out a few minutes later, she visibly pulled herself together and offered him a smile. So, it probably wasn't a work issue. I'd considered a strategy of befriending her to get closer to Zach, but she seemed to be something of a loner and barely left the house.

- *19:05 Tyler Peralta and Baylee Sarterfeld arrived at Torres property.*

Baylee was Peralta's girlfriend, according to social media. They'd been dating for over six months.

- *20:17 Pizza delivered by slim Black male driving red Honda Civic with sign for "Milano's Pizza" on door. Limited conversation, tip changed hands. Ref photo SP42.*
- *22:11 TP and BS left Torres property.*

Six thirty a.m. on Tuesday, and I finished writing up the logs for the past five days, attached those and the photos to my summary, and pressed send. Then yawned. Lone surveillance was tough, I was already shattered, and there was no end in sight. Damn, I hated mornings. Vegas came alive at night, and only the school run got me out of bed before nine.

Think of the money, Ari.

Plus the fact that this wasn't the most challenging assignment I'd ever done, not now that I'd found somewhere to stay and begun to settle into the role. Boring, yes, tiring, yes, but not technically difficult. I was a tiny cog in a big machine. Jankowski's men were running down the leads and determining whether anyone I spotted was a viable suspect. All I had to do was submit my reports on time.

So, where was I staying?

Right in Seagrass Point.

The small settlement sat between a redwood forest and the ocean a little way north of Santa Cruz. To call it a town would have been generous—there was no real infrastructure, no Main Street, just a surf store that sold a variety of boards, clothing, and accessories, and a general store-slash-diner that sold everything else. I suspected most of the trade came from tourists, either surfers or people passing through on their way to and from San Francisco. The place was pretty, I'd give it that. Cutesy in a driftwood-and-pastel-colours kind of way, and most of the homes were expensive. Big, fancy places in a mishmash of styles, each one unique. Think *Grand Designs* versus *100 Day Dream Home*.

When I'd checked the listings online, there were precisely three properties available for rental in Seagrass Point. No way would Rennick spring for the mansion, which left two. The first was a super-cool Airstream trailer, immaculately restored and rated five stars. Free Wi-Fi, utilities, and use of the pool included. When I was a teenager, I'd dreamed of buying a trailer like that, just hitching it up and taking off to see what the rest of the United States had to offer. Of course, fate had come up with other plans for me, and this week was no different.

The second option was a garage apartment that worked out four hundred dollars a month cheaper, and there was a good reason for that. Reviews mentioned the smell of mothballs, the intermittent hot water, and the landlady's attitude problem.

Can you guess which of the two was next door to the Torres place? I'd bought an air freshener, steeled myself for cold showers, and vowed to avoid Wilma Carrington at all costs. Cranky didn't even begin to cover it. But if I stood on the wobbly chest of drawers in the bedroom, a small round window in the eaves gave me a good view over the single-storey Torres home. A swathe of overgrown ivy meant Zach and Maya were unlikely to notice me watching, and at least I didn't have to hunker down in the forest to carry out surveillance. Things could have been worse. They could also have been a lot better, but when had my life ever gone smoothly?

The Torres property certainly fit with the locale. The long, low rectangle was nestled into a slope, the front a wall of mirrored glass that overlooked the ocean and the roof covered by an expanse of grass with a pair of lawn chairs perched on top. Red-and-yellow cushions stood out against the white frames. More chairs sat on a floating concrete terrace in front of the building, and skylights—glass domes topped with metal birds that rose from the immaculate sea of green—suggested the house went deeper into the hillside than it first appeared. A narrow pool ran the full length of the building, shimmering in the sunlight, and in between the terrace and the water, ribbons of ornamental grass wove through a strip of gravel. A small bridge crossed the pool, more decoration than of any practical use.

The drive led around the side of the main house to the double garage, which wasn't so different from the one I was currently living above, except it was painted white and had obviously been well-cared for. Maya Torres appeared to have made the garage apartment her home. I saw her coming and going, and she parked her silver Toyota outside. Zach usually left his Dodge Ram in a small pull-off near the pool. Nobody parked in the garage, and from what I could work out, that space was reserved for Zach's collection of surfboards. His quiver, according to the jargon I'd picked up. In the mornings —or at least, every morning since I'd been watching—he'd select a board, load it into the back of his pickup, and drive to a local surf spot.

With me following.

Outside, I heard the *crunch* of feet on gravel and clambered onto the chest of drawers, muttering a silent prayer that it didn't tip over. *Right on time.* Zach Torres strolled along the driveway wearing board shorts, a tight rash vest, and a pair of flip-flops. Dressed for the office. As I watched, he turned to stare at the ocean for a few moments. What was he thinking? Deciding where he wanted to surf this morning? In four days, we'd been to three different places. He seemed to favour a quiet beach a two-minute drive away, and I could understand why—when he ventured to the more popular spots, he spent more time signing autographs and posing for photos than actually surfing.

Maya's windows stayed dark while Zach loaded gear into his truck. She didn't appear to share his love of early mornings. Or surfing, or even beaches. On the internet, I'd found a single candid shot of her in a bikini, but that had been taken several years ago, and she'd put on weight since then. Now, she tended to favour long skirts and loose, floaty tops teamed with sandals.

The day before yesterday, she'd shown up at the beach three hours after Zach arrived and spent a quarter hour speaking with her brother, pausing every so often to point at her iPad. Some sort of scheduling meeting? Zach had nodded frequently, interspersed with the occasional grimace and head shake. I'd recorded the interaction from my position farther along the beach on the pretence of photographing surfers and seabirds. I wasn't the only person out with a camera that day. A guy up on the cliff—well, perhaps "cliff" was too generous a word, but there was a definite step—he was taking photos too. Seabirds mainly, judging by the angle of his camera. When I caught him looking in my direction, I waved, and he waved back.

Was I worried about being noticed? No, not really. If I was working a surveillance detail for a day or two, staying hidden had its advantages, but I couldn't skulk around in a place like Seagrass Point for months without raising suspicions. Better for Torres to see me around. To get used to my presence on the beach. That way, he'd tune me out. When I followed him to contests, then I'd have to keep out of his way and Maya's too, but for today, I could relax in plain sight.

Initially, Jankowski had taken that approach too. After I signed Rennick's contract, Lila had forwarded me copies of the Twilight Agency's reports, and Jankowski had sent a man in undercover as a surfer. I knew the guy, and yes, he was tanned and toned and looked the part, but he was also the world's biggest bullshitter. Five bucks said he'd lied about his surfing ability, which was probably why he'd ended up in the hospital with a broken leg two weeks into the job.

I wasn't dumb enough to try climbing onto a surfboard, no siree. If the weather was good, I might fulfil Rennick's wish and wear a bathing suit to the beach, but swimming was out of the question. Even the sound of the waves left me slightly nauseated. After my near-drowning, I'd had nightmares for years—murky water closing over my head, thrashing arms and legs followed by the paralysing fear of not knowing which way was up, my chest getting tighter, tighter until I couldn't hold my breath any longer. Then blackness. I later learned that a teenage boy had seen me fall into the lake and run to save me, but in those long moments while he searched, I'd been terrified. Even now, I much preferred showers over baths, and swimming pools were firmly off-limits.

But that was okay. I could work around my fears. Secretly, I'd set myself a goal of paddling at the water's edge before I went back to Vegas, but this was early days. No pressure. I had a cover story. Yesterday, I'd photographed the beach for the travel blog I'd set up—*Ari's Big Adventure*—and today, I planned to embrace my inner eco-warrior. This was a marathon, not a sprint. All I had to do was hover around the periphery of Zach Torres's world, note everything I saw, and collect a paycheck at the end of each week.

I watched as Torres pulled out of the driveway. The

tracking device I'd placed in his wheel well meant I could give him a head start while I gulped down a bowl of cereal.

Get close, but not too close.

Right?

Wrong.

CHAPTER 7
ARI

Today, I was counting nurdles. Yes, nurdles. Those tiny little plastic pellets that Torres had spat across the beach the first day I'd seen him. Erin had been right—there were trillions of the damn things.

Three days ago, I'd signed up to assist with the *Say No to Nurdles!* campaign, a project run by the California-based Making Waves Initiative. They were trying to build up a global picture of nurdle pollution, and anyone could volunteer to count the pellets and submit their data online. I hated those little plastic bastards already, and I hadn't even swallowed any. Worse, they tended to congregate below the high-tide line, so I had to sit on damp sand rather than finding myself a nice dry spot farther up the beach. Mental note: buy a waterproof cushion.

One, two, three, four...

The campaign website asked counters to measure out a one-metre-by-one-metre square—the campaign was international, so metric measurements were used—then mark the corners with pegs and the sides with string wound around the pegs. Super-keen participants could buy a set of *Say No to Nurdles!* pegs with tiny flags on the top—all profits went toward the project's costs—but I was using pencils I'd found in the general store. Once you'd measured your square, you had to note its location using latitude and longitude or the What3Words app—the website gave handy guides on both—and then you got counting. Branded notepads were available too. Once you'd either counted all the nurdles in your square or died of boredom, whichever came first, you recorded the numbers on the website. An app was coming soon, apparently.

Rinse and repeat.

Yawn.

But Torres was a supporter of the campaign—I'd found an old post on his Instagram page extolling the benefits of counting nurdles because "only by truly understanding the problem can we pressure plastics manufacturers to stop polluting our oceans." So he could hardly criticise my presence.

The beach was almost empty today, possibly because the weather was miserable. I'd felt several spots of rain when I first arrived, but it had dried up temporarily, and now the clouds were just menacingly grey. Torres was with his buddies again today—Peralta and Kealoha—plus a couple of other guys I didn't recognise. I'd dutifully taken pictures of them all. If the Twilight team identified them, would they feed the names back to me? Lila had been vague on the flow of information. My task was narrowly defined, and it seemed that she worked within a rigid set of rules. Probably lived by them too. I'd met her three times before I left Vegas, and although she'd been polite, she seemed to have a stick permanently stuck up her ass. Or, more likely, an Apple Pencil. She struck me as the efficient type. And even if the information was meant to be provided, it wouldn't surprise me if Jankowski held it back out of spite.

Twenty-one, twenty-two, twenty-three…

Torres paddled in the distance, gesturing to Peralta.

Discussing whose turn it was next? Apparently, there was a whole lot of etiquette about who got to catch a wave, and I didn't understand any of it. In the end, Peralta went first and did some fancy tricks that included getting airborne before gliding onto the beach to a smattering of applause from the few groupies who'd braved the inclement weather. The usual suspects—a big-breasted blonde who seemed determined to share her assets with the world, a brunette who had more energy than decorum, and an obviously fake redhead. I'd seen them all outside Haven's Rest at various points. Didn't they have homes to go to? Jobs?

Forty-six, forty-seven, forty-eight.

At the far end of the beach, a family played in the sand near the water's edge, building a sandcastle. Mom and two kids, a girl Haven's age and a younger boy. It should have been a happy day, but the mom didn't look pleased to be there. Twice, I'd seen her on the phone, pacing up and down as she argued with someone, and occasionally, a few words drifted in my direction. *You promised you'd be here. What am I meant to tell Bennie and Shiloh?* I wondered who'd skipped out. The kids' father? Asshole. One day, hopefully a sunnier one, I'd take Haven to the beach, but Maxwell Suker definitely wouldn't factor into that plan.

Fifty-three, fifty-four, fifty-five...

Hell, these nurdles were a real problem, weren't they?

A man bundled up in a coat walked a dog close by. The dog carried a stick in its mouth and did absolutely nothing that it was told. At one point, it ran up to the groupies and shook water over them—a bright spot in an otherwise dull day. *Poppy, come back.* Now the mutt was in the sea, paddling frantically toward the surfers, her head bobbing among the white foam. Torres finally caught a wave, and I watched as he swerved across the face of it before ending up at the front of the board with his toes hanging over the edge. Was that intentional, or was he having balance issues? No, he'd done it on purpose. He waved at the groupies as he hopped off the board onto the sand.

Dammit, I'd lost count.

Fortunately, I'd piled the nurdles into a small mound, so it wasn't difficult to start again, but I still cursed under my breath for getting distracted. Torres was just a pretty body stuffed into a wetsuit. A wetsuit that clung to every muscle, and those thighs… Shit!

One, two, three…

Dunes topped with grass bordered the beach—probably how Seagrass Point got its name—and a teenage boy flew a kite with a younger girl. Brother and sister? The kite was shaped like a butterfly with streamers fluttering out of its ass, and the girl squealed in delight as it swooped and turned. The boy handed the strings over to her, and she promptly crashed it into the sand. Oh well.

Sixteen, seventeen, eighteen…

Torres was already paddling out for another try, and today, his wetsuit was neon orange. Didn't he know how to do subtle? Even out of the water, he tended to choose bright colours. The complete opposite of my fashion choices—I went for bland, dull clothing to blend into the background. But Haven would love one of those funky shirts they sold in the surf store. I'd have to find the time to pick one up before I headed home. Plus a gift for Nana too, because she'd certainly earned it.

Thirty-four, thirty-five, thirty—

Who had screamed? My gaze darted toward the girl with the kite, but she was happily skipping along behind her brother. The groupies? No, they were clustered around a phone, probably watching a Zach Torres replay. And the scream had been one of fear, not excitement. The surfers were all accounted for, no accidents or spills, and Poppy the dog was wrestling with a lump of seaweed. Which left the mom and two kids, but where were they? The lumpy sandcastle showed where they'd been, one turret collapsed and a bucket and spade abandoned in the sand.

Then I saw it.

A hand.

In the water.

And I ran.

Where the hell was the mom? And the other kid? I scanned the beach, but they were nowhere in sight.

"Help! Help me!"

Could anyone hear? The wind whipped my words away, and the groupies were screeching again. My heart hammered as I sprinted across the beach, too terrified of a kid drowning to be scared of the water. Call it immersion therapy. Quite literally. With nobody else around, I had no choice but to get my feet wet.

All around, the surf boiled white, but the spot where I'd last seen the child was calmer than the surrounding water. Perhaps I could just wade out a little way? How deep was it? I stuck a toe in, sweat trickling down my brow and mingling with the salty spray.

There! The child spluttered to the surface, farther out this time, and I saw it was the girl. She tried to yell but swallowed a mouthful of water and went under again.

"It's okay, I'm coming. Help! Somebody help us!"

The ocean was lapping around my knees now, and the next wave nearly knocked me off my feet. Ouch! I yelped as I stubbed my toe on a submerged rock. Sheer determination kept me upright, and I began to float as I waded forward. Shit, shit, shit!

"Help!"

The girl flailed again, and I dove forward. *You can do this, Ari.* When I fell into the lake, I'd been a child, but I was bigger now. Stronger. If Poppy could do the doggy paddle, then surely I could manage it too? I tried and went under, the water stinging as it rushed up my nose. Gasping, I flailed frantically as I popped to the surface and sucked in a breath. How did I get so far from the beach?

Something hit my thigh, and I was about to freak out when I realised it was the child. I grabbed for her and caught an arm, then hung on for dear life, hers and mine. I couldn't scream for help anymore. A wave broke over my head and I choked, trying for one last lungful of air before I sank under again. My nightmares came to life as I kicked with my legs, but I didn't know which way was up. Was I pushing us to the surface or down into Neptune's grasp?

I caught sight of the girl's face, her eyes open, blonde hair floating in the water. Was she already gone? She was a dead weight, but still I refused to let her go. My vision blurred, and her face morphed into Haven's. I couldn't leave her. I *couldn't*.

Finally, finally, my head broke the surface, but I only had time to gulp one mouthful of air before I submerged again. The beach was so far away now. I spotted figures at the water's edge, but it was too late. Too late…

My energy was ebbing fast, my lungs burning. The current pulled me down, and a strange sense of calm washed over me. I couldn't fight the ocean; I knew that now. So why even try?

The last thing I felt before everything went dark was a band tightening around my chest, squeezing, squeezing. Neptune? Damn, he was strong.

I closed my eyes and let him take me.

CHAPTER 8
ZACH

Let's surf at Seagrass, Kai had said. It'll be chill, Kai had said.

He'd fucking lied, hadn't he?

First, Khloe, Alys, and Stacey had shown up, as they had every single day since school broke for the summer. At first, having fans had been an ego boost, but the novelty had soon worn off. Now, Zach found the attention tiring. Surfing was freedom, always had been, but ever since he'd joined the World Surf Tour, a part of that freedom had been exchanged for money and fame. The money was nice, but the fame? Not so much.

It's not forever. That's what he kept telling himself. He just had to play the game for a few more years, make enough cash to fund an early retirement for himself and Maya, then fade away into obscurity again. Of course, nobody apart from Kai and Tyler knew that little secret. Not even Maya, because success was always uncertain in this game—one bad wave could end a career—and he didn't want to promise her something he might not be able to deliver. Plus Zed Nelson, the tour's promoter, insisted on his surfers being committed.

Team players. Zach had already screwed up twice, and he couldn't afford to do it again.

Stick with the plan.

So, he sucked it up and exchanged a few words with the girls before he headed out to sea again. Why were they so fixated on him? Tyler genuinely loved the attention, and Kai was arguably a better surfer. As Zach paddled to the outside, he watched his friend drop into a wave and perform a perfect rodeo flip. Kai was riding a shortboard today, far more manoeuvrable than Zach's longboard. Zach preferred the shortboard too, but the WST had contests for both styles of surfing as well as aerial and the big-wave rounds at the end, so he had to practise. Tyler was on a longboard too, but he didn't have the pressure of the WST weighing on his shoulders. No, he'd followed a different path. Sure, he entered the occasional contest, even won on occasion, but Board Stiff was his main project. Can't chase monsters forever, he said, and after he'd broken his arm four years ago, he'd diversified his interests. Bought the run-down surf store the three of them used to work in and turned it into a success, and his hand-shaped boards were always in demand. Thankfully, Zach was always at the front of the line.

They'd even been offered a joint deal by Outside In, a big European surf brand—a mass-produced line of boards designed by Tyler with Zach's name plastered across them—but negotiations were currently at a stalemate. The company wanted too much. Multiple public appearances, rights tied up for years, and that was before Zach's lawyer had caught them sneaking in alterations to the exclusivity clauses between contract drafts. The whole thing left a bad taste in his mouth. Tyler was keen on the deal, but Zach wouldn't risk making the same mistakes his father had regretted.

Kai pointed and yelled, "Outside."

There was a big set of waves coming in. Zach paddled harder, easier on the longboard than a shortboard, and he was gonna make it. Another thirty yards, and— Who just screamed for help?

One of the drama queens?

Zach glanced toward the beach, but Khloe, Alys, and Stacey had their heads down, probably picking out pictures for their Instagrams. Or maybe TikTok or whatever else was popular these days? The three of them were obsessed with social media. The beach was quiet, and there weren't many people out on the water—only Zach, Tyler, and Kai, plus a handful of other regulars. All present and accounted for. Had he imagined the scream? No, because Kai was scanning the water too, searching for something other than his next wave.

"Over there," he yelled, pointing toward the sandbars.

And Zach saw it. A face appeared, gasping for air at the edge of a rip current before disappearing again. *Fuck.* Kai was already up on his board, and Zach caught the next wave, yelling to Tyler at the same time.

"Someone's in trouble."

"What?"

Zach pointed toward the spot where he'd last seen the face. Whoever it was, they hadn't resurfaced.

"Someone's in trouble," he repeated, screaming at the top of his lungs.

Now Tyler understood, and he paddled for the shore. Faster for him to run along the beach than stay on his board, but would they make it in time? Kai was ahead of them both, a good thing because he was more experienced with water rescue. While Zach had turned his back on the surfing world and moved to northern Virginia for several years, Kai had spent that time working as a lifeguard in Hawaii.

When Kai reached the rip head, he dove in, searching. That was where the current would have spit its victim out. As Zach arrived on the scene, Kai burst to the surface, arms wrapped around a woman, and thrust her toward Zach's outstretched arms.

"There's another one down there."

Two of them? Hell. Kai was gone before Zach could speak, and he grabbed the woman's arm. Blonde hair was plastered across her pale face, and he couldn't tell whether she was breathing. The instinct to drag her onto his board and paddle for the shore was strong, but that would be the wrong move. Every year, Zach and Kai arranged lifesaving courses for local surfers, and last summer, they'd flown in an instructor Zach had met in Brazil to train the participants. Snippets from the guy's teaching came rushing back… *Breathing will stop before the heart does. A person ventilated in the water has a three hundred percent greater chance of survival than one resuscitated onshore.* They'd practised the technique, and memory kicked in as Zach pulled the woman's head and shoulders onto the side of his board. No need to empty water from her lungs—when the salty tentacles of the ocean entered the airway, the larynx spasmed and sealed it off, sending water to the victim's stomach instead.

The woman didn't resist, her arms and legs limp, her eyes closed. Zach paused and counted to ten, watching for signs of breathing. Nothing. He gave two rescue breaths, vaguely aware of Tyler riding the rip current and arriving beside him as Kai heaved the second victim out of the water. Did Zach's girl have a pulse? Her hands were cold, her lips almost blue, but he detected a faint flutter.

Thank the gods above.

The vise around his chest unwound a notch as he breathed for her again, and then she spluttered, coughed, and puked all over herself. Zach turned her onto her side so she wouldn't choke on her vomit, then hauled her farther onto the board. She lay there, panting for a moment before her eyelids flickered open, revealing wide eyes the colour of the Caribbean Sea framed by thick lashes.

"What the hell were you doing out there?"

His fear at almost seeing a woman drown came out as

anger, something he wasn't proud of, but it wasn't the first time his temper had made an uninvited appearance.

"I...I..."

How was the second victim? Yet another wave of horror crashed through Zach when he realised it was a kid. A little girl. Kai had her up on Tyler's board, giving not only rescue breaths but CPR too, as Tyler kicked like a demon, pushing them toward the shore. Had someone called 911? Zach scanned the shoreline and saw the girls had followed Tyler over. Khloe was filming the rescue while Stacey and Alys just stared.

"Call an ambulance," he yelled.

"Huh?" Khloe seemed more puzzled than anything else.

"Call a fucking ambulance, you idiot!"

Alys came to life and pulled out her phone, and Zach had to trust she'd do the right thing. He still had a problem of his own to deal with. Was the blonde the kid's mother? He scanned the beach, but the only people watching were the three girls, the other surfers now helping Kai and Tyler to carry the kid out of the water, and a man with a dog.

The blonde groaned, and the sight of the lifeless child did nothing to quell Zach's fury. Sure, he took risks every day— some people even said they were stupid risks—but he never took his own flesh and blood swimming in a rip current.

"Hold the rails," Zach ordered.

"The...what?"

"The edges of the board."

Another cough. "Is...is she okay?"

"No, she's not okay. Don't you know anything about water safety?"

The blonde shook her head. "I c-c-can't even swim."

"Then why the fuck was your kid in the ocean?"

More screaming, this time from the shore. A brunette was running from the sand dunes, waving her arms, shouting at Kai and Tyler.

"What did you do to her? What did you do to my baby?" she yelled.

Her baby? Wait, *this* was the kid's mom? Then who was the blonde? A friend?

"She's not—" the blonde started, then shrieked as a wave rocked the board.

"Just hold on until we reach the shore. Nobody has time to rescue you again."

On shore, the brunette began thumping Kai on the back, still yelling, something about him being a paedophile and a child molester. Tyler tried arguing, and when she still wouldn't shut up, Stacey whacked her on the head with an oversized purse. Well, that was one way to handle it.

Zach's board hit the sand, and he offered the blonde a hand. She pulled herself to her feet, but her knees buckled, and he barely managed to catch her before she hit the deck.

"Why don't you just sit down?"

"Okay."

It came out as a croak. The blonde needed medical help, but she was breathing. She wasn't the priority right now. How was the kid? Zach glanced at Kai, and he shook his head. Tyler carried on with the chest compressions.

"Did you call the ambulance?" Zach asked Alys.

She nodded. "And I called my friend Emily. Her pop's a doctor, and he lives real close."

Good. That was good. Seemed he'd underestimated her. The brunette scrambled to her feet, mouth open, but before she could get a word out, Stacey pushed her down.

"Don't you dare touch him again."

"Where's..." The blonde was still coughing. "Where's your son? The little boy?"

"My son?" The brunette's eyes went wide. "My son!"

She stared around wildly, and Zach spotted a small boy meandering by the sand dunes, heading toward the road. What was wrong with this woman?

"If someone can hold Poppy, I'll fetch him," the dog walker offered. "Got kids myself."

Alys grabbed the leash, and he took off at a run. The brunette began sobbing, and in the relative quiet, old memories came flooding back. The bad ones. Rex, an old-timer who rode a wooden longboard, hauling Zach's father into a boat and bringing him back to shore. Rex's girlfriend crying as Zach begged the medics to fix his dad. To make him live again. But he'd been missing for hours by then, trapped underwater beneath some of the biggest waves on the West Coast. How long had this little girl been under? One minute? Two? Heaviness settled in Zach's gut, an ache he knew all too well.

Not for the first time, he questioned his decision to return to surfing. The ocean was a cruel mistress and an unforgiving master. But he'd tried staying away, and that hadn't exactly worked out either, had it? The world thought he led a charmed life, but the reality was very different.

CHAPTER 9
ARI

So much for staying on the periphery of Zach Torres's life. I couldn't get much freaking closer to him. Right now, I was debating whether waking up with his lips pressed to mine was better or worse than not waking up at all.

Haven, think of Haven.

My daughter still had a mom, but did this lady on the beach still have a daughter? No matter how irresponsibly she'd acted, nobody deserved to lose a child. A doctor arrived, not an EMT—he was wearing chino shorts and a golf shirt—but he'd brought a portable defibrillator and that was the important thing. Everyone stood back as he shocked the little girl, her small body jolting as the voltage surged through her.

Part of me wanted to slink away, to crawl back to Vegas with my tail between my legs, resign from the case, and never see the ocean again. But the other part was just…numb. I couldn't move. My legs were still trembling—hell, *all* of me was shaking—and I couldn't have run if I'd wanted to.

"We have a heartbeat," the doctor announced, and the three groupies began cheering, which wasn't in the best taste, but I guess I understood the sentiment. The girl's mom tried to get up again, but Tyler Peralta pushed her back down.

"Get your hands off me," she snapped.

"Lady, you need to keep your mouth shut," the brunette groupie said.

"They hurt my child! They—"

"Are you high?" the redhead asked. "They *rescued* your child. And where were you? Why'd you leave her on her own?"

"Bennie needed to go potty. What was I meant to do?"

"Take her with you?"

"She didn't want to come."

"So you thought it was better to leave her next to the ocean to, like, drown?"

"I told her to stay where she was."

She was a small child, for goodness' sake. Haven was generally well-behaved, but even she was liable to meander off when the mood took her, and this woman had barely paid attention to her kids since I arrived at the beach. I almost made a comment, but what was the point? If a near-drowning hadn't given her the wake-up call she needed, then a lecture from me sure wouldn't help, and I'd only draw more attention to myself.

The little girl coughed, and if her throat felt anything like mine, it would be burning too. Gingerly, I stretched out my limbs. Everything worked, although my head was pounding and my arm had a long scrape from a rock, or the sand, or maybe Torres's surfboard because the surface had been unexpectedly rough.

But my injuries were minor compared to the girl's—at least she was alive; that was what mattered. Even Digby Rennick couldn't get upset about that, surely? A life was more important than money. Although money was also necessary, and realistically, I knew I couldn't quit this case even if I wanted to.

Finally, *finally*, sirens sounded in the distance, and within a few minutes, the girl—Shiloh, her name was Shiloh—was being loaded into the ambulance. The hard part was over. Now I had to go back to my rented apartment, explain the situation to Lila, and work out how to extricate myself from this huge mess I'd created. I might get away with my nurdle counting in Seagrass Point, but now that Zach Torres had seen me up close, staying under his radar at the big contests would be tougher. What if he glanced up and saw me in the crowd? Would wearing a cap and sunglasses be enough? Or would I need to add a wig? Change my face shape? Distract him with my woefully inadequate boobs?

"I'm sorry I snapped at you," he murmured into my ear, breaking me out of my thoughts. Someone had wrapped a blanket around my shoulders, and I pulled it tighter. "I thought she was your kid and you hadn't been paying attention."

"I just saw her in the water and tried to help."

"Without being able to swim?"

"I didn't think it looked that rough."

"It looked calm because it was a rip."

"A what?"

"A strong current that tries to pull you out to sea."

And it had succeeded. "Oh."

"You should stay away from the ocean if you can't swim, especially around these parts. It can be unforgiving."

"Fine, I'm sorry I tried to save her." Despite the situation, sarcasm crept into my voice. "Is the lecture over now? I just want to go home."

"Home? You need to go to the hospital."

Oh, no, no, no. A hospital visit was impossible. Now that I was self-employed, I had no insurance, and another bill would leave me bankrupt.

"I'm fine."

"You were unconscious. I had to resuscitate you."

"And now I'm resuscitated, so thanks. Good job."

I got to my feet, intending to walk away because starting an argument with the target of my investigation was a really bad idea, but the world began to spin, sky and sand and relentless waves merging into a grainy blur. An arm snaked around my waist, and I found myself sitting on the beach again.

"Can we get a doctor over here?" Zach called.

"No, I'm—"

"Stop talking, uh… What's your name?"

"Uh, Arianna. Ari."

Telling him that much was okay. My travel blog was set up in the name of Arianna Dee—during undercover work, it was better to stick close to my real name because then my reactions would be more natural. Morty Coulson had taught me that. If I called myself Becky and then took an extra second to answer because my brain needed to process, the delay would only raise suspicions.

The EMTs were busy with Shiloh, so Dr. Golf Shirt poked and prodded me, shined a light in my eyes, and asked a hundred questions that my sluggish brain struggled to answer. Was that what nearly drowning did? Filled your head with sludge?

"Owww. Get off me."

I jerked away when he pressed the sore spot near my temple, and he nodded.

"You have a mild concussion." Mild? That was like a headache, right? I had Tylenol back at the rental apartment, so if I just took a couple pills, then— "You probably hit your head on a rock while you were underwater. And I understand you lost consciousness?"

"Not for very long."

"Any blurred vision, nausea, ringing in the ears?"

"She vomited," Torres told him. Traitor.

"I would strongly recommend that you go to the emergency room."

"I can't afford to go to the emergency room."

"What if I paid—" Torres started, but I cut him off. If he covered the bill, he'd find out my true identity, and I couldn't afford for that to happen either. Although the offer was generous. *Very* generous. Then again, if Rennick was right about the amount of money Torres was making from his betting scam, he could afford a few X-rays.

The doctor sighed. "I can't force you to go."

"No, you can't."

"Then you need to rest for two days, minimum. Get plenty of sleep and avoid looking at screens because that will make the headache worse. No driving or sports." His words were matter of fact, his tone resigned, but his expression belied his exasperation. "And make sure a responsible adult stays with you for the next twenty-four hours in case your condition deteriorates."

Avoiding sports wouldn't be a problem, but I needed to drive. How else would I follow Torres? Plus the only adult I knew in California was Wilma Carrington, and I'd rather swallow sulphuric acid than spend a whole day with my grouchy landlady.

But I nodded my agreement because what was the alternative? "Sure."

"I'll drive you home," Torres offered. "Where do you live?"

"I can walk."

"Sweetheart, you can't even stand."

I hated that he spoke the truth.

"I'm not your sweetheart," I said through gritted teeth.

Peralta grinned. "Feisty. I like that."

Torres cut him a glare. "Either I drive you home, or you call a friend to pick you up."

Where was my phone? I patted my pockets and quickly realised I wouldn't be phoning anyone. Would the "bowl of rice" trick work on a device that had been submerged in seawater?

"My car is here."

"In the lot over there?" Torres nodded toward the patch of gravel at the edge of the beach.

"The blue Honda." My chest seized. "My camera? Where's my camera?"

"The camera's over there." Peralta pointed behind me. "I'll get it."

"And I'll drive the car back to your place," Torres said. "Kai can follow in my truck."

"But—"

"Those are your options." His expression softened. "I was an asshole earlier, and I'm trying to make it up to you, okay? Let me do this."

"Trying to make it up to me? By ordering me around?"

Stacey batted her eyelashes. "You can totally order me around any time."

Seriously? We were at the tail end of a medical emergency, and she thought now was a good moment to flirt?

"It wasn't an open offer," he told her.

And just to annoy her, I said, "Fine, I'll take the ride."

Torres smiled for the first time since he'd fished me out of the water. "That's a better answer."

My heart skipped. Was that normal? Or another symptom of concussion? I considered asking the doctor, but I didn't want another lecture on why I should go to the emergency room. One was quite enough.

None of the groupies looked happy when Torres helped me to my feet again. This time, I managed to stay upright with relatively little dizziness. The ambulance had departed, leaving behind the detritus of a life saved—disposable gloves and plastic wrappers that Kai Kealoha was stuffing into a bag, his movements slow and methodical.

Torres followed my gaze. "Hey, buddy. I gotta drive Ari home. Can you pick me up?"

"From where?"

They both turned to me, expectant.

"I'm staying in the garage apartment at Coral Cottage. It's only two minutes away."

"You live next door to me?" Torres asked.

I played dumb. "Do I?"

"You're renting from Ms. Carrington?"

"That's right."

I didn't miss Kealoha's grimace. Yup, that about summed up my thoughts on Wilma Carrington as well.

"Then we're neighbours. I guess I should introduce myself properly—I'm Zach Torres."

This time, I got the proper photoshoot grin, not only from Torres but from Peralta too.

"For the record, Zach normally waits until at least the second date before he locks lips with a lady."

"Shut up, man."

"Just sayin'."

"Just don't."

My lips still stung, although that was probably due to the saltwater. "This wasn't a date, it was a near-death experience. And don't expect me to bake you cookies."

Peralta snorted. "I like her."

Something else the groupies didn't find amusing.

"Can we get out of here? Where's my camera?"

My head was throbbing, and I couldn't think straight. The wind nipped at my wet shirt and pants, and I was ten seconds away from shivering. Only Torres's arm around my waist kept me from turning to ice. The man gave off heat like a furnace. As well as changing into dry clothes, I needed to swallow some painkillers and maybe nap for twenty minutes before I resumed surveillance. Why was I barefoot? Dammit, my shoes had disappeared as well, and those sneakers had been almost new. Another expense. What were the chances of charging the cost back to Rennick? I *had* lost them while I was on the clock, even if lifesaving didn't form part of my regular duties.

Peralta held up the camera, and Torres's grip tightened as I swayed.

"Yeah, we can get out of here," he said.

CHAPTER 10
ZACH

Didn't bad luck come in threes? Zach hoped not, because Ari already had two problems to contend with this week, and worse than the concussion was renting an apartment from Ms. Carrington, who breathed fire every time her arthritis acted up.

How did Zach know that? Because he and Maya had rented the same garage apartment for a couple of months when they first moved to Seagrass Point, and he'd felt the lash of Ms. Carrington's tongue whenever his footsteps crunched the gravel too loudly or he left his boards "cluttering up the yard."

He'd always known that buying a property next door to her would be a risk, but he'd figured she was getting on in years. How much longer could she stay alive? Seven years later, he'd come to the conclusion that she was immortal. The old dragon had become unbearable, yelling every time they used the pool in the evenings or grilled in the yard, and he'd been on the verge of selling up. Of taking the loss and moving to a nice little cabin deep in the forest with no neighbours whatsoever. But one afternoon when she'd stormed over to complain, Maya had been home alone, and as a peace offering, she'd given Ms. Carrington a bag of freshly baked cookies. But the wrong ones. Too late, Maya had realised that her oatmeal-and-raisin were still sitting on the counter, and Ms. Carrington had gone home with Tyler's edibles.

Now they sent her a food parcel every week, and she'd mellowed out considerably. The cookies were her little after-dinner treat, she said, and by some coincidence, the pain in her fingers had eased recently. Wasn't that strange? Maybe it was the weather? Did Zach think it was warmer this year? He just nodded and agreed, and now whenever he had to travel overseas, he made sure her freezer was full of weed cookies beforehand—the investment was worth it.

Ari stayed silent on the ride back. Since she lived right next door to Haven's Rest, Kai had stayed behind at the beach to help Tyler pack up the surfboards, and Zach would walk home after Ari was safely settled inside.

"You need a hand up the stairs?" he asked after he'd opened her Honda's passenger door. The car badly needed a service—it made a knocking noise every time it turned left.

"I'm okay."

She wasn't, and he wished he'd just wrapped an arm around her again instead of asking. Now he had to watch as she struggled up the stairs, her knuckles white as she gripped the bannister.

"So, who are you staying here with? A boyfriend? Or a girlfriend?"

"It's only me."

"Then who's going to monitor your condition for the next twenty-four hours?"

"My condition is that I have a headache. All I need is painkillers and a nap."

"That's not how concussions work."

"What, are you a doctor now?"

"No, but I know how to listen to one."

"He had to say that stuff. He just doesn't want to get sued."

"Kai and I didn't fish your ass out of the ocean"—and a very nice ass it was. Walking behind her did have its advantages—"in order for you to act reckless over a head injury."

Ari ignored him and fumbled to get the key in the lock. Once, twice, three times she missed, and he closed his hand over hers to assist. Now that the adrenaline had worn off, she was in worse shape than she wanted to believe.

"There you go."

She walked inside without a word and tried to close the door, but Zach put his foot in the gap. Too bad he was wearing flip-flops.

"Fuck!" He staggered backward and nearly fell down the stairs. "Fuck, you broke my toe."

"Sorry! I'm sorry! Do you need ice?" Ari covered her face with a hand. "I don't have any ice."

"If I hop home and get ice, are you gonna let me in when I come back?"

"No?"

"Then I guess I don't need the ice that badly."

The garage was wider than a single but not as wide as a double. Downstairs, there was enough space for one vehicle and a workbench, but Ms. Carrington had filled the place with junk. Dusty chairs and broken appliances and dishes that belonged to her long-dead cat. In years gone by, she'd been a keen gardener, but now the flowers were gone and a service cut the grass every two weeks in summer. Ms. Carrington's son had moved to Houston. Zach couldn't blame him.

Upstairs, there was a small bathroom, but the rest of the space was open plan. Two single beds were pushed together in the far corner near a closet and a chest of drawers, with a curtain hung from the ceiling for privacy. The kitchenette was basic—an electric stove, a microwave, and a small refrigerator beside a sink in one corner of the living room. No dishwasher, no laundry facilities. There wasn't a laundromat in town, but Maddie at the general store would wash, dry, and fold for a few bucks. Ari had chosen to rinse her panties in the sink and hang them over the shower rail, and when she realised Zach had noticed them, her cheeks reddened and she slammed the bathroom door. Fortunately without his foot in the way this time.

"Look, thanks for saving me, but what are you planning to do? Watch me like a creeper for twenty-four freaking hours?"

"If that's what it takes."

"What if I told you I had a gun?"

"Do you have a gun?"

He held her gaze for a long, uncomfortable moment, and finally she looked away.

"I have pepper spray."

"Is it the good kind with the neon dye in it? Because pink doesn't really suit me."

"This isn't funny, Zach."

His lips twitched, but he swallowed the smile down. This stranger was…interesting. Courageous but impulsive, smart but pigheaded, snarky but not quite as confident as she made out. He'd grown so used to pushing women away that to have the roles reversed was quite a novelty. Perhaps that was why he felt so determined to make her see sense?

"Yes, I know. And I wasn't planning to perv over you all night. I'll ask my sister to come and sleep on the couch."

"Your sister?"

"She lives with me. Well, kind of. She has the garage apartment."

"The couch is lumpy."

Zach already knew that. Ms. Carrington hadn't changed the furniture in a decade, and it had been uncomfortable when he lived there.

Cedro Torres had always told his son that opportunities were like waves—the big ones were risky, but they could change your life. He hadn't been lying, but those changes hadn't always been for the better. Would today be any different? Zach hesitated to ask the question on the tip of his tongue and watched Ari as she dug through a suitcase, cursing softly to herself.

"What are you looking for?" he tried instead.

"Tylenol. I brought a bottle with me; I know I did."

"Want me to help?"

"No."

He sidled up to her, silently chastising himself for staring at her ass again. "I have Tylenol."

"Here?"

"At my place."

Damn, Ari had a nice smile. The purple bruise on her temple? Not so good.

"If you bring it, I promise I'll let you in again. Uh, I'm sorry about your foot. Is your toe really broken?"

"I think it's just bruised." He nodded toward the refrigerator. "You have food here?"

"What, now you're inviting yourself over for lunch?"

"Actually, I was gonna invite you over for lunch."

"Huh?"

"Come and have lunch with me, Ari."

"I'm not sure that's a good idea."

"You need to eat." He opened the refrigerator and found three cans of soda, an apple, and half a burrito. "Is this what you live on?"

"I'm not much of a cook, okay?"

"Now you're definitely coming for lunch." When she didn't reply, he closed the refrigerator and walked back to her, stopping close, maybe too close because she took a step back. "I have salmon niçoise salad and homemade chocolate cake."

"You cook?"

"Sometimes, but my sister made it. If you're worried about hands wandering while we eat, my housekeeper will act as chaperone."

Ari swallowed hard. "Are you saying that you lack self-control?"

That had never been a concern until today, but this morning's events had left Zach off kilter.

"No, sweetheart, I'm saying that most women have trouble keeping their hands off me."

Her mouth set in a hard line. "Well, Mr. Torres, I'm not most women."

Was it fucked up that he found her indignation a turn-on? Definitely. He didn't bring girls home with him, and he was careful to avoid *feelings*. They weren't compatible with his current lifestyle. If he wanted sex, he drove to San Francisco, where his old friend Brax owned Nyx, a private members' club with a secret in the basement. Above ground, the place boasted a fancy restaurant, a gym, a spa, and luxuriously appointed bedrooms for overnight stays. Membership was limited to the rich and famous, anyone with something to lose. Fees started at six figures, but patrons weren't paying for the elegant, old-world ambience or the first-class cuisine. No, they were paying for discretion. Because below ground, in the space nicknamed The Dark, anything went. If you had a kink, it was catered for, either by the hosts and hostesses or by like-minded members. Zach preferred his women blonde, compliant, and ideally tied up with a pretty little bow. Or handcuffs. He wasn't fussy.

The best part about the women in The Dark was that they came without strings. At this point in his life, he didn't need the distraction of a girlfriend. Emotions were dangerous. Just ask his father.

"It's only lunch, Ari. Bring your pepper spray."

She bit her lip, and he knew then that he had her.

Chocolate cake versus a soggy burrito—there was no contest. Ari bent over the suitcase again, and this time, she came back with a small canister in her hand. Shit, she really was bringing the pepper spray? He'd been joking, and the lack of trust, it…hurt.

"I need to change into dry clothes first."

"Take your time. We have all day."

CHAPTER 11
ARI

What was I doing? Had I lost my ever-loving mind? I was meant to be keeping my distance from Torres, not joining him for lunch. This damn concussion had scrambled my brain. Plus he'd bribed me with Tylenol and chocolate cake, and chocolate was my biggest weakness.

Inside, I was still jittery, and although I'd never admit it, I was glad Zach had offered me his arm. I leaned on him as we ambled slowly down Ms. Carrington's driveway, noting that he walked with a slight limp. Oops. Guilt niggled at me, not only for injuring his foot but also because he'd saved my life today, and I hadn't exactly been brimming with gratitude. The shock of almost drowning, then being rescued by a suspected fraudster who'd possibly been involved in a woman's death as well, and now finding myself pushed into having lunch with him... It had all left me off balance. Plus I felt a weird rush of heat whenever he got too close—the doctor hadn't mentioned *that*.

Lunch would be safe enough, wouldn't it? I had my pepper spray, and if Zach had been telling the truth about the housekeeper, a witness would keep him from trying anything untoward. Wouldn't it? I didn't have a phone, and although I was trained in self-defence, I was in no fit state to run or fight.

Okay, this was a bad idea.

No, a terrible idea.

"What's wrong?" Zach asked.

"Why would anything be wrong?"

"You just tensed up."

Oh.

"I'm wondering how to replace my phone."

"You need to make a call?" He fished a cell phone out of his shorts with his free hand and held it out. "Here."

Who would I call? Nana? What would I say? *Everything's going great—I almost drowned, but a hot criminal revived me and now I'm going to his place for lunch.* She'd have a heart attack, and then what would happen to Haven?

"I don't need a phone right now." Although I wouldn't mind taking a look at his later when he wasn't watching my every move. "But mine's gone to the great garbage dump in the sky, and I like having one for emergencies."

"We probably have a spare—Maya will know."

"Who's Maya?" Had to keep up the pretence, didn't I? "Is that your sister?"

"Yeah, my little sister."

We'd almost reached the gates when I heard a voice behind us.

"Arianna, you left the television on standby when you went out this morning. That's a waste of electricity, and do you know how much utilities cost?"

Of course I did. These days, I dreaded the arrival of every bill and budgeted carefully to pay them. Usually, I remembered to unplug the TV—Ms. Carrington had left a laminated sign on the coffee table to remind me—but it must have slipped my mind earlier. And of course she'd noticed. At first, I'd been pleased that the apartment rental included cleaning, but now I realised it was just an excuse for the nosy landlady to poke around. She put far more effort into snooping than she did into vacuuming, but if I complained, that would make my stay here even less comfortable.

I turned to answer. "I'm sorry, Ms. Carrington. It won't happen again."

"Young people these days, they have no respect for rules."

"Just ignore her," Zach murmured. "She's always like this."

"Is that you, Zachary?" Ms. Carrington adjusted her glasses and squinted. "You'd better not be corrupting my guest."

He took a calming breath. "I'm only feeding her lunch."

"Lunch? Next it'll be dinner, and we all know what that leads to, don't we?"

"What kind of cookies do you want today? Chocolate chip? Peanut butter? Ginger?"

"Chocolate chip, but Maya will need to leave them on the porch because I have my painting class tonight."

"I'll remind her." And to me, "Keep walking."

Although the encounter had been uncomfortable, as all encounters with Wilma Carrington were liable to be, at least she knew where I was going. If I didn't come back, she'd call the police. Not out of concern for my well-being, you understand, but to report nonpayment of my rent and abandonment of my belongings.

"Must be fun living next door to Ms. Carrington," I said once we'd made it to the relative safety of Zach's driveway. "Does she ever smile?"

"Nope. But I've gotten used to her over the years. Worked out how to keep things bearable."

"You bribe her with cookies?"

He chuckled. "Something like that."

"Have you lived in Seagrass Point for long?" I already knew the answer, but questions like this were expected by targets. "It seems such a friendly place, Ms. Carrington excepted."

"We moved here seven years ago."

"You and your sister."

"That's right."

"Did you have to move far?"

A shrug. "Far enough. What brought you to Seagrass Point? It's not much of a tourist town unless you surf."

Nice subject switch. "I needed a change of scene. Life hasn't been going so well lately, but I guess the bad luck just followed me here from Las Vegas."

"That's where you come from?"

"Lived there my whole life. Until now, anyway."

We reached Zach's front door, and rather than fish around for keys, he pressed his thumb to a scanner half-hidden by a trailing plant that was growing in a polished metal holder beside the video doorbell. A security-conscious surfer. Disappointing. I recognised the system, and it was a good one. Almost impossible to hack or disarm without the proper credentials. If ever I got the urge to snoop around the Torres home after hours, I wouldn't be able to simply copy a key or pick the lock, plus there would be photographic evidence if I so much as set foot on the property. Good thing I hadn't tried that yet.

"This is all very James Bond," I remarked.

"I kept losing my keys."

"You couldn't just hide a spare in a flowerpot like a regular person?"

Not that I'd ever recommend doing that, of course, although it did make my job much easier.

"I used to do that, and I came home to find a girl sleeping in my bed. Naked."

"Eeuw. She found the key?"

"She also stole my underwear off the clothes line, which is

why I have a dryer now." He pushed the front door open. "Come in and take a seat."

The whole house was built around the view. A horseshoe of couches in the living area faced the sea rather than a TV, and the dining table was perpendicular to the huge windows so everyone could enjoy a little nature with their meal. When Zach waved me toward the kitchen area, I climbed onto a padded stool at the breakfast bar in time to see a flock of gulls fly past.

The place was immaculate—spotless and minimalistic. The appliances were stainless steel, high-end enough to make a professional chef turn green with envy, and the accessories were few and carefully placed. An enamelled fruit bowl on the counter. A puff of giant white feathers in a turquoise vase. A pair of surfboards hanging on the back wall. A wide seascape I recognised as Seagrass Beach with a lone surfer balanced on a wave.

I nodded at it. "Are you the surfer?"

"Yup."

"Who painted it?"

"Ms. Carrington."

I did a double take. "As in, 'tiptoe when you're walking past my window' Ms. Carrington?"

"She's a brilliant artist. A total bitch, but a brilliant artist. One of the reasons she's so nasty is that it hurts her to paint the way she used to. Arthritis."

"Oh."

"As Maya puts it, the pain of having something she loves taken away from her tumbles out through her mouth."

"That's...that's so sad." I saw her in a new light. "The doctors can't help? Give her medication?"

"She says the pain hasn't been so bad lately." Zach grinned. "The painting was a thank-you for the cookies Maya makes her. How hungry are you?"

Honestly? Not very. "Do you think Shiloh will be okay? I mean, she was underwater for so long, and…"

Zach closed the refrigerator door and drew in a long breath. Until now, he'd seemed unaffected by all the drama, but in that brief, unguarded moment, he looked positively haunted.

"I don't know. I don't know how bad it'll be. But she's alive, and that gives her a chance." He pulled out the stool beside me and sat down. "Thanks to you, she's alive. I didn't even notice her on the beach. When I'm on the board, I'm just so focused on the waves and… I didn't see her."

"But you saved us. You and Kai and Tyler, you saved us."

"Kai did most of the work."

I touched a finger to my lips, remembering the moment I'd regained consciousness in the water.

"You definitely played your part."

"I've fished worse things out of the ocean."

"Did you go to charm school for that line?"

"No need, I'm a natural."

With that smile and the way his eyes sparkled, I might even have believed it.

"I'm sorry if I came across as ungrateful earlier. Thank you for rescuing me. Thank you for driving me home. Thank you for"—I waved a hand at the kitchen—"this."

Now Zach got up again, the moment over. "Can't let my new neighbour starve, can I?" He set plates on the counter, six of them, then answered my unasked question. "Kai and Tyler will be back soon, Maya too. And Gloria's already here."

"Gloria?"

"Our housekeeper."

Which meant Zach had told the truth—we wouldn't be alone. Okay, that was good. So why did I feel a pang of disappointment?

"I should thank Kai and Tyler properly as well."

"Don't fawn over them. You're just another notch on their lifesaving belts."

"They've done this before?"

"Kai used to work as a lifeguard, and Tyler drives a rescue ski for Sal's Army."

"What's Sal's Army?"

"The safety crew on the World Surf Tour. They work other events too, plus they're out around Santa Cruz whenever the swell gets big."

"You mean bigger than today?"

Zach snorted out a laugh. "The waves at Seagrass are small but fun. Good for aerial. You really don't know anything about surfing?"

"No, I really don't."

Other than the fact that people bet a lot of money on it. My YouTube studies hadn't prepared me well at all. I'd spent more time watching interviews with Zach Torres, trying to get a feel for him as a person, than watching surf videos. And even the interviews hadn't helped much—in person, he was less glib, more empathetic. I'd been expecting a shallow playboy, but what I'd gotten was boy-next-door with a six-pack.

"So, Arianna…" He leaned his elbows on the breakfast bar and looked me in the eye. "Why are you in surf country if you don't surf? You could have gotten a change of scene in a hundred other places."

"Uh…" I'd prepared my story so carefully, but my head was still sludgy. *Be careful, Ari.* Because something else had become clear—Zach was smarter than the image he projected. "Ever had a moment in your life when you just needed to get away from everything?"

"Several."

"All the little things piled up. A boss I hated, the death of a friend, an ex who made things difficult… Anyhow, I came into a little money—an inheritance—and I figured I'd make a fresh start."

It was a tangle of half-truths and one outright lie, a vague but plausible story that Zach would hopefully accept without pushing for further details.

"And you chose Seagrass Point for your fresh start? Most people would go somewhere with a Walmart."

"I prefer the peace and quiet. It's pretty here." I nodded toward the windows. "I had this idea that I'd spend some time in California, then head overseas. Maybe check out the Caribbean over winter. I started a travel blog."

"You should learn to swim before you do that."

"Starting a blog?"

"Ha-ha. Before you visit the Caribbean. Half the fun is in the water."

That was a commitment I didn't want to make. "So, why did *you* move to Seagrass Point? You're not a fan of Walmart?"

Zach waved his own hand toward the windows. "You're looking at it."

"The view?"

"The ocean and the solitude. At first, it was meant to be a temporary arrangement, but then this place came up for sale, and… Here I am."

"Buying a palace is way out of my budget."

"It was a wreck when we moved in. The roof leaked, the concrete was spalled, and the wiring was unsafe. I knew I'd taken on a project, but…" He shook his head. "There were times when I almost threw in the towel."

"Looks as if it turned out okay."

Zach smiled. "Yeah, it did. Out of the darkness came light. So, how long are you planning to stay with Ms. Carrington? Most people don't last out the week."

"I figured a few months, but after today…" I shuddered. "The ocean's gonna give me nightmares."

"Don't let one bad experience ruin the magic."

"It's actually two bad experiences, although the first one was in a lake. I'd hoped living here would be a healing experience—you know, getting over old fears by spending time near the thing that scares me."

"What happened in the lake?"

"I fell out of a boat when I was four years old. That day, a teenager rescued me, and I swore I'd never go in the water again."

Zach leaned forward and brushed a stray lock of hair away from my face. His touch made me shiver. Or maybe it was just the cold? Delayed hypothermia or something?

"Then what you did today was insanely brave."

Insane was right. "Or monumentally stupid."

His gaze fixed on mine. "I'm serious—if you plan to spend more time at the beach, you should take swimming lessons."

I was ready to swear off beaches for good, but avoiding the ocean completely wasn't an option, not if I wanted to get paid. And I should be doing my job, not sitting here trying to work out whether the main suspect's eyes were blue or green. Depending on the light, they could be either—a sort of aqua that started off jade in the centre and faded to turquoise around the edges. Fine lines at the corners were a reminder of his outdoor lifestyle, and the dark smudges underneath suggested he didn't get enough sleep.

"Uh..." I gave myself a mental kick. "Can you recommend a good teacher?"

Oh, brilliant answer. Totally what I meant to say. Had I lost my freaking mind?

"As it happens..."

The sound of an engine interrupted Zach, and his truck turned into the driveway a second later with Kai at the wheel. Tyler followed behind in his own vehicle. The spell was broken, and that could only be a good thing.

"I'd better go and unload my boards," Zach said. "You'll be okay on your own for a few minutes?"

"I'll be fine." But old habits died hard. "You said earlier that I could borrow your phone—do you think…?"

"Sure." He slid it across the counter, then opened the cupboard beside the refrigerator. "And here's the Tylenol I promised."

He poured me a glass of water too, added ice, and headed out the door, leaving me alone with his phone and a guilt complex. I'd snooped through a hundred phones in the course of my work, so why did I hesitate to pick up Zach's today? *He saved your life, Ari.* Yes, but I couldn't afford to let that overshadow the need for justice. Zach Torres's friendliness was just one more example of a man's deceit—I'd fallen into a pit of lies once with Haven's father, and every time I saw Maxwell spewing his bullshit on TV, I swore never to make that mistake again. On TV? Yes, because somehow after being released from prison, he'd managed to get himself elected as a member of the Nevada Assembly. Apparently, the folks in District Thirteen didn't care that their representative was both a sanctimonious jackass and a convicted fraudster, just as long as he had good hair.

Once Zach had disappeared outside, I scrolled through the call list, specifically to the week before the contest at Jeffreys Bay. That was the last time Rennick had detected anomalous betting patterns. Technically, reviewing Torres's phone usage came under Twilight's remit, but the more information I had, the better. Plus I didn't trust Jankowski. He wasn't a terrible investigator, but he wasn't a great one either, and his "do the bare minimum and collect the money" ethos filtered through the entire organisation. Unfortunately, like Maxwell, he also had a great line in bullshit, so he was never short of clients.

Calls to Tyler, Kai, Maya, Chuku, Zed... Who was Matt Morella? That name sounded familiar—he was a surfer if I recalled correctly. What about Pete? Macy, Macy, Macy... Was that a girlfriend? Ex-girlfriend? And Cheryl? Natty B, Nyx, Papa G—that last one sounded like a pizza joint. Dammit, I wished I had a pen and paper, but I couldn't see any stationery lying around in this immaculate home.

I memorised the names as best I could, head throbbing, then dialled Nana's number from memory. If I didn't call anyone and Torres noticed, that might arouse suspicions.

"Whoever you are, I don't want to buy any."

"Nana, it's me."

"Ari?"

She didn't have any other grandchildren. "I had to borrow a phone."

"What happened to yours?"

"I accidentally got it wet, and it might take me a day or two to replace it, so don't worry if I don't call tonight."

"Is everything okay?"

I took a breath, forced myself to smile because Morty always said that even if a person couldn't see your expression, they could hear it.

"Everything's fine. Honestly. It was just an accident."

"Do you want to speak with Haven? She's in her room, reading."

My heart ached to hear her voice, but Torres could return at any time. "Don't disturb her if she's settled. I'll call back as soon as I can."

"You're sure you're all right?"

Nana wasn't stupid, and she knew me too well to be fooled by my fibs. But she also wouldn't push for answers if I didn't volunteer them. She'd always respected my job and understood that there were some things I couldn't discuss.

"I'm fine, I swear. Tell Haven I love her?"

"She already knows."

"*Hola*, ma'am."

The voice from behind nearly gave me a heart attack, and Torres's phone flew out of my hand. Shit, shit, shit! I dove for it, head thumping, but the newcomer was faster, a petite Hispanic woman dressed in white shorts and a black polo shirt. I put her in her late thirties. The phone bounced off my foot, and she caught it before it hit the floor.

"Sorry, I didn't mean to scare you. You're a friend of Maya's?"

I took the phone from her outstretched hand, noting that it was locked again. "No, I came with Zach."

"Really?" Why did she sound so surprised? "Where is Zach?"

"Unloading the truck. Are you Gloria?"

Gloria with the silent footsteps. Or was it just my wonky brain that had made me miss her approach?

She bobbed her head. "Yes. Yes, I work here. Can I get you something to eat? A hot drink? You look cold. A sweater?"

I was about to decline out of habit, but then I realised my arms were covered in goosebumps.

"If there's a sweater I could borrow, I'd be grateful."

"I'll get you one of Zach's. Ah, here are the boys."

The front door opened, and the three of them trooped in, talking among themselves. This was the first time I'd gotten a good look at Kai and Tyler. On the beach, I'd had other things on my mind. Kai was the tallest, around six feet two, and he wore his black hair in a ponytail. Somewhere between the beach and the house, he'd lost his shirt, and I was treated to a close-up of the tribal tattoos decorating his hard muscles.

"What's for lunch?" he asked, and the housekeeper beamed at him.

"Today, it's salmon."

Tyler ran a hand through damp brown hair. "Do we need to cook it? Should I light the grill?"

"No, it's all ready. Sit, sit."

Zach took the seat next to me and pocketed his phone. A moment later, the front door opened again, and Maya walked in. These days, her dark hair was longer than in the few pictures I'd found, almost reaching her waist, and she looked nothing like her brother. Where his features were chiselled, hers were soft. His tan came from the sun, while her skin had a decidedly olive tone to it. And he appeared to be confident, outgoing, whereas she struggled to make eye contact.

"Maya, this is Ari," Zach said. "She's joining us for lunch."

Maya focused on her brother instead of on me. "She was the one who helped to rescue that girl at the beach?"

"You heard about that?"

"The video's already online. Fifty thousand views and counting."

One of the groupies—she'd been filming. Well, she hadn't wasted any time cashing in on her five minutes of fame, had she? I swallowed a groan. If the footage was online,

Jankowski would see it before the day was out, which meant I needed to email Rennick and explain the situation. That promised to be a fun report to write.

Maya hardly said a word as she helped the housekeeper to set out food on the dining table, although I noticed her sneak the occasional glance at Kai when she thought no one was looking. Was she just enamoured with his tattoos, or something more? Gloria sat down too, and from the lack of discussion, I realised this must be a regular occurrence. Curious. The only other person I'd known with staff was Maxwell, and he'd have kicked his maid out of a window before he invited her to join him for lunch.

"Will the girl be okay?" Maya asked after we'd all spooned food onto our plates and Zach had recounted this morning's adventure in more detail. "The caption at the end of the video said she was breathing, but…"

Tyler forked a piece of salmon into his mouth. "Baylee has a friend on the paediatric floor, and she'll keep an ear out. I know she's not really meant to, but…" He shrugged.

"Baylee is Tyler's girlfriend," Zach explained, and I didn't miss the slight curl of Maya's lip. They didn't get along? "She's an actress, but she also works part-time at the hospital."

"In the billing department," Kai added, and was it me, or did I detect the tiniest hint of animosity in his tone?

Baylee wasn't popular?

Whatever, Tyler didn't seem to pick up on it.

"Ari, how are you feeling now?"

"As if I just went five rounds with a cage fighter."

"Know how that feels. Every time I surf Peahi or Todos or Mavericks, I end up black and blue."

"Only because you keep wiping out." Kai laughed. "We brought your belongings from the beach, Ari. Your camera and the things you left in the sand—a notepad and the string with the sticks."

"Thank you, thank you, thank you. Is the camera okay? Any damage?"

"Looks good to me."

"String and sticks?" Zach asked.

"I was counting nurdles for the *Say No to Nurdles!* campaign. Doing my bit for the environment, you know? Where's the camera? I should check it."

Only once Kai had brought my camera in from the truck and I'd taken a few test pictures did I relax. And eat. The food was really good. Perfectly cooked fish, beans that weren't boiled to mush, and the tang of lemon. A thousand times better than a reheated burrito.

"There's a campaign?" Zach asked.

"I thought you knew about it? You promoted it on Instagram."

"I did? Maya runs my social media." Zach dropped his cutlery and narrowed his eyes. "You checked out my Instagram? Does that mean you knew who I was before we met today?"

Ah, *dammit*. Never again would I socialise while concussed.

And now everyone was staring at me, waiting expectantly for an answer. An explanation. *Think, Ari. Think.*

"Guilty as charged." My cheeks burned. "Soon after I got here, I paid a visit to Pleasure Point, and there was some kind of surfing event going on, so I stopped to watch. The girl standing next to me was your biggest fan, and okay, I got curious and looked you up. But I'd paid the deposit for the apartment next door by then. I swear I'm not a psycho stalker."

Technically, none of that was untrue; I'd just left a lot of stuff out. But would Zach believe the story?

"Now I know you're lying." Fuck. "No way were you standing next to my biggest fan. They're camped out at the bottom of my driveway, waving placards." He broke into a smile. Phew. "If you want to talk about nurdles, Kai's your man. He's Mr. Green."

"He converted his truck to run on cooking oil," Tyler said. "So instead of swinging by a gas station, he has to go to the 7-Eleven. Don't accept a ride if he offers one. He'll make you push the shopping cart."

"Don't listen to this asshole." Kai elbowed Tyler in the side. "A Chinese restaurant in Santa Cruz gives me all the oil I can use."

"He keeps it in drums in his garage. The place smells like a kitchen."

"Better than smelling like a weed farm." Kai conjured up a devastating smile. "So, Ari, you're counting nurdles?"

"It seems a worthwhile thing to do. Truthfully, I never realised that plastic pollution was such a problem until I came here. In one square metre, I found fifty-seven of them."

"That's nothing—head south to Sunset or Moss Landing, and you'll double that."

"I have no idea where those places are. I'm still finding my way around."

"Why don't you come with us? We were talking about going to Moss Landing in the morning."

"Zach can't surf Moss Landing tomorrow," Maya told him. "He has a photoshoot for Gold Rush clothing, and they want to do it by the jetty at Capitola."

Zach finished chewing his mouthful and cursed. "I forgot about that."

"That's why you have me."

"I can still go to Moss Landing, right?" Kai tried. "I don't have a photoshoot. Do I?"

"You're giving a surfing lesson to three beginners who entered a contest on the WST website. I'm sure they'll send a camera crew."

"Where? At Cowell's?"

Maya nodded her confirmation. "Ten o'clock start."

Kai's look of resignation let me know what he thought of that idea. "How about Thursday?"

"When we went over your schedule on Sunday, you both agreed you were going longboarding at Privates, Tyler too, and then you have a video interview with a blogger at three p.m."

Kai turned back to me. "Wanna count nurdles at Privates?"

"Private whats?"

"Privates Beach."

"I thought all the beaches in California were public?"

"That's just what people call it. At one time, you had to live in a house there or buy a key to the gate in order to use that stretch, but now it's open. Parking can be a bitch, though, which means it stays quiet. So, are you coming?"

Zach didn't look thrilled by the idea of me tagging along, and the polite thing would be to decline, but Kai was offering me the perfect surveillance opportunity. I couldn't afford to turn it down. How else would I monitor my prey on a quiet beach, especially now that Zach knew who I was?

Maya wasn't enthusiastic either. "Doesn't Ari have a concussion? Shouldn't she be resting?"

"I'm sure I'll feel better tomorrow." A yawn came before I could stop it, and I covered my mouth with a hand. "All I need is a good night's sleep. I'll head home after lunch and get some rest."

Home. If only.

"Maya, can you go with Ari this afternoon?" Zach asked. "The doctor said she shouldn't be on her own today."

"What about the cookies? I need to bake."

For a moment, Zach looked torn. "Right, I forgot. Yeah, you need to make cookies." Good to know where I came in his list of priorities. "Kai, what are you doing later?"

"Working on my new board with Tyler. Can't Ari just stay here? You have three spare bedrooms."

The housekeeper nodded. "Yes, yes, I can watch her."

Zach and Maya looked at each other, and unspoken words passed between brother and sister. Finally, Zach shrugged.

"I guess that would work."

Would it? "I don't want to be any trouble."

Tyler reached for the olive oil. "You'll be asleep, and Zach won't even be here. How could it be trouble?"

Another offer I couldn't afford to decline. Who knew what information Gloria might let slip?

All I needed to do was stay…awake…and…listen.

Yawn.

CHAPTER 13
ZACH

"Coffee or juice?" Maya asked.

"Coffee."

Too much was preying on Zach's mind, and he hadn't slept well. The WST, yesterday's rescue, the virtual stranger in his guest room...

Because Ari was still here. Yesterday evening when he'd tried to wake her, she'd just mumbled at him to leave her alone and rolled over. Then Maya had googled "treatment for concussion" and found out that rest was important, so they'd decided to respect Ari's wishes and leave her where she was rather than carrying her back to Ms. Carrington's place. The dragon would probably call the cops if a bunch of people trooped past her window, anyway.

Maya poured two steaming mugs of coffee from the French press and added milk—regular milk for her and oat milk for him. Lactose intolerance was no joke. She'd already made poached eggs and toast, and not for the first time, he wondered how he'd possibly manage without her.

The years they'd spent apart after their parents died had been hard enough. First, they'd lost their mama, and then— on the sixth anniversary of her death—their papa had joined her on the other side. Nobody wanted two foster kids, so they'd been split up, with Zach living in LA while Maya was sent to Santa Cruz. At sixteen, he hadn't been old enough to apply for custody of his sister, so they'd been forced to wait. To plan. And three times, those carefully made plans had been tipped on their heads.

The first blow had come two weeks after he turned eighteen. He'd filed the paperwork to apply for guardianship of Maya and gotten a job loading trucks with a local food supplier. Found a place to live, just a one-bedroom apartment that needed work, but he planned to sleep on the couch so Maya could have her own space. Then he'd gotten stopped by the cops. He hadn't known the junker he was driving was stolen—he'd borrowed it from a man he'd thought was a friend—but the judge didn't much care about that. And while Zach did thirty days in the county jail, his guardianship application got tossed out.

Unsuitable to care for a minor.

The second blow? Maya's foster parents had moved to Virginia. But they were good people, and rather than toss her back into the system, they agreed to do an ICPC transfer and take her with them if she wanted that. Zach's own foster placements had been less than stellar, and he didn't want Maya to go through the same hardship, so he'd encouraged her to take the offer. Better for him to move to Virginia than for Maya to go through a dozen more homes before she aged out of the system.

Which had led to the third blow.

He'd found a job in a clothing store and begun taking classes at community college with the idea that someday, he'd transfer to take a degree in marine biology and get back to the ocean. Selling clothes paid little more than minimum wage, but he lucked out and found a cheap place to live, a sprawling old Queen Anne mansion that had seen better days. The owner offered cheap rooms as long as Zach and the other tenants helped with renovations. The deal seemed too good to pass up—even if he'd gotten a second job, it wouldn't have paid what he saved in rent. And his roommates had become friends, all nine of them, including the owner. Levi had stayed there occasionally, but most nights, he'd gone back to his family home and his overbearing parents.

Zach had learned plenty about construction—something that had paid dividends when he bought his own rehab project—and weekends had been spent on plumbing and carpentry. The place looked pretty good by the time Ruby got murdered.

Yeah, murdered.

The fallout from that, well, Zach couldn't see it ending any time soon. Even now, people still brought up the Blackstone House shitshow, either suspicious that he'd been involved or morbidly curious like a rubbernecker at a car crash. Levi had gone to jail for the killing, but that still didn't stop the conspiracy theories, which had been fuelled in no small part by Levi's parents. They'd hired fancy lawyers and private investigators and tried to pin the blame on anyone but their son.

Those months had been hell.

Maya's eighteenth birthday had coincided with the end of the trial, and the two of them had caught the first flight to California. Back to the ocean. Back to their home. Thoughts of a steady career in marine biology fell by the wayside as Zach returned to his one true love—surfing.

Only fools attempted to make a living from surfing, his dad—a pro surfer—had always said. But Zach had tried the conventional route, and where had that gotten him? If he was going to be poor, he figured he might as well be poor and happy.

But fate had dealt him a full house, and he'd ended up... well, not rich and happy, but comfortable and reasonably content. His debts were manageable, and he got to do what he enjoyed most days. The fame, he could do without, but that was a necessary evil. The women too. He wasn't interested in commitment—love was dangerous. That final day at Mavericks, his dad had been preoccupied with memories of the past, of the wife he'd lost, and Zach would always wonder whether that distraction had cost him his life.

"What time is the shoot?" he asked Maya.

"Hair and make-up at ten thirty."

"Hair and make-up? What's the point of that? They want me in the water, don't they?"

She held up her hands. "I don't make the rules."

"They're stupid rules."

"Gold Rush is paying you six figures this year, so you'll have to put up with the eyelash extensions."

"Eyelash extensions? What the fuck?" Too late, he caught the twinkle in her eye. "You're messing with me."

She nodded, giggling. "At least, I think I am. I guess lash extensions are a possibility."

"Promise you won't let them do that to me."

"I bet the girls would dig it. And speaking of girls, what should I do about Ari? Walk her home before we head out? Or leave her sleeping? Gloria will be here soon."

Gloria was Zach's biggest indulgence. With his surfing commitments, he didn't have spare time to clean, and Maya worked hard enough without having to worry about cleaning the house as well. The arrangement suited all of them—Gloria came during school hours, which allowed her to care for her two young sons, and Zach was flexible during breaks. Gloria took some time off, and on other days, she brought the kids to work with her and they swam in the pool when she was finished.

She wouldn't mind keeping an eye on Ari, even though it was technically outside of her job description, but Zach still wasn't sure about the woman currently occupying his spare bed and his thoughts. She seemed a little too good to be true.

Beautiful, kind, brave, and not an "I Love You, Zach" sign in sight. But she'd hidden the fact that she'd known who he was…

"I'll go and wake her. No need to give Gloria extra work."

"You think I should put together lunch for Ari to take with her? If she still has a headache, she probably won't feel like cooking."

That would be the neighbourly thing to do. "There's lasagne left over from last night."

"I'll make a salad too. I still can't believe she went into a rip when she couldn't even swim."

"She didn't know it was a rip."

"We should teach her, don't you think? I mean, if she's gonna be here for a while, she should learn about the ocean. Not everyone is lucky enough to have parents who are part marlin."

Maya said that "we" should teach her. She liked Ari? Zach took a sip of coffee and buttered his toast. Last summer, his sister's friend Tonya had gotten married—Maya had been maid of honour—and Tonya's new husband had been deployed to Germany three weeks after the wedding. Maya hadn't been the same since they left. Would having another girl around, one close to her age, help to ward off some of the loneliness Maya would never admit to feeling? Every time Zach asked whether she was okay, she said she was fine, but the spark had gone out of her.

"What do you think of Ari?"

"She seems nice. I found her blog—it's new, but she takes good pictures."

"What kind of pictures?"

"Wildlife, artsy sunsets, a few of the sea. No close-ups of you, if that's what you're asking." Maya knew him so well. "I don't think she's a gold digger like Baylee."

"Don't say that in front of Tyler."

Maya rolled her eyes. "As if."

Tyler wasn't rich, but that didn't stop Baylee from spending his money. Like Zach and Kai, he was comfortable. He'd decided that the pursuit of happiness was more important than a fat bank balance, and he spent his spare cash chasing waves rather than building a stock portfolio. If he needed more money, he could make more boards—he had a waiting list bigger than the waves at Nazaré—but he never liked to miss a good swell.

Zach chewed thoughtfully and found he didn't hate the idea of spending time around Ari—no, correction: of *Maya* spending time around Ari. Maybe some good could come out of yesterday's trip to Seagrass Beach after all?

CHAPTER 14
ARI

Just five more minutes…

I hadn't slept this well in years. The bed was so cosy, so soft and comfortable… Which was strange, because it sure hadn't been snug for my first week in town. My foggy brain was mulling over that puzzle when the edge of the mattress dipped, and I knifed up in an instant.

Opened my eyes.

Then it all came back.

I was in Zach Torres's guest room, and I'd probably overstayed my welcome. Was it time for dinner? I hadn't eaten much for lunch, and there was half a burrito waiting with my name on it.

"Morning." Torres placed a mug on the nightstand. "How are you feeling?"

Slightly giddy. Mental note: don't try any fast moves today, and definitely don't go anywhere near water.

"Morning?"

"You've been asleep for seventeen hours."

I lay back and groaned. Yes, I'd wanted to get close enough to Torres to carry out surveillance, but I hadn't planned on staying overnight at his house. Or for the guilt that came with it. Investigating a suspect was so much harder if you were actually starting to like the guy.

He's a criminal, Ari. A thief and possibly worse.

"Sorry. I'm so sorry."

"You looked as if you needed the rest." He nodded at the mug. "I wasn't sure how you took your coffee, so I made it black."

"Black is fine. Give me two minutes, and I'll be gone."

"No need to rush. If you have a concussion, you should take it easy. Stay away from electronic screens. And drink plenty, but not alcohol."

Dammit, I hadn't sent a report to Rennick either.

"What are you? My doctor?"

"Dr. Torres? No, but I have an associate degree in biology, so I understand the importance of staying hydrated."

"You went to college?"

None of the bios I'd read on Torres had mentioned a college education. Which made me wonder what else was missing from the available information?

"You sound surprised."

And he sounded disappointed.

"I'm just surprised you found the time to study. Don't professional surfers travel a lot?"

"I haven't always been a professional surfer." A pause. "I took a break for a few years. Figured I'd give the conventional route a try—college, steady job, nine to five. Guess I shoulda known better."

"What changed your mind?"

"Circumstances changed it for me." Was he talking about Blackstone House? During my research, that period had produced the least information on Torres. One article had mentioned him working in retail, but it hadn't gone into detail. He'd enrolled in college too? "But that's in the past. Can't say I regret the life I have now."

"I can understand why. You don't get this view from an

office." I propped myself up against the pillow and tried a sip of coffee. Freshly ground, not instant. "Thanks for this."

"Any time," he said, sounding as if he meant it.

On paper, on screen, Torres came across as confident, even cocky, a man who knew he'd been blessed with both looks and surfing ability and intended to make the most of it. But up close, he was…softer. Even though he was right on the edge of my personal space, I didn't feel uncomfortable.

"Well, I'll get out of your hair, and I truly appreciate the hospitality." I swung my legs out of bed, a move that made my head throb. "Maybe I'll see you around?"

"Your head still hurts?"

Was it that obvious? "A little."

"Why don't you take some Tylenol and come to Capitola with us today?" He hit me with that smile. "Maya's worried about leaving you on your own."

Maya? Really? I had to suppress my own grin. Being invited along on surveillance detail by the main suspect's sister was a first, but I'd take it. Skulking around in the shadows was so clichéd.

"If you're sure I won't get in the way, a day on the beach might be exactly what I need."

"You can sit with Maya. Between you, me, and the deep blue sea, I think she gets lonely sometimes, but don't tell her I said that."

Interesting. Torres wanted me to keep his sister company? That was the insinuation, and it would certainly take my plans in a whole new direction. But what better way to monitor Zach than to spend time with his closest relative and personal assistant?

"I won't say a word, I swear."

To think I'd been dreading this job… With the exception of a brief undercover stint in a luxury resort—a businessman had wanted evidence of his wife's infidelity and was willing to pay anything to get it—this was the nicest day I'd ever had at work.

The sun was shining, the photographer's assistant brought a cooler full of drinks, and I had a deckchair in prime position as Zach walked out of the sea for the seventeenth time, shirtless, flicking water out of his hair with practised ease. I had to watch. I was getting paid to do so.

"Will he have to do any actual surfing?" I asked Maya.

"Oh, for sure, but they usually like to get the other pictures done first. In case he gets any cuts and bruises later, you know?"

"Does that happen often?"

She nodded. "Most weeks. Surfing's basically a contact sport, but your opponent is the ocean."

"And people do this for fun?"

"Like so many things that are bad for you, it can be addictive."

"Do you surf?"

"Not much, not anymore. I spend all my time managing my brother's schedule."

"Kai's and Tyler's too?"

"Kai, yes. Tyler, when he needs extra help. Plus I do some work with Sal's Army."

"That's the rescue crew, right? Zach mentioned the name."

"Tyler helps to run it. Do you want another drink?"

"Is there a Coke?"

"Diet or regular?"

"Diet."

Maya fetched drinks for both of us from the cooler and passed me a dripping bottle. A small crowd had gathered to watch the activities, a handful of surfers and a bigger group of girls. The three groupies from Seagrass Beach were missing, but that was because they had more important things to do today. When Zach, Kai, and Tyler had all declined to be interviewed by the local news station, their fan club had stepped in instead. The blonde's video had been playing on TV while I ate a hasty breakfast, with the girls providing an excited—and somewhat exaggerated—commentary. At least nobody was interested in the part I'd played.

"Your brother seems tight with Kai and Tyler. Have they always been close?"

"Since we moved to Seagrass Point. The three of them worked in the surf store together, and they hit it off right away. You have no idea how relieved I was. We came here without knowing anyone, and the two of them made us feel so welcome."

"Did they grow up in this area?"

"Tyler did. Kai moved north after his father passed away and he needed a fresh start, and he rented a room from Tyler and his then-girlfriend until he could afford his own apartment."

"When you say the surf store, do you mean Board Stiff?"

"You know the place?"

"Next door to the general store? I remember looking in the window and feeling intimidated."

Maya laughed. "Tyler bought the place after the previous owner retired. Glenn moved to Wyoming to be near his daughter, but he only lasted six months there before he got sick of horses and grandchildren and came back. Now he works three days a week and keeps an eye on the place when Tyler's away."

"What does he do the rest of the time?"

"Surfs. Glenn's a longboard guy. And when he's not surfing, he waters his plants and watches the world go by."

"You're never too old to surf, huh?"

"Not if it's in your blood." Maya sounded sad, and I

wondered why she didn't surf anymore. "You really don't know how to swim? Zach said you didn't, but…" Her voice trailed off, but I hadn't missed the incredulity. "Mom and Dad had me in the water from the moment we met."

"Met?"

"I was adopted, Zach too. You didn't wonder why we look completely different?"

I nearly blurted out that none of the articles I'd read had mentioned much about their family history, but I stopped myself just in time.

"Genetics sometimes gets creative."

Haven had inherited her father's dark hair and my blue eyes. His confidence and my sneakiness. I only hoped that as she got older, none of Maxwell's many personality defects made an appearance.

Maya shrugged her acceptance. "Genetics doesn't matter. Zach's the best brother I could ever have hoped for, and our parents were amazing too."

A spike of jealousy drove through me, just for a second, but it was there. Their parents had wanted them. Loved them. My mom had treated me as an annoyance, and my dad barely knew I existed. What was worse—to feel that love and lose it, or to never experience it at all? Once again, I felt guilty for leaving Haven behind at home. What if she thought I didn't care?

"I never really knew my mom. My nana raised me, and she can't swim either."

"It's never too late to learn."

"I grew up in Sin City. Drowning didn't seem like a risk I'd have to face."

"You used to live in Las Vegas? I've always wanted to visit. Just for a week because I'd probably lose all my money in a casino, but I'd go to a show every night. Tyler's brother saw Cirque du Soleil there, and Indigo Rain. Luna Maara too, and I've always wanted to hear her sing live. Did you go to many of the shows?"

"I was always too busy working, plus the tickets were out of my price range."

"Where did you work?"

"I waitressed in various places. From what I heard, Luna Maara's manager is a lousy tipper."

"Figures. Head honchos get to their position by stepping on the people beneath them."

The way she said it, I knew she'd had personal experience. I was about to agree when her phone rang—no, not *her* phone, Zach's phone—and she paled a shade as she checked the screen.

"It's Maya. … No, he's busy. … Okay, I'll get him." She cursed softly as she stood. "Zach, Zed's on the phone."

Zach's smile turned into a scowl. Interesting. Zed Nelson was the promoter of the World Surf Tour, and Zach's de facto boss. Despite Zach's praise of the man in the press, they didn't get along?

"Give me five minutes, guys."

Zach abandoned the surfboard propped on the sand, and when he took the phone from Maya, there was no mistaking the tension in his frame. He listened for a moment, his expression growing blacker with every passing second.

"I helped to save a girl's life, and that's your takeaway? That I called Khloe an idiot? I said it in the heat of the moment, and I doubt she even noticed." A pause, and Zach blew out a long breath. "Okay, I apologise. I wouldn't have fucking sworn if I'd known the video would end up on the internet."

In my opinion, Zach's comment had been justified—Khloe *had* been an idiot, filming instead of helping. And Zed Nelson sounded like a first-class whiner.

"I don't have time," Zach continued, then listened to some high-pitched babble. "Fine, one interview. *One.* Send them over." He glanced across at me. "Yeah, I do know who she was. Sure, I'll ask her." Zach put his hand over the phone. "Ari, you wanna do a news interview?"

"Hell no."

"She said no." A soft snort. "Good luck with that. She doesn't have any *contractual commitments*." He tossed the phone onto the deckchair, and it bounced off into the sand. "Ari, you might want to keep your head down later. They're sending a news crew to the beach in front of the house."

"I bet Ms. Carrington will be thrilled."

"That's what I'm counting on."

"You can hide out in my apartment if you want," Maya offered. "It's probably the safest place if Ms. Carrington goes on the warpath."

Maya was a sweetheart. Genuinely nice, the kind of person I'd love as a friend if I were in California for pleasure rather than business. And spending time with her might give me more of an insight into her brother. One thing that bothered me about Jankowski's investigation into the betting irregularities was that he'd spent a lot of time considering the "who" and the "how" but no time wondering "why?" What was Zach's motive for throwing the contests? He didn't strike me as a man who'd be driven by money alone.

"Thanks, I really appreciate it."

CHAPTER 15
ARI

"Could you pass a screw?" Zach asked.

"A long one or a short one?"

"Long."

I picked a screw out of the box, and Zach took it with slim fingers, the electric screwdriver in his other hand as he balanced on the ladder. Turned out that surfing wasn't his only skill—he was pretty good at DIY too.

We were in Maya's living room, installing the floor-to-ceiling bookshelves she'd longed for ever since she was a little girl. I'd learned plenty about the Torres siblings over the past two weeks.

The night I'd hidden out in Maya's apartment, I'd found it was still a work in progress. A project. They'd spent years fixing up the main house, she said, and until last year, Maya had lived there with her brother. But she'd always dreamed of having her own space, and when Zach had bought the property all those years ago, he'd promised to convert the garage loft into an apartment for her someday. And he didn't break promises.

This job was getting both easier and harder. Easier because Maya was likeable and kept inviting me over to hang out, plus Zach and the others would happily give me a ride to whatever beach they were surfing at so I could count nurdles and take photos for my blog. Zach—or rather Maya—had mentioned the blog on his Instagram page, and now my hurriedly set-up website was getting more visitors than I ever imagined. The founder of the *Say No to Nurdles!* campaign had even sent me a thank-you note.

But it was harder because of the guilt. I was living a lie. Zach and Maya were helping me, and sooner or later, I'd have to betray them, a prospect that left me feeling sick. A part of me wanted to quit, to make this life in California real, but with Haven waiting for me back home, that was out of the question. And if Rennick's suspicions were correct, then Zach was a fraudster himself. Although not a car thief—Maya had told me the full story about that, her voice indignant, how Zach had been set up by a so-called friend and the judge decided to make an example of him.

At least Rennick was happy. Well, I assumed he was. I dutifully sent my reports to Lila, and he paid each weekly invoice on time. He hadn't said a word about the rescue drama, and only once had he asked a question—a request for me to monitor Zach's spending habits if possible. Did he use cash or cryptocurrency, anything that wouldn't go through regular, traceable channels? So far, I hadn't seen any evidence of that. Maya did most of his spending for him.

Lila had thawed a tiny bit, thankfully. She'd signed off her last email with "Hope you have a good weekend" instead of "Kind regards," so it felt as if I was making progress there.

Today, Maya was preparing lunch in the main house while Zach and I worked on the shelves. Earning our keep, he said. Kai had gone to Santa Cruz in his truck to pick up more lumber and a new saw blade. Zach reckoned the shelves would take another week or two to finish, and then I could help Maya to paint them.

"If the surfing thing doesn't work out, you could always turn to carpentry," I kidded.

"You should see my plumbing skills. If you need a bathroom installed, I'm your man."

"Any tips for fixing a shower? Mine only runs hot when it feels like it."

"Hit it with a wrench? But do it quietly."

"I don't have a wrench. Would a hardback copy of *DIY for Dummies* work?"

Zach laughed. "If you can find me a set of body armour, I'll take a look."

Body armour was necessary when it came to dealing with Ms. Carrington. The memory of her steaming down her driveway to yell at the news crew who'd dared to set up their camera an inch onto her property still made me giggle. The broadcast had been live, and now everyone in Santa Cruz and the surrounding counties knew to give the place a wide berth.

"You'd run the Carrington gauntlet to do that for me? I'm touched."

"On second thought, you can just take a shower at my place. I'll leave towels out."

I wasn't sure whether he was serious or not, and I didn't want to push him. Not when I already had reasonable access to the property. But I was curious to learn more about Zach. His past fascinated me.

"I promise not to use all of your hot water. Where did you learn plumbing? And carpentry? Is there anything you can't do?"

"Those years I went to college? That was in Virginia. Money was tight, so I lived in a shared house with a bunch of other people, and we were renovating the place in return for a discount on the rent." He put down the screwdriver and met my gaze. "If you've googled me, you know where that was."

Zach would probably think it was weirder if I *hadn't* googled him.

"Blackstone House."

He sighed. "Yeah. I had nothing to do with Ruby's death, I swear."

"If I thought for a moment that you did, I wouldn't be here alone with you."

I spoke the truth. Now that I'd spent time with Zach, I could accept that he might be involved in a betting scam, and I could believe he might lose his temper on occasion, particularly if an asshole like Zed Nelson rubbed him the wrong way, but stabbing a roommate after sex and carving satanic symbols into her chest? No way. He wasn't a psycho.

"Not everyone thinks that way."

"But the guy who did it got convicted, didn't he? And went to prison?"

"Yeah, he did, and he's not getting out. But his legal team tried to muddy the waters and blame the rest of us."

"Why you? Why not some mysterious stranger? Wouldn't that have been easier?"

"How much did you read online?"

Everything I could find, but I still wanted to hear what Zach had to say on the matter. I'd become a PI because I loved mysteries, and—as Nana always said—I was too nosy for my own good.

"An article or two. But if you don't want to talk about it, that's fine. I'm just morbidly curious. True crime podcasts are a guilty pleasure."

"Well, Ruby died on a Tuesday, and we didn't find her body until Friday. But we know that nobody else came or went from the house during that time. The windows were locked from the inside, and there were cameras over every door, good ones."

"You had a high-end security system on a half-renovated house?"

"It was in reasonable shape by then—ten of us had been

working on it for two years. And one of my roommates was…
How do I put this? A little paranoid."

Which one? I knew all of their names except one—
Dawson Masters, Braxton Dupré, Justin Norquist, Greyson
Meyer, Jerry Knight, Nolan de Luca, and Levi Sykes, plus an
unidentified minor who never should have been there. Sykes
had been sentenced to life in prison. The only housemate with
an alibi was Greyson Meyer, who'd been away visiting family,
so the others had naturally fallen under suspicion.

I was ready to probe deeper when the door opened.

"Lunch is ready, and I mean *ready*," Maya told us. "I put
the omelettes in the oven to stay warm, but they'll rubberise if
you don't come and eat them."

"What about Kai?" Zach asked. "We're not waiting for
him?"

"Kai's already eating. Plus we need to go over the final
arrangements for the Huntington Beach Classic."

"Did you book the hotel rooms?"

Maya gave him a *look*. "No, I thought we could camp on
the beach. Ari, are you coming? My room has two beds, so
you can share if you want."

I hadn't realised I'd be invited, so I'd booked a single at a
budget motel on the outskirts of town. But Maya's offer was
much better.

"I've never watched a surfing contest before. If it's okay
for me to join you, I'll gladly chip in toward the room."

Zach waved a hand. "Just carry a clipboard around, and
we can write it off as a business expense. Right, Maya?"

"No problem. And if you don't mind running the
occasional errand, we can cover your meals too."

"Tell me what to do and when to do it, and I'll run errands
all weekend."

Maya beamed at me. "I won't say no to that offer. We're
driving down on Tuesday with Kai so everyone has time to
acclimate to the chaos."

"What about Tyler and Baylee?"

"They're leaving a day earlier," Zach said. "Tyler needs to talk to a guy about buying a surf store."

"Doesn't he already own a surf store?"

"Yeah, but he's thinking of expanding. Turning Board Stiff into a brand rather than just selling other people's stuff, and if he's gonna add to his portfolio, then Surf City is the place to do it. The owner of Big Break wants to retire, and Tyler needs to check out the location and discuss the price he'd be looking for."

"While Baylee just wants to shop," Maya muttered under her breath. Brother and sister exchanged a look.

But Baylee did have her uses—she'd reported that Shiloh, the little girl I'd helped to rescue from the rip, had regained consciousness and was expected to make a full recovery. I only hoped Shiloh's mom had learned her lesson about watching her kids.

"I'd love to get a ride down for the contest."

And maybe, just maybe, I'd see something useful while I hung around behind the scenes.

CHAPTER 16
ARI

I f I'd thought the Zach Torres exhibition at Pleasure Point was a circus, the Huntington Beach Classic was the Las Vegas Cirque du Soleil of surfing contests. It came complete with jugglers, a dance troupe, and a trio of fire-eaters to entertain the crowd, and at nine a.m. on Saturday morning, we gathered in the WST equivalent of the Big Top. And if the surfers were the acrobats, then Zed Nelson was the ringmaster, an over-tanned loudmouth with a soul patch, a suspiciously smooth forehead, a ponytail, and gold earrings. I put him in his late forties, but he dressed twenty years younger. His sneakers probably cost more than I made in a month.

I'd figured I was unimportant enough to hover on the periphery, unnoticed, but Nelson ruined that plan when he spotted Maya and asked, "So, who's this lovely lady?"

After Maya introduced me as a friend from out of town, he kissed me on both cheeks, European-style, instead of shaking hands. I disliked him immediately. In Vegas, I'd met a thousand Zed Nelsons, and the veneer of money and expensive aftershave did nothing to hide his true nature. The man was slime in a skin suit.

"And how long are you staying here in California, Ari?"

I shrugged, noncommittal. "I haven't decided yet."

"Well, I hope we see more of you on the tour. We'll be back here for the Surf 365 Special in September. If you need a ticket, just have Maya call my people."

"Thanks, I appreciate that."

He looked me up and down, his gaze lingering on my breasts. "We'd give you VIP access, of course."

"As I said, I don't know if I'll still be here."

Maya looped her arm through mine. "We have to go check on Zach's stuff."

As soon as we were out of earshot, I made a gagging noise. "Is he always like that?"

"Yes."

"How come nobody's punched his teeth out yet?"

"Because he's the boss."

"He's a lawsuit waiting to happen."

Although a man like him would probably settle out of court. An NDA, a payoff, and he'd be free to molest his next victim.

Outside the tent, Maya paused to study the water. To my untrained eye, the wave was merely…well, a wave, but Maya picked up on the nuances.

"The ocean looks good today."

"I guess that's a matter of perspective. To me, it just looks wet."

"See the way the wave angles in a semicircle toward the beach? The pier makes it do that. It's a nice, consistent wave, quite slabby and a little better in the winter, but scheduling means we're here in August."

I'd always assumed that surfing was a summer sport, but since I'd begun hanging out with Torres and his buddies, I'd found out that the opposite was true. Winter meant bigger waves. And also thicker wetsuits.

"What's a slabby wave? Is that good or bad?"

"Depends. Slab waves are fast, not so great for beginners, but fun for experienced surfers."

"Glad I'm staying on the beach, then."

"Zach will get you on a board someday."

"There's a better chance of me ice skating in hell."

Maya stared out to sea for a moment longer, then cut her eyes sideways. "He likes you, you know."

"He's been very kind. I moved here without much of a plan, and he—and you—have made everything so much easier. I'd still be taking cold showers and living on burritos otherwise."

"No, I mean he *likes* you."

I stiffened. That couldn't be right. Yes, Zach and I spent plenty of time talking, and he'd added my fingerprints to his home security system, and last week, he'd left his boards behind and driven me a few miles up the coast for a picnic at his favourite non-surfing beach. But he'd never tried to touch me. Not really. The occasional brush of his hand when we were both moving around the kitchen, or him covering my eyes to surprise me with the view, or that time he'd carried me to bed when I was exhausted, that was only him being friendly.

Wasn't it?

Oh, shit.

What if Maya was right?

No, she couldn't be right.

"I think he's just acting neighbourly."

"Okay, you keep telling yourself that."

"I'm only in Seagrass Point temporarily. My aim is to travel."

Maya shrugged. "Zach travels." Then she checked her watch. "We should listen to the briefing."

I wanted Maya to be wrong. *Needed* her to be wrong. But I'd been so focused on work and memorising every freaking person Zach talked to for my reports that perhaps I hadn't paid as much attention to his words and actions as I should have.

Back in the tent, Nelson was standing on a platform, aiming a laser pointer at a schedule projected onto a screen beside him. Surfers would head out in groups of six for ninety minutes at a time, four groups each for men and women because this was an *equal opportunities* tour, he stressed. Competitors got points for each wave they surfed based on technical ability and style, with the best three scores being added together to give an overall total. The top two from each heat would go through to the knockout rounds tomorrow.

From what Zach had said, the World Surf Tour was the toughest surf contest ever created. Four disciplines were covered—longboard, shortboard, aerial, and big-wave—and each round was physically gruelling. Nelson was all about the show, and he liked the spectators to get their money's worth. Because ultimately, that meant more money for him.

But the WST had also made Zach Torres famous, and sponsorship and endorsement deals had followed. Occasionally, I overheard Maya on the phone, discussing finances, and Torres had to be pulling in high six figures each year, if not seven. Which should have made risking it all for a betting scam unthinkable, but I also knew he had debt. The Twilight file told me he'd remortgaged Haven's Rest to invest in Surf 365, an inland surf park that offered perfect waves all year round, as well as an on-site hotel, camping facilities, three restaurants, a gym, and weekly entertainment. Torres wasn't poor, but he wasn't rolling in cash either.

Although he didn't seem to care much about money. Yes, he had a beautiful home, but I understood now that he'd done a lot of the work himself over the span of several years. He'd hired a specialist firm to repair the concrete and waterproof the structure, but the plumbing, the carpentry, the painting and decorating, that had all been Zach. Nor did he have expensive tastes. Most of his clothes were gifted by his sponsors, Tyler gave him deep discounts on his boards, and he drove a six-year-old truck.

In short, Zach Torres was a conundrum.

A conundrum who was currently sitting in the front row of the briefing, legs outstretched, jaw clenched as Zed Nelson went over the clothing rules.

"Shorts for the men, bikinis for the women. Wetsuits are for pussies—we're in California, folks, and the water temperature is sixty-eight. Ladies, I noticed several one-pieces in the line-up in J-Bay, and apart from Rebecca's effort with the cutouts, I wasn't impressed. Let's make this ratings-friendly, okay? And gentlemen, a reminder that rash vests aren't permitted without prior authorisation. There are fifty thousand women on the beach today, and they're all screaming for abs."

"Equal opportunities," Maya muttered. "Nobody's allowed to wear comfortable clothing."

"Why do they put up with this?"

"Because if they don't, there are a hundred others waiting to take their place."

"Would he really kick a star off the tour?"

"Yes. Matt Morella was the reigning champion, and Zed booted him over an argument about sunglasses."

"Sunglasses? Are you serious?"

"Everyone has to wear Le Ray branded sunglasses, and Matt said they made his face look weird. There was a massive fight, and he got replaced by Will Strohe." Maya tipped her chin toward a guy sitting ramrod straight, nodding as Nelson talked about meet-and-greet sessions. "A team player."

Ass-kisser, more like.

"Each competitor will need to participate in two selfie sessions over the weekend," Nelson said. "Preferably one each day, but if interview commitments get in the way, speak with Destiny and she'll shuffle things around. Don't forget, we all share responsibility for collective success. Let's spread the load."

Spread the load. Nelson's words reminded me of another question I had regarding the case, one that nobody had managed to answer satisfactorily. According to Rennick, all the wagers against Torres had been made with AnyBet and its sister companies. To him, the reason was simple—they were the best and accepted any bet a gambler cared to make. But would a layperson think the same way? Why wouldn't they try making bets with other sportsbooks, entities outside of AnyBet's network? Or laying bets on a peer-to-peer exchange? That way, their activities would be harder to detect. Anyone who'd reached the pinnacle of their career and then decided to risk everything to make a quick buck must surely have studied the world of sportsbooks as much as I had, so what was I missing? Why weren't they spreading the load as Nelson had just instructed his competitors to do?

Was I seeing something that others had missed?

And what was the damn motive?

Morty Coulson had always said that motives could be condensed into the four Ls: love, lust, loathing, or loot. Okay, so he was mostly talking about murder, but in my experience, the theory worked pretty well for other types of crime as well.

Love could lead to mercy killings, a hastened end of a loved one's suffering. Lust could push a person to do the unthinkable in the pursuit of a sexual payoff—harm a rival or destroy an innocent life for kicks. Loathing... Well, revenge was one hell of a motivator. Many, many years ago, a playwright said that hell hath no fury like a woman scorned, which had always struck me as kind of sexist because men could be assholes too. I'd seen it over and over again—a mild-mannered accountant who set fire to his ex-business partner's home following a fallout, a teenager who vandalised his father's car after a fight about his allowance and then tried to blame the damage on his cousin. Who were Zach's enemies?

And loot… As a society, we'd been trained to want more, more, more. Ads pushed the luxury lifestyle, and people practically worshipped billionaires. Some people would do anything to achieve the American dream.

Rennick and Jankowski both assumed we were dealing with a "loot" crime. A common or garden thief, albeit a wealthy one, committing a crime they saw as low risk. AnyBet, a corporate entity, was the only victim, and who cared if a corporation lost a few bucks in profit? Quite honestly, I wasn't particularly bothered if Digby Rennick could afford one less rock for his zen garden either, but I also took pride in my job. And my curiosity knew no bounds.

Which was why I'd begun to wonder if someone was targeting Rennick personally. He was a bit of a dick, after all. Had he kicked any business partners to the kerb? Did he have a scorned ex-lover or two lurking in the background? Nobody with that amount of money got through twenty years in the corporate world unscathed.

On stage, Nelson was droning on. "And we need to keep the rescue crew out of sight this weekend. In J-Bay, a jet ski passed in front of the camera right as Kai did a cutback and ruined what would have been an excellent shot."

"It was a layback snap," Maya said under her breath. "He knows nothing about surfing."

"So, this weekend, let's keep the jet skis on the other side of the pier with the fast boat, and they can slide in when necessary."

There was a chorus of dissent, not only from the safety team but from the surfers too, and who could blame them? Zach's voice was the loudest, and I was oddly proud of that.

"Is this a joke? We're risking our lives out there."

"We're talking five-foot waves. It's hardly Mavericks."

Ouch. That was a low blow, considering Zach's father had died there. Maya didn't look too impressed either.

Kai jumped in, and I noticed he kept a hand on Zach's

arm. "You know that someone can drown in a puddle if they're unconscious, right?"

"Let us do our job," Tyler added. He was a key member of the safety team, and I knew that having him there let Zach breathe easier.

Eventually, Nelson buckled under the weight of popular opinion, not least the reminder from one of the female competitors that making the safety team stand back could lead to a nasty lawsuit in the event of an accident. But the disagreement left a dark cloud hanging over the day when everyone filed outside.

And I knew my initial assessment had been right on the money: Zed Nelson was an asshole.

CHAPTER 17
ARI

I barely saw Zach for the rest of the weekend, at least up close. Maya found me a pair of binoculars so I could watch him and Kai compete. They both won their heats on Saturday for an easy ride into the knockout rounds. I had an easy ride too. Rennick had messaged via Lila to say that all looked normal in the betting patterns this weekend, so although I had to be vigilant, it was unlikely that Torres would throw the contest by prior arrangement.

On Saturday evening, the competitors were expected to eat together, with the tour sponsors invited along as guests and the media in attendance. Zach and Kai had seemed distinctly unenthused by the event while Maya was on edge, pacing our shared room as we waited for room service to arrive.

"They'll be okay," I told her. "It's just dinner."

"Will they?" Maya stopped mid-stride and spun to face me. "It's a room full of testosterone and alcohol. Shane Lotter's on the tour this year, and Kai can't stand him."

"Really? Kai's always come across as an easygoing guy."

"He is, but not when someone drops into a wave on top of him and breaks his arm."

"Shane really did that?"

"Yes, he really did, five years ago, but he never apologised. And last year..." Maya closed her eyes for a moment. "Last year, Zach punched out one of the sponsors. Well, his son, but same difference. And the year before, he gave Scottie Stenson a black eye."

"What? Why?"

Had Rennick been right in his assessment of Zach's character, and I was wrong? The thought gave me chills. In my line of work, being able to judge a person quickly and accurately was vital.

"Scottie always makes horrible comments about women. And the sponsor's son was hitting on Macy Burton—she was a newbie, only nineteen—and he wouldn't take no for an answer. So Zach got involved, and it was a mess. Somebody called the cops, and then the lawyers got involved. A *real* mess."

In all my research, I hadn't heard a whisper about any altercation, but at least I hadn't been wrong when it came to Zach's morals. Good for him. I had no idea who Macy Burton was—possibly the Macy I'd seen listed in Zach's call log?— but if I'd been on the receiving end of unwanted attention, I'd have done the same as Zach did. If nothing else, my brief relationship with Maxwell Suker had left me with little tolerance for jackasses.

"I had no idea."

"Zed covered everything up, and believe me, he hates having to grovel." Maya flopped backward onto her bed. "Can we talk about something else?"

Sure. Because although I was here to work, I also wanted to be a friend to Maya—at least temporarily—and right now, she sounded wretched.

"When we get back to Seagrass Point, how do you feel about taking a day away from the beach?" Rennick couldn't expect me to work twenty-four-seven, and even though this job was far from the worst I'd had, I was still tired. Emotionally drained. "I read that there's a butterfly preserve nearby?"

"It's beautiful, but the butterflies are only there in the winter. We could go in October?"

"If I'm still here, I'd love that." Great, reminding Maya that I planned to leave only made her frown. "How about visiting a vineyard? Aren't there one or two nearby?"

"If you want to visit a vineyard, we should go and see Zach's friend Nolan. He owns a vineyard in the Sierra Nevada foothills."

Zach's friend Nolan… Could that be Nolan de Luca? There was little mention of him online after the Blackstone House affair, but what if he'd relocated to California too?

"He offers tours?"

"Not, like, organised ones, but he'll show us around."

"Think we could drive there and back in a day?"

"Better to stay overnight. He has plenty of space. I'll ask Zach to call him, assuming he doesn't end up in jail this evening."

"Let's watch a movie, okay? Everything will be fine."

At least, I hoped it would. And now I had something interesting to look forward to.

Damn, I needed earplugs. The crowd on Sunday was twice the size of Saturday's, and it felt as though every single person was screaming as Zach leapt off the top step of the podium. He'd had a wild ride in the final against Kai, but when he caught a monster wave, one Maya called "the bomb," it was all over. Zach shot out of a barrel, performed a frontside air reverse, and took a bow as he rode the wave to shore. Even Kai had been cheering as Zach hopped off the board, and they'd hugged each other at the prize ceremony too. Shane Lotter hadn't looked so happy on the third step, but that was his problem.

The downside of winning was that Zach had a hundred more interviews to do before he could leave, but Maya had planned ahead and booked a table in the hotel restaurant, and we weren't due to drive home until tomorrow anyway.

"Ari, Ari, Ari!"

Who was yelling my name? As I headed toward the exit, I turned to see a girl waving frantically over the barrier, and it took me a moment to place the face. It was Erin, the girl I'd met at Pleasure Point on my first day in California, except now her hair was green. I elbowed my way past a group of drunk VIPs and went to say hi.

"What are you doing here?" she asked. "I thought you knew nothing about surfing?"

"I still don't, but it's growing on me. Your boss let you take time off today?"

"Oh, I totally got fired from that job. But don't worry; I found a new one. The manager wanted me to work this weekend, but I told him at the interview, no way, not when the Huntington Beach Classic was on."

"Another grocery store?"

"Nah, now I'm serving drinks in a strip club, but the money's way better, and I'm already used to cleaning up gross spillages. Plus I get every Sunday off, so I can go to the beach."

"Strip clubs don't open on Sundays?"

"Nah, all the customers go to church then." I stared at her for a beat, and she started giggling. "Just kidding. Although we do have one pastor who comes in for lap dances."

"Are you serious?"

"He removes the collar, but it's definitely him. He takes the dollar bills off the collection plate and stuffs them into Roxy's G-string. Ohmigosh, is that Maya Torres?"

I turned to see Maya heading in our direction. "Yes, she's—"

Huh. Erin had disappeared. Weird.

But thirty other girls had taken her place behind the barrier, and they were all begging for posters of Zach, stickers, postcards, even locks of his freaking hair. Judging by Maya's sigh, this was a regular occurrence. By the time we escaped an hour later, we had a list of eighty names split between Maya's iPad and various scraps of paper, and a whole lot of mailing to do. But at least the fans were happy.

"I'm so sorry about that," I told her. "I stopped to talk to one person, and the others just appeared from nowhere."

"Relax—providing Zach Torres memorabilia is my job. The girls love it."

"I swear I'll help to pack the posters."

"That's sweet of you. Then maybe we can take that trip to the vineyard we spoke about?"

"Deal. What time is dinner?"

"The table's booked for eight o'clock."

At eight o'clock, there was still no sign of Zach or Kai, but when Maya and I walked into the hotel bar at seven forty-five, Tyler and Baylee were already seated in the restaurant area. Maya groaned at the exact time I did. Tyler was a good guy, but honestly, what did he see in that woman? Yes, she was stunningly pretty, but hospital gossip excepted, she was also a pain in everybody's ass.

Maya checked her phone again. "Zach says they won't be long."

"We could sneak out and come back later?"

"Too late." Maya waved. "Tyler and Baylee have seen us. There isn't enough Tylenol in the world for this."

"Is your headache getting worse?"

She nodded, then winced. "I think it's because I've been squinting at a screen in the sun all day."

"Why don't you go and lie down for a while? I'll tell them you're not feeling well."

I expected her to shrug it off the way she always did, but instead, she gave an apologetic smile.

"Would you mind? If I don't get some rest, it'll be ten times worse tomorrow."

If I could wait tables at a third-rate diner in Vegas, I could handle Baylee for fifteen minutes. Probably if I asked a question about her designer purse, she'd talk for that long by herself. Or her acting roles, although I'd looked her up on IMDB, and her biggest claim to fame was a single line as a bartender in a Scott Lowes romcom. I glanced across at the table and saw that Tyler had already ordered water and a bottle of wine. Smart guy. But who were the other two seats for? Zach, Kai, Tyler, Baylee, Maya, and me—that was six. But the table was set for eight.

"Who else is coming?" I asked.

"Oh, Zach's friend Dawson and his girlfriend are in town. They're nice, though. Not all pretentious like some Hollywood people."

Click, click, click. Another piece slotted into place. Dawson must be Dawson Masters, another Blackstone House alumnus. He'd made the news again when he began dating up-and-coming actress Violet Miller, the same Violet Miller who'd been pictured riding tandem on a surfboard with Zach earlier in the year. In a plot worthy of a movie, there'd also been a stalker involved, and a kidnapping, but Violet had refused to discuss the details publicly.

Was it strange that the Blackstone housemates had stayed in touch? If I'd been involved in that mess, I wasn't sure I'd want a reminder of the past. Let sleeping dogs lie.

Before I'd finished that thought, whispers began in the

dining room, and there they were. A Hollywood star with a huge, hot guy at her side. Not quite Zach Torres hot—I was staying objective here—but certainly sizzling.

Violet spotted Maya at the bar and waved, then the crowds parted as Dawson followed her toward us. She wore navy-blue capri pants and a pink beaded top, casual but stylish, and Dawson was dressed in jeans and a faded T-shirt with *Sun of a Beach* written across the chest.

"Maya? It's good to see you again."

The two embraced, and Violet's warmth seemed genuine. Dawson followed up with a kiss on the cheek, but not the sleazy kind.

"Zach's not here yet?" he asked.

"He's running late. Uh, this is Ari. A friend of ours."

Violet took both of my hands in hers. "It's lovely to meet you. Are you having dinner with us?"

Somebody pinch me. Nana would have a fit when I told her I'd been speaking with Hollywood royalty. She went to the movies twice a month with her friend Reba, come rain, come shine, and they'd seen *Hidden Intent* twice, probably giggling like schoolgirls at the dirty bits. Reba snuck snacks into the theatre in her prosthetic leg because she "didn't work for fifty years to pay ten bucks for a package of M&Ms."

"Yes, although I didn't realise you were coming. It's nice to meet you too."

Dawson held out a hand and introduced himself, and I shook it. The guy was built like a tank. No wonder Violet seemed relaxed with him around—the way he scanned the restaurant, ever vigilant, nothing would get past.

"Should we sit down? Or get a drink first?" Violet asked.

"Our table's ready. Maya, are you...?"

Violet picked up on my concern. "Are you okay?"

"I have a headache."

"Do you need Advil? I have some in my purse."

"Painkillers aren't really helping. I thought I might lie

down for a few minutes, but…" Maya waved at the restaurant. "I don't want to be unsociable."

"If you're not feeling good, then you should rest. We can catch up another time. The cottage is more or less habitable now—we have couches and everything—so whenever Zach gets a break from surfing, we'd love to see you both."

"I'll check his schedule and call you?"

"Great."

Maya took a step backward. "Thanks for being so understanding."

And then she was gone, leaving me alone with a first-class diva, an A-list actress, the Hulk's brother, and Tyler. Thank goodness for Tyler—at least there was one person I could talk to.

CHAPTER 18
ARI

Our table was a large round one, much nicer than the usual rectangular version where someone got stuck on the end and you wound up talking to the person next to you all evening. Dawson tucked himself and Violet into the corner, backs to the wall, the position that clearly made him the most comfortable, and I reached for the chair beside Violet because the other option was sitting next to Baylee. A waiter practically sprinted across the room and yanked the seat out, huffing out an apology to Violet that he hadn't managed to get there in time.

"Oh, it's fine." And when he'd left, she added under her breath, "Get nominated for a couple of awards, and people think I can't work a chair anymore. Or a door, or even my own feet."

Dawson laughed. "Vi isn't a fan of golf carts."

"I just feel like such a fool riding around in one, and even more of an idiot when they get stuck in the freaking sand."

"Was that the commotion over by the pier?" Tyler asked. "I heard the marshals call for help on the radio."

"Guess which pictures will be splashed across the internet tomorrow?"

"Where did you get your purse?" Baylee interrupted. "Is it a Valentino?"

"Uh, I'm not sure? I think someone gave it to me."

"It's definitely a Valentino, but last season."

"I only brought it because it has a shoulder strap."

Baylee rolled her eyes. The bottle of white in front of her was almost empty, and I was fairly sure she'd drunk most of it. Tyler didn't seem to touch alcohol at all.

"This season's purses are prettier. More flowers and gold studs. You can never have too many studs."

Violet's mouth said, "Really? I haven't seen them," but her expression said, "Help me." Fortunately, Zach and Kai picked that moment to arrive, although it took them five minutes to reach us because they kept stopping to pose for photos and sign autographs. But they finally made it, and I wasn't quite prepared for the brush of Zach's hand across my back. His touch made me shiver.

"Hey."

"Congratulations on winning."

"The wave did the hard work. Where's Maya?"

"She had a headache, so she went to lie down."

"You think one of us should check on her?" Kai asked, and was it me, or did he sound a little too disappointed by her absence?

"I think she just wants to sleep."

Zach took the place next to mine, and Kai sat on the other side of him, leaving an empty spot beside Baylee. Smart move. Although if she kept drinking at the same pace, maybe she'd do us a favour and pass out before dessert?

Violet, though, was a sweetheart. Incredibly down to earth and not at all like the prickly airhead the gossip websites made her out to be, even when Baylee not-so-subtly tried to hit her up for a role in her next movie. Once she'd politely explained that the casting director made those kinds of decisions, she chatted happily over an appetiser of grilled goat's cheese, no airs or graces whatsoever. Dawson seemed to be the strong, silent type. He didn't say much, but he watched everything. The papers said he was former special forces, and I could believe that. He had this *aura*.

A waiter came to clear the plates, while a second placed a magnum of champagne into the ice bucket beside the table.

"Who ordered that?" Baylee asked. "I didn't order that."

And she'd been ordering most of the alcohol, as well as drinking it. The woman's bladder must have the capacity of Lake Superior.

"It's from Alexa," the waiter told her. "It was ordered by telephone."

"Who's Alexa?"

Zach obviously knew. "An old friend."

He didn't elaborate, but I caught the look that passed between him and Dawson, as well as Dawson's quiet mutter of, "Fuckin' Alexa."

Colour me intrigued. Who exactly was Alexa? I hadn't heard Zach mention the name before, but now wasn't the time to pry, not with Baylee at the table. Another point of note? Violet didn't seem puzzled. She also knew who Alexa was.

And after the entrée, I got the chance to ask her.

I was washing my hands in the bathroom when she walked out of a stall, straightening her top. She smiled at me in the mirror, then grimaced at her own reflection.

"SPF fifty, and I still get sunburned."

"It might just be the lighting in here."

I looked kind of pink too, and my skin usually had an olive tone, thanks to my non-father.

"I hope so, otherwise tomorrow's headlines will be talking about my hot flashes. 'Is Violet Miller menopausal?' Which would make a change because last month, I ate too much cake and they thought I was pregnant."

"I guess most people only see the good parts of life in the

public eye. The huge homes, the glamorous outfits, the red-carpet shindigs."

"'Violet Miller unblocks toilet' doesn't sell papers."

"Plumbing problems?"

"All part of rehabbing an old house. Here's a tip: whenever a reporter asks you a question, just smile and walk away. It's fifty-fifty whether you get labelled as 'standoffish' or 'mysterious,' but either is better than the press twisting every word you say."

"Oh, I don't have to worry about that. I'm a nobody."

"Now that you're Zach's nobody, that makes you a somebody."

"What?" I quickly realised her mistake. "Oh, no, no, we're not together. Actually, I'm more of a friend of Maya's."

"Really?" Violet turned to face me. "You haven't noticed the way he looks at you?"

First Maya and now Violet... Could it be true? The thought made my heart sink. Not because I didn't like Zach, but because I did. He was the type of guy I'd always dreamed of meeting—kind, generous, laid back, and damn, he was sexy. But I was a fake. Cut me and I bled lies. Nothing could happen, and I had to keep my distance for both of our sakes.

"We're neighbours, that's all." And I needed to change the subject. "Any idea who Alexa is?"

"Do I detect a hint of jealousy?"

Violet didn't give up, did she? I had to laugh.

"No, just curiosity. I checked the wine list, and that bottle of champagne cost six hundred bucks."

"It did? Wow. Can you actually tell the difference between twenty-dollar wine and six-hundred-dollar wine? People talk about bouquet and complexity, but they taste the same to me."

"You're partly paying for the heritage, but more expensive wines tend to be aged in oak barrels, plus they use higher-quality hand-harvested grapes, which gives a more intense flavour. Uh, I dated a wine snob once." My cheeks heated, partly with embarrassment but mostly with anger. Haven's father would happily drop hundreds of bucks on a bottle of Chateau Fonbel St. Emilion, but he'd refused to pony up for diapers. "It's all a matter of preference, though, and Alexa's gift was very...thoughtful."

"You don't need to worry about her—she's not an ex-girlfriend or anything like that. Dawson said Zach's never gotten serious over a woman before. Like, he mostly does no-strings hook-ups, not dinner dates." Violet clapped both hands over her mouth. "Shoot, I shouldn't have said that."

"Relax—as I said, there's nothing going on between us."

Violet's look said *yeah, right*. "Alexa used to room with Dawson and Zach years ago, that's all. I don't think she even lives around here."

Jackpot. They used to be roommates? As far as I knew, the only home Zach and Dawson had shared was Blackstone House, but there was nobody named Alexa on the published list of tenants. Unless... Had I just found the "unidentified minor"?

"You don't *think* she lives around here?"

"Well, I've never met her in person, but the housewarming gift she sent us was postmarked Japan."

The bathroom door opened, and a group of women walked in, ending what had been an interesting conversation. All those little snippets Violet had revealed, and she didn't even realise she'd done it.

Back at the table, it didn't escape my notice that Zach's hand stayed on the back of my chair after I'd sat down, and he'd also moved three inches closer. Fuck. If Violet and Maya were right, then taking this job might turn out to be the worst mistake I'd ever made. Because hurting Zach would be my biggest regret. If only he could have met the real me, then maybe— Oh, who was I kidding? If I'd served him a burger at the Big Bite Diner, he wouldn't have given me a second glance. Plus most men ran faster than Usain Bolt when they found out I had a daughter.

"Another glass of wine?" he asked.

"I shouldn't. We have a long drive tomorrow."

"I'll take the first stint. You can sleep it off."

"Okay, one more."

This bottle wasn't expensive, but it was good. I swallowed a sigh as Zach reached past to pour, brushing my arm in the process. I could so easily fall for this man. Not because of his looks or his fame or his money, but because he had a good heart. Too bad mine was black.

Or red.

Wine slopped over my boobs, soaking my top as Zach lurched forward.

"What the…?" he started, but a vapid giggle cut him off.

"Oops."

Dawson was already on his feet. "This is a private dinner."

"I totally know that, but I just came over to give Zach my friend's number."

"He's not interested."

"Can't you see he's with someone?" Violet added.

"Yeah, but my friend's way hotter. Look, there she is."

Still dripping, I turned out of morbid curiosity to see a Baylee clone with bigger hair give a coy little wave from the bar. Zach didn't bother to look. He was trying to blot wine off my boob with a napkin, but then he froze.

"Shit, sorry. I didn't mean to grope you."

"It's fine."

Dawson snatched the paper from the girl's hand and tore it up. "Your presence isn't welcome."

"That's polite for 'get lost,'" Baylee yelled, and the few people who weren't already staring at us turned their heads to gawp, camera phones at the ready. I needed to get out of here, fast.

"I'd better go change my top."

"You want my jacket?" Tyler asked.

"No, it's fine."

I practically ran out of the restaurant, heading for the stairs instead of waiting for the elevator. I didn't want to be a YouTube star—been there, done that, nearly died in the process—nor did I have any desire to listen to other people discussing my non-relationship with Zach. How did celebrities stay sane? Upstairs, I could tiptoe into my shared room, change my top, and while away twenty minutes on the balcony so I didn't wake Maya. That should be enough time for Dawson to clear the dining room of groupies, and I had no doubt he'd do that. He had a quiet authority that even Barbie's cousin wouldn't mess with.

The door opened with a quiet *click*. Did I dare to turn a light on? Maybe the bathroom light with the door half-closed? I winced as I stubbed a toe on my suitcase, my own fault for leaving it in the way, and felt for the switch. Dammit, I forgot there was an automatic exhaust fan. I glanced toward Maya's bed as the fan began buzzing, hoping she hadn't stirred, and…found it empty.

Where was she?

I turned on more lights and checked for a note. Nada. Nothing on my phone either, and her bed didn't look slept in. Her pyjamas were still neatly folded by the pillow.

My chest seized, my first thought that something bad had happened. But what could have happened between the dining room and our bedroom? The hotel was full tonight, packed with people in town for the surfing contest. The elevator and stairwell both had cameras, as did the lobby. Could someone have grabbed her and pulled her into a room? It was possible, but there were only three doors between ours and the elevator, so unlikely. Which left another option: that Maya had gone somewhere voluntarily. That she'd lied when she said she was going straight to bed.

Had she been here at all? I spotted the shoes she'd been wearing earlier neatly placed by her closet, noted the giant tote she used to haul her stuff around sitting on a chair. So, she'd come back and then gone out again? That lent credence to the "voluntary" theory.

My first instinct was to call her, but when I did, her phone went straight to voicemail. Should I try Zach? I almost did, but there were no signs of a struggle and Maya obviously didn't want anyone to know where she was. I paced the room, considering my options. What was Maya doing? Was her disappearance innocent? Or was she up to something altogether more shady? She seemed so nice, so honest, but I was proof that appearances could be deceptive. That agendas could be hidden.

In the end, I came to a decision. It was half past nine, and if Maya had snuck out on purpose, she probably thought I'd be gone until ten at least. Three courses with wine and friends, that had to take two hours, spillages excepted. But I'd come back early.

Had I ruined whatever plan she'd made?

I'd eat dessert, and if she hadn't returned by eleven, then I'd raise the alarm. And if she *was* back? I'd just have to keep a closer eye on her. Find out what she was hiding.

Maybe I wasn't the only fox in the henhouse…

CHAPTER 19
ZACH

Most women fell at Zach's feet after he won a surf contest, but not Ari. Which was both a good thing and a bad thing. Good because he never wanted more than five minutes with those other girls. Bad because he had no fucking clue how to take things further with the only woman he'd had feelings for since he left Blackstone House. And the girl he'd dated when he lived in Virginia hadn't been a patch on Ari. He was young back then, inexperienced with both women and life in general, and what he'd felt was lust, not…whatever this was. Ari was different.

And this evening, he'd thrown wine all over her. *Way to go, dude.*

Fame had a lot to answer for. Tyler had entered Zach in his first competition, the only aim to get a win on his résumé so he'd stand out among the crowd of surf instructors plying their trade in Santa Cruz. But one thing had led to another, and now here he was. Fit, famous, and followed everywhere he went.

Ari had come back after she'd changed her clothes, but for the rest of the meal, she'd seemed distracted. Fidgety. And the moment she finished her coffee, she'd yawned and run off to bed.

Her bed, not his, unfortunately.

"Drink this."

Dawson passed him a glass of Scotch, two fingers poured over ice. They were sitting in the living area of Zach's suite, a suite he hadn't booked, but the girl at the front desk was a fan, apparently, and he wasn't going to say no to a free upgrade. Violet had gone to slather herself in aloe vera gel, leaving Dawson to commiserate.

"I can see why you like Ari. She's pretty normal—although that's unusual for you."

"I'd never date one of those hustlers from the bar."

"I was thinking of your efforts in Virginia. Remember the girl who made the hair necklace?"

A groan slipped out. Zach wasn't sure what had been worse—that his girlfriend had set a lock of his hair in resin and worn it as an amulet, or that she'd snipped off the hair as he slept without him noticing. Or that he hadn't realised she was a lunatic for the three months they'd been dating.

"How could I forget?"

"Or the one who hit on Justin without realising you were roommates?"

"Can we focus on the current problem? Should I tell Ari how I feel?"

Was it better to ask her out on a date and risk rejection, or carry on as they were and hope that friendship turned into more? Zach had grown to enjoy lazy evenings on the terrace with her and Maya. Kai often showed up, and Tyler too. But sometimes, the others would leave and he'd find himself alone with Ari, just talking about everything and nothing. She showed genuine interest in his life, and for the first time, he found himself spilling secrets from the past he'd tried to bury. Sharing was strangely cathartic.

"Violet reckons you've been friend-zoned."

"Fuck."

"Maybe Ari just needs time? Can't be easy, moving to a different state when you don't know anyone."

Yeah, and Zach didn't want to make her uncomfortable. How much longer did she plan to stay in California? He had to strike a delicate balance, weighing up the risks of scaring her off against the chance of her leaving anyway.

"I can give her time." He drained his glass and coughed at the burn in his throat. "Pass the bottle?"

"No."

"No?"

"You won't thank me if you end up driving with a hangover tomorrow."

Dawson was right. Dawson was always fucking right. Out of all of his roommates in Blackstone House, Big D had been the level-headed one. Brax had paid lip service to legality, while Justin could be moody at times. Perhaps he'd matured now? Nolan used to pop anxiety pills he got from Levi, and Greyson was smooth, too smooth. It was no surprise that he'd become a politician. Alexa was cunning, while Jerry had been colder than a polar bear's nuts, a quiet character who'd disappeared before the court case was over.

"Did you tell Alexa we'd be here tonight?"

"Nope."

"Neither did I."

"She probably hacked your email again. Found the reservation."

"I should change my password."

"Not sure that'll help."

Right again. The last time he'd tried, Zach had used a twenty-digit string of random letters, numbers, and punctuation that he'd carefully written down on a Post-it because no way in hell could he remember the combination. The next morning, he'd woken up to a message on his desktop: *Nice Try :)*

As Dawson would say, *fuckin' Alexa.*

"I don't feel so good." Maya leaned against Zach's kitchen counter. "Maybe it's better if I stay at home."

"You're sick? Need me to drive you to the doctor?"

"No, no…" Her voice dropped to a whisper. "It's just that time of the month."

Whoa, okay. "You want to cancel the trip? We can reschedule for another week."

"Your calendar's pretty full, and you need a break. Besides, Ari's looking forward to the wine tasting."

On Monday evening, after they'd arrived back in Seagrass Point, Maya had announced that she and Ari wanted to visit a vineyard later in the week, and wouldn't the Dionysus Estate be perfect? Zach hadn't spoken with Nolan for months, but Nolan loved to talk about grapes, and he'd been happy to offer a tour and a bed for the night. Then Maya had suggested that Kai and Zach come along too because they needed to let their bodies recover for a day. The WST contests *were* gruelling. Zed insisted on providing a two-day show with action on the water from dawn till dusk, and the currents at Huntington Beach made the paddle-out tough. Saturday's ninety-minute heat plus a quarter-final, a semi-final, and the final on Sunday had left Zach aching. Kai too, although like Zach, he would never admit it. They just shared a bottle of Advil.

So they'd planned to take a trip to Sierra Nevada on Thursday, but last night, one of Kai's neighbours had fallen and broken her leg, and he'd promised to help out for a few days until her daughter could fly in from Georgia. Georgia the country, not Georgia the state. And now Maya was pulling out too?

"We could do something here instead?" Zach suggested. "I'll pick up wine in Santa Cruz. Bread and olives too."

His diet could withstand one carb overload.

"No, you should go."

"I'd feel bad leaving you behind. The trip was your idea."

"For goodness' sake." Maya raised her gaze to the ceiling. "Can't you see I'm trying to do you a favour here?"

"Huh?"

"You like Ari, yes? So go hang out with her."

Ah, shit, was it that obvious? Zach thought he'd been subtle. But the chance to spend some quality time alone with Ari was impossible to resist. Unless, of course, she didn't want to go with him alone. What if the idea made her uncomfortable? They'd only known each other for a month.

Only known each other for a month.

That was the moment Zach realised that what he felt for Ari ran past lust and a simple need to get his rocks off and into something far deeper. When had he ever considered a woman's feelings before? Other than his sister's? He bedded women at Nyx and the occasional groupie, no strings, no small talk, and certainly no second date. His idea of commitment was buying a hook-up breakfast before he left in the morning.

Yeah, yeah, judge as much as you like—it was what they asked for and all he promised.

But with Ari, he wanted more.

He wanted everything.

"If she still wants to go, then we'll go." Zach began walking away, then turned back. "Maya? Thanks."

CHAPTER 20
ARI

"There it is," Zach announced, slowing as we approached a pair of weathered stone gateposts. Wrought-iron gates hung between them, firmly closed, the metal hammered into twisted vines. On a small wooden sign, the letter D curled into a bunch of grapes.

D for Dionysus, Greek god of wine, pleasure, and festivity.

Zach pressed a button on the intercom, and after a pause, a woman spoke. "Can I help?"

"Zach Torres to see Nolan."

Another pause, longer this time. "Please take the right-hand track and continue to the house."

I'd looked the place up online, of course. Nolan de Luca's name was rarely mentioned, but his winery had become one of California's most celebrated boutique producers, taking the wine world by storm with a Robert Parker score of ninety-six on its first bottling. Which apparently meant it was pretty damn good.

Dionysus produced limited amounts of Syrah and Zinfandel, focusing on quality over quantity. The vineyard wasn't open to the public—Nolan hadn't cashed in on the tourism boom by offering lunches, and tastings were available by invitation only. The website needed some improvement. There was no "about the owner" section, no virtual tour, no news and events page. The online store sold vintage bottles starting at three hundred bucks, or you could join the waiting list for a future allocation.

This clearly wasn't the kind of place that sold box wine.

The awkwardness of coming with Zach alone had been tempered by my curiosity about Nolan de Luca. Zach had given me the option to back out of the trip, but the opportunity to meet another player in the Blackstone House affair had been too good to pass up. Yes, I knew I was being paid to investigate Torres, but I couldn't help being intrigued by the older case. As far as I'd been able to ascertain, the ten housemates had lived together for two years before Levi Sykes flipped out and killed Ruby Costello, and details were still vague on the motive. He'd had sex with her before she died but claimed it was consensual. Satanic symbols were found. Plus there were allegations of a cover-up by the others in order to hide the fact that they were members of a devil-worshipping cult.

Having met Zach, I didn't believe the cult thing, but there was still enough weird stuff surrounding the case to make it fascinating. The knife used had belonged to Dawson. A stack of cash had been found in the fireplace in Ruby's room. The locket she always wore was missing, and Tina, her best friend and the last person to speak to her, had disappeared right after the murder, never to be seen again.

No wonder there were conspiracy theories.

Although it was sometimes difficult to tell the lies from the truth. Take Maya, for example. On the last night in Huntington Beach, I'd returned to our shared hotel room at eleven p.m. and found her in bed, pretending to sleep. I say "pretending" because just for a second, I saw her watching me. She'd come back, taken a shower—the shower tray was still wet—and then pretended she'd been there the whole time.

Something was off about her.

"Do you come to the vineyard often?" I asked.

Zach shook his head. "Don't have the time. I visited when Nolan opened the first bottles, but that must have been three years ago."

"It's a brand-new vineyard, then?"

"Yes and no. Nolan inherited it from…I think it was an uncle, but the place was a wreck. He had to replant half of the vines, restore the buildings, and buy new equipment."

Grapevines stretched into the distance on either side of the gravelled driveway, carrying on up the hills in front of us. Beyond them, mountains rose from the green, monsters' teeth dark against the clear blue sky. We rounded a bend, and the driveway split into three. The left track wove among the fields and disappeared, destination unknown. Straight ahead, I saw a stone-sided monitor barn set against the hillside, the design rustic but the build new. Zach took the right-hand turn, and we drove past a small grove of twisted trees before pulling up in the courtyard of a two-storey L-shaped home made from the same stone as the barn.

"This place is a ghost town. Should we knock?"

"Yeah."

I reached for the door handle, but before I could exit the truck, a dog shot toward us, a German shepherd, and began barking like crazy. I took one look at its teeth and hit the locks.

"On second thought, maybe I'll just stay right here."

"There's Nolan."

A man ambled around the end of the house, running a hand through messy brown hair. His tan said he spent a lot of time outdoors. The buildings of the Dionysus Estate might have been impeccable, but perhaps its owner had fallen on hard times—Nolan's T-shirt had holes in it, his shorts were covered in muddy paw prints, and his sneakers had different-coloured laces. Safe to say nobody was sponsoring *his* clothing.

"Juno, sit."

The dog sat.

Zach rolled down the window. "Is it safe to get out?"

"Sure. She doesn't much like strangers, but she'll be okay now that I'm here."

"Never figured you for a dog person."

"Never figured myself for a dog person."

"And yet…"

"She just showed up one day. I printed flyers, and one of the neighbours said he saw her get thrown out of a car. So, you want the tour?"

"The house looks better than when I last saw it."

"Couldn't have looked much worse."

"Nolan focused on getting the vineyard up and running first," Zach explained. "The last time we came, there was a storm, and we spent all night emptying buckets because the roof leaked."

"I had a new roof put on. Got rid of the spiders too, so you don't need to run screaming to Alexa anymore."

Wait, what? "Zach doesn't like spiders? He never mentioned that."

"We're here to talk about wine, buddy."

Nolan laughed and reached through the truck window to unlock the door. "My favourite subject. You want to put your bags in your room first?"

Room? That was a slip of the tongue, right?

Wrong.

Nolan led us into the house, through a spacious hallway and up a wide flight of stairs into a luxuriously appointed bedroom, complete with a king-sized four-poster bed. Gauzy white drapes hung from the frame, bright in the sunlight that streamed through the window. A generous balcony lay beyond, more of a raised terrace really, with stairs that led down to a twinkling blue pool surrounded by lavender. I could smell the fragrance from the second floor.

"We finished the pool two months ago. Feel free to swim after dinner."

Uh, no. "I'll have to pass."

When Nolan looked puzzled, Zach explained. "Ari likes water as much as I like spiders."

"But you're a surfer."

I forced a laugh. "Awkward, I know. Where should I put my bag?"

"Here?" Nolan waved to a space at the bottom of the bed.

"I meant, which room? Assuming Zach's sleeping in this one."

"You're not together? When Maya called, I figured…"

"We're just friends."

Nolan and Zach exchanged a look.

"Just friends," Zach confirmed. "Ari can have this room. I'll take one of the others."

Nolan gave us the full tour. I'd assumed the winery was small, a modest operation that fit into the barn we'd seen, but that was only half the story. Because there were caves. Seven thousand square feet of caves, cool, dark, and slightly humid, half of them full of oak barrels. The rich aroma of wine permeated throughout, and we stopped in the larger of the two tasting rooms, an underground lair with a thick granite table as the centrepiece. The polished stone gleamed under the chandelier overhead, the light bouncing around until the rock walls sucked it into their claret-painted depths.

"We're still quite a young operation," Nolan said. "If you try the Syrah again in a few years, you'll taste the difference."

"It's a little out of my price range," I said.

"Take a bottle home with you."

I shouldn't have been surprised that Nolan came across as a nice, normal guy. After all, he was a friend of Zach's, although markedly more private. What impact had the Blackstone affair had on his life? The press had pushed him hard when they found out his father was in jail, and for murder, no less. Was that why he hid away on this vast estate? Or had he always preferred the quieter life?

Underground, there was silence apart from the *clink* of glasses and Nolan's commentary on the various vintages we tried. Maxwell Suker would have walked over molten lava for a trip here. According to Nolan, we were meant to spit the wine out, but why would a girl do that? This stuff cost, like, five hundred bucks a bottle. No way was I gonna waste it.

At first, I tried to take in what he was saying about tannins and grape varieties and ageing and notes of jasmine and huckleberry, but in the end, his words ran together in a liquid trickle. *Just smile, Ari.* Men always told me to smile more.

"This is good." I held up the glass in what I thought was Nolan's direction. The cave needed better lighting. "Dee-lish."

"I think we should call it a day with the tasting."

"Awwwww. Please, one more?"

Zach wrapped an arm around my waist as I stumbled sideways. "No, that's enough."

"You have a pretty chest. Did I ever tell you that?" I twisted to run my hands over solid muscle. "Kind of smooth and also bumpy."

Nolan coughed behind us. Or it could have been a snort.

"You want me to bring a handcart?"

"I'll carry her."

Huh? "Carry who?"

Zach didn't answer, just plucked me off my feet. I wrapped my arms around his neck to steady myself, and boy, did he smell good. Sort of coconutty. That was his shampoo. Sometimes I borrowed it when I used his bathroom, but shhh, don't tell anyone.

"If you're gonna vomit, tell me and we'll stop."

"I never vomit. My stomach's made from cast iron, that's what my nana says. One time when I was little, I ate a slug. Never puked at all." Oh, wait. Hadn't I puked on Zach's surfboard? "Okay, maybe if I drown, I puke, but that's the eskech...exeshp..."

"Exception?"

"Yes, that."

This was the best day of my life. Fancy wine and blue skies and mountains and a hot man and a tiny vacation and fruit and spooky caves and a view that came off one of those TV shows—you know the kind, with the houses nobody could afford. We *crunch, crunch, crunch*ed down the driveway and around the oh-so-expensive villa and OMG, there was a freaking hammock? I loved hammocks. Okay, so I'd never actually been in one, but I loved the idea of hammocks. So swingy and sunny and—

"Wait, where are we going?"

"Bed. I'm taking you to bed."

"Aw, but I wanna go in the hammock."

"Not sure that's a good idea, sweetheart."

"Please?" I squinted at Zach's face, half-blinded by the sun. His lips were an inch away from mine, and when he didn't say anything, I closed the gap. Just for a moment. His kiss was so soft, so sweet, and he didn't try to get gross and stick his tongue in my mouth right away. "Please?"

CHAPTER 21
ZACH

The hammock swung slowly in the breeze as Zach stroked Ari's hair. His leg had gone to sleep half an hour ago, but he didn't care to move, not when she looked so peaceful. And at least she'd kept her word about not puking.

Earlier, Nolan had steadied the hammock as Zach hauled Ari into it. The kiss had caught him by surprise, wine-stained lips and a soft, breathy moan that made his cock harden instantly. Luckily, Ari had been too drunk to notice his reaction, too sleepy to object when he wrapped his arms around her to stop her from falling onto the hard ground as she shifted this way and that, trying to get comfortable.

"Just friends, huh?" Nolan smirked as he carried over a parasol to give them some shade.

"Shut up."

That had been three hours ago. This wasn't the afternoon Zach had planned, but he couldn't think of a better way to spend a lazy Thursday by the pool.

The dog padded back and forth, and there were chickens somewhere. Zach could hear clucking. The occasional *crunch* of gravel sounded as a vehicle came or went, but otherwise, there was peace. No groupies, no cameras, no nosy neighbours. He loved his home in Seagrass Point, but privacy wasn't one of its plus points. Years ago, when he'd been a nobody, he used to sit on the terrace, watching the waves, but that had come to an end after he spotted a drone hovering outside one morning. He'd had to install a mirrored coating on the windows as well. But this… *This* was paradise.

Ari stirred slowly in his arms. Mumbled something unintelligible, then stiffened.

"Hey."

"What happened? Where are we? Why are we in a hammock?"

"You drank a little too much wine, we're at Nolan's place, and you insisted on lying in the hammock." When she tried to scramble away, he tightened his arms. "Take it easy, or we'll both fall out."

"I… Why are you in the hammock with me?"

Because at the time, it had felt right, but now Zach was beginning to rethink that decision.

"After you kissed me, it seemed…comfortable, I guess."

"I kissed you? What? No."

Ari didn't remember. Fuck, and now the way she was looking at him… She thought he'd taken liberties he had no right to take. But then she screwed her eyes shut.

"Sorry. I'm sorry, I shouldn't have done that." She *did* remember? "I'm not sure what came over me, I mean… Uh, I don't know what I mean."

Zach helped her to sit up, then balanced the hammock as she swung her legs over the side.

"There's nothing to apologise for. I wanted it too."

"No, there is. I can't… I can't do this." She pointed between them. "You and me, this can't happen."

"Why not? I like you. Ari, I really fucking like you." When she took a step back, his chest seized. "I thought you liked me too?"

"I do. I do, but I'm not in the right place right now. For any kind of relationship, or even something superficial. There's so much going on in my life that you don't know about, and...and..." A tear rolled down her cheek. "If I was in the position to...you know... You're the perfect man, but..."

"Hey." Zach got to his feet and offered a hand, but she just stared at it. "Hey, it's okay. I understand. I can't pretend I'm not disappointed, but I understand. And I'd hate to lose you as a friend."

She didn't speak, but she did stop backing away.

"Ari, can we at least stay friends?"

Finally, she nodded. "Friends."

"You know how I feel now. The ball's in your court. If you ever want more, you only need to say the word, but let's just go back to how things were. Okay?"

Another nod.

"Want to get dinner? You haven't eaten since breakfast."

"I think I'm not very good at wine tasting."

"You were meant to spit."

"I never spit."

If things had gone differently today, those words would have been music to Zach's ears, but as it was, he struggled to muster up a smile.

"Let's go find Nolan's kitchen. I can make omelettes."

If there were chickens, there had to be eggs.

"Can I have mushrooms in mine?"

"Anything you want, sweetheart. Anything you want."

A tickle woke him. A stray hair of Ari's? Only in Zach's dreams. Events of the past week had caught up with him, and he'd followed her lead and fallen asleep right after dinner. His room was next to hers, slightly smaller but still with the same monochromatic colour scheme. Nolan had played it safe. He never had been adventurous when it came to decor. Someone else had helped him with the tasting room, Zach would put money on it, but Nolan hadn't said who.

And at that moment, Zach didn't much care about furniture.

The bedside lamp was on, and it cast enough light for Zach to see the eight-legged freak walk across his pillow.

Fuck!

He leapt out of bed in an instant, ready to yell for Maya, then realised she wasn't there. And no way was he asking Ari for help. In Blackstone House, Alexa had done the honours—the brat had loved bugs, and Zach wouldn't be surprised in the slightest if she had a houseful of pet tarantulas. That was, if she had a house at all. He got the impression she moved around a lot.

Anyhow, he knew his fear was irrational. But ever since he'd watched *Arachnophobia* as a kid, he'd been waiting for the day that spiders would take over the world.

Breathe.

Breathe.

Breathe.

Okay, staying in this room was out of the question now, but there was a sunlounger by the pool. The temperature was in the low sixties—with a blanket, he wouldn't freeze if he slept outside. Plus he could look at the stars. When he and Maya were kids, their parents had taken them camping most weekends in the summer, and he missed the outdoor life.

The pool looked inviting, lit by underwater bulbs that left the water shimmering. A waste of electricity? Probably not. Nolan had solar panels everywhere—on the roof of the house and the barn, and another array on the hillside. Plus there was a small lake for irrigation, and a wind turbine for bad-weather days. Zach bet one of the caves was filled with long-life supplies. Nolan had always believed in being prepared, and the shit that went down at Blackstone House had only made him more determined to be self-sufficient.

One a.m.—it wasn't too late for a quick dip. Zach climbed down the steps into the water and swam a few lengths, then just floated, watching the universe above. The twinkling heavens. Was there life after death? He wasn't convinced, but if there was something beyond this mortal realm, he liked to think that his parents were watching his achievements in the world of surfing, and he knew they'd be proud.

His dad had taught him how to pick out the constellations, and he traced Capricornus in his mind. His mom had been a Capricorn, read her horoscope religiously, not that Zach believed in—

What the fuck? He slipped under the water as an almighty splash sent waves in his direction, then spluttered to the surface in time to see Ari trying to drown herself again. He made a grab for her and clung to a handful of wet T-shirt as she frantically gasped for breath.

"Put your feet down."

"Can't…can't…"

"You can. The pool isn't that deep. Sweetheart, look at me. Put your feet down."

"I…I… Oh." Then she sucked in a shaky breath and shoved him backward. "You asshole."

"What? What did I do?"

"I thought you were dead! You were just…just floating there, and you weren't moving, and…"

"I was watching the stars. It's relaxing."

"How? How can that be relaxing? What if you sink?"

"I won't sink. The human body has natural buoyancy."

"Mine doesn't."

"It does. I can prove it." Zach closed the distance between them. "Do you trust me?"

"I…" Ari fixed those big blue eyes on his and swallowed hard. "Yes, I trust you."

"Then lie back." He placed a hand between her shoulders, pressing gently. "Relax. I've got you."

"What if I—"

"You won't."

She didn't break their gaze as she slowly lay back in the water. Zach kept his hand steady, taking a little of her weight until she became more confident. He'd never been scared of water—in awe of the power of it, yes, and sometimes wary, but not scared. But even in a swimming pool, Ari was terrified. Her breathing was ragged, and he could see the pulse beating in her neck, as well as… Shit.

"Your shirt…"

"What about it?"

"It's gone see-through."

She cursed under her breath and tried to cover herself with a hand, then quickly gasped when her head began to slide under.

"Don't panic, sweetheart. I'll close my eyes. Just breathe."

Okay, maybe he told a small fib. He definitely peeked. Like the rest of her, Ari's breasts were perfect, two firm handfuls, or possibly mouthfuls, depending on your taste. Zach was a mouth man.

Ari gradually relaxed, and when she was calm and still, he slowly let go, leaving her suspended in water still warm from the sun. When she didn't react, he took her hand and floated next to her, staring up at the cloudless sky.

"Next step, backstroke."

"I think I'm more of a doggy-paddle girl."

"Only because you've never taken swimming lessons. Backstroke's more comfortable and less tiring."

"Is that your favourite way to swim?"

"No, I prefer"—do *not* say breaststroke, asshole— "freestyle. When we get back to Seagrass Point, I'll teach you."

"In the pool?"

"To start off with. Saltwater's actually easier to swim in because it gives more buoyancy, plus the waves make it more fun."

"You and me, we have very different ideas of fun."

"Wait until I get you on a surfboard."

Ari choked out a laugh. "That's not happening."

"Give it time."

Time they might not have. Ari wasn't staying in California forever, and now that she'd knocked him back, Zach knew it wouldn't be easy to change her mind about her future plans. He tried to push away the sense of dread and live for the moment. Whatever happened would happen. Or not. What had his dad said about the big waves? Those monsters surfers waited half a lifetime to see? That they'd come when they came, and not a moment sooner.

The two of them floated in the dark for nearly an hour, but when Ari's teeth began chattering, it was time to call it a day. Or night. Zach stood, then steadied Ari until she'd found her footing.

"I'll go get you a towel," he said.

"I think there's one on the chair by the stairs."

"That's a blanket."

"Why is there a blanket out here?"

If it had been anyone else, Zach would have lied. Said he planned to sleep under the stars in a throwback to his childhood or sit outside for a while because he couldn't sleep.

But this was Ari.

He wouldn't lie to her.

"There's a spider in my bedroom."

"A spider?"

"It walked across my pillow."

She didn't laugh—okay, she did smile a bit—and for that, he was grateful. "When you said you disliked spiders, I didn't realise it was full-blown can't-stay-in-the-same-room-as-one."

"People swallow eight spiders a year as they sleep."

"That's an urban legend."

Funny, that was what Alexa had always said. "But the story must have come from somewhere, right?"

"There are only three or four species of spider that live in American homes, and they hang out in their webs. They probably find humans terrifying."

"Now you're a bug expert?"

Yeah, Ari and Alexa would get along well.

"My, uh, my friend's daughter had to do a school project on bugs, and I helped with the research." She hadn't let go of his hand, and now she gave it a squeeze. "Want me to go put your spider outside?"

"It's dark. What if you can't find it?"

"Then we can trade rooms. C'mon."

When Baylee had found out about his fear of spiders, she'd laughed, and she still teased him mercilessly. Tyler had spoken to her, tried to get her to stop, but she still slid in a barb at every opportunity. Ari was so matter of fact about the whole thing that Zach's chest ached.

"Do you want to count nurdles in England?" he blurted.

She froze. "What?"

"The next round of the WST is in Cornwall, England. We've rented a house there."

"And you want me to de-spider it?"

No, he just wanted her, period.

"You sure know how to sweet-talk a guy."

After the knock-back this afternoon, he figured she'd turn down the invite, but she surprised him.

"I've always wanted to visit England."

"Then you'll come?"

A nod, and then she slipped her hand out of his.

"I should go and find the spider."

CHAPTER 22
ARI

Since Zach had bought my airplane ticket, I figured I should make myself useful. Oh, I'd tried to pay him back, but he refused to accept the money, which was why I was currently sitting in his bedroom, packing clothing into a suitcase. T-shirts, shorts, boxer briefs… Maya had printed me a list—Zach needed two items of clothing from each of his brand partners. Yes, even his underwear was sponsored.

And *maybe* I'd googled the ads with him wearing it.

It felt a bit weird, going through his closet, but Maya said it was either her or me, and Zach didn't care in any case. He was surprisingly open for a man suspected of a crime. I had access to his home, his truck, his credit card. Even his computer. He'd given me the password yesterday so I could email the airline about food preferences—vegan for Baylee, a new thing, apparently, and no dairy for Zach. So far, I'd resisted nosing through the rest of his files, but the temptation was burning away inside me.

And you know who wasn't quite so open? His sister. Maya guarded her devices fiercely, and so far, I'd never seen her leave any of them unlocked.

All food for thought.

I could hear her in the other room, talking on the phone, presumably to a sponsor or a journalist or someone else who wanted a piece of Zach.

"Yes, he can do the shoot, but not at Mavericks. That's non-negotiable, I'm afraid." A pause. "Why? Because he never surfs Mavericks. Yes, he'll do Jaws or Killers if you're willing to pay the costs, which includes a safety team. Okay, think about it and get back to me."

For the trip to England, Maya had rented a house near Fistral Beach, a famous surfing destination that I'd never heard of. The property came with four bedrooms, off-road parking, a yard full of flowers, and a hot tub. I'd room with Maya again—she was happy for me to share her space, just not her electronics.

She leaned her head around the bedroom door. "Did I put sunglasses on the list?"

"Two pairs, Le Ray."

"I forgot them one time, and Zach had to buy more at the airport."

He was down on the beach at the moment with Kai, Tyler, and a longboard. I'd thought of tagging along, but he rarely spoke to anyone while he was surfing, only the groupies who followed him, and I couldn't see Khloe, Alys, or Stacey masterminding a financial scam.

"I already packed them."

"Thanks for helping with this. I know you didn't sign up for packing, but organising the logistics takes more time than I ever thought possible."

"It's the least I can do. It's me who needs to thank you guys for letting me come along."

"Might as well fill the house. Uh, I was thinking of letting Tyler and Baylee have the master suite. Usually, I'd give it to Zach or Kai, but it's on a different floor and I hate listening to

Baylee's sex noises." Maya made a gagging sound. "She's so freaking loud."

"I'm sure Zach and Kai would rather have a good night's sleep than a clawfoot bathtub."

"Right. So I'll put Tyler and Baylee on the third floor. Do you need anything from the grocery store? We're almost out of eggs and spinach, plus I need to pick up a new suitcase for Kai. The airline broke the handle off his last one."

"Can you pick up a bag of potato chips? I have a craving."

"Which flavour?"

"Cheddar and sour cream if they have them, plain if they don't."

"Got it."

The front door opened and closed, and I was alone in the house. Gloria had gone to pick her eldest boy up from activity camp—he'd gotten into a fight with another kid, and being sent home early was his punishment. She'd apologised twenty times for taking off, but nobody minded.

Especially me.

Because I couldn't resist the lure of Zach's computer. I hated myself for doing it, but I had to take a look. If Maya needed to buy a suitcase, that meant she'd be going to Santa Cruz rather than the general store in Seagrass Point, so I'd have at least an hour and a half to investigate.

I made coffee and settled myself at Zach's desk in the small office he officially shared with Maya but rarely used. His workplace was the ocean. What was I looking for? Correspondence discussing the sportsbook scheme, spreadsheets with calculations, bank records... I started with his emails and searched possible keywords. Yes, theoretically Twilight had already covered this part, but I went over it again, just in case. *AnyBet, betting, dutching, odds, transfer, funds...* Nothing useful. Next, I checked the messages around the dates Rennick had given me, hunting for correspondence with the e-wallets that had deposited money at AnyBet. Zilch.

Zach wasn't big on spreadsheets either. He kept records of contest results, and there were details of his investment in Surf 365. Haven's Rest was mortgaged too, with nearly a million bucks outstanding. Hardly chicken feed, but Zach made good money.

How did I know that? Well, his tax returns were there on the hard drive, neatly filed in date order. Bank statements too. Strangely enough, he hadn't declared thousands of bucks in illicit earnings, but he had made seven figures last year between payments from the WST and various sponsorships. The same the year before. His income had climbed steadily, starting eleven years ago when he'd worked as a retail assistant in Virginia, taking yardwork on the side. Minimum wage, minimum wage, minimum wage... No, that couldn't be right. He said he'd bought Haven's Rest seven years previously, but he'd been dipping into his overdraft most months back then. Even as a rehab project, this place couldn't have been cheap. And he'd said repairs were needed, a new roof, work on the concrete. How had he paid for it? There was a big gap in Zach Torres's finances that couldn't be explained by the documents in front of me. Had I missed something? Had he borrowed money? Not from a bank, because no reputable institution would have given him a loan with this credit profile, but—

"You want more coffee, Ari?"

I jumped out of my skin at the sound of Gloria's voice and tried desperately to steady my heart rate as I minimised Zach's bank statement. How much had she seen? I'd angled the screen away from the door, but she'd crept right into the room.

"I thought you went to pick up Luis?"

"*Sí*, but I brought him back here. The laundry is still in the washing machine, and I have ironing to do."

"I could have put the laundry in the dryer."

She glanced out the door, and her voice dropped to a

whisper. "Alvaro is sleeping, and I didn't want Luis to wake him."

Alvaro was her husband. "Is he okay?"

A shake of the head. "The doctors, they don't know what's wrong with him."

Weight loss, tiredness, weird aches—Maya had quietly told me that he'd been to the hospital for tests a few times recently.

"I'm sorry to hear that. How about Luis?"

"Some other kids made fun of his glasses. I always tell him to walk away, but today, they followed him."

"So why did *he* get kicked out? Why not the bullies?"

Gloria shrugged. "This is life. Do you want the coffee?"

"I'll make it."

Phew, that had been a close call. And my snooping had raised more questions than it answered. Something weird was going on with both Zach and Maya Torres, and I intended to find out what.

CHAPTER 23
ARI

I'd been looking forward to the trip to England, but now? Not so much.

The bad news came on Wednesday afternoon, two hours before we were due to board the red-eye to London. Rennick called me personally, which was a first and also served to highlight the gravity of the situation.

"We're seeing preliminary indications of unusual betting patterns on the UK WST event."

"Betting against Zach? I mean, against Torres?"

Dammit, I was getting too close. Some days, I almost forgot why I'd come to Seagrass Point in the first place. Only my nightly calls with Haven and Nana kept me grounded, and on the last of them, Nana had muttered darkly about Stockholm syndrome. But I didn't have Stockholm syndrome. Zach wasn't my captor. I was here because I wanted to be. Uh, no, because I was getting paid to be.

Thankfully, Haven had interrupted before I said something stupid. "Mom, you *are* coming home for my birthday, aren't you? You promised."

"I wouldn't miss it for the world."

Although I knew I'd have to answer a thousand more questions from Nana.

"Yes, against Torres," Rennick said, snapping me back to the call. "Your report this weekend will be critical. We need to know where he goes, who he speaks with, every last detail about his frame of mind."

"I'll make sure the report is detailed. It'll be with you on Monday, as soon as I can find enough privacy to write up my notes."

"And you said you'd be in Las Vegas next week?"

"That's right. Only for two days, and then I'll get right back on the job."

If Rennick was going to try and stop me from going to Haven's party, that was a dealbreaker. I'd already told him—via Lila—that my attendance was non-negotiable. But that wasn't his plan.

"Good. While you're here, we'll hold a progress meeting—Lila will arrange a time."

Another weird chat in his zen garden? I could hardly wait.

But first, I'd have to watch the man I'd come to care about cheat for cash in Cornwall.

Right now, I was wedged between him and Maya in coach class, trying to catch a few Zs. Of course, Zach had been offered an upgrade, Kai too, but they'd declined because—in Zach's words—we were a team.

Some team, when one person was a traitor. Rennick's call had brought me right back down to earth from…wherever the hell I'd been. Planet Zach. I'd actually begun to believe in him. To wonder if Rennick was wrong and the betting losses had been a weird fluke.

But now the pattern was repeating, and this weekend, I'd have a front-row seat as the action unfolded.

"Can't sleep?" Zach asked.

"I've only flown a handful of times. Guess I'm still getting used to it."

Before I'd "screwed up" by getting pregnant, which was somehow all my fault, Maxwell would occasionally take me on business trips. The fact that he'd always treated me to hotel stays but never taken me to his home was yet another red flag I'd been too young and infatuated to notice. He'd always claimed to have decorators in, or a problem with the AC, or—on one memorable occasion—an infestation of scorpions. Anyhow, all of those trips had been domestic, and also business class, and this was the farthest I'd ever travelled.

Zach twined his fingers through mine. "We'll be on the ground before you know it."

I should have reclaimed my hand, but I couldn't bring myself to shake him loose. This fantasy life I'd been living, it wasn't real, but I wanted to pretend for just a moment longer. I'd never had friends like these before. At school, bullies had driven me to become a loner, and after Haven was born, I'd had no time for anything but work and motherhood. Now, I'd tasted a different life, and giving it up would be hard. With three hundred sleeping passengers as my witnesses, I was never surveilling a hot guy again.

"Everything's so small," Baylee exclaimed for the millionth time since we arrived. "The cars, the houses, the food, the roads…"

"Your mind," Maya muttered under her breath.

"That's because there's less space, babe." Tyler pressed various buttons on the coffee machine, but nothing happened. "How does this thing work?"

"Here, let me."

Maya took over making the drinks, and Baylee kept talking. Unfortunately.

"And nobody speaks proper English. Like, I can't understand what they're saying. I told a guy yesterday that we had better gelato in California, and he told me to 'giss on.' What does that even mean?"

I could take a guess, but I was diplomatic enough to keep my mouth shut. And besides, I had bigger things to worry about, like Zach's movements and activities. It was Sunday morning, and Zach had come through the heats in first place, half a point ahead of his closest rival on technical ability and a full point in front for style. Kai was sitting in seventh place after a wipeout cost him his best wave. But the money didn't lie—according to Rennick's latest message, AnyBet would hand another hundred thousand bucks to the suspected scammers if Zach lost. *When* he lost. Rennick was convinced he'd throw the contest.

But Zach wasn't acting like a man who wanted to lose. No, he'd given the first round his all yesterday, and after the evening meet-and-greet with the VIPs, he'd stayed up for hours watching reruns of his performance and checking buoy reports and weather forecasts. This morning, he'd woken early and taken a walk down to the beach to get a feel for the conditions. I'd snuck out and followed in case he planned a clandestine meet, but he'd just watched the sea for a quarter hour, then returned to the rental house alone. Why would any of that matter if he wasn't allowed to win?

"Maybe you should buy a guidebook?" Kai suggested to Baylee.

"Why? I already know where the beach is, and there's nothing else to do around here."

She'd spent yesterday evening moaning about the lack of designer boutiques in Newquay, which she kept pronouncing as *New-kway* even after I'd corrected her. The multitude of castles, restaurants, and national parks that the area had to offer appeared to hold no interest.

I sipped my coffee and stayed out of the conversation.

Nobody ever won an argument with Baylee. She just kept going and going and going—I had to assume that Tyler wore earplugs at home.

"Want me to take Zach's coffee up to him?" I offered, looking for any excuse to get out of the kitchen.

Maya slid it over. "Thanks."

Upstairs, I knocked on his bedroom door, and when there was no answer, I pressed my ear against the wood. The shower wasn't on, and neither was the TV.

"Zach?"

Nothing, but the door swung open an inch.

"Are you there?"

The bathroom door was closed, so I figured I'd leave the coffee on the chest of drawers by the window. But I paused for a moment to enjoy the view of the sea, and that's when I heard it.

The farting.

The farting followed by a waterfall that sounded suspiciously like diarrhoea.

"Zach, are you okay?"

"Fine. Just get out of here."

Well, that was a first. He'd never told me to take a hike before, and of course I ignored him.

"What can I do to help? Do you need pills? Should I call a doctor?"

The smell was beginning to seep under the door now, and it wasn't pleasant. But I was a mom—poop was a big part of my life.

"I said I'm fine."

"I have ears, Zach."

And a nose. And a stubborn streak that Haven had inherited. Which meant I'd also had experience at dealing with embarrassment, like the time she'd peed in her pants at the Children's Museum and didn't want to tell me in case I made her go home. No, she'd locked herself into a bathroom stall and sobbed instead. Fortunately, a kind-hearted tourist had run out and bought a fresh pair of shorts while I assured Haven that everybody had accidents at some point in their life.

"Leave me alone."

"Did you leave me alone when I jumped into the pool at Nolan's vineyard? No, you helped me to float instead. What kind of friend would I be if I didn't return the favour?"

I heard a quiet snort, followed by retching. "I already know how to float."

"Lifting people up comes in different forms, Zach. I'm not going anywhere."

He didn't speak again, and I began to wonder whether he'd stay in the bathroom all day. But ten minutes later, the toilet flushed and the door opened, releasing another wave of stink. Boy, that was some stomach upset. Zach stood there with a towel wrapped around his waist, silent, and he wouldn't meet my gaze.

"How are you feeling?"

The question was unnecessary—his pale face and hunched shoulders told the story. His stomach was bloated too— probably from the gas.

"Honestly? Like shit."

"Come and sit down. I'll speak with Maya and get her to call Nelson."

"No, you fucking won't."

His vehemence shocked me, and I took a step back.

"Well, someone needs to tell him. Your withdrawal will impact other competitors."

"I'm not withdrawing."

"Zach, you can't seriously be thinking of getting on a surfboard in this state. You've said it yourself; the ocean's dangerous."

"Yeah, well, it's not the first time I've surfed while I'm under the weather."

Those ten minutes had given me time to think, and I wasn't certain I liked the possibilities I'd come up with. This whole time, everyone—me, Rennick, Jankowski—had been working on the assumption that Zach was an integral part of the betting scheme. A willing player. But what if we'd been wrong? What if he'd lost those contests not out of a desire to cash in on a fraud but because he was sick? Unless he was the world's best actor, he wasn't faking these symptoms.

And his words had just fuelled my suspicions.

"This has happened before?"

He doubled over, holding his stomach and groaning, and I watched helplessly. What the hell had happened? If he wasn't a knowing participant in the AnyBet scam, then someone had done this to him. Someone had made him ill, and my blood boiled just from thinking about it.

"Getting the shits right before a contest? It's happened once before," Zach admitted, his voice weak. "I got through it."

Only once? Well, crap. Maybe my theory wasn't valid after all.

"Why surf today? You're unlikely to win, so why push yourself if you don't have to?"

"Because Zed introduced a bonus for competing in every round. A quarter million bucks. The first year, I didn't get it because I refused to surf Mavericks, and last year, I got suspended for one round." He closed his eyes for a second. "I lost my temper with somebody, and that was the punishment." Was he talking about the incident Maya had mentioned? The one with the sponsor's son? "But this year, I've stayed out of trouble, and Mavericks isn't on the program. Nelson replaced it with Todos Santos. Yeah, I know the money shouldn't be important, but I mortgaged my place to invest in a new surf venue, and I also want to help with the expansion of Sal's Army."

"The rescue team?"

Zach nodded. "Safety's important, and skis cost money. Sleds cost money. Plus drivers need to be paid, and we're competing with the photographers. There's always a guy with a camera willing to pay hundreds of bucks for a ride. If I can clear my debts, that frees up more cash for the Army."

"So you want to risk your own safety today to help save others in the future?"

"I don't need to win. All I need to do is catch a few waves. It's longboard, not big-wave, and Tyler's out there to pick me up if I fall."

"What if this sickness… What if it gets worse?"

"I'll be careful. And you should stay back too, because I don't want to pass it on."

"You think it's contagious?"

A shrug. "The first time it happened, I figured I'd accidentally eaten something that contained milk. But I'm so fucking careful now. I bring half of my food with me." That was true—Gloria had spent a day organising items from Maya's list, taping the packages and bottles in bubble wrap and packing them into their own case. "So I probably caught a bug on the plane. Maybe I should wear one of those face masks next time."

I wanted to interrogate Zach, to ask when exactly he got sick, but that was impossible at this point in time. I couldn't say a word about my suspicions. No, all I could do was find him Imodium and painkillers—thankfully, I'd brought a first-aid kit—and then watch helplessly as he headed to the beach.

This job had just gotten a whole lot more confusing.

CHAPTER 24
ZACH

This was the side of his life that Zach hated. The loss of control. He loved surfing for its freedom, but there was nothing free about being allocated a one-hour time slot with whatever waves happened to be there and then performing like a contractually obliged circus animal when all you wanted to do was puke up your guts. On Sunday, he came eighth out of eight after a vicious stomach cramp fucked up his balance and sent him headfirst into the surf.

And worse, he'd sent clouds of noxious fart in Ari's direction, and although she'd reacted with sympathy rather than horror, he'd still wanted to jump out the bathroom window rather than face her. At least Kai had been blessed with a better day. Top step of the podium again.

A knock came at his bedroom door.

"Do you want anything for dinner?"

Ari.

And the answer was no, he wanted to stay in his room alone and nurse his wounded pride, but he got up to let her in.

"Hi."

"Hi." She smiled at him. "So, dinner? How's your stomach?"

"Still slightly delicate, but the cramps have stopped."

"You still think it's a bug?"

"I don't know." The quick recovery pointed to a lactose issue, but how could that have happened? For as long as Zach could remember, he'd suffered from a severe intolerance. Even a splash of cow's milk in his morning coffee left him doubled up in pain on the toilet. But he hadn't drunk any cow's milk. No, he'd brought his own oat milk from California and, as he always did, stuck to basic foods in the days before the competition. No unknown brands, no restaurant meals that could contain lactose. And it crept into all kinds of products—cookies, cakes, soup, salad dressing, breakfast cereals. As usual, he'd brought his own granola with him. "I guess it must be. Or food poisoning?"

"I've eaten the same foods as you since we left the US, and I'm not sick."

"You had a sandwich for lunch yesterday, and I had the tuna salad."

"Kai had the tuna salad, and he's fine too."

Zach thought back and realised it was true. Ari was observant. "Then it must be a virus."

"You said it presented the same as lactose intolerance. There's no way milk could have snuck into a dish?"

"I've spent my whole life living with this—I know which foods might be suspect, and either I check the ingredients, or I don't eat them. Plus Maya briefs the caterers for the tour before every round."

"What about on the airplane? There were no ingredients listed on the in-flight meal, and I'm not even sure what that pink stuff in the cup was."

"It was vegan raspberry mousse. Maya checked with the flight attendant while you were in the bathroom. And besides, the flight was too long ago—if I accidentally consume lactose, the symptoms show up within hours, not days."

"What did you eat this morning?"

"Coffee that I made myself with oat milk. Granola, also made with oat milk, a banana, and toast with olive oil spread." Zach held up a hand. "Bread can be a problem, I know that, but Maya ordered it from a vegan bakery we found the last time we were here, and they delivered the loaves plus a bunch of shit for Baylee before we arrived."

"I think Baylee's given up being vegan. I saw her eating a mozzarella-and-tomato panini at the airport in San Francisco."

"Figures. She tried a juice diet once, and it lasted three days." Zach's stomach gurgled, and he groaned. "A juice diet sounds tempting right now."

"You said this happened once before?"

"Yeah, the year before last, in Tahiti." He'd left the hotel maid one hell of a tip. "I wasn't so careful back then, and we ate in a restaurant the night before. Are you coming to Tahiti this year?"

"Am I invited?"

"You're always invited, sweetheart."

Zach held his breath as Ari pondered the question, realising just how much he wanted her to be there.

"It's in October?"

"Yeah, and there's also a round in Portugal next month. I know we agreed to stay friends, nothing more, but I'd really like you to come."

She smiled, and warmth spread through him.

"Well, I did say I wanted to travel. Maybe bite-sized visits will help me decide where I want to spend more time?"

"I can recommend California. Santa Cruz is fantastic at every time of year."

"Nice try. Did you decide about dinner?"

"I guess I could try something plain."

Should he apologise for inflicting the stink on her this morning? Or forever block it from his mind and hope she did the same?

"I'm sorry about…you know."

"Forget it. Shit happens, right?" Ari clapped a hand over her mouth. "Sorry, that was the worst pun in the history of puns, and I didn't mean it, I swear. Uh, I'll help Maya with the food. Is an omelette okay? A plain one?"

"Plain chicken would be better, maybe some boiled potatoes and a green salad."

"Vegan mayo?"

He nodded. Not for the first time, he wondered how he'd cope when Ari left. Sure, he'd managed before, and Maya would be there, but Ari had slotted so perfectly into his life that losing her companionship would be hard. Today, she'd barely left his side, and when he went to surf, the worry in her eyes had been genuine. She cared. And so did he. Perhaps he could visit her, wherever she ended up? Or would that be creepy?

He'd get a taste of what it was like to miss her this week when she headed back to Las Vegas for her friend's baby shower. She only planned to be gone for two nights, but… Fuck, he never used to be clingy like this.

"You want me to bring your meal up here?"

"No, I'll come downstairs."

"I should warn you that Baylee's started on the champagne."

"As if the day hasn't been bad enough already." Zach rolled his eyes to the ceiling. "Damn. Forget I said that."

"So I realise this might be an inappropriate question to ask, but…*why*?"

Zach knew exactly what Ari was asking, and he also knew the answer. Tyler didn't want to be burdened by a serious relationship, not after getting his heart broken by the only woman he'd ever truly loved. They'd dated for two years, been engaged for one, and she'd dumped him a month before the wedding. Last Zach heard, she was shacked up with a management consultant from Baltimore. After the split, Tyler had tried hook-ups, but those left him miserable. Then he met Ginger, then Tifanii, then Baylee—opportunists, all of them—and found he preferred the transactional arrangements they offered. He bought Baylee purses; she looked pretty on his arm and fucked in any position his dick desired. Maya said Baylee was a gold digger, and that was no lie. Baylee also didn't care who knew it.

But still, Zach decided to be diplomatic. "Because of her stunning intellect and philanthropic tendencies."

Ari just laughed and held out a hand. "Nice dodge. Come and eat? If Baylee won't shut up, I'll start watering down her drinks. I used to work at a dive bar in Sunrise, so I know how to do that."

"Sunrise is in Las Vegas?"

"Yup, and not the good part. The owner was a pervert, and he used to encourage women to dance on the bar so he could look up their skirts. Plus he used to collect their underwear to hang from the ceiling. His idea of decor."

"Sheesh."

"Wait, it gets worse. When the bar hit hard times, he started selling the underwear on the internet. Do you realise how much men will pay for used panties?"

"I swear I have no idea."

"That's a good answer. You can stay."

Oh, he intended to. Zach wanted to stay in Ari's life forever.

CHAPTER 25
ARI

Most kids wanted parties at Wet 'n' Wild or King Putt or the movie theatre, but not Haven. She'd begged to take three friends to the Coral Reef Aquarium. Her fascination with the ocean was a new thing, and according to Nana, Haven had begun watching nature documentaries to understand why "Momma moved to the beach." When I heard that, my heart ached. Now do you realise why it was so important for me to come back home, even for a few days? The guilt at leaving my daughter for so long was almost overwhelming, compounded by the hug she'd given me after she tore open the carefully wrapped gifts I'd brought her: a box of candy from Cornwall, a windowsill garden, a sea monkey tank, a United States jigsaw puzzle, a pony necklace, and a Junior Detective Fingerprint Kit—might as well start her young.

"I don't need all this stuff, Momma. I just want you here."

The words had cut right to my core, and I'd nearly called Rennick and quit on the spot. But I wasn't rich. I didn't have the luxury of being able to pick and choose my jobs. By sacrificing this time with Haven and working seven days a week over the summer, I'd be able to keep a roof over our heads and build up a cushion of savings too. A just-turned-nine-year-old didn't understand how close we'd come to getting the electricity cut off, or that our landlord would evict us if I kept paying the rent late. Rennick's money would buy us time and maybe even a short vacation.

"I know, munchkin, and I miss you too. When this job is done, we can take a trip together. A break outside the city. Someplace with horses."

Haven had been asking for a horse since she was four years old, but the closest we'd gotten was the petting zoo. Riding lessons were out of reach at the moment, but in Cornwall, I'd noticed flyers for a pony trekking centre in the lobby, no previous experience necessary. If I could find something similar in a neighbouring state…

"I don't want a horse anymore."

"You don't?"

"No, I want a dolphin."

Aw, crap.

"I don't think you can keep a dolphin as a pet."

"My dolphin would live in the ocean, and we'd swim together every morning. Momma, can you teach me to swim?"

"If I knew how to swim, I would."

"Can't you learn?"

Couldn't I learn? She made it sound so simple. Oh, to be a child again. At least I was able to get into a pool now, and I'd become proficient at floating. It had become my and Zach's little ritual. As the sun went down, we'd bob around the pool at Haven's Rest, counting the stars.

He'd offered to teach me to swim as well, but so far, I'd been too chicken to try. The thought of the water running over my face terrified me. But the way Haven was looking at me? I knew that when I returned to Seagrass Point, I'd be taking advantage of Zach's generosity one last time before I stabbed him in the back.

And the moment of reckoning was surely growing closer.

Little clues were popping up.

On two of the days Zach had performed badly, he'd been sick, and although he'd written the most recent episode off as a virus, he was surely in a position to understand the effects of lactose intolerance. Yes, the first time could have been an accident as he thought, if not for one little issue: the amount of money bet against him before the symptoms even appeared. I'd checked with Rennick—the wagers on the Tahiti contest the year before last had been placed before the heats began. And the past weekend, he'd been careful with what he ate, so careful. Once I realised what had happened, I'd tried to collect the milk container for analysis—the most likely culprit for contamination, in my opinion—but the others had already finished the contents. I'd found the carton lying in the recycling box, rinsed clean.

A coincidence?

Or had someone tried to hide the evidence?

Because if Zach's performance had been sabotaged, then the prime suspects were the people close to him—Maya, Kai, Tyler, or Baylee, with Gloria a possibility too, seeing as she'd packed the food. I couldn't rule out somebody connected with the tour either, but the timing didn't quite fit. If Zach's food had been spiked at a tour event on Saturday, he'd have spent the night on the toilet, not the morning.

All this time, I'd pegged Zach as the traitor, but what if it was one of his friends?

One of *my* friends.

Yes, I needed this time in Las Vegas. A moment away from the bubble I'd been living in.

A reset.

"Maybe I could learn to swim," I told Haven. "Are you ready to go to the aquarium?"

"Yes!"

Today I was a mom first and a PI second.

Why the hell had I come back to Vegas?

I'd been shown into Rennick's inner sanctum by Meryl, his second assistant, a perfectly coiffed, rail-thin lady in her early forties who whispered that Lila was sick today. Perhaps there was something in the water? Other than kiwi and strawberry, anyway. Lila's sidekick had set the tray of refreshments on the floor before backing out of the room, closing the double doors behind her.

I'd arrived on time, but Jankowski was already there, leaning against a wall with his hands in his suit pockets and one leg crossed over the other at the ankle. An illusion of nonchalance. I didn't miss the clenched jaw or the scowl he gave me.

The small table and the stools had disappeared, and with Rennick occupying the only remaining chair in the room, I picked up a glass of fruity water and perched on a rock, leaving footprints in his carefully raked sand. Well, he should have been more accommodating to visitors, shouldn't he? He was a multimillionaire—was a couch really out of the question?

Jankowski gave his report first, and although he used plenty of words, they all boiled down to a whole lot of nothing. His team had checked out the addresses used on the questionable accounts, which were dotted across the world. The properties existed, but the folks living in them were definitely different. Those residents that Jankowski and his team had interviewed—in Toronto, Ancona, Seville, Edinburgh, Cannes, Venice, and St. John's—denied any involvement.

"How did the perp get ahold of the addresses?" I asked, which earned me another glare from Jankowski. "Is there any common thread? Or were they picked at random?"

"The folks we spoke with don't know."

"Some of the accounts were open for years."

"So either the scammer was playing the long game, or those accounts belonged to previous occupants and got hacked."

"Did you check out the previous occupants?"

"That information wasn't readily available."

So look harder, idiot.

"Have there been any data breaches?" I asked Rennick. "A large-scale hack?"

"Customer accounts are locked down tight. In our database, payment details and passwords are encrypted."

Then the person—or group of people—we were hunting had harvested the information piecemeal, by either accessing existing accounts or setting up new ones over a period of time. And I knew from Jankowski's earlier reports that they suspected the use of VPNs to mask the perp's location. Payments and withdrawals were made using e-wallets to hide the origin and destination of the funds. The e-wallet functioned as a payment intermediary, an alternative to a credit card.

I didn't envy Jankowski's task—he was digging for a needle in a digital haystack, and without subpoena power, he couldn't compel the providers of the e-wallets to give up information about their users. And technically, no crime had been committed. The only evidence was Rennick's statistical analysis and the fact that Zach had, on several occasions, had a really bad day.

Conversely, I had to admire the perp's plan—unless AnyBet began limiting wagers, our opponent could keep extracting dirty money. And as Rennick said, imposing limits would cost the group more in bad publicity than they were losing to the scammer.

Meanwhile, Jankowski was chasing his tail, and I was listening to Zach shit in a bathroom.

We moved on to my report, and I summarised the events in Cornwall—Zach's sudden illness and the fact that this was the second incident of the same nature. Predictably, Jankowski wasn't impressed.

"That's it? Two months of work, and all you've come up with is 'Guy with lactose intolerance drinks milk'?"

"He didn't drink the milk. Not voluntarily, anyway. And don't you think it's strange that he got sick on the morning of the contest? As the betting was being manipulated?"

"Maybe he was faking?"

"He wasn't faking."

"And what about the other staged losses? Your theory doesn't cover those."

"I don't have an answer for that," I admitted. "Yet."

"You don't have answers to much, do you? Just a half-baked theory and a suntan. How was your little jaunt to England?"

"Great, and how was Antigua? Did you stay all-inclusive?"

"I didn't eat dinner with the main suspect, if that's what you mean."

"Eating dinner with the main suspect is my *job*."

Rennick tapped a pen on the desk, a small sound, but it snapped me out of the argument. Jankowski too. I'd never seen him look so contrite. Rennick regarded us with a look that might have been curiosity or mild amusement, and I wanted to sink right through the rock I was sitting on. But the rock was solid, so I took a deep breath and brought the conversation back on track.

"All relevant details of my conversations with Zach Torres have been included in my reports."

But with Jankowski denigrating everything I did, I decided that now wasn't the right time to bring up what I'd seen right before I left for Las Vegas. Or *thought* I'd seen. I wasn't certain.

Maya's phone had rung, and when she glanced at the screen, the briefest flicker of shock had crossed her face. But rather than decline the call, she'd scuttled outside to answer it. Five minutes later, she'd strolled back in, phone in hand, composed once more.

"Why can't these photographers get the message?"

"That's who was on the phone? A photographer?"

Maya nodded. "Every month, I get another call asking if Zach will do a shoot at Mavericks. Even in the summer when the wave doesn't break, he won't go there."

"Maybe you should put a note on his Wikipedia page?" I joked, but inside, I felt as sick as Zach had on Sunday because it wasn't some random photographer's name that had flashed up on her screen, or even an unknown number. No, it was *Zed Nelson*. Why had Maya lied? If she'd said that Zed had called, it wouldn't have been strange at all, so why the subterfuge?

Fear makes people think irrationally, Morty had always said. Had Maya panicked? If so, what was she trying to cover up?

To the world, she appeared to be the devoted sister, but what if there was resentment bubbling underneath the surface? While Zach got fame and fortune, she'd given up surfing to run around after him. They'd spent their teenage years apart—how close were they really?

That was the puzzle I had to solve, but I'd do it without Jankowski's input. I didn't trust his judgment anyway.

Rennick took a sip of his water. He was barefoot again today, and dressed in what looked like pyjamas. A late riser, or just a rich eccentric?

"Arizona, your theory has some merit, but Dale is correct in that it only covers a fraction of the timescale. You need to dig deeper."

"I plan to."

"And, Dale, I don't believe any more overseas trips are required. We've established that the residents of the addresses used on the accounts aren't involved, and the funds are untraceable. You'll have to try a different approach."

"I know a guy who can have a word with Torres."

What the hell?

The zen master's eyes narrowed. "Are you advocating violence, Mr. Jankowski?"

"Uh, no, no, not at all." Jankowski backpedalled in a hurry because that was exactly what he'd tried doing. At Twilight, it was an open secret that Jankowski bent the law, and he wasn't afraid to inflict a few bruises while he did it. "I'm just saying that Torres must know who's involved."

"Arizona is handling that part of the investigation."

Rennick had stuck up for me. He'd actually stuck up for me, and greater than the surprise was the relief. Jankowski was a king in the world of private investigation, and I was a mere serf. But if my ex-boss was considering an underhand approach, I'd have to watch Zach's back, and my own too. Mental note: remember to carry a stun gun in my purse alongside the pepper spray.

"Mr. Rennick, I promise I won't let you down."

CHAPTER 26
ZACH

"Take a deep breath, and exhale steadily as you put your face in the water. Keep one hand on the edge of the pool."

"What if I go under?"

"You're wearing a floatation device, sweetheart. You can't sink."

Ari was back in Seagrass Point. For two irrational days, Zach had been worried that she was gone for good, especially when she didn't show up for dinner on Friday, but when he cracked and called her, it turned out there was an accident on the interstate. A semi had overturned, and there were eggs all over the road. "Cooking on the damn asphalt," Ari said on the phone. "I won't get there for hours."

Zach had stayed up until she arrived, waiting with a cold drink, a hot meal, and an offer of a bed for the night because if Ms. Carrington woke after the witching hour, she'd turn into a gremlin's angrier cousin. Ari had brought him a gift too, a *Kiss My Wrasse* bumper sticker that he'd stuck next to the *Can't We All Just Get A Longboard?* decal on the back of his truck. And she'd also changed her mind about learning to swim. Tyler had taken her to Board Stiff and kitted her out with half a dozen new bathing suits and a bikini—be still Zach's twitching dick—and Maya had dug out a spare buoyancy aid. Kai offered to stand by, ready to give the kiss of life, and Zach had jokingly threatened to punch him. Okay, half-jokingly. But he'd gotten the message and left them alone.

Ari sucked in a lungful of air and dipped her face under, blowing bubbles, and Zach kept a hand on her stomach, a connection he hoped would give her confidence. Three seconds, four seconds, five, and she popped up again, dripping water as she flung her arms around his neck.

"I did it! I'm still alive!"

"Don't sound so surprised."

"Why? Two out of the last three times I put my face in the water, I ended up getting CPR."

"I can give you CPR if you want."

"Nice try."

While Zach still felt a simmering attraction, Ari joked about the chemistry between them instead. But she kept an arm around his neck as they settled into the shade of the new metal planters he'd installed to give them some privacy, troughs filled with palm trees and bamboo and tall grasses that rustled in the breeze. Learning to swim was hard enough without photos appearing on the internet. And at least Khloe, Alys, and Stacey had gone home. Khloe had left a note in the mailbox—*We still love you, but we thought you'd be more fun.* What had they expected him to do? Sunbathe naked by the pool and then invite them in for a four-way?

Anyhow, the peace suited him just fine.

"Seriously, though, I'll keep you safe. I promise."

"I should have said this before, but I'm so grateful for everything you've done." Ari nibbled on her bottom lip as she pushed wet hair away from her face. "I've never had

someone who looks out for me the way you do, and I guess…
I guess I don't find it easy to give up control. To rely on
anyone other than myself."

"Who was he?" Zach asked softly.

"Who was who?"

"The asshole who hurt you."

"Nobody." A sigh. "I try not to think about him. He liked
to be in control too, and when I didn't conform to his
expectations, he left. Just abandoned me. I found out later
that he'd cheated as well."

"I'm so sorry, sweetheart."

"Don't apologise. You're not the asshole."

"But I'm still sorry that happened to you." He leaned in
close and kissed her on the forehead. "And I won't abandon
you."

"Don't say that."

"Why not? It's the truth. You know I like you." Zach held
up a hand before Ari could reject him again. "I also know you
need space, so that's what I'm going to give you."

"You'll abandon me in the end."

"My heart says otherwise, sweetheart, but I'm not going to
start a fight. Try putting your face under the water again."

"I promise I'll find a way to repay your kindness
someday."

"You're already doing more than you know."

Sea, sun, and a sexy travel blogger—that was all Zach
needed to be happy.

"Hey, what did you do that for?" Baylee faced Ari, hands on
hips. "That was Zach's coffee."

"It had milk in it."

"*Oat* milk, duh. That's what he drinks."

"Not this weekend, he doesn't." Ari grabbed the carton and poured the contents down the sink. "Where did you get this? We didn't bring it with us."

"I bought it at the grocery store."

"Well, this weekend, he's not drinking oat milk, rice milk, almond milk, or any other type of milk."

"Who made you the boss?"

"Didn't you see how sick he got in Cornwall?"

"Yeah, so?"

"Milk might have caused that."

"It was a virus; Zach said so himself."

Zach watched the confrontation from the kitchen doorway. A rack full of pots and pans hung over the central island in the Portuguese villa, blocking him from view. He hadn't seen this fiery side of Ari before, but he kind of liked it.

"Or his food might've gotten contaminated," she told Baylee.

"Are you always this paranoid?"

"I'm just looking out for Zach."

"Are you? Before you showed up, he used to come over to our place for dinner and go to parties. Now he stays at home every freaking night."

"That's his decision."

"Is it? Because from where I'm standing, you look like a manipulative bitch. Our group was tight until you shoved your way into the middle of it."

Okay, whoa, too far.

"Baylee, that was a shitty thing to say."

Both women spun to face him. One looked horrified, and the other was spoiling for a fight. Take a guess which was which.

"Why? It's the truth. You spend all your time with her now."

Zach hadn't realised he was meant to carve up his free time according to someone else's schedule. Having to surf on someone else's orders was bad enough. And as for the parties… He realised now that he'd always been searching for something, that missing piece in his life, but he'd found it closer to home than he ever expected. With Ari around, there was no need to go out on the hunt anymore.

"That's my choice."

"So you're ditching your best friends for a girl?"

Was he? True, he hadn't spent as much time with Kai and Tyler lately, but Tyler had been busy shaping boards. The last time Zach invited him over, he'd dropped by for one non-alcoholic beer and then headed back to work. Did Baylee know that? Or was the communication problem hers?

And Kai's second love was music. When he wasn't surfing, he sang in an Eagles cover band, and while they usually took a gig a month, they'd played five in the past four weeks. Zach and Ari had attended the beach party they'd headlined, plus another show at the Coco Bar in Santa Cruz.

Kai and Tyler were his friends and always would be, but the three of them didn't have to spend every waking moment together. Fuck, Zach had to be at the beach in an hour. He didn't have time for this shit, and he didn't appreciate Baylee sticking her nose into his business either.

"If you have a problem with the amount of time I'm spending with Kai and Tyler, try talking to Kai and Tyler."

"Don't you think it's weird? The way Ari just showed up?"

"What's weird about it? That she moved to Seagrass Point and happened to use the beach?"

Hadn't he done exactly the same thing?

"She has an apartment, but she still spends most of her time at your place."

"Yeah, well, I'm in love with her. She can spend her whole damn life at my place if she wants to."

Silence.

Dead. Silence.

You could have heard a shrimp sneeze.

"And I'm taking my coffee black now."

Baylee stormed out, slamming the door behind her and leaving a room full of bad vibes in her wake. Shit. Zach had imagined someday telling Ari how he felt, but not like this. Worse, her horrified expression had ratcheted up a notch.

"So…" His voice came out as a croak. "Now you know."

Hers was a whisper. "Now I know."

"I don't expect you to suddenly fall at my feet. Nothing needs to change."

"Right."

He wished he could take the words back, but at the same time, he didn't. That they'd tripped so easily off his tongue showed the depth of his feelings, and holding them in had caused a dull ache in his gut. Before, spending time with her had left him feeling almost…deceitful, dancing around the truth with declarations of "like." As if he were pulling a bait-and-switch.

But now she knew.

"I'll make the coffee," he offered. "You want a cup?"

The machine was out of beans. Before he could pour more in, Ari put a hand on his.

"It's not you; it's me."

"Espresso or Americano?"

"Zach, I know this isn't easy. Not for either of us. If…if you still feel the same in six months, then I'm yours."

He froze. "You mean…?"

"I mean that a lot can happen in six months. I'll skip the coffee."

"Wait, we need to—"

But Ari was already backing out of the room. "Don't you have a beach to get to?"

Yeah, he did.

That weekend in Portugal, the waves didn't matter. The trophy he won didn't matter, and neither did the prize money. Ari had given Zach hope, and although she'd backed off again, she was still very much in his life.

And he intended to keep her there.

CHAPTER 27
ARI

With hindsight, getting into a fight with Baylee had been the wrong move. But I'd panicked. I'd panicked when I saw her putting milk in Zach's coffee and stopped her in the quickest way possible. And the dumbest part of the move? Nobody was going to spike Zach's milk this weekend. Lila had reported that betting patterns were normal.

The aftermath of the contest in Peniche had been uncomfortable, the airplane ride back almost unbearable. I'd nearly fled from the departure gate and caught another flight, but I hadn't wanted to hurt Zach by running out on him.

In the end, Maya had calmed me down in the bathroom.

"We don't all think like Baylee, you know."

"You heard about the fight?"

"Zach told me. She thinks the whole world revolves around her."

"I didn't set out to monopolise his time, honestly."

"You're good for my brother. And if Zach didn't want you there, you wouldn't be around, trust me. Do you realise you're only the third woman in seven years that he's brought back to the house?"

"I didn't know that."

"He's picky." Maya rolled her eyes. "Tyler, not so much. This'll blow over, don't worry."

Her words gave me some reassurance, but since we arrived home, I'd begun spending more time in my rented apartment—quietly, because Ms. Carrington was blessed with superhuman hearing. We'd been back for a week, and Baylee still hadn't said more than two words to me, and while I wasn't her biggest fan, I was also a huge liar who'd only end up hurting the entire group when I left.

Why had I made that dumb six-month promise?

I'd given Zach hope, I saw it in his eyes, and that only made my job harder. At least I had a hard deadline now. Whether I'd solved the case or not, I'd be gone by next February.

I was about to reheat the leftovers that Maya had sent me home with and settle in for an evening of report writing when I heard an engine start, followed by the *crunch* of tyres on gravel.

My first thought? *I hope Ms. Carrington doesn't blame me for that.*

My second thought? *Where's Maya going?*

And it was Maya, not Zach. Zach had left an hour ago to spend the evening watching sports with Kai and Tyler, and Maya said she was going to send a few emails and then get an early night. But now she was leaving?

Sure, it was possible she had a sudden craving for ice cream, but she'd bought groceries earlier. What was so important? I thought back to her disappearance from our hotel room in Huntington Beach—could tonight's excursion be connected?

Screw dinner. I needed answers more than I needed spaghetti bolognese. A moment later, I was in my car, mentally preparing myself for the ear-bashing I'd get from Ms. Carrington later.

A tracker would have been nice, but I didn't have that luxury, not on Maya's car. Mental note: swap the unit currently on Zach's truck. Thankfully, the streets were reasonably quiet, and I'd had plenty of practice at vehicle surveillance. Day had turned to dusk, so even if she glanced in the rear-view mirror, which she rarely did—I knew that from riding with her—she probably wouldn't recognise my Honda.

Maya headed for Santa Cruz, but instead of swinging by a restaurant, she bypassed downtown and drove to Carbonero Estates, an upscale neighbourhood of multimillion-dollar homes nestled among the forested areas near the golf course. She'd never mentioned having friends in this neighbourhood, but its name rang a bell. Where had I seen it before? In Jankowski's files? Maya slowed and turned into a driveway, then paused as a pair of imposing wooden gates slowly swung open. Who lived there?

The smart thing to do, the sensible thing, would have been to note down the address, go back to the apartment, and look up the information I needed. But Jankowski had once accused me of being stupid, and when I rolled past the property and saw a walking trail winding its way through the trees, I figured I might as well live up to his expectations.

Was this the kind of place where residents would report a suspicious car parked on the street? Probably. But a quarter mile away, one of the neighbours was having a party, and guests' cars had overflowed onto the nature strip outside. I tucked mine onto the end of the line, feeling out of place among the Mercedes, Audis, and Lexuses.

In a masterstroke of planning, I'd left the apartment wearing a yellow T-shirt, so I grabbed my black windbreaker out of the trunk and slipped it on. In this age of instant gratification, I figured that if I could just get close enough to the house to glimpse the occupant through a window, my curiosity would be satisfied.

Too bad there was a wall in the way.

Eight feet of solid brick with the occasional security warning. Cameras! Patrols! Alarm system! Well, I wasn't planning to break into the house, not tonight, and patrols would make their rounds every couple of hours at most. Cameras... Well, they couldn't cover every angle, and Morty had taught me how to work out their field of view. This wasn't my first rodeo. Uh, I meant this wasn't my first wrong turning while trying to find a friend's place.

Tucked into the shadows, I listened carefully for a dog. Electronic protection had predictable weaknesses, but dogs did their own thing. I heard a bark in the distance and waited, but there was no return volley from the mystery house. Phew.

A little way off the trail, a sturdy oak grew beside the wall, and back in Vegas, Morty had sent me on a training course at the Red Rock Climbing Center to prepare me for situations just like this one. Oh, sure, PIs weren't technically meant to trespass, but everyone broke the rules on occasion. Not getting caught was the critical part.

Damn, I was unfit. Back in Vegas, I used to go to the gym several times a week, and when I couldn't afford a membership anymore, I'd taken up running. Plus picking up after Haven had kept me fit. Now? Now climbing one tree left me breathing hard.

Things needed to change.

The house was a good size, three thousand square feet at a guess, with a separate two-car garage. The yard was tidy but soulless, an expanse of perfectly manicured lawn edged by clumps of shrubbery. A pool at the rear was designed for aesthetics rather than functionality—a kidney bean shape with a waterfall was no use for serious swimming; I understood that from watching Zach in action.

Morty Coulson's first rule of nosing around: always plan your exit route. A storage shed near the pool—one I assumed held the filtration equipment—would give me enough height to get back over the wall, and a cluster of ornamental rocks beside it practically formed a stepladder. All I had to do was run up and over.

I skirted a table and chairs and approached the house. The red light of a security camera glowed from the roofline, but it was fixed in place, a cheap system with the field of view set too high to be useful. The owner would get a great picture of anyone crossing the lawn and not much else. I hugged the fence line until I reached the terrace, then cut across to the house. A light blinked on, and I froze, playing statue in the shadows cast by a leafy vine as it wound its way over a pergola.

Nothing.

Fortunately, few people paid attention to security lights after the first few false alarms. Most folks assumed the intruder was a bird or a fox or even just the wind. Only in the presence of other concerns—a strange noise, perhaps, or a worried call from a neighbour—did they bother to look outside.

When there was no reaction from the house, I carried on circling, checking each window as I went. Whoever lived here, they weren't concerned about the size of their electricity bill—every chandelier was blazing.

Ah, there he was.

In a dual-aspect living room, a man sat on a couch, watching TV. *Brooklyn 99*—I recognised the show. I could only see the back of his head, but there was something familiar about the longish brown hair. Did I know him?

I pulled out my phone and started videoing the scene as I moved around the corner to the next window, just in case the man's identity proved important for my report. And while I tiptoed carefully past the pool, I did have one niggly little thought—where had Maya gone?

Then I found out.

And I wished I hadn't.

Zed Nelson relaxed on the leather couch, head lolling back, pants around his ankles. The perfect profile shot. Maya was on her knees in front of him, one hand on his bare thigh and the other wrapped around the base of his cock as he fucked her mouth.

Shit!

I mean, what in the hell?

Maya and *Zed*?

This was her secret?

But...but Maya was so sweet, and Zed was a world-class dick. Actually, no, I take that back... From what I'd just witnessed—and somebody *please* wash my eyes out with bleach—Nelson's dick was anything but world class.

I stumbled backward in shock, horror, whatever, and fell over a lawn chair. The metallic clatter as it crashed into a tiny table was followed by the glare of a security light, and I realised I had roughly five seconds to get the hell out of there. Ten if I was lucky and Zed paused to pull up his pants.

I wouldn't make the shed roof. Hell, I wouldn't even make the nearest tree, and if Zed came out to investigate the noise, the whole undercover job was screwed. I needed to hide, but...but...

There was only one possible place.

I saved the video and shoved the phone into my pocket, then ducked and rolled into the pool as a shadow appeared at the window.

Panic sent my heart into my throat, but I forced the fear back where it belonged—into my stomach so it could tie my guts up in knots. Zach had spent his spare time training me for this, helping me to feel comfortable in the water, and *I could damn well handle a little dampness.*

Focus, focus, focus. I had ten seconds of breath left, and I pushed off the edge of the pool with my feet, gliding under the water until I reached the waterfall. *Find your footing.* Five seconds left, and I rose slowly behind the curtain of water, giving myself enough room to breathe while I watched the house. Maya was still at the window, her face pressed to the glass, and a moment later, Nelson appeared outside with a gun in his hand, sending a fresh wave of terror through me. If he saw me, would he shoot?

The tumbling water sent up enough splashes to hide my shape, and I held my breath as Nelson made a circuit of the yard, checking behind each bush as he went. As he came closer, I noticed he kept his finger on the trigger, which indicated poor discipline as well as frayed nerves.

Keep going, keep going.

"Probably just a cat," he called.

Thank goodness.

I stayed frozen to the spot as he tucked the gun into his waistband and stalked back inside, and only when he appeared in the living room again did my pulse begin to slow from its wild gallop. Zed and Maya. Sheesh. Did Nelson have a surprise altruistic side that he'd managed to keep well hidden until now? Or had Maya been seduced by money and power?

Guilt washed over me like a chlorinated waterfall because I shouldn't even be asking myself that question. I'd spied on a private moment that I had no right to see. Unless… Unless Nelson was somehow tangled up in the AnyBet scam. There was no love lost between him and Zach—what if he manipulated the losses not only as a way to make money, but in order to make Zach look bad too?

I made the mistake of glancing at the window again, and now Maya was topless. Hell, I had to get out of here. Slowly, slowly, I slithered out from behind the waterfall and crawled across the pool deck, keeping low until I got to the shed. A hop, skip, jump, and I was over the wall. At least the phone Maya had given me to replace my old one was water resistant.

Boy, tonight's report was gonna be a doozy.

CHAPTER 28
ZACH

"You want this?"

"Huh?"

Zach pushed the bottle of Surf Star Liquid Energy he'd been about to drink across the kitchen table toward Ari, avoiding Maya's laptop and notepad.

This weekend, they were staying in his second home, which sounded much flashier than the reality. Yes, he owned the modern, five-bedroom villa that overlooked the wave pool at Surf 365, but for most of the year, he rented it out to tourists and banked the income. Maybe someday he'd move there—a prospect that looked more attractive by the day, seeing as Britney and Angela had replaced Khloe, Alys, and Stacey outside the gates of Haven's Rest—but for the moment, he used it for just two or three weeks per year.

Last night, he'd gotten a decent amount of sleep despite the band that had played into the early hours two hundred yards from his bedroom window, and he was ready to tackle the semi-final. But Ari looked as if she needed a nap.

"You need the caffeine more than I do."

"Uh, thank you? I think."

Not only were there dark smudges under her eyes, but she

also seemed surprised to see him. Zach wasn't surprised by her surprise—she'd avoided being alone with him at any point in the past week, and this morning, she'd waited until she thought everyone had left before she made her appearance downstairs. Probably because Baylee had spent yesterday afternoon drinking Mai Tais in the VIP bar and then made another snarky comment when Ari began checking the contents of the refrigerator in the evening.

"Are you obsessed or something?" she'd asked as Ari held a bottle of soda up to the light to examine the liquid. "It's cola. There's no freaking milk in it."

Tyler's snicker didn't help matters, but Ari had stayed calm.

"You say obsessed; I say careful."

"More like paranoid."

Then Maya had come steaming in, powered by a single lemon drop martini. She never had been able to hold her liquor.

"Yes, Ari actually cares about my brother and not just his money—difficult for you to comprehend, I know."

"Wait a minute…" Tyler tried, but Maya wasn't done.

"And what's your contribution to this team, anyway? Besides sleeping with Tyler, I mean?"

"I…I carried half the bags in from the truck."

"Half of the bags were *yours*. You brought more clothes than the rest of us combined."

"By quantity or by volume?"

"What's that supposed to mean?"

Baylee looked Maya up and down. "Isn't it obvious?"

"Babe, that's too far," Tyler told her as Maya burst into tears and stormed out.

"I only said what everyone else is thinking."

The media had nicknamed Kai "Sub-Zero" because he never lost his cool, but even he looked pissed.

"Not everyone, Baylee." Then to Zach, "I'll go after her."

What Zach wanted to do was haul Baylee out the door and dump her into the lake, but there were journalists everywhere, plus a hundred thousand people with camera phones. So he gritted his teeth and tried diplomacy instead.

"Why don't we—"

Ari jabbed Baylee in the chest. "Bitch at me all you want, but do *not* bring Maya's weight into this."

"Why should I listen to you?"

"Oh, I'm sorry, do I have to buy you a designer purse first?"

"You don't even have a job!"

Finally, Tyler had gotten his act together and picked Baylee up. Of course, she struggled and whined, but he held firm.

"Come to bed, okay?"

"She just insulted me."

"I'm surprised you even noticed," Ari muttered, then put the cola back in the refrigerator and slammed the door. "I'm done here."

Zach had been left alone in the kitchen, staring into a glass of apple juice that Ari had blessed with her approval. Maybe she'd become a little obsessive about his diet, but that just showed she cared, right? At least, he hoped she did. Lately, he'd felt as if he was losing Ari, and he didn't know how to fix things.

And it wasn't only his imagination; Maya had noticed her pulling away as well. Since the first spat with Baylee, she'd begun distancing herself, spending some evenings alone next door and early mornings jogging along the shore. Sure, she still came over to swim and shower, but only when Maya was there, and she never quite relaxed.

If Maya went out, Ari vanished too, almost as if she was watching. Was she that worried about Zach braving Ms. Carrington's wrath to visit? He wished he could turn back the clock and tape Baylee's mouth shut because the day she'd started bitching was when things had begun to go wrong. Tyler had spoken with his girlfriend and reminded her that bros came before hoes, including her—although he hadn't used that exact phrase—but she'd clearly failed to take his words on board.

Zach's friendship with Tyler and Kai was solid. But that didn't mean there wasn't enough room in his life for Ari too. The question was, did she have room in her life for him? Baylee swore she'd seen Ari having lunch with another man in Santa Cruz, pizza at an Italian restaurant near the hospital, and Zach wasn't sure whether Baylee was telling the truth or just stirring. And so far, he'd been too much of a coward to ask Ari for her side of the story. No news was better than bad news.

At least she'd agreed to come to the Surf 365 Special this weekend, and although the venue couldn't offer any nurdles for her to count, he was proud of the surf park he'd helped to build. If there was one wave he wanted her to be impressed by, it was this one.

This was only the second time Surf 365 had been included on the WST calendar, and although the venues rotated from year to year, he hoped it would become a permanent fixture. And it had advantages over the traditional contests—the on-site accommodation, a natural amphitheatre with a permanent stage for entertainment, and guaranteed water conditions. They could alter the profile of the wave depending on who was surfing, with smaller, gentler sets for beginners and gnarly barrels for the pros. And safety was a priority. To Zach, that had been the main attraction of the place, the reason why he'd invested. The park had a dedicated water rescue team, plus a medical centre, and the only sharks were in the gift store.

"Have the others already left?" Ari asked.

Zach checked his watch. "Five minutes ago."

"Why didn't you go with them?"

"Because I wanted to speak with you first."

"Oh." She gave a weighty sigh. "I'm sorry about last night. I shouldn't have snapped at Baylee, but what she said to Maya was low."

"Yeah, it was."

"Are you okay? I mean, not too stressed?"

"Baylee apologised to me this morning. I think Tyler put her up to it, but I told her she should be apologising to you and Maya instead. Has she done that?"

"She hasn't said a word."

Disappointing, but not unexpected. "She also promised that she'd stay out of the bar today."

But that still didn't get to the root of the problem, Zach knew that. He hated that Baylee had judged his sister. Yeah, Maya had put on a few pounds in the past year, but so what?

Ari's roll of the eyes said she felt the same way. "I honestly don't know what Tyler sees in Baylee."

"He loved a girl once, but it didn't work out. If I was gonna play amateur psychologist, I'd say that he's punishing himself. That he's scared to get close to another good woman in case he ends up hurt again."

"So he dates Baylee as a defence mechanism? That's so sad."

"The last chick was worse. Tifanii. One F, two I's. She left him for a cage fighter."

"Ouch."

"I think he was actually relieved." Zach didn't know whether to sit or stand, so he leaned against the counter. "I used to think he was crazy for dating women that he didn't see a future with, but now I understand why he guards his heart."

He held his breath, waiting for a reaction. Would Ari back away literally as well as metaphorically?

No.

No, she moved forward. Hesitantly, but it was a step in the right direction.

"Zach, don't do this…"

He cupped her cheek in one hand, and she leaned into it. This… This was what he'd missed. The connection. The heat that built when they were together. He'd felt it the first day they met, and the initial flames had only grown in intensity. And while Ari's mouth might resist, her body told a different story.

"I love that you care enough to read every ingredient list in the kitchen. I love that you stuck up for Maya. And that dig at Baylee made me hard."

Ari managed a tiny smile. "You're not upset?"

"The only thing I'm upset about is that you slept in your bed last night instead of mine." He hooked an arm around her waist and pulled her closer. She didn't resist. "I've never felt this way about anyone before, and…and it scares me."

"It freaking *terrifies* me. Zach, if my life was different, if… if…I didn't have…future, uh, commitments, then I'd—"

"There's somebody else? Fuck, is there another man?"

"No! No, there's no other man. How could you even—"

She grabbed his face with both hands and kissed him. Not a "let's just be friends" kiss or an "I'm sorry but I'm trying to let you down gently" kiss, but a full-on tongue fucking. All the tension he'd been storing up for the past two and a half months napalmed through his veins as Ari twined her arms around his neck and pressed her body against his, soft, delicate, a butterfly with iron wings. He'd spent long nights imagining this kiss, but the reality surpassed every dream. Ari tasted of mint toothpaste and hope.

Zach nibbled her lips and ran his fingers through her hair. Somewhere, his phone rang, but he ignored it. What could be more important than kissing his girl? But Ari slowly pulled away.

"Don't you have to go surfing?" she asked.

"No."

"Liar."

"One thing I learned from my parents is that love is more important than anything."

His dad had never taken the big risks until after his mom passed away. Maybe if she'd still been alive, he wouldn't have paddled out to catch one last wave at Mavericks. Maya had been too young to see the change in him, and he'd tried to keep the sadness hidden, but it was there. And a tiny part of Zach would never forgive him for leaving them, for numbing his pain with death and leaving them to face theirs alone.

"I'll still be here when you get back," Ari whispered.

"Will you?"

"I promise. Now that I've had a taste of you, I have to finish the package."

Zach pressed a soft kiss to her neck. "My package is yours."

"You're so charming."

"And you're my lucky charm."

"Let me take a shower." Ari opened the bottle of Surf Star and swallowed a mouthful. "I'll come and cheer for you."

"I love you."

Ari didn't say the words back, not that he'd expected her to, but she did smile.

"Get out there and win."

CHAPTER 29
ARI

What the...? Where the hell was I?

Damp. Somewhere damp... Soft... My hair hung around my face, tickling me, and my eyelids felt so, so heavy. Every limb, leaden. Faint shouting sounded in the background, music rising and falling. I tried to move an arm, and the effort left me drained.

How long had I been sleeping? I replayed disjointed memories—Rennick's call about his numbers being off again, an argument, a kiss, standing in the shower... Holy fireballs, that kiss... I'd tried so hard to resist temptation, but I was weak. I was Eve in the garden of Eden, faced with forbidden fruit and a one-eyed trouser snake.

But...but...I was meant to be watching Zach on a surfboard now.

Why was everything dark?

Tiredness had seeped into my bones, and for a brief, nightmarish moment, I wondered whether I'd been kidnapped, but when I forced an eye open, all I saw was mint-green cotton. Bed. I was in bed, and I'd been drooling.

I...I didn't understand.

Why wasn't I outside, cheering Zach on? I'd even taken

five minutes to borrow Maya's Sharpies and create an "I Heart Zach" poster because I knew it would make him laugh and also annoy Baylee.

Now I was in bed?

And why did I feel so freaking shattered?

Even though I was awake now, my head still felt sludgy, every thought a chore. What time was it? I scrabbled around on the nightstand for my phone and squinted at the screen. Four o'clock in the afternoon. I'd been asleep for nine hours straight.

Think, Ari, think.

Okay, the last thing I remembered was washing my hair. Could I have fallen and hit my head? Possibly? Then how did I get into bed? The poster... I'd made the poster after I showered, and I'd eaten a banana while I was colouring the hearts. Chased it down with a bottle of that energy drink Zach got paid to promote.

The bottle he'd passed me.

The bottle he'd been about to drink himself.

Suddenly, I was wide awake.

No, no, no... It couldn't be... Had someone tried to drug Zach?

Rennick said the numbers were messed up this weekend. That Zach was meant to lose again. I'd gotten rid of all the milk and tossed out anything that might contain dairy, plus Zach had humoured my efforts and double-checked too. Had the enemy tried a different approach?

And make no mistake, they were the enemy. If Zach had climbed onto a surfboard feeling as tired as I did, he could have been seriously injured.

Where was the bottle? Where was the damn bottle? I needed to have the contents tested, to check whether my theory was correct. But what other explanation could there be? I hadn't spent the entire day unconscious for no reason.

I spotted the bottle lying on the floor and crawled over to

it, sending silent thanks skyward when I saw the teaspoonful of orangey-yellow liquid in the bottom. Even with Zach's higher body weight, a tranquilliser would have left him dazed.

Four o'clock...four o'clock... Dammit, the final had been scheduled to start at three. Had Zach won? Because...because if I'd been drugged instead of him, then he'd stood a chance. And if he'd snatched first place, then I'd won too. Because the scammer would have lost. Lost every single one of their bets.

Pants, I needed pants. And a T-shirt. No, a bra first, didn't want to give Zach the wrong idea. Except I'd already given him the wrong idea, hadn't I? I'd kissed him. Me. The girl with a nine-year-old daughter, a three-year dry spell, and no self-control whatsoever. Oh, but I had stupidity. Yup, I had that in spades.

I guess I harboured a dumb hope that if I could take down the gang ripping off Rennick, then maybe I could just sort of...slide into the new life I'd created. I'd have to tell Zach about Haven, obviously, but I could spin a story about a custody battle or something. Say she'd been living with her father while I was in California.

Yeah, Ari, tell more lies. Terrific plan.

Okay, so perhaps coming clean would be the right approach. If I explained that what started out as a job had turned into so much more, that I felt the same way about him as he felt about me, then we might stand a chance.

But first, I needed to get outside. See whether he'd taken the top spot. Fuck, what if more than one drink had been spiked? I'd been checking for milk, for cloudiness that might indicate contamination, not for dissolved pills. A wrong assumption. So far, the scammer—well, they were more of a poisoner now because who knew what I'd ingested?—had always stayed one step ahead.

Not for much longer.

If my future happiness with Zach depended on solving

the case, then I had to make it happen. Even if it meant exposing one of his closest friends as a traitor. Maya, Kai, Tyler, and Baylee were at the top of my suspect list. Who else would have known that Zach liked to pep himself up with an energy drink before each contest? And somebody had made sure that particular bottle was in the refrigerator, waiting for him. I couldn't risk tipping them off by interrogating Zach, not yet, but the clock was ticking.

I was the hunter, and they were my prey.

CHAPTER 30
ZACH

She'd gotten cold feet, hadn't she?

All day, Zach had been hoping that he'd just missed Ari in the crowd, that she'd been hidden in the sea of screaming fans among banners making lewd suggestions. But surely she'd have been there for the trophy presentation? She had a VIP pass, and there were still empty seats in the reserved area—those folks who'd forked out thousands for an all-inclusive package tended to spend more time in the bar than watching the action.

The moment he stepped off the podium, a blonde in a bikini approached. One of Zed's minions.

"Zach, please follow me to the press conference."

"Give me a minute."

"Uh, Mr. Nelson said—"

"I'm sure he did, but he'll have to wait for a minute."

Where was Maya? Zach spotted her holding Kai's third-place trophy and pushed his way through the drunken crowd, ignoring requests for autographs and selfies.

"Where's Ari?"

"Back at the villa?"

"Are you asking me or telling me?"

"I called her at lunchtime to see where she was, and she said she was too tired to come watch. And she sounded *really* sleepy. I mean, she mumbled so much I could barely understand what she was saying."

"And you didn't check on her?"

Maya's cheeks reddened. "I meant to, but Kai lost his leash, and Tyler needed my help with the radios because two of them malfunctioned and they couldn't find the spares, and — Zach, where are you going? You need to get to the press conference."

"No, I need to find Ari."

"But it's live."

And his future with Ari might be dead. What if she'd left the surf park? He ran toward his villa, shouting, "Back in five," to another of Zed's people. They could interview Scottie Stenson first—he'd taken the runner-up spot, and that asshole always had plenty to say for himself.

Someone thrust a microphone in Zach's face, and he shoved it away. The WST was the least of his concerns right now. If he got suspended, he'd deal with it. Surf 365 was operating in the black now, and although the company carried a lot of debt, his old friend Brax had arranged the financing on favourable terms. Zach's mortgage would get paid off. It would just take longer, that was all.

He hopped over the low wall that surrounded his villa and ran up the path, cursing when he realised he didn't have a key. Maya kept his belongings safe while he surfed. And she'd be at the press conference, apologising for the fact that Zach was an asshole. He kicked the door, except he didn't because it suddenly opened and then Ari was hopping backward, clutching her shin. Fuck!

"Are you okay? Shit, I'm sorry. Sweetheart? I'm so sorry." He slammed the door behind him and managed to catch her before she hit the deck. "Do you need ice? I'll get ice."

"I'm fine. A tiny bit bruised, but fine."

Zach buried his face in her hair. She smelled faintly of vanilla and something fruity. Strawberries?

"I thought you'd left. When I didn't see you all day, I thought you'd left."

"I promised I'd stay." Great, now she sounded hurt. "I just…" Ari paused to yawn. "I just got really tired."

"You've been asleep?"

"All day. I…I don't know what happened."

"Did you sleep last night?"

"Not really," she admitted.

"Then it's good that you got some rest. Let this place work its magic."

"Magic?"

"One of my co-investors has an aunt who's into crystals, and when she came to the opening, she told us this place was built on a ley line. That it vibrated with earth energy and if we opened our minds to its power, it would heal us. Honestly? I thought it was bullshit until I experienced it for myself."

"You did?"

He'd almost tossed out the giant pink crystal Aunt Maggie had gifted him, but Maya liked it, so it had taken up residence on the living room windowsill. He figured a guest would walk off with it someday, but it had stayed put so far.

"At the Surf 365 Special last year. Maya warned me I'd been partying too hard, but I was a fucking star, right? Number one. I deserved all the shit people were throwing at me. That's what I told myself, anyway. I stayed up until two a.m. drinking and…" And fucking, but Ari didn't need to know that part. "And in the morning, I felt like shit. A chewed-up piece of string. I barely made it to the semi-final, and after I'd fallen off the board three times, I crawled back to bed and slept for hours."

"Wow."

"It was a wake-up call." And one that Zach had badly

needed. Looking back, his life had come dangerously close to derailing. At the time, the experience had freaked him out—not just the bone-weary exhaustion, but the virtual blackout that accompanied it—so now he appreciated the surf park's calming effects. Being here was the opposite of Saquarema—during last year's aerial round in Brazil, he'd been wired. Fucking shaking uncontrollably. Maya had blamed it on too much caffeine, so he'd cut down on energy drinks too. "I live cleaner now."

Plus he'd met the girl of his dreams, and he wouldn't have Ari if he'd still been cavorting with groupies and drinking himself into a stupor after every big win.

"You think I needed a wake-up call?" she asked. "I only have the occasional glass of wine."

"Not that kind of wake-up call. I'm just saying that this place has a way of making you reevaluate your life." Zach feathered soft kisses along her jaw. "You felt it in the kitchen this morning, didn't you? The energy between us? The ley line amplified it."

"You really believe that?"

"Tell me, Arianna, why did you suddenly decide to taste my tonsils this morning after months of resisting my many, many charms?"

"I...I don't know."

"Because of the magic."

Zach fisted her hair in his hand, tilting her head to give himself better access to her throat. He traced her racing pulse with his tongue, and she leaned into him, yielding in a way she never had before. Maybe he *should* move here permanently?

"Did you win today?" she gasped.

"Oh yeah, I won. You're my prize."

"I mean the contest. Did you win the contest?"

"That too. The reporters are probably losing their damn minds because I'm not at the press conference."

"What?" Ari pushed against his bare chest with her palms. "You're meant to be doing interviews?"

"I'd rather be here."

"You have contractual commitments."

"Now you sound like Zed."

"Get out of here."

"Kiss me first."

"No, you—" Ari stood on tiptoe and wrapped her arms around his neck. "Okay."

This time when their lips met, it was altogether softer but somehow needier than their frantic clash that morning. Zach kept one hand in Ari's hair but slid the other down to her ass, tipping her forward so she could feel what she did to him. Her breathy little gasp told him that she'd gotten the message.

"Holy fuck, Zach."

She was impressed? Good. Without wanting to brag, he had nothing to be embarrassed about in the showers.

"It's all yours, sweetheart."

Ari tore her lips away and looked down. "I meant, holy fuck, you can't seriously be thinking of going to a press conference like that?"

He followed her gaze and saw not only the tent in his swim shorts but also her point. The world's media was waiting on the other side of the door. If he stepped out of it, nobody would care that he'd just won a surfing contest.

Shit.

"I should pay a visit to the bathroom."

"Or..." Ari bit her lip, which did nothing for Zach's cock issue. "Or..."

His mouth dropped open as she sank to her knees, dragging his shorts down with her. She wasn't going to...

She was.

Happy fucking Sunday.

Zach groaned as she took him into her mouth, got even

harder as she squeezed his ass with both hands. Her tongue circled the sensitive head, and if she kept that up, he might not be late for the press conference after all. Because no way would he last long. She caressed his balls, then tightened one fist around the base of his cock in a move that almost made him come on the spot. He had to lean against the wall for support because his knees threatened to give way. He'd been blown a hundred times before, but not like this.

Not by her.

Not by the woman he loved.

He watched as those plump pink lips tightened around his shaft, burning the image into his retinas. Their gazes met, but she wasn't trying to impress him, seeking his approval. No, she was enjoying herself. And the mischievous twinkle when she took his cock all the way into her throat said she knew the effect she was having on him.

"Good girl," he murmured.

She released him for long enough to speak. "Give me more, Zach."

"You're killing me."

"It'll be a pleasurable death, I promise."

He thrust into her mouth, matching his rhythm to hers as he approached his climax. In that moment, it wasn't the earth that held the power; it was her. Did she realise that she was his kryptonite?

"I'm gonna come."

Zach choked out a warning so she'd have time to pull away, but she didn't. No, she moaned as he spilled into her throat, then smiled as she stood to kiss him. He could taste himself on her lips, and fuck if that wasn't the sexiest thing he'd ever experienced.

"Now go to your press conference," she murmured against his cheek.

"Don't you want me to return the favour?"

"Later. You can return the favour later, with interest."

"And dinner. Let's get out of here and find a quiet restaurant, just the two of us."

"I can't think of anything I'd rather do." Ari pulled up his shorts and pressed a chaste kiss to his lips. "Or anyone."

"I love you."

"And I'm…getting there."

CHAPTER 31
ARI

"So now you're the girlfriend, huh? If you'd shown this amount of dedication to the job at Twilight, maybe I'd have kept you on."

"I quit, asshole. Remember?"

On Monday afternoon, less than twenty-four hours after I'd feasted on Zach's cock at Surf 365, I sat in the passenger seat of Jankowski's BMW, sipping coffee from a to-go cup. The car was a compromise—he'd suggested meeting in his hotel room, and I'd told him to go to hell. See how professional I was being? In my head, I'd told him to go fuck himself with a cactus.

And perhaps I'd have spoken my mind if I didn't need his help. Firstly, he'd offered to take the Surf Star bottle to the lab for testing—he had better contacts in that field than I did, and he knew a guy who would rush it through the system—and secondly, he'd sent a team to Santa Cruz to assist with the Nelson angle because I couldn't follow more than one person at a time. And much as I hated to admit it, his men were competent when it came to surveillance. Of course, he'd had to come and "evaluate their performance," which was Jankowski-speak for getting away from his wife for a week.

He probably had half a dozen local call girls on speed dial by now.

"Fired, quit… We both know what really happened—you just got over-emotional."

"Are you kidding?" My voice rose to a squeak. *Breathe, Ari.* "Over-emotional? You molested me."

"There you go again."

"And then you blackballed me all over town."

"I figured you might need an incentive to apologise."

"Apologise? For what? You hitting on me in your office?"

"You were the one who did the hitting—I couldn't stand straight for a week."

"Really? Good."

"Which brings us to today. Nothing in life is free, Arizona."

Stupid, stupid me. Over the past three months, I'd kept my emails to Jankowski civil, and he'd done the same to me. Even after the bickering in Rennick's office, I'd harboured hope that we could salvage a working relationship, that he'd undo some of the reputational damage he'd caused me back in Vegas, but I should have known better. Men like Jankowski didn't change. Once they'd revealed their true selves, it was hard to pack the snake back into the basket.

And could such catastrophic damage truly be undone?

After Surf 365, I had my doubts. There was no turning back the clock on my dalliance with Zach, even though it was doomed to crash and burn. *Tick, tick, tick.* All I could do was hang on and try to enjoy the ride, knowing that I'd be shattered beyond repair in the not-too-distant future.

Our relationship was official now. At the press conference, he'd apologised for his lateness and told the world that his girlfriend hadn't been feeling well. Sure, he'd dodged the inevitable questions about my identity, but reporters had set up camp outside Haven's Rest when we arrived back this morning, and now there were blurry photos all over the internet of me scurrying into the house. Ditto for my departure this afternoon. Maya assured me they'd get bored in a week or two, and she was happy to run errands for me while I hid out behind the mirrored glass, but that was no way to live, and it would mean I couldn't do my job properly either.

Although Rennick was thrilled by the latest developments. Over the damn moon. By accidentally getting drugged, I'd ensured that he made back all the money AnyBet had lost, but he still wanted to find out who was behind the scheme, and so did I.

So while Rennick sat in his ivory zen garden, I was out in the real world, wondering if a pissed-off scammer was lurking in the shadows, watching me. However inadvertently, I'd cost them a small fortune.

Would they give up and slink away?

Or would they be looking for revenge?

"Is your hotel around here?" I asked. Jankowski had given me the name of a side street in the east of Santa Cruz, a residential area rather than tourist central. "I thought you'd have a view of the beach."

"Thanks to your joke about Antigua, Rennick started paying attention to the expense budget. Now we're stuck at some dump next to the hospital."

"Shame."

"The place is full of crying parents and cancer kids."

Didn't the man possess a shred of empathy? "Do you have any actual information for me? Or are you just gonna whine about the lack of room service?"

Jankowski glowered, but I didn't care. He wasn't my boss anymore. "Maya Torres went to visit Zed Nelson again last night. She was in his hotel room for an hour."

While I'd been in Zach's bed. Almost unconsciously, I pressed my thighs together at the memory.

"She told me she was going to meet a potential brand partner."

"Zach Torres doesn't do that himself?"

"Maya screens any offers first."

"Pretty darn thoroughly." Jankowski chuckled. "Next time, make sure you get photographic evidence."

Urgh. Knowing that Jankowski would read the report and also that he was a dirtbag, I hadn't submitted the video of Maya and Zed. Instead, I'd encrypted it and stored it on my hard drive, and there it would stay unless I found a reason to use it. I treated his remark with the contempt it deserved.

"Have you considered seeing a therapist?"

"You sound like my ex-wife."

Hopefully, she'd taken him to the cleaners in the divorce.

"How long will it take for the lab results to come back?"

"Two weeks?"

"That long? I thought you said the guy owed you a favour?"

"Maybe I could hurry it up, but that depends on how nicely you ask me."

"You want me to say please? Fine. *Please* can you do your job?"

His gaze darkened, and in that moment, I realised that Jankowski was more than a harmless pervert who overstepped the mark. No, at heart he was a predator. I'd given him a message loud and clear, and still he tried to manipulate me. To use my desire to excel at my job as a way to exert control.

"No, sweetheart, I want you to pucker up."

When Zach called me "sweetheart," it was, well, sweet, but hearing the endearment from Jankowski's lips, I wanted to vomit. Instead, I steeled myself with a long breath. A thousand thoughts flashed through my mind. Thanks to the lies he'd spread about me, I knew I had no professional future in Vegas, and now that I had no job, what was keeping me in Nevada? Before, I'd been scared to jump into the unknown, but now I'd experienced life in a different state, and it wasn't so bad. This morning, I'd talked to Nana, cried a few tears too, and told her how everything had gone so right with Zach yet so incredibly wrong. And she'd made a confession too—she was sick of Vegas. She'd grown up in Montana, and she missed the countryside. Since our sweet next-door neighbour, Miriam Timperley, had passed away from the big C last year, Nana had become a little lonely, and the stairs in our third-floor walk-up were a struggle now. Her words set me free—we didn't have to stay in Sin City. Even if I lost Zach, I wanted to move. Haven had a handful of close friends, but last year, she'd broken down in tears and confessed that she also got bullied at school. I'd spoken with the principal, and she assured me they were handling the problem, but Haven still had bad days. Maybe she'd be okay with moving too? If we found a place near the coast, she'd love the beach. I could teach her to swim. And who knew, we might even see dolphins?

One thing was certain; I'd never get my old life back.

Jankowski took my hesitation as consent and leaned in, eyes gleaming. This time, I'd send the message in block capitals, highlighted and underlined. I let him stick his tongue in my mouth as I rummaged in my purse, gagging on the taste of stale tobacco that his breath spray hadn't managed to hide. The man kissed like a raw trout.

Ah, there it is.

I jammed the stun gun into Jankowski's crotch and fired ten million volts into his dick. He spasmed and pissed himself, and I was glad we'd used his vehicle for the meet and not mine. I didn't have time to get my Honda detailed today.

"Do not *ever* touch me like that, do you understand?"

"You bitch! You'll never work in Vegas again!"

"I want those lab results in one week."

"Fuck you."

"We've just established that's never going to happen. And in case you get any ideas about ditching my sample, you should know that I recorded this little interaction, audio and video. Screw with my investigation, and I'll send it to your wife."

"*Your* investigation?"

"I answer to Rennick, not you." I picked up my purse and climbed out of the car. "One week," I reminded him and slammed the door, trying not to show Jankowski how badly I was shaking. Had I solved the harassment problem for good? Or tanked my entire future?

Only time would tell.

"Sweetheart, are you okay?"

"Why wouldn't I be?"

"You seem unsettled."

Well, it wasn't every day you got to roast your former boss's genitals, was it?

"I can't get used to these reporters trailing me everywhere."

Usually, it was me who did the following. I'd had to drive a surveillance detection route to and from Santa Cruz and take evasive manoeuvres to shake them off.

"Did you get your paints?"

In an effort to maintain neighbourly relations and also to take my mind off impending doom, I'd signed up for Ms. Carrington's beginner painting class. One hour a week, starting with basic watercolour techniques. Plus painting would give me an excuse to spend some time away from Haven's Rest. If I needed to follow up a lead, my alibi would be a wonky tree and a stormy sky on cold-pressed paper.

Although the biggest clues were potentially closer to home. I needed to take a look at Maya's laptop. Jankowski had researched her finances, and for all intents and purposes, she didn't appear to be wealthy. Her bank account contained low six figures—probably saved from her salary since her living expenses were close to zero—plus she owned five percent of Surf 365 versus Zach's fifteen percent, although she didn't appear to have taken on any debt to purchase it. A gift from Zach? It seemed like the sort of thing he'd do, but had she repaid him in the worst possible way? By working with Nelson to fix the WST results?

In second place on my list of suspects was Baylee. Not only was she the newest member of Zach's group, but I could also see her selling out for money. Last week, Maya had complained that Baylee had been around for "two years too long," so it seemed she'd also had the opportunity to get close to Zach, although she and Tyler had only been an official item since last October. Their one-year anniversary overlapped with this year's Pipeline contest, so of course she'd talked Tyler into taking her to Hawaii for a free vacation.

Kai came in third. He had no debt and a comfortable cushion of savings, but was the money his goal? Since he was currently sitting in second place in the WST standings, he had one hell of a motive to take Zach out of the competition. If he got a cut of the betting profits, well, that was just a bonus.

I couldn't take Tyler off the suspect list either, although I wasn't sure of his motive. Did he need cash to build his surf store empire? Possibly, but according to Zach, he'd only begun considering expansion in the last year. Or could there be a hint of jealousy, perhaps? He, Zach, and Kai had all worked together at Board Stiff, but Zach had eclipsed the others when it came to financial success. Tyler lived in an apartment above the store now, while Zach had a fancy home by the ocean. How much money did Tyler make from retail?

Not much, according to Jankowski, and Baylee spent most of it.

Gloria was fifth on the list, but a distant fifth. Yes, she packed Zach's food and drink, but she didn't have control over when he consumed it. Although she'd have known that only Zach drank that particular flavour of Surf Star. And she had a motive—Jankowski said her husband was sinking under medical debt. Had someone bribed her?

Four months into the investigation, and although I'd inadvertently left AnyBet in profit, I didn't feel as if we were close to solving the mystery. Jankowski hadn't got very far either, which was the only saving grace. Plus I'd prevented Zach from suffering a possible injury at Surf 365.

Oh, and fallen in love.

Fallen in love with a man I couldn't keep. Because without confessing all, how could I explain Haven? What kind of mom would abandon her child with a relative while she learned to paint and counted nurdles at the beach? Without the excuse of working to provide for my daughter's future, I'd look like a cold-hearted bitch.

The only plausible explanation was the story about shared custody, which Nana would go along with, but Haven was nine years old. What if she let the truth slip? Maxwell sure wouldn't back me up.

Hell, this was all such a mess.

"Sweetheart?"

"Huh? Uh, yes, I got the paints. The assistant at the art store was super helpful. There's another bag of stuff in the car, and an easel."

"I'll go get it. Bet the assistant was on commission."

"Probably. Now you know why I don't watch the shopping channel—I'd end up buying everything."

"I always wanted the frying pan set and the five-way ladder."

"What about the ab trainer?"

Zach tensed his muscles and pressed my hand to his stomach. "What do you think?"

"I think that the easel can wait."

His grin turned filthy. "Why? Do you have something else in mind?"

"You still owe me the interest on that favour, and I'm about to become California's nakedest loan shark." I squealed as he picked me up and headed for the bedroom. "At least let me lock my car."

"If someone steals it, I'll buy you a new one. Lose the underwear."

Zach might have let me take the lead on that first day at the surf park, but I quickly realised that wasn't how he liked things to work. In the bedroom, he preferred to be in charge. Last night, I'd been wary because Maxwell's control freakery had scarred me for life, but Zach's commanding nature didn't extend beyond the bedroom, and I realised that sometimes, just sometimes, it was nice to relinquish power to somebody else. Since I was eighteen, I'd been responsible for supporting the family, for taking care of Haven, for building my career. I'd never trusted a man with my pleasure before, probably because none of the handful of men I'd slept with had been very good at providing it, but Zach delivered in every way.

If he told me to lose the underwear, it was gone. The rest of my clothing too.

I lay back on the bed, and for a moment, Zach just watched me, backlit by the setting sun. The million-dollar view from his bed made me nervous. What if a stranger saw my naked ass? There were still a dozen photographers at the end of the driveway, waiting with their long lenses and bated breath.

"What's wrong, sweetheart? You're still worried about the car?"

"How good is the mirror coating on that glass?"

"Unless someone has their face pressed right against it, they can't see through."

"Are you sure?"

"If I thought for a moment that anyone but me would see what I'm about to do to you, I'd lower the blinds." Zach beckoned, and I sat up to meet him. "Mine."

"Yours," I whispered.

He kissed me roughly, then ran a hand along his cheek, checking the beard situation. Clearly it was satisfactory because he spread my legs and dove right in, running his tongue between my slick folds and sucking gently until my back arched off the bed. With every brush of his fingers, he wiped away the dirt left by Jankowski until the events of the afternoon were just a bad memory. The earth at Surf 365 wasn't magic; Zach Torres was magic. The healing energy was all his.

My first orgasm came from his tongue, then he flipped me onto my stomach and raised my ass into the air. I stretched languidly like a cat, high on dopamine and oxytocin, ready for round two. The sting of Zach's hand on my butt cheek made me flinch, but the rush that followed left me purring.

"You have the perfect ass." Another smack. "Nice and pink."

Being spanked had never made my wish list, but damn, it was hot when Zach did it.

"Give me your cock."

"Patience, sweetheart." He fisted my hair in his hand and pulled my head back. "Or do you want me to gag you?"

"Is that an option?"

"Not today. I have plans for your mouth today."

He teased my legs apart, and I felt his hardness pressing into my back as he leaned over and kissed my shoulders. Even though he bossed me around, he was a giver, not a taker, and when he finally rolled on a condom and slid inside me, he hit exactly the right spot. Deft fingers circled my clit as he thrust, and when I crested the wave once more, he was right there with me.

Zach Torres was the whole filthy package.

And out of boss mode, it turned out he was a cuddler. He shattered me, and then he completed me. Afterward, we snuggled in his king-sized bed, watching the waves breaking on the shore. There were no surfers out today. A flock of seagulls flew past, and the occasional car puttered along the road, but I was safe in his arms, cocooned against the outside world, safe from the problems waiting beyond the horizon.

Then Zach's phone buzzed.

"How do you feel about a movie night tomorrow?" he asked after he'd checked the screen.

"Where? The theatre in Santa Cruz?"

"Here. Baylee's offered to bring dinner."

I couldn't help grimacing.

"Tyler says it's a peace offering."

Although Baylee was a piece of work, Tyler was one of Zach's closest buddies, and I had to respect that. I didn't want to get in the way of their friendship.

"I'll make popcorn."

Zach kissed my temple. "Thanks, sweetheart. I'll make sure we get an early night."

I rolled onto my side and studied the man next to me, my gorgeous, tanned surfer dude, and a lump stuck in my throat.

"I love you," I blurted before I could chicken out. Even though our relationship was doomed, I had to tell him.

He gathered me up in his arms again. "I love you too."

CHAPTER 32
ZACH

"Couldn't you have told her no?" Maya asked. "I can't believe Tyler's still dating her."

"We both know why."

"He has to stop punishing himself like this, for everyone's sanity."

Yeah, well, Tyler didn't see it that way. He'd fucked up five years ago when one stupid mistake cost him his fiancée, and he'd been self-flagellating ever since. The mistake? He'd drunkenly let slip that he didn't like Juliette's father—who, let's face it, was a complete jackass—and the man had overheard. Next thing they knew, he'd begun cancelling the wedding he'd paid for, and rather than settle for a smaller ceremony, Juliette had freaked out and called the whole thing off.

"Maybe in time…"

"How long does he need? Can't you—"

The conversation came to an end as Baylee carried bags of food into the house, followed by Tyler with a stack of pizza boxes. The *clink* of bottles told Zach that Baylee had brought wine too. Heaven help them all.

She stopped in front of Maya. "Uh…uh, I'm sorry that I was rude to you."

If Baylee had expected a gracious acceptance, she'd misjudged. Maya had put on weight after their parents died and been bullied throughout her teens for that, but when she finally left foster care, it had been a fresh start for both of them. She'd stuck to a rigid diet for years, only to loosen her self-imposed rules last summer. Zach was glad she'd finally decided to relax and embrace her curves, and beyond pissed that Baylee had criticised his sister for her choices.

"Don't do it again," Maya told her.

Good. She'd stuck up for herself.

Baylee backed away from the kitchen and almost walked into Kai, who'd just arrived. He sidestepped and watched her retreat, impassive. No, he hadn't forgiven her either.

"I'll go set up the screen," she said, then scuttled over to the living area.

Unlike many people, Zach hadn't arranged his couches around a flat screen TV. He preferred to watch the ocean. But for the rare occasions he felt like watching a movie, he had blackout blinds and a screen that lowered from the ceiling, plus a wireless projector that hooked up to a laptop. Baylee knew how everything worked, and she busied herself with the setup while Zach contemplated pouring the wine down the sink.

"I hope she's planning to apologise to Ari as well."

Tyler shrugged. "She feels bad for what happened."

"I get that she's your girl, but I can't stand by while she insults mine."

"You and Ari are together now? Together-together?"

"Yeah, we are."

"Where is she?"

"In the bedroom, waiting to see which side of the bed Baylee got out of today."

"She promised there won't be a repeat of Saturday."

Half a year ago, Zach's life had been easy, no drama. But would he trade the current ups and downs for the old status quo? No way. Ari was the missing piece of the puzzle he hadn't known he was looking for until he dragged her onto his surfboard that day at the beach. Smart, down to earth, and definitely compatible in bed... Not to mention gutsy. She'd conquered her fear of water and learned to swim. Next challenge: teach her to surf too. And maybe Maya would get back into the water someday? She used to work on the safety team at the WST, but she'd taken a step back last year when running Zach's life got too demanding. He'd offered to hire another assistant, but she'd steadfastly refused, saying she didn't trust anyone else to get things right. Yet she let Ari help out. Not that Zach expected his girlfriend to work, but she seemed to like staying busy, and he made enough money that she didn't need to get a job or spend her inheritance.

He headed for the bedroom, where Ari was sitting on the couch by the window with his laptop on her knees.

"Is it safe out there?" she asked.

"Baylee seems repentant. She brought pizza."

"Give me five minutes? This airline sure isn't making it easy to specify meal preferences."

"Is that for the flight to Tahiti?"

She nodded. "I booked seats in the exit row."

"If I win the tour, next year we'll fly business class." Zach kissed her softly. "I'll save you a chicken wing."

"Boy, you really spoil me."

Baylee had curled up beside Tyler on one couch, a glass of wine in her hand. Great. Tyler had juice—he'd been teetotal since the incident with Juliette's father. Maya shared another couch with Kai, leaving the third empty for Zach and Ari. He grabbed a slice of the vegan pizza with added pepperoni that Baylee set in front of him and took a bite. Almost cold. He was about to get up and reheat it when Baylee started the movie.

"Hey, wait a second. Ari isn't— What is this?"

It wasn't a Hollywood blockbuster, that was for sure. Ari appeared on the screen, sitting in a car with an older man Zach didn't recognise. It wasn't her Honda, either. No, it was an expensive-looking BMW, black with the sport kit. Were they arguing? At first, he thought so, but then the stranger leaned in and kissed her.

And she kissed him back.

What the fuck?

The clip ended, and Zach couldn't move. He felt rather than saw Ari at his elbow, but he couldn't bring himself to look at her. The location on-screen had been familiar—a side street near the hospital where one of his surf buddies used to live. When had Ari been there? The day they met, she'd claimed it was her first time in California, and the red-and-yellow foliage in the video said "fall." So the video was recent.

Tyler spoke first. "What the hell, babe? This isn't *Point Break*."

Zach wanted to wipe the self-satisfied grin off Baylee's face, but he was frozen. As was Ari when he finally managed to turn his head and look at her.

"Who is he?"

She came to life. "You bitch! Show him the rest of the tape."

"Oh, I cut off there. I couldn't bear to watch anymore."

"Who is he?" Zach asked again, his voice hollow.

His *chest* hollow.

Now he knew how Tyler had felt when he lost Juliette. Sick, his emotions in free fall, just waiting for the sickening *thud* as he splattered all over the blacktop.

"I saw them yesterday when I was leaving work," Baylee said, her tone saccharine. "I thought you'd want to know."

Ari stepped forward, hands on her hips. "He's my ex-boss. A predator who uses his authority to target women.

And you deliberately cut off the part where I stun-gunned his dick because you're a vindictive little witch."

Kai and Tyler both winced, but Baylee was unrepentant.

"You looked as if you were enjoying yourself to me."

Then Maya came to life. "Get out of here! Both of you, get out of here!"

She launched herself at Baylee first, arms outstretched, and knocked her back onto the couch. The wine went flying. Kai leapt after Maya and wrapped her up in a bear hug while Tyler tried to pry her hands away from Baylee's hair. A chunk came loose, and Baylee began shrieking.

"I'm sorry," Ari whispered.

"You said there was nobody else."

"And there isn't, I swear."

"If he's your ex-boss, what was he doing in Santa Cruz? And if he's a predator, why did you get in a car with him for a cosy tête-à-tête? Something doesn't add up, Ari."

She turned away, and that gave Zach his answer. She'd lied to him. She'd gone behind his back for a rendezvous with another guy, and she'd been caught. Now she was trying to wriggle out of the problem.

How far would she twist the knife? She'd already sliced through his heart—did she want to take a few other vital organs too?

If he'd known how bad the tale would be, maybe he'd have done the intelligent thing and kicked her straight out the door. But, a sucker for punishment, he needed to hear what she had to say. Perhaps deep down, he hoped she'd be able to justify her deception? That he'd somehow be able to have the future he'd imagined with her?

But he should have known it was an impossible dream.

CHAPTER 33
ARI

uck, fuck, fuck!

There and then, I made it my mission in life to toss Baylee Sarterfeld into an active volcano. One with an acid-filled crater and sulphur deposits that stripped out the lining of a person's throat. But for now, I had to be content with Maya tearing out handfuls of her hair and ripping off her false eyelashes.

How had she recorded that clip? I hadn't noticed her following me, and I was pretty good at spotting tails. Then I realised… I'd met Jankowski near the hospital. Four p.m. must have been quitting time, and I'd walked right past her place of work. In the car, I'd been too focused on my jerk of a boss to watch passers-by.

And now I had a huge mess to deal with.

I had my own video showing the true nature of the meeting, of course I did, but playing that would only make matters worse. Four of my suspects were watching me, shocked, disappointed, and disgusted, and I couldn't risk tipping them off. I still loved Zach, just as I always would. And even though his love was fast turning to hate, I wouldn't risk his future safety. Somebody close to him—apart from me —was a traitor.

"We'll have this conversation in private."

"Will we?"

"Please? I owe you an explanation, but I'm not speaking in front of *her*." I nodded toward Baylee. Kai and Tyler had untangled Maya's fingers from her hair now, and Maya was glaring daggers at both of us in turn.

"If it wasn't for my quick thinking, she'd still be lying to everyone." Baylee folded her arms, smug. "You should be thanking me for showing that she's a manipulative psycho."

A manipulative psycho? Well, it took one to know one.

"Tyler, get her out of here." Kai stayed calm, just as he always did. "She isn't helping."

"Did you know about this?" Zach asked Tyler. "This video?"

"Nah, man, I swear. I'd have stopped her. I mean, I'd still have told you because, you know… But not like this."

He took Baylee by the wrist and pulled her toward the door, ignoring her protests. She stopped resisting when Maya wriggled out of Kai's arms and went after her again, and the door slammed so hard the glass in the windows rattled.

"We'll leave you two to talk," Kai said, and it was Maya's turn to object.

"She lied to my brother."

"Let her explain."

"Okay, fine, explain."

"Maya, they need time alone."

"But—" Maya started, but Kai took her hand, considerably more gently than Tyler had taken Baylee's, and Maya softened. "Okay. Okay, I'll go." Then she narrowed her eyes at me. "But if you hurt Zach, I'll *never* forgive you."

I deserved her contempt. Every ounce of it. I tried—and failed—to swallow the lump in my throat as the two of them exited and headed for Maya's apartment, no doubt preparing to dissect this evening's events. Tempting though it was to reach for Baylee's half-empty bottle of wine, I resisted the urge and took a seat instead.

Zach remained standing. "Tell me you have an explanation."

"I do, but you're not going to like it."

In the brief moment of calm after Baylee left, I'd considered my options, although in truth, I'd been preparing for this moment for a long time. I couldn't—*wouldn't*—lie to Zach again. Rennick would be annoyed, but he had his money back, and I didn't plan to work in Vegas again.

"Well?"

"I didn't move next door by accident. I... I'm a private investigator, and my brief was to get close to you."

"Are you kidding me?"

"I wish I was."

"Why? Why the hell would you investigate me?" Zach's eyes widened, and he took a step back. "Shit, you're working for the Sykes family? Levi was convicted in a court of law, can't they understand that?"

Ah, crap, he thought this was about Blackstone House?

"No! No, I've never met the Sykes family. This is to do with the WST."

"The WST?" Anger turned to confusion. "Why would they investigate me? If this is about that prank with Zed's Ferrari in Huntington Beach last year, it wasn't me, and I'm not snitching on a buddy."

"What happened to Zed's Ferrari?"

"Someone pissed in the gas tank. That's not why you're here?"

"No, and I'm sure he deserved it."

"Then why? What did I do?"

"Nothing, as it turns out. I think you're a victim."

"You're not making any sense."

So I explained. I left out any details that identified my client and went through the sportsbook manipulation in vague terms, then told Zach about my suspicion that his food and drink had been spiked, first with milk and then with some kind of tranquilliser.

"The man in the vehicle really was my ex-boss. We were both hired to work different angles of the same case. He's taken the Surf Star bottle for lab testing."

"Let me get this straight—you think a shadowy con artist broke into my villa at the surf park two years running and put a tranquilliser in my drink bottle? And switched my milk in England and Tahiti? That's ludicrous. Did you see how many people were outside last weekend? They would've taken three thousand pictures of the suspect."

"No, I think the culprit is a little closer to home."

"What are you saying?"

"I'm saying that you need to watch your back. Check every item in the refrigerator. When you're at contests, drink water from the faucet only, and check each food package for tampering. I'll get an early warning if the betting patterns go screwy, so you'll know when to be extra careful, and—"

"Ari, stop. *Is* your name even Ari?"

"Yes. Yes, it is, but it's short for Arizona, not Arianna."

"Then stop and listen to yourself, *Arizona*. You say the culprit is closer to home? Are you accusing my oldest friends and my *sister* of poisoning me? Have you lost your mind?"

"The evidence—"

"Is circumstantial. Isn't that what they call it when it's tenuous at best and completely fucking made up at worst? Those contests aren't the first time I've had a bad reaction to lactose, and they won't be the last. And last year at the surf park, I was tired, but I've felt shittier after a night of partying."

"Did you drink Surf Star?"

"Probably. Who knows? It was over a year ago."

"How much of the bottle would you have drunk?"

"Just drop it. My friends didn't do this."

"What about Baylee? How well do you know her?"

"Baylee? You think Baylee's a criminal mastermind?" Zach spun away and tore both hands through his hair. "Actually, she might not be as dumb as I thought she was—she was right about you, wasn't she?"

His words cut right to the bone.

"My feelings are real, Zach. The only things I lied about were an inheritance and my initial reason for being here. Hell, I was planning to move to California when this job was over."

"Yeah? Well, now you don't need to bother."

My heart cracked, and all the pain I'd been trying to keep inside spilled out, along with a whole lot of tears. Zach paced behind the couch and I turned to watch him, wishing there was something I could do or say to change things, but knowing that there wasn't.

"Well, I'm not staying in Vegas."

A shrug. "I can't make you. Try San Diego—I hear it's nice down there."

"Zach, I'm worried you might be in danger. Whoever's behind the betting scam lost a hell of a lot of money when you won last weekend. Maybe they'll fade away to lick their wounds, or maybe they'll be angry enough to try something stupid. Please, promise me you'll be careful. You can't trust anyone."

"No fucking kidding. Look, people probably bet against me at Surf 365 this year because I fell there last year. And you say people bet against me in Cornwall too? It's no secret that longboard isn't my strongest discipline. Whoever you're working for, they're making a big deal out of nothing, but I'll give you ten out of ten for dedication to your job."

"Zach, don't do this…"

"Get out of my home. Pack your shit and leave."

"There's still so much you don't know. I followed Maya, and—"

"And I don't *want* to know. I was doing fine until you came along. We were all doing fine. Now you've driven a wedge between Tyler and Baylee, which she arguably deserves, but he doesn't. And you've... Fuck, I thought we'd get married someday. Have a couple of kids and spend our days on the beach. And now *this*... You're telling me not to trust anyone? Good news—I don't think I'll ever trust anyone again."

"I'm so sorry."

"Just leave."

He strode into his office and slammed the door, rivalling Tyler's effort from earlier. And now I had to go. What choice did I have? I couldn't hurt Zach further by staying where I wasn't wanted. Sobbing, I walked into the bedroom and began stuffing my belongings into my bag, realising just how much I'd made myself at home. My toothbrush was by the sink in the bathroom. My shampoo was in his shower. He'd cleared out half of his closet and bought me a bathrobe. Maya had gifted me my phone—should I leave that too? My Honda was still being temperamental, and the thought of getting stranded on the way back to Vegas terrified me. I'd have to drive through the night. In the end, I decided to take the phone and mail it back tomorrow.

When I was done, I left five notes on the dining table, one each for Zach, Maya, Kai, Tyler, and Gloria, apologising for everything and wishing them happiness in the future. Five wholly inadequate attempts to right some of the wrong I'd done. No words would ever be enough.

I'd always regret the way this had ended, but I couldn't regret loving Zach. He'd shown me that there were good men out there. That white knights weren't just a cliché from romance novels; they walked and talked among us.

Maybe someday, I'd cross paths with another dreamboat, but I doubted I'd be that lucky. One thing was for sure, though—I'd never settle for a mule now that I'd ridden a prize stallion.

Zach had taught me many lessons, and I'd treasure every single one of them.

CHAPTER 34
ZACH

"Vodka and Coke?" Violet exchanged a look with Dawson. "Are you sure? It's nine o'clock in the morning."

"It's seven p.m. here," Alexa chipped in through the speaker. Nobody had invited her to the conversation, but she'd called Brax about a business-related issue earlier—apparently, she acted as a consultant on occasion—and now they were stuck with her.

"Where are you?" Dawson asked.

"Norway. *Somebody* wanted to see the fjords."

Brax gave Zach a look of mild distaste. "At least swap the Coke for orange juice."

"Fine, just make it a double."

"Don't forget the cocktail umbrella, Violet," Brax said.

"Where do you want me to stick it?" she asked sweetly, and Brax wisely didn't answer that question.

Why was Zach in Los Angeles? He wasn't sure. He only knew that after last night's revelations, both those about Ari and those made by her, he couldn't stay in Seagrass Point. If he hadn't left, then Maya, Kai, and Tyler would have asked him a thousand questions, and he didn't have any answers.

Trust no one, Ari had said, but of course she'd been overreacting.

Hadn't she?

He'd had time to think as he drove, too much time. And once the shock wore off, he'd considered her allegations in greater depth. Her actions too. Back at Haven's Rest, with Baylee screeching and that image of Ari in a stranger's car still frozen on the screen, his first instinct had been to fight. To assume that everything Ari had said and done was wrong because her betrayal hurt so deeply.

But she'd obviously believed in her theory. The amount of time she'd spent learning about lactose intolerance, the way she'd gone head-to-head with Baylee over the milk in his coffee... Zach had written the bathroom episodes off as carelessness, the exhaustion last year as a hangover. But what about that Sunday at Bells Beach when he'd been puking his guts up? Or earlier in the year in Jeffreys Bay when he'd been so wired that he was seeing double? He'd been out partying the night before, and Kai had even joked about him picking up the wrong drink. They'd both figured that it was better for him to get spiked than some poor woman. After that, he'd started being more careful in clubs. Ordering bottles rather than glasses and making sure Kai or Tyler kept an eye on them if he was busy, while he did the same for them.

Ari seriously thought one of his two best friends could have sabotaged his WST rounds? No way. And she'd also started to say something about Maya before he cut her off, which was another ridiculous suggestion. But Baylee... After the stunt she'd pulled yesterday, he wouldn't put anything past her. He ran through past trips in his head, those occasions when he'd felt "off." Had she been there for all of them? The contest in Tahiti, when he'd been stuck in the bathroom until five minutes before the quarter-final, had been the first time she'd travelled with Tyler. So it was possible she was involved.

"Are you gonna tell us what happened?" Dawson asked. "Or just keep drinking until you pass out?"

"Can I pick option two?"

"No," Violet and Alexa said together, although Alexa wasn't really Alexa—she was speaking through a cartoon avatar wearing a grey fedora. She always had liked to stay in the shadows. Brax had set up his laptop on the kitchen table at Mulberry Cottage, Violet and Dawson's half-renovated home, a cutesy two-storey Victorian on a three-acre lot. At one time, it had belonged to a renowned artist, and they'd bought it after his daughter had moved into a retirement home. The place was habitable now, if a little bare.

Zach took a deep breath. In a way, it would be good to get things off his chest, and if he could trust anyone, it was Dawson and Brax. Two of his oldest acquaintances, friends who pre-dated his surfing career and the circus of the WST. They'd gotten through the aftermath of Ruby's murder by sticking together, and he needed to share that strength again.

"I just found out that the woman I fell in love with was a PI sent to investigate me."

"*What?*" Violet spluttered, spitting coffee across the table. "Ari? Ari's a PI?"

Brax snorted, and Alexa's avatar wore an annoying grin.

"Oh, this is gonna be good," she said.

"It's not funny."

"Yeah, it is. Out of all the bikini-clad bimbos who throw themselves at your feet, you managed to pick the one woman who was paid to be there."

"Ari isn't a bimbo," he growled.

"Alexa, don't start," Brax warned. "Do you want me to unplug you?"

Cue a sulky look from the avatar. Why did Alexa always hide behind technology? Zach hadn't seen her face in nearly eight years. She'd been the second to disappear after the murder, escaping from foster care and vanishing into the night as soon as the trial was over. For years, he'd worried about her, wondered where she was and if she was okay. But Alexa was a survivor. And, it had turned out, a devious little sneak.

"What happened?" Dawson asked. "Why would anyone send a PI to investigate you?"

Zach told the story, starting with the weird episodes that had happened during WST contests before moving on to the rescue at the beach and the way Ari had slotted so neatly into everyone's lives, Baylee's bitchiness and subsequent unravelling, and the accusations Ari had levelled at Zach's closest friends.

"If anyone poisoned me, it must've been Baylee, right? But Ari messed with my mind. I thought I knew her, that I could trust her, and my judgment sucked. So how can I trust anyone now?"

Violet reached across the table to squeeze Zach's hand. "If it was Baylee, then isn't the problem solved? I can't imagine that Tyler would keep dating her after the bait-and-switch she pulled with the movie. I mean, she used him too."

"Baylee wouldn't have to get near Zach if she wanted to poison him," Alexa pointed out. "She could just pay someone else to do her dirty work."

Zach groaned. He hadn't thought of that.

"Does she have the money?" Dawson asked. "Ari said the culprit—or whoever they were working with—lost it all after you won at the surf park."

Brax took a sip of espresso. "We don't know if that was their only capital. That's the first rule of investing—never spend what you can't afford to lose."

"They're not investing; they're running an amoral enterprise."

"Isn't everyone on Wall Street? Same rules apply."

"Why does life always have to be about the money?" Zach

asked. "I shoulda bought a shack in Hawaii and fished for my supper."

"Because money makes the world go round." Brax's world, anyway. "And what's stopping you from moving to Hawaii? You could sell your hobbit home and buy a place in Maui tomorrow."

"As I'm constantly reminded, I have contractual obligations. Can we stick with the current problem? What am I supposed to do about this betting thing?"

As usual, Dawson was the voice of reason. "Buy your own food and keep it under lock and key. When you're at a contest, check the seal on every bottle and eat protein bars for lunch."

"Seals on bottles mean nothing," Alexa said. "It's easy to replace those. Drink from cans. And check the wrappers on the protein bars for needle marks."

"Have you been talking to Ari? You definitely share the same paranoia."

"You call it paranoia; I call it self-preservation. And Ari was right, wasn't she?"

"I don't know that for certain."

"Okay, on balance of probabilities, she was right. You're sure she didn't say who her client was?"

"No. I mean, I wasn't thinking straight, but I don't recall a name."

Brax leaned back in his seat, steepling his hands. "Playing devil's advocate, could Ari have been behind the contamination? A double agent? And when she got caught, she tried to shift the blame?"

"She wasn't around until the summer."

"Correction: you didn't notice her around until the summer. And this scam had to be a team effort."

"You didn't see the way she monitored the refrigerator, or the dressing-down she gave Baylee for putting oat milk in my coffee. But...but I guess it's possible. And more likely than

Kai or Tyler or…hell, Maya being involved." He closed his eyes for a moment, wishing this nightmare was over. Or better yet, that it had never begun. But then he'd never have met Ari, and… "I really thought she was the one."

Violet offered a smile, sympathy with a hint of pity. "I don't see Ari being involved either. *She* was the one who got sick last weekend. And I don't think she set out to hurt you either. When I spoke with her, she said you were just friends, but the way she said it… She was fighting a battle with herself."

"So why does it feel as if she scooped out my heart with a melon baller?"

"We only have her word that she was sick," Brax said. "Did anyone actually see her that day?"

Zach sifted through the memories, but all he could think of was her lips around his cock in the hallway. If it had just been a job to her, why would she have done that? And the time they'd spent in bed—those orgasms hadn't been faked, of that he was certain.

She'd said she loved him.

But she'd also lied.

"No," he said finally. "Nobody saw her sick. What the hell am I meant to do?"

"Win. Watch your back and win. If you're winning, then the scammer isn't."

Brax made it sound so simple.

"I don't think I can live like that. I don't *want* to live like that."

"And don't let on that you know what happened, otherwise Baylee and whoever she's working with might change tactics. Come at you from a different direction."

"This is a never-ending nightmare."

"It's not forever. Win the championship at the end of the year, and then reevaluate. If you get your name on the trophy, nobody can take that away from you, and it'll open up new career opportunities and options for product endorsements."

"Maybe you could hire someone to help keep you safe?" Violet suggested.

Dawson grinned. "Like a bodyguard?"

"I was thinking more of a chef."

"What would I tell Maya?"

"The truth? I mean, your sister wouldn't harm you, would she?"

"Ari mentioned something about her, but I didn't listen, and now…" Zach gave his head a shake. "No, you're right. Of course you're right. Maya wouldn't have done this."

Although she had changed in the last year. Become quieter, more withdrawn. Started going out to visit friends that Zach never met. And she'd stopped surfing. For years, she'd avoided the hordes of photographers at the more popular beaches, instead preferring to head down the coast with Tyler to find a quiet break, but this was different. She'd quit her active role in Sal's Army too, although she still did the bulk of the admin.

How well did he really know his sister?

"Can I stay here for a few days?" he asked. "I need to think things through."

Violet didn't hesitate. She might have become Hollywood's darling, but fame hadn't changed her, and underneath, she was still the same sweet country girl that she'd always been.

"Stay as long as you need. Do you need more clothes? Toiletries? I can get them delivered."

"I didn't bring anything with me."

Packing for a trip had been the last thing on his mind when he ran out of the house.

"I can have my PA send clothes," Brax offered. "We're still about the same size, aren't we?" Brax eyed Zach critically. "I'm a touch narrower in the shoulders."

"A touch? And I don't wear suits unless I'm getting paid to."

"I do occasionally dress in casual attire, you know." Said the man who was wearing a vest with a pocket square that matched his tie. "And if you feel the need to exorcise your demons, let me know, and I'll book you a room at The Dark."

Zach's stomach turned at the thought, although he knew his old friend meant well. "No, thanks."

"Too soon?" Brax asked, studying Zach's expression.

"Too soon."

A new voice sounded, male, but too quiet to make out the words. Alexa's avatar waved.

"Gotta love you and leave you, folks. Apparently, there's a waterfall I have to look at."

And the brat was gone.

"A boyfriend?" Zach asked, one eyebrow raised.

Brax shrugged. "Who knows? Chase has been around for a while, but I have no idea of their relationship. Alexa never talks about her personal life."

"Probably because she's too busy poking her nose into other people's," Dawson added.

Violet slid a highball glass toward Zach, orange juice with a splash of vodka, nowhere near a double. She'd skipped the umbrella too, but she had arranged slices of kiwi on the edge of the glass. It felt as though he'd stepped back in time. How many times had he, Brax, and Dawson sat around a table trying to puzzle out the answer to a mystery? Nolan and Justin were missing, but Violet made better drinks. Nolan would have poured a glass of red, and Justin had been a smoothie connoisseur.

"Try to get some rest," she said. "I know it doesn't seem like it right now, but things will get better."

Maybe. But would they get worse first?

CHAPTER 35
ARI

"Momma, I made this for you." Haven squashed beside me on the couch and gave me a hug before tying a bracelet around my wrist, one made from knotted string and colourful beads, blue and yellow and green. "It's to remind you of California. Blue for the sea and yellow for the sun and green for the trees and blue for the sky."

"You already said blue was the sea."

"That's why there's two different kinds of blue. See? And it's okay if I don't get a dolphin yet."

At least someone was happy to see me back in Vegas. Nana had remained stoic, but she knew I'd blown the job and we'd all have to tighten our belts again. Of course Rennick had fired me. I'd spoken with him on Thursday, and he'd listened to my explanation, thanked me for my efforts, and then terminated my contract. What else could he have done? I'd lost my access, and Zach knew my face now, so lurking in the background was out of the question. Jankowski had probably opened the champagne when he heard the news. That was another reason to hightail it out of town—if I saw his smug face, I couldn't be held responsible for the consequences.

The satisfaction of being right offered little comfort, and I *had* been right. Yesterday, I'd received a report from the lab with the results of the drug test—it seemed that Jankowski had forgotten to have my name removed from the email list—and Zach's bottle of Surf Star had been laced with Eszopiclone, a powerful sleeping pill. It was only available on prescription, but easy enough to buy on the street if you didn't have a friendly doctor. No wonder I'd been groggy last Sunday.

Now it was Saturday, and despite the mess I'd created, I was determined to put a brave face on things for Haven, even if the last thing I wanted was a reminder of my time with Zach. That wound was still too raw.

"Thank you, sweetie. What do you want to do today?" After four months away, I had a lot of time to make up. "How about the Play Zone at the Container Park?"

"Mom, that's for *kids*."

Uh, yes? "Okay, then what about the circus show? Or the flamingos?"

One advantage of living in Vegas: the free shows at the big hotels. I'd seen them all ten times over, but Haven still enjoyed them, and my wallet thanked me.

"Can we go to the mermaid show? Casey's mom took us while you were away, and I don't want to be a cowgirl anymore. Now I want to be a mermaid. Or we could go swimming? You promised you'd teach me to swim."

"Of course we can go see the mermaids. Swimming lessons might have to wait for a while, but why don't we go to the chocolate factory too?"

I *really* needed some of those free samples.

"Can I get a rocky road slice? And one for Nana too?"

The budget would just about run to that. I'd spent

yesterday doing the math—there would be no ocean view for us, but with my income and Nana's social security, we'd be able to afford an apartment in Eureka. Or if we went farther inland, Clovis or Chico were other options. I'd checked out the employment situation, and there were waitressing jobs available, plus I had my California PI licence. Maybe in the future, I'd be able to find work in my chosen field again—it all depended on how far Jankowski's slimy tentacles had stretched. On the positive side, he wasn't getting any younger, and rumour said his cholesterol levels were through the roof.

If we moved fast, the three of us could get settled in a new home before we burned through the money I'd earned working for Rennick. Two bedrooms would be enough—in Vegas, I'd been sleeping on a fold-out couch for years, while Haven had a curtained-off corner in the living room, so there'd be no difference for me. I could sell some of my stuff and rent a box van to take the rest with us. José who lived downstairs would help to carry the furniture if I bribed him with beer. Next up, I had to check out the schools—Haven's education would be a factor in our final destination. My little girl was bright, and I wanted to give her the future she deserved.

"Sure, we can get rocky road. Milkshakes too."

I held it together until Saturday evening. Researching the pros and cons of California—Nana had insisted I check out Montana too, just in case—had kept my mind off Zach for a few days, but when Haven's channel-hopping had turned up a clip of a surfer defying gravity on a giant wave, I'd been forced to hide in the bathroom. Nana had followed with tissues, and she sat next to me on the edge of the tub.

"I…I don't know what's wrong with me. I mean, the guy on TV wasn't even Zach."

"You just had your first experience of love, and losing him hit you hard."

"I was ninety percent sure it would happen, and I thought I'd prepared myself, but I still feel as if my heart got cut out with a rusty butter knife."

"It doesn't feel like it right now, but I can tell you from experience that it does get better."

"From experience?"

Nana had once confessed that the only reason she'd stayed married to Grandpa was because neither of them could afford rent on their own. Thankfully, he'd lasted until I turned sixteen, and I was already bussing tables by then, evenings and weekends. Nana had shed a tear at the funeral, but the next day, she'd taken his clothes to Goodwill and begun painting the living room, grumbling that she'd always hated that horrible beige wallpaper he'd picked out. Like being dead already, she said.

But now she gave a sad smile. "I've never told you this, but before I met your grandpa, I was engaged to another man."

"What? No way?"

"Adrian. He was a marine, and ever so handsome. We'd planned to marry when he came home from South Korea, but all I got was a phone call." She shook her head, eyes glistening. "A training accident. I never did hear the details, and his parents kept the flag."

"I'm so sorry."

"I'll give you one piece of advice, Ari. Don't settle. A part of me will always regret that I didn't run off to New York and start a new life when I had the chance. I wanted to, you know. I saw myself working in one of those huge skyscrapers and drinking cocktails at the Plaza."

"I can't believe you kept those secrets from me."

"What good would telling anyone have done? Adrian was gone, and in those days, girls from my high school got married and had babies. They didn't run off to the big city alone. But you…" Nana smoothed my hair in that calming way of hers. "You're still so young. I don't want you to grow old alone, but there are worse things in the world than being single."

"I know. Maxwell taught me that lesson."

"The adventurous streak might be genetic, but just promise me you won't abandon your family the way your mother did."

"I absolutely swear I won't do that." And even though I was devastated by the way things had ended with Zach, I loved being home. And by "home," I meant with Nana and Haven. The location was irrelevant—home wasn't a crappy Las Vegas apartment, it was the people inside it. "And if you weren't happy to leave here, we wouldn't go. You know that, right?"

Nana nodded. "I know. But I'm still young enough for an adventure too. Surfing might be a bridge too far, but I'd like to paddle in the ocean before I need a walker."

"You'll still be running through the waves when you're a hundred."

Nana squeezed my shoulder as she got up, her knees cracking. "Don't let one little mistake ruin your life, my love."

"I won't."

No, I had to pick myself up. I couldn't afford not to. And who knew, maybe in the years to come, I'd be able to look back on my time with Zach and smile? Maxwell had called Haven a mistake, but she was the most wonderful thing ever to happen to me. Yes, the timing had sucked, but my daughter was not a *mistake.*

Every cloud had a silver lining.

What if the months in Seagrass Point had been a stepping

stone? A catalyst to change my life? Once Haven was settled in a new school, and—

My pocket vibrated.

Who was phoning me? I hadn't given anyone but Nana my new number yet—I'd decided on a fresh start, out with the old—and I groaned at the thought of a sales call. It was Saturday night. Didn't these people have lives of their own?

I picked up and channelled my mother. "Whatever you're selling, I don't want any."

"Arizona Danner?"

The voice was female and unfamiliar. Had I forgotten to check the "no marketing" box when I signed the contract?

"Who is this?"

"My name is Alexa."

CHAPTER 36
ARI

"Alexa who?"

"Just Alexa."

"Whatever sales list I'm on, take me off it, okay?"

"There's no list."

"Then how did you get this number?"

"You're a private investigator—use your imagination."

I gripped the phone harder, my palm sweating. Who was this? I didn't know anyone named Alexa. In fact, I'd only heard the name once recently, and that was… No way. It couldn't be.

"Are you Zach's Alexa?"

"I'm certain he'd object to that categorisation."

"But you do know him? You sent champagne to his table in Huntington Beach?"

"You're observant. Good. I wanted to send Möet, but they only had Cristal. What did you think? I'm not much of a drinker anymore, but my companion assured me it would taste okay."

Her *companion* thought Cristal was *okay*? Even Maxwell

had bowed down to those flat-bottomed bottles. Who was this woman? And why was she calling me?

"What do you want?"

"I want to hire you."

Huh? I nearly choked on my own tongue. "I'm sorry?"

"I presume you have a fairly clear schedule following the unfortunate hiccup in your previous investigation, coupled with the fact that your former employer seems to be bad-mouthing you all over the state. He's a massive dick, isn't he?"

"Yes, although I'm not sure it's as big as he thinks it is. Wait, you want to hire me? What for?"

"To finish what you started."

"I don't understand."

She sighed, a soft sound that said *do keep up.* "It's simple. Somebody tried to harm Zach, and I want to know who."

"But I can't help you, not anymore. He won't even look at me now."

"Yes, I appreciate that does make things more difficult. But you're in a unique position—aside from everyone on the suspect list, you're the only person who's spent a significant amount of time with him in the past several months. I want to understand the dynamics of each relationship he has, and that's difficult from... Chase, how far are we from Santa Cruz?"

I heard a man's voice in the background, clear enough to tell me she was using a speakerphone. Whoever Chase was, the two of them didn't have secrets.

"Approximately nine thousand kilometres."

"From nine thousand kilometres away. And I'll also need you to do any necessary legwork."

"Legwork?"

"I can do most of the digging around myself, but I don't do legwork."

She planned to take an active role? This got weirder and weirder.

"Are you an investigator too?"

"No, I'm an entrepreneur, but I'm really good at finding things out. What are your rates?"

"I haven't said I'll do the job."

"No, but if you love Zach the way you claimed to, it's a given."

"He said that?"

"Was he lying?"

Sheesh, this girl was sharp. And slightly scary, if I was honest. She had a way of keeping a person off balance. Of tipping you onto the back foot.

"He wasn't lying."

"Were you lying?"

"I wasn't lying either."

"Good. Now that we've established the basic facts, what are your rates?"

I wasn't sure whether to laugh or tear my hair out.

"Chase, is she always like this?"

"Yes."

Alexa did at least laugh. "I can see why Zach liked you." Past tense. Oof. "Now, what are your rates, or should I make something up?"

"Look, I don't want to spend months alone on the road. My daughter missed me enough the first time."

"Your daughter?" Alexa gave a low whistle. "Does Zach know you have a kid?"

"I could hardly take her to work with me, could I?"

"Yikes. This should be interesting. Can she stay with her father again?"

"Her father couldn't pick her out of a line-up. Not that it's any of your business, but she stays with my grandmother when I'm away."

"Sweet." Alexa's voice softened infinitesimally. "I'm not

anticipating any extended travel. A trip or two, but it won't be full time, and some of the work can be done remotely."

"How many hours are we talking?"

"I'd want you on a retainer. This job gets priority. How about twenty thousand a month, plus expenses?"

"Twenty thousand dollars?"

That was more than I'd earned in my life. Twice as much as I'd been billing Rennick, and she was saying I wouldn't even need to be on the job full-time?

"I'm hardly going to pay you in pesos, am I?"

"How long do you think the job would take?"

"Who the fuck knows? It depends on whether the asshole who screwed with Zach crawls into a hole and hides or comes back to try again. A month? Two months? I'll pay you for a month, minimum."

Even after tax, an extra twenty thousand bucks would give me more options. A bigger apartment deposit, and maybe even a new car. The Honda had come dangerously close to overheating on the drive back to Vegas. And anything left over, I could tuck into a savings account for the inevitable emergencies that would crop up in the future.

"That sounds reasonable." *Play it cool, Ari.* "But if the perp doesn't strike again, I'm not sure how easy it would be to track them down. I practically lived with Zach for months, and I still had a list of five possibles."

"Five? Zach gave us four."

"Which four?"

"Kai, Tyler, Baylee, and Maya. So really, that was three because Maya wouldn't have done this."

"You know Maya?"

"A little." A pause. "From when she was a kid. She worships her brother, and no way would she ever risk harming him."

"She was actually near the top of my suspect list."

"Why?"

Nice try. "I'd prefer to have a contract in place before we get into the specifics."

And quite honestly, I still had reservations. How would Zach react if he found out I'd gone behind his back yet again? And it wasn't only Zach I'd have to watch out for—Jankowski's team would be baying for my blood too.

"Send me the contract and your bank details," Alexa said. "My lawyer will get back to you within the hour."

She had a lawyer? Oh, who was I kidding? Alexa had twenty thousand bucks lying around to waste on a potential wild goose chase; of course she had a lawyer. Although I'd never known a lawyer who worked on a Saturday night. Morty's lawyer, who was also his poker buddy, had rarely managed to reply to an email within a week. Although Morty had paid him in beer and brisket, so perhaps that was part of it.

"Give me your email address."

Alexa read it out, and that was the first indication I got of how fiercely she guarded her privacy. Rather than a gmail account or even a personalised domain name, Alexa read out a random string of letters, numbers, and punctuation, followed by "dot com."

"Are you sure that's the email address and not the password?"

"The password is far more complex."

Sheesh. "I do have one more question: why are you doing this?"

The silence went on for so long that I thought Alexa wasn't going to answer. Had I annoyed her? And worse, kissed twenty thousand bucks goodbye? What if—

"Because at one time in my life, I had nothing and nobody. Zach was one of the people who showed me I wasn't alone."

Interesting answer. And having experienced Zach's kindness firsthand, not one that shocked me.

"Won't he be upset if he finds out you hired me to work on the case again?"

"Probably. But left to their own devices, people don't always do what's best for them, and right now, Zach's letting emotion cloud objectivity. And I'd rather have him pissed off than quadriplegic." Well, that made sense. "Go have dinner. We can talk afterward."

And then she was gone, leaving me to wonder whether I'd imagined the whole damn conversation. Alexa, friend of Zach, likely resident of Blackstone House, wanted to pay me an obscene amount of money for less work than I'd been doing before. I truly had stepped into the twilight zone.

The job wouldn't be sunshine and rainbows, though. I knew that every time I saw Zach, even on a screen or from afar, the pain would come rushing back. But at least I could work with Alexa to stop him from falling victim to a money-hungry monster. She was right—better irate than injured.

My ass cheeks were numb when I stumbled out of the bathroom and into Nana.

"Was it him?" she asked. "Was it Zach?"

"Huh? Oh, no. No, it wasn't."

"I thought he might've come to his senses."

There was little chance of that.

"No, but I think I've lost mine. I'm back on the case."

"Really? That strange man with the rock garden changed his mind?"

"Turns out he isn't the only person who wants to get to the bottom of the mystery." I told Nana about Alexa, how she'd offered me money that I couldn't turn down to work with her. I only hoped she wasn't a back-seat driver. There was nothing worse than a client giving orders without understanding the job.

"Does this mean we're not going to California?"

"Not right away. In a few months, hopefully? Maybe after

Christmas, which would work out better for Haven's schooling anyway."

"As long as we leave by next summer. You know that landlord of ours is never gonna fix the AC properly."

"I'm so sorry that I wasn't here to deal with it." No, I'd been living in luxury. "Whatever happens, we won't be here beyond spring."

CHAPTER 37
ARI

Alexa's lawyer did indeed get back within the hour. He crossed out the clause about client testimonials —Alexa didn't provide those, apparently—and sent me the mother of all NDAs to sign. I'd have to be careful when it came to confidentiality and the work I'd done for Rennick. Obviously, I couldn't disclose the precise details of the scam, the amounts involved, or the names of the entities; but the poisonings themselves, those were fair game. Zach could give that information to Alexa himself, and my thoughts on the suspects weren't specific to AnyBet either.

By midnight, the contract was signed, twenty thousand bucks had landed in my bank account, and I'd installed Alexa's preferred chat app.

Surreal.

Alexa viewed time as something of an abstract concept— her words, not mine—and our first meeting began at seventeen minutes past one, with me sitting on a cushion in the bathroom and talking quietly because Haven and Nana were asleep. But if I'd been curious to see what she looked like, I was disappointed. Alexa was a cartoon wearing a grey fedora. Big head, tiny body like a Japanese chibi. The character was white with blonde hair and big blue eyes, and I made the assumption that Alexa would have stuck reasonably close to her own ethnicity when she created her avatar.

"Good morning."

Cartoon Alexa gave a coy wave. "Let's pick up where we left off earlier. You said Maya was at the top of your suspect list? Why?"

No small talk, no pleasantries. Alexa got straight to the point, but I was growing used to her bluntness. And at least if she didn't waste words, I might get some sleep tonight.

"Because she's having… Well, I guess it's not an affair because she's not cheating on anyone, but she's seeing Zed Nelson."

Silence. As if Alexa was waiting for the punchline. Then the frantic clicking of keys. Was she running a search?

And finally, "Euew. That old dude with the Botox and the ponytail? He runs the WST?"

"That old *rich* dude."

"Maya never cared about money."

"I thought that too, but trust me when I say she isn't with him for his good looks or charming personality."

A pause. "Okay, so let's assume that Maya's taste in men has degraded significantly. How does that make her a suspect?"

"Because she's lying to everyone about the relationship, including Zach. Every time she goes to see Zed, she says she's somewhere else. A business meeting, a shopping trip, that kind of thing."

"How did you find out she was with Nelson?"

"I followed her one night. I didn't even realise it was his house she'd gone to until I looked through a window and saw them… Uh, let's just say I wish I could unsee."

"That still doesn't explain why she would risk Zach

surfing while he was sick. And if Nelson's already rich, why would he mess around with a betting operation?"

That was a question I'd asked myself as well.

"I'm not sure the money would have been the primary motivator, but more of a bonus. Nelson's all about the show, and if the title battle goes down to the wire, that could only be good for viewing figures."

"Did you spend much time with Maya?"

"As much time as I spent with Zach. You?"

"A reasonable amount. Zach and I were roommates for a while, and Maya came over whenever he wasn't at college or working. Her foster parents were cool with it until—" Alexa halted mid-sentence. "She was there quite often."

"You were going to say 'until the murder'?"

Silence, and once again, I wondered if I'd overstepped the mark. Cartoon Alexa might have looked cute, but she struck me as a prickly character and also one who was used to getting her own way.

"Zach mentioned Blackstone House?"

"It's public information."

"My presence there isn't."

So she *was* the unidentified minor.

"Zach told me a few more of the details." I took a shot in the dark. "The cameras were yours?"

"Why does it matter? The case is closed."

"I'm just curious. The papers were full of conspiracy theories, and Zach said that Levi Sykes's lawyers tried to blame the rest of you."

"Zach had nothing to do with it, if that's what you're worried about."

"I'd already come to that conclusion on my own. Dawson and Nolan don't seem the type to strangle a woman and carve her up either."

Alexa's tone turned from barely concealed annoyance to curiosity. "Nolan? You've met Nolan?"

"I visited his vineyard with Zach. We only stayed for one night, but Nolan was very hospitable."

"What's it like? How is he?"

Now she was the one with all the questions? Interesting.

"I don't know much about wine, but it seems like a really professional setup, and the caves where the casks sit to age are fascinating. Apparently, it started out as a natural network of tunnels and then got expanded by prospectors. Nolan gave us a tour, but I've forgotten most of what he said because I overindulged during the tasting."

"The wine's good. Did you know the first bottling of Syrah got a score of ninety-six from Robert Parker?"

"Yes, I'm aware. But I thought you weren't much of a drinker?"

"I'm not." But she'd obviously followed Nolan's journey into the world of wine production, even if she hadn't spoken with him recently. Did she keep tabs on all her old roommates? "Let's get back to the issue at hand." Nice subject change. "I still don't like Maya for this, but I also see where you're coming from. And Zach… I think he sees it too. When we were going through the suspects, he hesitated before he ruled Maya out. Something about her current behaviour bothers him, even if he won't admit it. Who's next on the list? Baylee Sarterfeld? The way Zach described her, she sounds like a real piece of work."

"After the way she arranged that fake movie night to expose me, I bumped her up the list. Until then, I had her down as bitchy but not sneaky, and she's definitely motivated by money. Damn, I'd love for her to be the culprit."

"She has debts to pay off."

"Not a significant amount. I ran her credit report when I started the investigation. Mostly, she just spends Tyler's money."

"Yeah, and she did the same with her ex, but he wasn't so relaxed about paying for her lifestyle as Tyler is. After they broke up, he claimed that all the money she spent on his credit card was a loan, while she said it was a gift. Rather than go to court, she agreed to pay him five hundred bucks a month for six years."

"Thirty thousand bucks? That's a lot of purses."

"Apparently, one of them came from Hermès."

"How do you know this stuff?"

"I still have access to Zach, remember? He thinks Baylee did it too, and he's not gonna let her anywhere near him in the future, which makes our lives both easier and harder."

"Easier because we don't need to worry about Zach being poisoned by her again, and harder because we won't be able to catch her in the act?" I asked.

"Exactly."

"What if Baylee or whoever she's working with recruits someone else? What if they don't decide to cut their losses?"

"Go big or go home? That was my thought too."

I nodded. "Baylee knows plenty of people on the tour. She could pass a bottle of water to one of Nelson's assistants and ask them to give it to Zach. I used to get a warning from my previous client whenever he saw the numbers were off, and then I knew to stay extra vigilant that weekend, but now I'm feeling my way in the dark."

"I'll make sure Zach declares her persona non grata."

"It's not that easy. Have you ever been to a WST event? There are tens of thousands of people there. With a wig and make-up, Baylee could easily blend into the crowd."

"And so could you."

"What?"

"You could go to the next round of the WST and keep an eye on Zach. He'll be fine on his own this week—he's staying with Dawson and Violet, and Dawson won't let him do anything dumb."

My heart lurched. The thought of seeing Zach again sent me into a tailspin. I was just getting used to the new reality, and now Alexa was determined to upset the fragile equilibrium I'd settled into.

"The risks might outweigh the benefits. What if he does see me? Either he'll think I've turned into a stalker, or he's going to realise I'm still investigating. He definitely doesn't know you hired me?"

Alexa snorted. "What do you think? Look, if you go on the trip, we'll take precautions. We can make sure you stay out of his way."

"Why don't we see where we get to over the next few days?" Much as I didn't want to leave Haven again, I knew what my next move had to be. "I should go and talk to Baylee's ex. See what he has to say. Do you have a name?"

"Steven Shaw."

Damn, that was a reasonably common combination.

"Any other information? Did he live in Santa Cruz?"

"I'll email you his picture, current address, phone number, the make and model of his vehicle, and an outline of his finances. He moved to Fresno."

My jaw might have dropped. Alexa already had that information? Then what was she paying me for? "That's… that's thorough." And then I felt a spark of excitement—Clovis was a suburb of Fresno, and one of the places on my list of possible future homes. When I went to visit Steven Shaw, I could spend an hour or two in Clovis and get a feel for the place. How long would it take me to get there? Six hours? Seven? "Provided I can find someone to check out my car on Monday, I can drive down on Tuesday and look for Shaw. I'll need to stay overnight."

"What's wrong with your car?"

"It's overheating."

"Hire a car and go on Monday. Chase can make the arrangements."

"Uh…"

"Who was the fifth suspect on your list?"

Talking to Alexa was like playing mental ping-pong, and I was the one getting smacked with a paddle. On the head. My brain was careening around inside my skull, and everything hurt. But she was my client, albeit a fairly unconventional one, so I forced my thoughts back on track.

"Gloria. Zach's housekeeper."

"Surname?"

"Sanchez."

"Does she live-in?"

"No, she has a place near Watsonville. Her husband does something agricultural, but he's been sick."

"Ah, medical bills. That's the motive?"

"I thought it might be. Zach takes half of his food with him to each contest, and she's the one who packs it. On the last trip, I checked all the seals, and she has no way of knowing when over the weekend he might eat or drink a particular item, so I put her at the bottom of the list. But I couldn't rule her out completely."

"And the other two are Kai and Tyler." Not a question; a statement. "Kai's the one with the motive. Zach's his competition."

"Yes."

Alexa really didn't need me, did she? And yet, for the next month at least, I was at her beck and call.

"Do you have any evidence of their involvement other than proximity?"

"Not at the moment. My next step would have been to install hidden cameras, but there always seemed to be someone around. Whenever we were away together, Maya used to set up her laptop on the kitchen table at the rental house, and people kept coming to talk to her."

"I could get Zach to install the cameras, but if Baylee *is* the fucker who poisoned him, then it'd be pointless. We missed the boat on that one."

"I know, dammit. Four months, I've been working on this, and I've only been able to rule out one suspect."

"Who was that?"

"Zach himself. Although there's something hinky about his finances. I know he's your friend, but I think he might be hiding some debt."

"What makes you say that?"

"Seven years ago, he was barely earning enough money to eat. Yet suddenly, he was able to buy an architect-designed home by the ocean. In California. Yes, it was a fixer-upper, but it still cost a small fortune."

Laughter wasn't the reaction I'd expected. Shock, perhaps, or an irritated instruction to stay on track. But not Alexa giggling through the phone.

"You don't need to worry about the source of the funds."

"Wait, *you* know how he bought Haven's Rest?"

"Yes, and it has no bearing on this case."

"But—"

"Chill, we'll catch our man. Or woman. Get some sleep—Chase will email you in the morning, your time."

And once again, she was gone, leaving me alone with a few misgivings, no small amount of puzzlement, and a whole lot of regret.

CHAPTER 38
ARI

I watched with my heart in my throat as Zach dropped into a wave and sprang to his feet. Months ago, Erin, the girl I'd met on that first day in Santa Cruz, had told me that Zach had magic. Flair. A connection to the ocean. Back then, I hadn't had a clue what she was talking about, but now I understood. Zach was hypnotic on a surfboard.

Today, he was taming the waves in Teahupo'o, French Polynesia. I'd never been to Tahiti before, and…I couldn't see myself ever visiting.

Right now, I was slouched down in the back seat of my rental car, hidden behind darkly tinted windows as I studied a video on YouTube. Zach had arrived in Tahiti several days early, and he'd been using the time to practise before the WST contest began tomorrow. I hadn't been able to resist torturing myself by checking out the clips his fans uploaded.

Research. It was *research*.

The Mercedes coupe had appeared outside my home last Sunday morning. I'd rolled groggily out of bed to answer a knock at the door, only to find a bemused man in a suit standing outside with a key fob, no doubt trying to work out why he'd been asked to deliver a car whose monthly payment was undoubtedly more than my rent.

This job sure did come with perks.

And challenges.

In the restaurant opposite me, Baylee leaned closer to the man seated across from her. They'd arrived separately, and he'd greeted her with a kiss on the cheek before a server led them to a table near the window. Now he fed her a spoonful of whatever they were eating for dessert with one hand, then adjusted his crotch with the other.

Dammit.

Steven Shaw had been right, hadn't he?

Baylee had moved on from Tyler already, and they'd only parted ways a week ago. The news of the breakup had come from Alexa, who'd heard it from Dawson, who'd heard it from Zach.

Rather than taking the softly-softly approach, I'd risked visiting Shaw at home in Woodward Park, an upscale community on the edge of Fresno. Lots were large and streets were lined with trees. I knew from my enquiries that schools were excellent and crime rates were the lowest in the city, and I also knew that I couldn't afford to live there.

Shaw was a doctor, according to Alexa's research, which was surprisingly thorough. As I read through her notes and observations, I'd known one thing without a doubt—this wasn't the first time she'd prepared a background check. And still she'd given nothing away about her own history. Six days after first speaking with her, I knew little more than her name and that she was younger than me, she had a "companion" named Chase who could have been an assistant or a boyfriend or both, and she was probably somewhere in Europe, judging by the time differences she mentioned.

Anyhow, once I told Shaw who I was and spun a plausible story—that I was working for the ex Baylee had just bankrupted—he was only too happy to talk. And talk, and talk. And by "talk," I mean "rant." He and Baylee had met when they both worked at the Greenfield Hospital in Salinas, and she hadn't been employed there for long before they began dating.

"She's that woman a man dreams of, you know? Beautiful to look at, outgoing, adventurous in...you know, in bed," Shaw told me. "But did you ever hear that proverb about the frog in boiling water? Drop it straight into the pot, and it'll jump out, but put it in tepid water to start with, and it won't realise the danger before it's gently cooked to death? That's what being with Baylee was like."

"Did she ever harm you?"

"Sure, she kicked me right in the wallet."

"I mean physically?"

"That's not Baylee's style. She's manipulative. Reels you in and then traps you in a web of narcissism. Makes you believe that every problem is either your fault or your imagination."

"What made you finally break up with her?"

"There was a new psych resident at work, and she saw through all the bullshit. Later, other people said they knew Baylee was bad news too, but Maria was the only one to speak up." He smiled for the first time as he held up his left hand, showing me the gold wedding band he wore. "We've been married for three months now."

"Congratulations."

"Knowing the bad makes you appreciate the good more."

That was a sentiment I could agree with. The only problem? I'd screwed up and lost both.

"It sure does. I understand you have a financial agreement with Baylee? That she still owes you money?"

"I was going to cut my losses, but Maria said that if I let Baylee get away with what she'd done, she'd never learn her lesson. In truth, I thought Maria was wrong because a leopard never changes its spots, does it? But Baylee had run up so much debt in my name, and one of my buddies is a lawyer. He thought I had a reasonable civil case, and it was enough to push her into a settlement." Shaw groaned. "Don't tell me she's been stealing from your guy to pay it?"

I made a face. Shaw had just given me a plausible reason for being here. "As you said, some people never change."

"Man, I'm sorry about that."

"When she was working at the hospital, did she have any access to drugs? A couple of times, my client felt extraordinarily sleepy, and he wonders if she put something in his drink to mess with him."

"As in, she drugged him?" Shaw raked a hand through his thinning hair. "Whoa. She's still working as a hospital finance assistant?"

"Yes, in Santa Cruz now."

"Unless the procedures are sloppy, she wouldn't have access to drugs. And I can't see her doing anything criminal. She bleeds men dry, takes them for every cent she can extract with her feminine charms, but she wouldn't risk jail. No, she'd just move on and find a new victim. You know why she works in a hospital? Because doctors are an easy mark. Good-paying jobs, spend most of their time with patients, bigger things to worry about than checking a credit card statement line by line. Maria found out I was the third medical professional she'd targeted. Is your guy a doctor?"

"No, he's a businessman."

And Baylee had probably seen an easy mark in Tyler too—laid-back, generous with his cash, happy to keep things relaxed rather than jump into marriage. Zach said the two of them had met at one of Kai's gigs. *Come for the music, stick around for the free vacations.*

"But he has money, right?" Shaw asked.

"A reasonable amount."

"Did you ever see that alien movie with Will Smith? *Independence Day?*"

At least ten times. Nana had a crush on President Whitmore, and possibly I did too, although I'd never admit it to her. And now the US had its very own Whitmore. James Harrison had flown helicopters in the US Air Force before he turned to politics, and although I didn't always agree with his policies, I couldn't deny that he was movie-star handsome.

"I saw it."

"Well, Baylee's the alien queen. She finds a host planet, sucks the life out of it, and moves on."

"Just without the biomechanical suit, huh?" I joked.

Shaw gave a mirthless laugh. "Doctor number one was a cosmetic surgeon. Apparently, she talked him into a *lot* of free work. Tell your guy that I'm sorry he fell for her bullcrap, and there *are* good women out there."

"I'll pass on the message."

So, even though Shaw didn't have a kind word to say about Baylee, he'd been quick to dismiss the idea of her causing a man physical harm. Which was almost disappointing. I'd wondered whether Shaw had misjudged her again. Everyone agreed she was motivated by money—how much would the accomplice's cut of the betting profits be? Whoever put up the cash was taking the financial risk, but our poisoner had opened themselves up to a different kind of jeopardy.

In the restaurant, Baylee's date reached across the table and took her hand. A sigh escaped my lips. Yes, Shaw had been right about her habits. The huntress had found a juicy piece of prey. Should I drop the new guy a warning? Maybe after the case was finished—I'd have to discuss it with Alexa first. Plus I'd need to do a little more research on the man to rule him out as a player in the sportsbook scam, but it didn't look hopeful. At least we were reasonably confident that Zach wasn't a target this weekend. On Tuesday, when Alexa and I were torn over whether I should hightail it to Tahiti or stick with Baylee, I'd tried contacting Lila. I wouldn't say we were friendly, exactly, but she'd warmed up slightly over the months we'd been liaising. She called me back later from an anonymous number, her voice hushed.

"We shouldn't be speaking. You got taken off the list."

"What list?"

"Mr. Rennick has a list of people who we're allowed to correspond with. Anyone else gets bounced down to the customer service team."

I didn't want to get her into trouble, but at the same time, I needed her help.

"So why are you speaking to me?"

"Because…because I feel bad for the position you were put in. And that other man… Ugh."

Wow, a rare show of emotion from Lila.

"Dale Jankowski has that effect on most women."

"Indeed. But I'm sorry, I'm not sure I'll be able to assist. I can't risk my job by sending you confidential reports."

"I'm not asking for reports, only one tiny piece of information." Perhaps the desperation in my voice would convince her. "Whenever the betting patterns went haywire, that's when Zach got poisoned. Could you just tell me if it happens again? I'm not in contact with him, but I still talk to some friends who are. Really, it's a win-win for both Zach and Mr. Rennick because if Zach doesn't end up sick, he's more likely to win the contest."

There was a long pause, and I steeled myself for rejection, but finally, Lila came through.

"Just that one thing?" she asked.

"Yes, only that."

"I can't pass along any other details, but I don't want an innocent man to get hurt."

"Thank you. I swear that's all."

With no alert from Lila this weekend, Alexa and I had figured that following Baylee made more sense than trekking to Tahiti. It reminded me of my original brief from Rennick—

follow the suspect, see who they meet. We already knew that Jankowski hadn't dug up anything useful from his initial cyber research into Ms. Sarterfeld.

The problem was, Baylee herself wasn't giving us anything useful either. No, she'd found some other poor schmuck to bedazzle with her fake boobs, and the ploy was definitely working. When he handed his credit card to the server, I snapped a picture and sent it to Alexa with a caption:

ME

Victim #5?

She replied within a minute. Didn't she ever sleep?

ALEXA

Can you find out who he is? I feel like we should send a note.

ME

I'll follow him when he leaves.

ALEXA

We'd be doing a public service.

Alexa might have been even stranger than Rennick, but I kind of liked her. And I now realised just how much I'd missed working with a partner. In the past, I'd had Morty to bounce ideas off, plus we'd helped each other with research when the need arose. At Twilight, it had been every man for himself, competition rather than teamwork, and Jankowski wouldn't have pissed on me if I was on fire. Or maybe he would? I wouldn't have been surprised to find he had some weird kink hidden under his ageing-frat-boy exterior. And he wasn't even a skilled investigator. No, his father had built up the Twilight Agency, and Jankowski had merely kept it functioning since the old man's retirement six years ago.

But now I had…well, not a partner, but Alexa didn't act like a typical client either. Rennick had been totally hands-off, while Alexa sent over research better than anything Jankowski had provided. Was she performing the searches herself? Or did she have a small army of staff at her disposal? I'd only heard Chase's voice in the background, but she obviously wasn't strapped for cash, and I had no idea what she did for a living. Hell, I didn't even know her surname. The contract I'd signed was with 1812 Enterprises, Inc., which had an address in Nevis. I'd looked up where that was and found a tiny dot in the Caribbean. Did Alexa live there? Or had she merely chosen to set up her company in the most secretive financial system in the world? I was inclined to believe the latter.

Only time would tell, and at the moment, time was moving frustratingly slowly.

CHAPTER 39
ZACH

For the first time in a year, Zach hadn't qualified for the semi-finals of a WST contest. *Fifteenth.* He'd come fifteenth, his worst result in years, probably because he'd spent the entire weekend on edge, wondering if his headache was due to stress or drugs, or if that ache in his chest had been caused by a slow-acting poison.

His phone buzzed, and he checked the message.

Where was he? Lying in bed in their rented villa. Where should he be? In the fan village, smiling for photos while random women groped his ass. If a guy tried the same with a female surfer, there'd be a lawsuit, but Zed turned a blind eye to the double standard in pursuit of the almighty dollar. At least the groupies were distracted today. The wave at Teahupo'o was a heavy, glassy monster that rose from the deep and barrelled over a shallow reef, and this weekend, it had wiped out several big names. Cheryl Campion had needed six stitches in her face after being flung headfirst into the coral yesterday, and this morning, the wave had claimed another prize—Marc de Bruin's board shorts. He'd been sucked over the falls and tossed around like a rag doll before he washed up in the lagoon, minus his clothing and several chunks of skin. The live-stream had captured his junk in full HD before someone remembered to switch cameras. Or maybe Zed had stayed with the shot deliberately to boost viewing figures?

Whatever, Marc was the star of the weekend. After Tyler fished him out of the water, they'd done several laps on the jet ski, waving to the screaming crowd, and now #HangingOutInTahiti was trending on social media. A female reality TV star had offered ten thousand bucks for the shorts if they ever showed up.

ZACH

Got a headache.

MAYA

Tylenol is in the first-aid box in the kitchen. Are you coming out for pictures? Asking for ten thousand women.

He swallowed a groan. Even after everything Ari had done, there was still only one woman he wanted. Was it possible to both love and hate a person at the same time?

ZACH

Give me an hour.

At least he wasn't shitting his guts into the toilet today. Or passed out from exhaustion. Or bouncing off the walls. Whoever had tampered with his drinks—if Ari had been telling the truth about that—they hadn't struck again this weekend. Which meant the culprit was probably Baylee. Tyler had finally ditched the bitch, but now he was miserable too. And not only because it had been a bad breakup. No, he'd forgotten to take his credit card away from her, and she'd driven straight to San Jose and spent six thousand bucks on shoes out of spite. Plus he'd acted as guarantor for her car payments, so he was on the hook for another fifteen thousand over the next two years.

Zach had offered to pay if Tyler struggled—it was the least he could do after Tyler had acted as his tow driver and safety guy for the last seven years—but Tyler refused the offer. Maya said he was embarrassed. Kai said he was depressed.

But at least he'd finally seen the light.

And so had Zach.

Getting mixed up with a woman was a bad idea.

MAYA

Do you need to see the doctor? Are you sick? Or sleepy?

He'd had to tell Maya the truth about Ari. Tyler and Kai had respected his reluctance to discuss the details of the split, but not Maya. A week after Baylee's movie night, his sister had still been furious with Ari for cheating, and Zach had felt an irrational need to defend his ex.

"She didn't cheat, okay?"

"But the video—"

"The guy Baylee saw was Ari's old boss. She quit working for him because he wouldn't take no for an answer, and he thought they had unfinished business."

"That's what she told you?"

"Yes."

"And you believed her?"

"Yeah, I did. Look, Ari wasn't a cheat, but she was a liar. The woman we knew wasn't real. Her name's Arizona, and she was a private investigator sent to infiltrate my life."

Maya's mouth had dropped open. "That's what she told you? I mean, wow, that's some story. Do you think she needs to see a therapist?"

"No, she doesn't."

Zach was thinking straight now. Whatever an outsider

might have suspected, he knew that his sister wouldn't have gotten involved in any half-baked scheme Baylee had cooked up. And it *must* have been Baylee. He was ninety-nine percent certain that Tyler and Kai hadn't been involved either, assuming Ari was right about the poisoning. He wanted so badly to believe that she'd made a mistake, but he also knew how he'd felt. Five separate contests, five times he'd gotten onto his surfboard feeling rotten. And it wasn't only the physical sickness; it was the timing too. Always on a Sunday morning, right before the quarter-final or the semi.

But after he'd explained all the lies to Maya, she became a little more sympathetic to Ari.

"So she was acting in your best interests?"

"She was also getting paid to be near me."

"Do you truly believe that? I mean, maybe at first, but you think she faked falling in love?"

"How the hell should I know? I've never been to detective school. I don't know what they teach there. And nothing changes the fact that she was here under false pretences. Nobody should lie to a person they love, right?"

"Right."

But Maya hadn't sounded quite so certain.

And now she'd stepped into the role of food police, even though it was probably unnecessary. To keep her happy, Zach had promised to only eat snacks and meals that she brought him, accompanied by canned products that he opened himself. No Surf Star. Boy, was he sick of tepid water from the faucet.

ZACH

> Apart from the headache, I'm fine.

Now he was the liar. He wasn't sure he'd ever be fine again.

Zach lay down on the couch, and one hour turned into two. Three. Four. He'd pay for his absence next time—Zed would probably make him attend a foam party for Instagram models or something—but at that moment, he couldn't bring himself to care.

He'd deal with the penalty when it came.

Two weeks ago, he'd been on top of the world, fresh from victory with the woman of his dreams at his side. Now? He'd lost everything.

His surfing mojo, his girl, his sanity…

Everything but his friends.

What the…?

Light cut into the darkness as Kai opened the blinds, and a few last rays of sunshine glinted off the oversized trophy he held in his hand. Oh, good—he'd beaten Scottie Stenson to the win.

"Congratulations. Now leave me alone."

"Can't do that, buddy."

"Says who?"

"Says Maya."

That was playing dirty. Kai knew Zach would do everything possible to make his sister happy. There were so many years when he hadn't been able to be there for her—her first, nerve-racking day of high school, the moment she flubbed her lines in an amateur theatre performance of *Grease*, in the aftermath of a disastrous date with her ninth-grade crush. Jonny Whelan had called her frigid after she refused to kiss him in the Megabowl parking lot, and Maya had called Zach for comfort. All he'd wanted to do was hug her, but they'd been three hundred miles apart. Although Zach had the last laugh. Ten years later, that prick Whelan had emailed

Maya to ask if she could get him VIP passes to the WST, and Zach had taken great pleasure in replying in the negative.

But those events paled into insignificance beside the many occasions she'd called him in tears after the death of their father.

He sighed. Time to stop feeling sorry for himself and get off the couch.

"Is there a plan? Or does she just want me to put pants on?"

"Yeah, there's a plan. You'll need pants and a shirt as well."

CHAPTER 40
ARI

Sunday night, and the end of a weekend that had been disappointing all around. Zach hadn't even made the quarter-final in Tahiti. And Alexa and I hadn't found any definitive evidence against Baylee. She'd spent the whole of yesterday shopping, mostly for clothes, but she'd swung by the grocery store too. On Friday evening, she'd been on a date with Dr. Benjamin Flanders, a work colleague who'd recently moved to the area, not dining with a mysterious co-conspirator.

After their cosy meal, I'd watched them smooch in the parking lot, but it seemed that Dr. Flanders either had an inbuilt sense of self-preservation or was more of a gentleman than Baylee wanted him to be, because he didn't follow her home or invite her over to his place. No, he meandered back to a McMansion not too far from Zed Nelson's, driving five miles per hour under the speed limit the whole way. Perhaps that natural caution was what had saved him? Or was he just worried about getting a DUI? He did wobble over the white line a time or two.

Anyhow, I followed him home, then did a reverse lookup on his address to find out his details. This morning, before I left Santa Cruz, I'd sent him a personalised card from one of those online services. Chase had helped out with the artwork —a frog sitting in a pan of water with the gas on high. Alexa had clearly told him about our conversation because he'd added arrows pointing to the frog and the heat, annotated with *You* and *Baylee*. The message inside? *Get out unscathed while you still can.* I'd signed it from Steven Shaw and added his phone number, just in case Flanders needed clarification. I didn't think Shaw would mind.

And now?

Now, I was pinching myself at the Hyatt Regency in Huntington Beach, waiting for the manager to knock on the door and tell me there'd been a terrible mistake. That I wasn't meant to be in this deluxe room with a private terrace and a view of the Pacific. Or worse, that I'd shown up at the wrong hotel entirely.

I wasn't even certain why I was here. Chase had emailed the reservation details, apologising for Alexa's absence— something urgent had come up, apparently—and telling me that she'd call later to explain. The eight-hour drive from Santa Cruz wasn't exactly a chore in the Mercedes, and I took a break in San Luis Obispo and another near Oxnard. Even though I'd arrived in the dark, the lights from the hotel twinkling on the waves reminded me of the ocean's beauty. I'd learned to appreciate the water now. Zach had given me that.

The chat app pinged: Alexa was online.

"Evening," I said. "Or is it morning in Scandinavia?"

She'd mentioned a fjord earlier in the week, which, combined with the time difference, meant she must be in Norway or thereabouts.

"I'm not in Scandinavia. Chase wanted to go to an Indigo Rain concert in Kraków."

So they were in Poland now?

Chase cut in, and tonight, I saw his avatar as well. Short

blond hair, tanned skin, black-rimmed glasses framing blue eyes. "She lies. Alexa was craving pierogi, so under duress, I booked a table at her preferred restaurant. The Indigo Rain concert was merely a happy coincidence."

"Pier-what?"

Alexa didn't try to deny it. "Little dumplings."

They'd flown hundreds of miles because Alexa wanted dumplings? These people lived on another planet. And how did they afford it? If Alexa had family money, she wouldn't have been living in Blackstone House, which led me to conclude that Chase was the wealthy one. She called him a "companion," which covered a multitude of sins. Were they lovers? Married? How strange that he acted more like an assistant.

"Did you eat dinner?" he asked me. "I can recommend the sea bass."

So he'd stayed here at the Hyatt Regency himself? With Alexa? Interesting. Was that why he'd chosen this particular hotel for me? Because it was tried and tested?

"I stopped at a diner on the way."

Alexa's tut said *what a waste*. "Try the waffles for breakfast."

"Or the avocado toast," Chase suggested.

"You're such a fucking hipster."

Hmm, the bickering made them sound almost like brother and sister, and if their avatars were true to life, they shared the same eye and hair colour. But curious though I was about Alexa and Chase, it was late, and I was tired.

"Why am I in Huntington Beach?"

The avatars exchanged a glance.

"There's good news and bad news," Alexa said. "The good news is that we've ruled out a suspect."

"And the bad news?"

"That suspect is Baylee."

"Tell me you're joking."

"I rarely joke."

"She has a weird sense of humour," Chase put in.

"So…" I couldn't help sighing. "Why do you think Baylee is innocent?"

"Apart from the fact that she doesn't have the brainpower or the connections to pull off a scheme like this one? I reviewed each of Zach's WST contests—both his results and any available footage."

"I'm sorry, *who* reviewed the footage?" Chase asked.

"Okay, *we* reviewed Zach's contests."

"The hardship of having to watch half-naked surfers… Do they pick out their own bathing suits?"

"There are rules," I told him. "And those rules say no rash vests or T-shirts or wetsuits. Muscles and cleavage are good, modesty's bad."

Alexa stayed businesslike, and something told me that she wasn't the type to get distracted by a six-pack and tight pecs.

"We've already established that there were six problematic rounds. You attended two of them and were able to vouch for Baylee's presence, so we focused on the other four. At three of them, we caught glimpses of her in the background, but at Bells Beach last year, she was nowhere to be seen."

"Bells Beach—that's Victoria, Australia, right?"

"Yes."

"Which is a fifteen-hour flight, so maybe she didn't go?"

"She was in Noosa two weeks before. That's Queensland."

"Baylee has a job. It's possible she couldn't get that much time off work."

"It's also possible that she went to an Atomic Pirates concert with a group of girlfriends and hooked up with the lead guitarist."

"*What?*"

"It appeared to be a bachelorette party, so I'm sure alcohol was involved."

"Tell me you're not serious."

"Do you want to see the video?"

"How the heck did you get a video?"

"It's on the lead singer's YouTube account; it's hardly a secret."

A moment later, the avatars vanished, replaced by shaky footage of a club or bar. The caption read "Behind the Scenes: Last Night's Atomic Pirates Afterparty, LA." I checked the upload date, and sure enough, it was the Sunday that Zach had lost his semi-final in Queensland.

"Hello, me hearties. We've just got off stage here in LA, and now it's time to get smashed. Our mate Vinnie sorted out this orgy of drinking and…" The camera panned around the room, showing a crowd of sweaty men and short-skirted women. "Nice one. Hey, Jason, come and talk to the fans. You all know Jason, yeah? Our sound engineer—couldn't do the show without him."

The videographer—presumably the singer himself—was moving around the club, narrating as he went in his oh-so-British accent, but Alexa zipped through the footage, then paused five minutes in.

"Where's Mattie? Has anyone seen Mattie? Man, it's hot in here." The singer paused to swig from the bottle of champagne in his other hand, then zoomed in on a couple kissing in the corner. The man sported a shock of red hair, and I mean scarlet, and the woman wore a gold sash with *Bridesmaid* written on it in fancy script. The butterfly tattoo on her left shoulder blade, together with the blonde hair, skyscraper heels, and designer purse, told me exactly who she was. Just in case there was any doubt, she turned as the singer approached, and for a few seconds, her expression of shock was clear before she ducked away from the camera.

"Oi, knobhead. Put the girl down and talk to the fans."

The scene paused.

"Need to watch it again?" Alexa asked.

"No, I've seen enough. What a bitch."

"Tyler Peralta is still on the suspect list, so I'll reserve judgment on how much sympathy I have."

"Have you found any more information on him?"

"I'm still digging," Alexa said. "My research is primarily electronic, and Tyler and Gloria spend the least time online, although Kai's earlier life is still something of a mystery. Did you know his father is dead?"

"Maya mentioned it, yes."

"Okay, then did you know he was poisoned?"

Oh, hell no. For the millionth time, I cursed Jankowski—background research had been his job, and like a fool, I'd trusted him to make at least a half-assed attempt at the task. Although Alexa and I were casting our nets beyond my initial, narrow brief of "follow Zach" now, precious early months had been wasted.

My expression must have given my answer away.

"Thought not. Anyhow, I'm ninety percent sure it's the same guy. Manu Kealoha's an unusual name, isn't it? Someone laced his Kool-Aid with ethylene glycol."

"Antifreeze?"

"Yup. Colourless, odourless, sweet-tasting."

"Holy shit."

"It happened over a decade ago."

"Was anyone convicted?"

"Nobody was even charged. The lead investigator retired, and he moved to San Clemente."

Which was a forty-minute drive away. The reason for my trip south suddenly became clear.

"And you want me to speak with him?"

"I understand that people often respond better to questions asked in person than over the phone." A pause. "Also, I've been told that I'm too blunt."

A laugh escaped before I could stop it. "I can't disagree with that."

"I'll send you the detective's name and contact details.

Don't forget to try the waffles."

"Okay, you've twisted my arm."

"I have to go now."

And she vanished without another word. Alexa was one strange woman.

CHAPTER 41
ZACH

There was a plan, Kai had said.

The part he left out?

That Tyler had made the plan, which was why they were sitting in a tiki bar, drinking Zombie cocktails from mugs shaped like Easter Island statues that weren't much smaller than the real thing. Fake parrots perched in real palm trees, and a guy was playing a guitar beside the firepit out front, although the music was barely audible over the buzz of conversation. And there were women *everywhere*.

Two years had passed since Tyler's previous breakup, which was perhaps why Zach had forgotten about his old friend's "if you fall off the horse, get right back on again" mantra. For the same reason as he drank Bloody Marys to cure a hangover, Tyler surrounded himself with beautiful girls to take his mind off the pain.

When life gives you lemons, toss them aside and find a peach. Although Baylee had been more of a grapefruit—impressive on the outside, sour on the inside.

Sometimes, Zach wished that Tyler would pause to think things through, but the impulsiveness that made him rush into rebound relationships was the same trait that sent him into the crash zone on a jet ski to save Zach's ass, and Zach couldn't have it both ways. No, Tyler was who he was, and a big part of friendship was about accepting people for who they were. Zach's mom had taught him that.

A petite brunette tried to sit on Zach's lap, and he shook his head.

"Not tonight."

"Awww."

She pouted, and Tyler held out a hand. "Plenty of room over here, sugar. Maybe he'll change his mind later."

"No, I won't."

Although Zach's natural caution had hardly paid dividends when it came to Ari, had it? Three months, he'd waited to be sure that she was The One, and he'd still been burned in spectacular fashion. Recovery wouldn't happen in two weeks. Hell, it wouldn't even happen in two years.

But that didn't stop Tyler and Kai from sending a parade of beautiful women in his direction. Curvy women, slim women, blondes, brunettes, redheads. American, British, French, Brazilian, Spanish women. A model, a nurse, a dog trainer, a scuba diving instructor, a shoe designer, a kindergarten teacher. In the end, Zach turned the farce into a drinking game. If the woman gushed over his surfing achievements, he took a sip. If she mentioned her zodiac sign, he took a mouthful. If she left a phone number, he swallowed the whole damn mugful. He got a brief respite when Tyler disappeared for an hour with a chirpy Canadian and Kai took a break from matchmaking to focus on a dinner of poisson cru, which was the French Polynesian version of sushi—raw tuna marinated in lime juice served with vegetables and coconut milk—but by the end of the night, Zach was still seeing double.

"You didn't like *any* of them?" Tyler asked. At least he was smiling now, probably a result of getting blown in the bathroom. "Not even Mindy?"

"Mandy," Kai corrected.

"She was smart. Something to do with books? And hot."

Which one was Mindy-Mandy? The blonde with the huge breasts? No, that was Missy. Wasn't it? Zach sifted through memories, but nothing got any clearer. Even the Easter Island mug looked fuzzy. Was that why the drinks were called Zombies? Because they turned your brain to Jell-O?

"I'm not interested in women anymore."

"No way." For Tyler, the idea of going without female company for longer than a week was unthinkable. "We just need to find you the right one."

"I had the right one." Zach let his head *thunk* onto the table. Maybe he could sleep right here? "Kind of. And now she's gone."

"If you miss Ari, why don't you call her?" Why did Kai always have to sound so fucking reasonable? "She could be missing you as well."

"Because Ari doesn't exist anymore."

Tyler and Kai exchanged glances.

"Buddy, Las Vegas is less than a day's drive from Santa Cruz," Kai said. "Why don't you take a trip there? Yeah, I know the video Baylee made was bad, but I've been thinking about that. The guy was her ex-boss, right?"

Tyler nodded. "That's what she said."

"So what if there was some weird power dynamic going on? Like, he was forcing her into doing things that she didn't want to do?"

"She could sue for that. Didn't he ever hear of the #MeToo thing?"

Fuck, Zach's head hurt. "No, you don't get it. Ari was a figment of her imagination."

"You're not making any sense," Kai said. "We all saw her. She hung out with us for months."

"*Arianna*, she was the one who hung out with us. *Arizona* is a private eye who told lies."

Another glance, and Zach laughed at the shock on their faces.

"Yeah, that's how I felt too."

"Just because she didn't tell you about her old job doesn't mean she lied about everything. She quit for a reason."

"Maybe the boss," Tyler reasoned. "If he was a jerk."

They didn't get it, did they? They didn't understand what she'd done. "Ari didn't quit. *I* was the job. The fucking *job*."

"Wait…" Kai's brows pinched together, and he glanced at Zach's empty mug. "How many of these have you drunk?"

"Not enough."

"Are you saying that Ari was investigating *you*?"

"Uh…" Dawson had told him not to talk about this, hadn't he? Or was it Brax? Probably Dawson. Dawson had his shit together. Brax *looked* as if he had his shit together, but his wife was a bitch and he couldn't get a divorce because of the prenup. "Never mind. It was all bullshit." Baylee-related bullshit, and he didn't want to mention her name in front of Tyler. "What happened to your Canadian?" he asked in an attempt to change the subject.

"She has an early flight tomorrow."

Kai didn't take the hint. "Can we go back to the investigator thing?"

"No."

"You know what we need to do?" Tyler came to the rescue. "Take a trip. How long since the three of us went off-grid and just fuckin' surfed?"

A year at least. "Too damn long."

"So why don't we get the hell out of here?"

"Now?"

Tyler's initial enthusiasm faded a little. "Uh, so I need to check that Glenn can cover at the store. Plus my brother promised to swing by on Wednesday to help me write a business plan. How about Thursday?"

Kai gave a wry laugh. "Adulting sucks. And also I have

band practice on Wednesday evening. Is the business plan for the new surf store?"

"If I can get the financing. Troy's gonna set up a meeting with the bank."

"Is he okay at the moment?"

It was a fair question. Troy, Tyler's older brother, was what Maya called "smart-stupid." He had enough brains to pass whatever exams he'd needed to take to become a CPA, but lacked the common sense to hold down a job for long. Zach had lost count of the number of times he'd succumbed to the same impulses that affected Tyler. Addicted to addiction, that was Troy. But while Tyler lived for women and waves, Troy had tried drinking, drugs, and—strangely—baseball cards, to name but a few bad habits.

"He's been better." Tyler shrugged. "And also worse. But he's good with numbers, and my math sucks."

"So why don't we fly to Oahu on Thursday?" Kai suggested. "Get there ahead of the contest and acclimatise for a week? Pipeline, Backdoor, Sunset Beach?"

In late October, the North Shore wouldn't quite be at its winter best—the big swells tended to come from November through January, but even without Waimea breaking, there were still plenty of decent waves to be found. Getting barrelled at Pipeline would be the perfect cure for the post-Ari blues.

When Tyler voiced his agreement, Zach nodded too.

"Sure, let's go."

CHAPTER 42
ARI

rnold Wise lived in a single-storey, clapboard home with a wide front porch. The Stars and Stripes fluttered from a flagpole in the immaculate front yard, and somewhere inside, a small dog yip-yip-yipped when I rang the bell. While I waited for an answer, I studied the place. The siding was freshly painted in pale grey, the small front lawn a vibrant green. Colourful flowers exploded from pots on either side of the front steps, and the windows sparkled. Someone clearly took pride in the place. But the empty driveway was concerning. The only movement inside came from the dog, its claws skittering across a wooden floor as it ran back and forth.

"Are you looking for Erna?"

The voice came from the side, and I turned to see a dark-haired woman peering over the fence, gripping the top as if she was standing on tiptoe.

"Actually, I'm here to see Arnold. Arnold Wise?"

"They're not at home."

I'd begun to suspect that was the case. "I don't suppose you know where they are?"

"Phoenix." A slight widening of her eyes told me she

realised that telling a stranger that her neighbour was out of town wasn't the best idea. "But they have a guard dog."

Ah, now I saw the pooch. It had run around to the side gate—presumably, it had a doggy door—and now it was leaping up and down, snapping at the air.

"What is it? A chihuahua?"

"She's a chorkie. A chihuahua crossed with a Yorkshire terrier. But don't be fooled by her looks—if anyone climbs the fence, she'll chew their ankles to the bone."

"The Wises went to Phoenix and left their dog home alone?"

"Their daughter's boyfriend has a real bad allergy. And my son feeds Cocopuff before and after school, walks her too, so she hasn't been abandoned."

So, they were staying with their daughter. Could Alexa find the address? How far away was Phoenix? Five hours? Six? Although if I showed up there stalker-style, that was more likely to scare Wise off than encourage him to help.

"Your son still has ankles?"

"When he first began helping out, he wore ankle guards and shin pads—he plays hockey—but now she tolerates him."

"Do you know when the Wises will be back?"

"Tomorrow afternoon." A note of curiosity crept into the neighbour's voice. "Should I tell them you called?"

But I left her disappointed. "Thanks so much for your help —I'll come back and see Arnold then."

I waved cheerily as I walked back to my car, but I shared in the disappointment with an added dose of frustration. A whole day, wasted. The clock in the background was tick-tick-ticking, and I had no choice but to wait.

The hotel was beautiful, and sleeping in a king-sized bed for another night sure beat the fold-out couch in Vegas. If only Haven had been with me... She'd have loved staying in a place like this. I carefully packed the complimentary toiletries away in my bag to take home, then called her, both relieved and disappointed when Nana said she was downstairs playing with Isabel Rodriguez and Isabel's huge collection of Barbie dolls.

Relieved because she was happy.

Disappointed because I hadn't gotten to speak with my little girl.

"Is everything okay?" Nana asked. "I thought you wouldn't have to travel so much with this new job."

"So did I. But it feels as though I'm finally getting somewhere with the case. This new client is a much better investigator than Jankowski ever was."

"Is that normal? For the client to investigate?"

"Nothing about this job is normal."

"Did you hear from Zach yet?"

Why did my chest still seize every time I heard his name?

"No, and I don't suppose I ever will. Can you tell Haven I'll call her tomorrow?"

"I promised we'd go to the mermaid show tomorrow."

"Again? We just went there last month."

"You know what Haven's like—once she finds something she loves, she wants to do it over and over again. Remember Elvis?"

How could I forget Elvis? For three long months, Haven had become obsessed with Elvis Presley. I'd lost count of the number of times we'd stood outside the window at Harrah's Piano Bar, listening to the tribute show—Haven was too young to actually go inside—and we both knew all the words to his greatest hits, Haven by choice and me under duress. And then, just like that, she'd moved on to Kelly Clarkson, but thankfully only for two weeks.

"At least the mermaids are quiet."

We said our goodbyes, and I checked my watch. Four p.m. Too early to eat, but I could take a walk along the shore to the pier. Maybe one of the stores there would have a mermaid gift for Haven? Plus I could pick up dinner from a café nearby. The restaurants in the hotel were lovely but expensive, and I didn't want to take advantage of Alexa's generosity, no matter how relaxed she seemed to be about expenses. Okay, I didn't want to eat alone in such a fancy place either. People would think I'd been stood up.

And I missed eating with Zach.

Returning to downtown Huntington Beach was bittersweet. Even as the sun dropped, surfers were out on the water, and although I knew Zach was probably still in Tahiti, I couldn't help looking for him. For him to pop up on a wave, grinning as he rode toward me.

Stupid.

Stupid.

I'd planned to walk along the pier, but instead I circled away, past half a dozen classic cars grouped together at the edge of the beach and toward Main Street. The place was so much quieter today. During the Huntington Beach Classic, the city had been packed, patrons spilling out of restaurants onto the sidewalks, the chatter inescapable, the energy overwhelming at times. I much preferred it this way. Perhaps because I felt so vulnerable now—alone, away from home, my only ally a faceless woman who hid behind a computer screen.

I wouldn't stay out late. Just long enough to pick up a gift for Haven and grab a bite to eat. When I was with Maya, we'd bought burritos from a colourful Mexican place, a little hole in the wall with the menu written on a wooden cactus that stood outside the door. I couldn't remember the name, but it was somewhere around here. I headed up one street and down another, past the Matrixx nightclub and the Big

Break Surf Store. The Big Break Surf Store… That name was familiar. After a moment, I remembered—it was the business Tyler was interested in buying. On impulse, I walked inside. The place was a treasure trove, not some soulless chain store but a hodgepodge of surfboards and clothing and accessories stuffed into every available space. One corner was full of scuba gear, and gadgets I couldn't identify hung from the ceiling. Posters and framed photographs filled the wall behind the counter, and this time when I looked for Zach, I found him.

"Can I help you, ma'am?"

I really hadn't considered this properly, had I? But Morty had taught me to think on my feet, so I dredged up a smile and shoved my sweaty hands into my pockets so I wouldn't fidget. Was this guy the owner? I put him in his late fifties, his grey hair pulled into a ponytail and his face weathered by the sun. He grinned back, showing crooked teeth to match his crooked nose.

"I'm not sure. Uh, I don't really know where to start…"

Mainly because I was still trying to come up with a plausible story.

"You need to buy a surfboard? I'd recommend a soft top for a beginner."

"Oh, no, no, I've been surfing my whole life." I was so going to hell. "I'm here in Huntington Beach on vacation, and I was talking to a group of guys on the beach about my absolute dream, and they said I should come talk to you because… Oh, shoot—I should start from the beginning."

The guy waited expectantly.

"You see, I've always wanted to run a surf store, and one of the folks I talked to, he thought that maybe you were looking to retire. Although I guess he might have been wrong because you look too young for that, but…" My cheeks heated. Good. "Sorry if I'm not making much sense, I'm just…"

"Excited?"

"Yes, that. And I've loved the time I've spent here in Huntington Beach."

Now I clasped my hands together and waited for him to talk. To hopefully take the bait.

"Have you run a store before?"

"Not, like, managed it, but I've been a shift supervisor at the Surf Shack in Cocoa Beach for the past three years. My grandma left me some money when she passed away"—the fake inheritance was doing a lot of heavy lifting on this job—"and I'd love to take the next step by running my own business." I paused for a moment. "You probably think I'm crazy, walking in off the street like this. I mean, I don't even know your name."

"The name's Memphis."

"It's good to meet you, Memphis. I'm Kristina. I know this is definitely an unorthodox approach, but a wise man once said that you'll never ride a monster wave if you're scared to leave the shore."

Thanks for the quote, Zach. I waited, hoping Memphis would throw me a bone. I only wanted to know whether Tyler was serious about buying the store. If he was, then he'd need money, but if he wasn't, it would be another tick in the "nope" column and drop him farther down the suspect list.

Memphis chuckled. "Not so unorthodox. How do you think I got my first job here?"

I knew then that I had him. With a combination of spunk and stupidity, I had him.

"No way—you just walked in off the street?"

"Didn't wind up owning the place right away, of course, but I bought it ten years later. And I admire your courage, young lady. I wish I could give you the same chance I was given, but we're fully staffed at the moment, and I have another buyer interested."

I let the smile slip off my face. "Oh, I'm sorry to hear that.

Uh, I mean, I'm happy for you and everything, just a little disappointed. The contract's already signed?"

"Not yet, but the fella's coming over with his accountant on Wednesday to go through the business plan, and he has a meeting lined up with the bank. You want me to pass on your number? He might be looking for a manager."

"He won't do that himself?"

"Not full-time. He already owns another store up near Santa Cruz, so he'll need a hand."

That confirmed it—Memphis was definitely talking about Tyler. And if what he said was true and Tyler was looking for a bank loan, then he wouldn't be funding the purchase by illicit means. Another check in the minus column.

"Uh, sure, that would be great." At least I might get a heads-up if the transaction progressed. "Could you also call if the deal falls through?"

"That I can do, missy."

I jotted down the virtual phone number I kept in reserve for situations exactly like this one, then mooched around the store. If I was going to be in town for another day or two, an extra T-shirt would come in handy, and I picked up a pink "Surf Princess" shirt for Haven too.

"Could you point me in the direction of the Mexican joint with the giant cactus outside?" I asked when I went to pay. "I know it's around here somewhere."

"Turn right out of the door, take a left at the stoplight, and it's fifty yards along the street."

At least I'd achieved one thing today—I'd found a burrito.

The next day, it was Mrs. Wise who opened the door. I began to explain who I was and why I was there, but before I finished, she was already shaking her head.

"I'm afraid that's just not possible."

"Your husband isn't here?"

"He's here."

"I realise that the investigation is still technically active, and that he can't give me any information that might compromise the case, but I'm worried about a man's safety. His food and drink have been tampered with six times already, and there's going to be a serious accident if I can't find out who's doing it."

"Oh, sweetie, you don't understand—Arnold has Alzheimer's. He has good days and bad days, but this morning, he couldn't remember who I was, let alone the details of a cold case from a decade ago. If he was able to help, I'm sure he would, but..." Mrs. Wise spread her hands. "He can't."

So near, yet so damn far, and a prime example of the limitations of cyber research. Alexa's efforts had given me the raw facts, but they couldn't tell me the state of a man's brain.

"In that case, I apologise for disturbing you."

"It's no bother. I hope you find the information you're looking for. You obviously care about this young man."

"I really do. I don't suppose you can remember the name of anyone your husband might have worked with during that time?"

"He did have a partner. A young rookie, I recall. Joe? Jeff? Something like that. We went to his wedding. Jake? I think it was Jake. He and his wife had a baby just before Arnold retired."

"Do you know his surname?"

"Smith."

Good that she'd given me the name, bad that it was such a common one.

"Where did he live?"

The Riverside County Sheriff's Department served over seven thousand square miles, and we'd gleaned little information on Manu Kealoha's life and untimely demise. Alexa had found birth and death certificates—he'd been born in Hawaii—plus the short paragraph in the *High Country Journal* that had mentioned Arnold Wise. The article hadn't said much, just that a body had been found and the investigation was ongoing. There'd never been a follow-up.

"Over in Aguanga," Mrs. Wise said. "After the wedding, the Smiths bought an old ranch-style home and set about rehabbing it. Arnold helped with some of the woodwork. He always was good with his hands."

"Do you remember his wife's name? Or the child's?"

"My memory isn't what it was, either. I'm sorry I can't help more."

If Alexa worked her magic, it might be enough.

"Honestly, you've been very helpful."

I wished her a good day and headed back to the rental car, patting it on the hood on my way to the driver's side.

"You and me, we're gonna be together for a whole lot of miles yet."

CHAPTER 43
ARI

"Manu Kealoha? There's a name from the past."

Jake Smith leaned on the half-polished police car parked in his driveway. He still lived in the same home that Mrs. Wise had recalled, although it was in good shape now, neatly painted in pale green with white accents. A basketball hoop was fixed above the two-car garage, and a small pink bicycle with streamers on the handlebars had been abandoned near the front porch.

As for Smith, he was a strapping guy, over six feet tall and with the muscles to match. Alexa's bio said he was thirty-two, but he looked a decade older. Had the job aged him? Or the kids? He had three now, two boys and a girl.

"Do you remember much about the case?" I asked.

"It was a strange one, all right."

When I'd swung by the sheriff's station a half hour ago, the deputy at the front desk told me that Smith had the day off, so I'd prepared myself for a long wait. But for the first time this week, luck had been on my side, and better yet, Smith seemed willing to talk.

"Ethylene glycol poisoning, right? Is the case still open?"

"Yup. And between you and me, I doubt it'll ever be closed."

His tone said what his words didn't: you're wasting your time.

"I'm not trying to solve that particular case. The name came up in connection with a different matter, and there's a… I guess you could call it a similarity. It's a long story, but someone's been spiking a sportsman's drinks, and I've been hired to look into it."

Smith gave a low whistle. "Spiking drinks? With ethylene glycol?"

"Nothing that drastic. Tranquillisers, lactose—because he's lactose intolerant—and maybe some type of upper." Alexa had watched the video of the J-Bay contest, the second round where Rennick had noted unusual betting patterns, and she thought Zach looked manic. Wired. Most un-Zach-like. Chase had suggested amphetamines or ivory wave as possible candidates. "But he's a surfer, and if he's off his game even a little, it could have disastrous consequences."

"If ethylene glycol isn't involved, then how did Manu Kealoha's name come up?"

"Because the victim is friends with a man we're ninety percent sure is Manu's son. A fellow surfer."

A few spots of rain fell, and Smith glanced at the half-polished vehicle, cursing under his breath.

"My wife told me not to wash the car. Shoulda listened." He put the lid back on the bottle of Auto Shine. "You wanna talk inside?"

His wife was home—he introduced her as Carolyn—and she made us coffee. Rather than vanish into the house, she leaned against the kitchen counter, curious, as I took a seat opposite Jake at the kitchen table.

"It's about the Kealoha case," he explained, and she snorted.

"Oh, that weirdo."

An interesting comment. "Why do you say that?"

"Those People's Promise folks? They're all..." She whistled and whirled two fingers by her temple in the universal sign for "cuckoo."

"People's Promise?"

"A thousand nutcases on a ranch in the desert, all dressed in pyjamas. Blue for the men, pink for the women. No TV, no AC, no microwaves. The women aren't even allowed to speak."

Jake tactfully tried to shush her. "Some people just prefer a simpler way of life, Carolyn."

"There's simple, and there's needlessly difficult. Mary-Ann's sister saw them out there with a horse and plough. *A horse and freaking plough.*"

Hoo boy.

"Are you saying Manu Kealoha was in a cult?" I asked.

Jake nodded. "The whole family was. Mom, Pop, and the two kids."

Two kids? Kai had a sibling? Wow. He'd never once mentioned a brother or sister, but then again, if he'd grown up in a cult, then I could understand why he didn't want to discuss his past. Especially if he'd murdered his father before he left. Assuming we had the right person, of course.

I tried not to seem too surprised in front of Jake and Carolyn.

"Can you tell me more about what happened? I mean, as much as you're able to. I appreciate that it's still an open case."

"There's not a huge amount to tell. Manu Kealoha collapsed with a seizure in Norm's Feed Store, right by the layer pellets. Norm called nine-one-one, but Manu died in the emergency room. We figured it was natural causes, but then the autopsy results came back and...well...sheesh. Turned out he'd been drinking antifreeze."

"Any idea how much? Could it have been an accident?"

"The toxicologist said about a soda can full."

Carolyn chipped in again, and I realised there were definite advantages to having her present. Jake had obviously broken the rules and discussed the investigation with her, and she spilled *all* the beans.

"Sheriff Richardson tried to say it was suicide, but what kind of man poisons himself and then goes out to buy chicken feed?"

"Honey, don't you have to hang up the laundry?"

She gave him a *look*. "It'll wait." Then to me, "Richardson was a political hack."

"Was there any suspicion that Kai might have been involved?"

"Sure was."

"Carolyn, please." Jake paused to take a calming breath. "If I thought there was any chance of the sheriff's department solving this case, we wouldn't be having this conversation. And it has to stay off-record, but if you think the son might be involved in another crime..."

"I'll keep your name out of it, I promise."

What could he tell me?

"Okay, so there were three main suspects—the son, the mother, and a neighbour. Kai was seventeen at the time of his father's death. But the Prophet—that's what they call their leader—he threw up obstructions at every turn. Nobody from the ranch would speak to us. Plus weeks went by before we received the toxicology results, and the crime scene had already been cleaned up by then. As in *scrubbed*."

"Why would Kai have fallen under suspicion?"

"Manu Kealoha wasn't a good man. That was the first time I had to break the news of a loved one's death to a relative, and I still remember the bruises on Sarah—that's his wife. A black eye and marks around her wrists."

"He tied her up," Carolyn added. Jake didn't try to quiet her this time. He'd probably realised it was a losing battle.

"We don't know that for certain. The Prophet hired a fancy lawyer, and we didn't have enough evidence for an arrest warrant. The boy didn't say a word, and neither did the little girl. Joy, they called her, but I never did see her smile. She was only twelve years old. A shy little thing, just stood behind her momma, watching us. We did search the house right after Manu's death, though, and the techs found empty packages of Kool-Aid in the trash and noted antifreeze in the lean-to garage."

"In southern California." Another snort from Carolyn. "I can't remember the last time it froze here."

"Did you find out who bought the antifreeze?" I directed my question at Jake, although it should have gone to Carolyn because it was she who answered.

"Nope, they didn't. No fingerprints either."

"The fingerprints were too smudged to be of any use. But from what we understand, the folks at People's Promise have strict gender roles. A woman's place is in the kitchen or the fields, so Arnold thought Sarah made the Kool-Aid. It would have been normal. But I always wondered if the boy tried to protect his mother."

"Or it could have been anyone else on the ranch because nobody ever locks their doors there, or so I've heard. They have no privacy. Can you imagine that? The freaking Prophet can meander in at any time he chooses."

"It was kinda strange," Jake admitted. "Even stranger if the son took up surfing. Not many people leave that place, and all money they make goes to the Prophet, so the disciples can't just go buy a bus ticket."

"You said there were three suspects—how did the neighbour come into it?"

"Arnold thought there was something going on between him and the wife."

"An affair?"

"Exactly. I'm not sure how the Prophet would've felt

about that. There're plenty of rumours coming out of that place, everything from polygamy to child brides to human sacrifice. He might have been fine with it."

"You think?" Carolyn again. "I bet two wives is fine, but two husbands? Marnie Coleman says that temple thing in the middle contains an alien spaceship."

"I don't know about the little green men, but I'll tell you one thing for sure—none of them use soap or deodorant."

"Can you remember the neighbour's name?" I asked.

I could request Alexa to take a look. It'd be interesting to see whether the man's name popped up anywhere else in Kai's life, if he'd influenced the boy or the man Kai would later become.

"Not offhand, but it'll be in my notes. Give me a minute."

He exited the room, leaving me alone with Carolyn, much to my delight. I took a sip of my coffee and tried not to smile as she slid into the seat her husband had vacated.

"Jake won't tell you this, but I don't think Arnold tried too hard to solve the murder. Manu Kealoha was an evil son of a bitch. Norm's dog used to bark at him in the feed store parking lot—dogs always know, don't they?—and Manu kicked her when she got too close. The poor thing ran off limping." Carolyn leaned in closer. "I don't think you should try too hard either."

"I swear I'm not trying to dig up the past. My only concern is what might happen in the future, and if Kai Kealoha is somehow involved in the current poisonings, he needs to be stopped."

"He's probably messed up in the head. My friend Tammy found one of those pink-pyjama girls crying by the side of the road last year. Couldn't have been more than sixteen. Didn't want to go back; wouldn't go to the cops. Me and Tammy, we cleaned her up, gave her a couple hundred bucks, and took her to the bus station in Hemet." Carolyn glanced toward the doorway. "Jake doesn't know."

"Was she okay? Where would she go?"

"She said she had a cousin in Colorado. Although I don't know if that was a real cousin. They're all brother, sister, cousin over at the ranch. The Promised Land, they call it. Bunch of pseudo-religious hokum, if you ask me."

"Did you ever meet any of the Kealoha family?"

She shook her head. "What would I even say to them? Offer help? Condolences? It's the kids I pity the most."

Footsteps signalled Jake's return, and Carolyn sat back in her chair. This mystery had the potential to be even messier than I first thought. Had Kai really been raised in a cult? He seemed so normal. Maybe he'd been deprogrammed or whatever it was they called it? Did he see a therapist?

Jake placed a thin cardboard folder on the table. "There are only my notes. The actual file is in the archive room at the station."

"He's very organised," Carolyn told me. "Everything in his office is tidied away just so."

As Jake opened the file, a piece of paper fluttered to the floor. No, not a piece of paper, a photograph. I picked it up to hand it back, then stopped short as I recognised the figure at the front of the picture. Not a boy, not quite a man. Teenage Kai had worn his hair long, but even when he sported an unkempt beard, there was no mistaking the face.

But that wasn't the only person I recognised.

Peeping out from behind her mom was a little girl. Joy Kealoha, I assumed. Except I didn't know her as Joy. I knew her as Erin, and I'd last seen her at the WST contest in Huntington Beach.

CHAPTER 44
ARI

"You're sure it's the same girl?" Alexa asked. It was the middle of the day, and she sounded tired. Had I woken her up?

"I'm seventy-five percent certain." Joy's hair had been very different from Erin's—long waves versus a pixie cut—and Erin wore dark make-up and a nose stud, but Morty Coulson had taught me to look past the things that could easily be changed and focus on the underlying features. "They have the same face shape. The same bone structure. Same skin tone, same build, same mouth."

"Erin… What else do you know about her?"

"Not much. We only had two brief conversations. She's a big Zach Torres fan, or so she claimed, and she picked me out as a hodad—"

"A what?"

"A hodad. Someone who hangs around the beach but doesn't surf. So I guess she does surf. She used to work in a grocery store, but she got fired for skipping a shift to go watch Zach surfing, and now she serves drinks in a strip club Mondays through Saturdays. Or at least, she did two months ago."

"Erin Kealoha. Or maybe Joy. Or she could have changed her surname… I'll take a look. Did you say there was another guy too?"

"Carson Hodges." That was the name Jake had given me for the neighbour, but his name hadn't come up anywhere else in the investigation. I'd double-checked Jankowski's reports. "He's probably in his fifties now. The deputy didn't remember much about him, but he was pretty sure Hodges came from Utah originally."

"Who gets priority?"

That was an easy question. "Erin."

Because *she* was the person following Zach around. Could she be working with her brother somehow to sabotage Zach's chances of winning the WST? If the two of them were colluding, it would be even more difficult to prove. They'd be able to cover for each other. Had she been at Surf 365 too? She could easily have stayed out of sight in a crowd of thousands, especially if she wore a wig. And if Kai left the back door of Zach's villa unlocked, she could have snuck in and switched out the Surf Star bottle, while Kai would have had the perfect alibi: Zach himself.

"Any idea where she lives?" Alexa asked.

"Not for definite, but during our first conversation at Pleasure Point, I got the impression she was local. She mentioned the big-tech crowd, so maybe try toward San Francisco?"

"I'm about to board a plane, but I'll let you know as soon as I have something. Are you going back to Santa Cruz?"

"I don't think there's much more I can do in Aguanga at the moment."

Out of interest, I'd driven past the Promised Land. The compound was surrounded by a chain-link fence topped with barbed wire, and when I tried buzzing the intercom at the gate, a camera atop the gatepost had swivelled to look down at me, but nobody answered. The place gave me the creeps.

"Chase will make a hotel reservation."

Another day, another fancy place to stay. This time, I was at the Forest Lodge Hotel and Spa. Halfway back from Aguanga, I'd gotten a call from Chase, apologising profusely for the lack of five-star accommodation in Santa Cruz. Would I rather have four stars beside the beach again, or four stars nestled in the forest? I'd told him to go with the cheapest option, which was why I was currently listening to birdsong on my private terrace among the towering redwoods.

Oh, I could definitely get used to this.

Although a sleep-in would be nice.

"Wherever Erin-slash-Joy is, she's living off-grid." The frustration in Alexa's voice was evident. "There are no breadcrumbs online. Zero. Zilch. For all intents and purposes, she doesn't exist."

"Not everyone in the world has internet access."

"Okay, we're talking the United States here. Weird cults aside, the majority of the population uses the Net. Which means she's hiding."

I was inclined to agree. But the question was, who from?

Right now, we had so many questions that it was overwhelming. There were only two of us, three if you counted Chase, and although Kai and Erin had jumped to the top of the suspect list, they weren't the only names on it. We needed to find her quickly and either rule her out or obtain proof of her involvement.

Time was of the essence. With every passing day, we got closer to the next contest, to another opportunity for the culprit to strike. But Erin was a ghost. A ghost who worked in a strip club, which meant there was only one thing left to do.

"How many strip clubs do you think there are in Santa Cruz?"

"None. Zoning doesn't allow them. But there are seven in San Jose and another three in Santa Maria." Why didn't it surprise me that Alexa already knew that? "Otherwise, we're talking Los Angeles."

"That's too far. More expensive to live there, too."

"I'll email a list with the details. You've got bikini bars, topless bars, and fully nude. I'd suggest starting with the seediest because those are the most likely to pay a server cash in hand."

There were times when men had a definite advantage in this business. I'd been to one or two strip clubs in Las Vegas—when you were hired to find evidence of infidelity, it was part of the job—but Morty had taken most of those cases. Not because I was a prude, but because most joints in Vegas didn't allow unescorted women to enter.

I'd spoken to a few of the performers, and while some tended to be wary of dancing for women, others said their money was just as good as men's, and apparently they tipped better. One girl from the Hustler Club had given me a good piece of advice—pretend to be a dancer myself, there to check the place out because I was thinking of auditioning. Easier said than done. Back in March when I'd been offered a job as a dancer instead of a cleaner, I'd tried one of those pole fitness classes just in case I was good at it, and looking sexy while hanging upside down was a lot harder than it looked.

"Don't forget to take your dollar bills," Chase called.

"It might not be that simple. Not every strip club welcomes a woman on her own."

"Do you have a friend you can take?" Alexa asked. "I could pay them for their time."

How embarrassing to admit that I really didn't have friends. Between working with Morty and taking care of Haven, I'd had no time for a social life, and before Zach, dating hadn't been on my bucket list. Perhaps that was why I missed Seagrass Point so much? Because I hadn't only lost the man I loved, I'd lost that whole support network.

"There isn't anyone. But I'll be allowed into some of the clubs, and I can stake out the others from the parking lot. It might take a bit longer, that's all." I tried to lighten the mood. "I'm not sure I'll be able to get a receipt for the dollar bills."

Alexa laughed. "I trust you. Do you need me to wire more cash?"

She trusts me. It might have been meant as a joke, but in the past week, I'd begun to trust her too. Even though we'd never met and I hadn't even seen her face, we worked well together. She was probably the most intriguing client I'd ever been involved with, even more so than Rennick. Alexa was an enigma. Down to earth yet mysterious, blunt but oddly thoughtful, an old head on young shoulders.

"More cash would be good."

San Jose:
Nip and Tuck
Blue Moon
Sunset Strip
Chubbys Sports Bar
Scores Gentlemen's Club and Steakhouse
Venus Cabaret
Secrets

Santa Maria:
Sin City
Heaven's Door
Cheetahs

Two cities, ten bars, nine days until the next round of the WST. Alexa and I had discussed the possibilities, and we both agreed that if our opponent was going to stay in the game, then he—or she—would strike in Hawaii. It was the last of the scheduled contests for this year. After that, the tour moved on to the big-wave format, and those dates were dependent entirely on the ocean swells. Crews remained on standby, and when the monsters began breaking, surfers had a couple of days to get their asses to the next venue. Maya said big-wave season was chaotic, and the betting would be equally frenzied.

Our scammer liked order.

Nip and Tuck sounded more like a cosmetic surgery clinic than a strip club, but the flashing *GIR S G RLS GIRLS* sign over the door gave the game away. The establishment scored a solid two-point-five stars in online reviews, with most of the better reviews coming from the "extras" offered by the women in the VIP rooms.

If Erin worked here, I felt sorry for her.

I glanced at the clock on the car's dash. Five to nine, and my "date" would be here soon. Yes, my date. Alexa had done the math. If I checked the clubs alone, I'd be able to do three a night if they let me inside, but only one if I had to sit in the parking lot, waiting for staff to come and go. And not only was time of the essence, but it was also money in Alexa's book. So she'd arranged for an escort to accompany me, because going to a strip club with a complete stranger was totally normal.

A red sports car pulled into the parking lot, and a man stepped out. Tall, lean, in his late thirties or early forties. Dark hair slicked back and scrappy goatee. He stubbed out a cigarette and flicked the end at a trash can, missed, and glanced around the lot, scratching his balls as he did so. *Oh, please no.* I held my breath until he headed for the club's entrance alone, then let it out in a whoosh. Damn Alexa and her mysteriousness. "He'll find you," she'd said. "Just chill out and wait for him to arrive."

A knock on the window made me jump out of my skin. My first thought was "cop," and my second thought was "wow."

Putting bias aside, if Zach was hot, then this guy was incendiary. Even in the shadows of the parking lot, that much was clear. Was the newcomer my fake date? Or a serial killer here to give me a pleasurable death? With one finger on the button of my rape alarm, I stepped out of the car. There was a bouncer standing in front of the club's entrance. A security camera mounted on a pole. This wasn't a good place to try any funny business.

The stranger shared the same blond hair as Zach, although his was a shade lighter and he wore it slicked back rather than all mussed up. A little preppy. Piercing blue eyes studied me, and he had cheekbones to die for. After a moment, he broke into a smile, displaying a row of perfect white teeth.

"Ari? It's good to finally meet you."

"What do you mean, 'finally meet me'?"

He held out a hand. "I'm Chase."

Holy fuck. *This* was Chase? This...this living god? He stood patiently, waiting for my brain to catch up, and after a mortifying length of time, I managed to shake his hand.

"I'm... I don't know what to say. I had no idea you were even in the US."

"Alexa's original idea was to hire an actor, but the first one we auditioned asked if the strippers were off-limits, and the second kept wanting to put his own spin on the role, whatever that meant. This seemed like the easiest option."

"Where is Alexa?" I glanced around, half expecting her to pop out of a parked car. The two of them did seem inseparable, after all.

"Oh, she's safely tucked up out of the way." Chase offered me an arm. "Let's go and check out the drinks menu."

He paid the cover charge at the door—fifteen bucks each —and we headed into the gloom, my heart pounding. I wasn't nervous, just…unsettled. Borrowing someone else's "companion" was weird, and even though this was work, spending time with another man when my heart belonged to Zach felt somehow disloyal.

The hostess—who wasn't Erin—showed us to a table near one of the stages, and I tried to ignore the gyrating dancers and focus on the other staff. Hell, there had to be thirty women in here, and the lighting was terrible. At least the servers wore halter tops and booty shorts. Staring at them would have been even more awkward otherwise. Would Erin wear a wig? Many of the staff seemed to do so.

Chase waved at a server, also not Erin, and when she hurried over, he ordered soft drinks. The girl—and no way was she older than twenty—couldn't take her eyes off him, although he seemed oblivious to her attention. I barely warranted a glance. And honestly, I couldn't blame her for that.

Chase was here. I had a million questions, and most of them had nothing to do with the case. While he spoke with the server, I took another moment to study him. He'd worn a tailored dress shirt tucked into slim grey suit pants, no tie. Broad shoulders and a taut stomach told me that despite Alexa's demanding nature, he still found the time to work out. How old was he? Twenty-six? Twenty-seven? Definitely no more than thirty.

"She seems to be enjoying her job." He nodded toward the stage, where a topless redhead ground against a pole as Beyoncé sang in the background. "Do you see anyone who could be Erin?"

"Not yet. This place is like a cave."

"There's a reason they keep the lights low."

Chase's tone was clinical, and apart from an initial, cursory glance, he didn't spend time looking at the dancers.

When Alexa had first suggested her "take a random man" plan, I thought I'd feel uncomfortable, but that wasn't the case. No, I felt safe. In person, Chase came across as detached, but he gave off calming vibes.

"Have you spent much time in strip clubs?" I asked him.

"No, but I worked in a bar once. Same vibe."

The server came back in record time and carefully placed Chase's drink in front of him on a paper coaster. Lemonade slopped over the edge of the glass as she set mine down, but Chase still gave her a twenty-dollar tip.

"Can I get you anything else, sir?"

"Not at this moment. Is Erin working tonight, my sweet?"

Puzzlement. "Erin?"

"Short hair, nose stud, loves to surf?"

"Sorry, I don't know her, but I'm new here."

"Maybe I got the name of the club wrong? We met at a party a few weeks ago, and she told me to look her up if I ever dropped by."

"You want I should ask around?"

He flashed her a smile, and even in the dim light, I saw her blush.

"If you wouldn't mind. Thank you…" He leaned forward to read her name badge. "Thank you, Misty."

Well, that was easier than I thought it would be. There were definite perks to having Chase tag along. The server skittered off, and he took a sip of his cola, then made a face.

"Who waters down soft drinks?"

"I don't think people come here for the beverages."

"So you read the online reviews too?"

"It's my job." I tried my own drink, and Chase was right. The lemonade was definitely on the weak side. "Are you allowed to tell me exactly who you are to Alexa? I've been hella curious, but she doesn't seem to invite questions."

"Who I am?"

"Personal assistant? Lover? Brother?"

"You don't mince your words, do you?"

"I thought you'd be used to that by now."

That got me a smile, but not the hundred-watt version. This was softer, somehow more intimate.

"Yes, I guess I am." He straightened his collar. "The answer is, I'm whatever Alexa wants me to be."

"That's not a real answer."

"It's the only one I'm able to offer at this time."

She had him well-trained, huh?

"Where are your glasses?"

"Why do you ask that?"

"Your avatar wears glasses."

A quiet chuckle. "Contacts."

Thank you. He'd just confirmed that his avatar had been designed as a reasonable likeness, which meant there was a good chance that Alexa was a blue-eyed blonde as well. Yet he hadn't reacted with horror earlier when I suggested they might be lovers, so I could probably rule him out as a sibling. Incest was the kind of thing a man would deny.

A dancer sidled up to him. "You wanna lap dance, sugar?"

"Not right now."

Undeterred, she turned to me. "How about you, honey-pie?"

I nearly choked on my drink, then realised I was meant to be playing it cool.

"No, thank you."

Chase tucked a fifty in her thong and gave her one of *those* smiles, which was worth another hundred.

"We'll let you know if we need anything."

But it turned out we didn't. Misty, the waitress, returned to confirm that nobody named Erin had worked at Nip and Tuck for at least a year, and the only female employee with short hair was "Destiny up on the stage." Even without the pumps, Destiny had to be at least six feet tall, so that definitely ruled her out. Chase gave Misty a hundred-dollar bill, and we headed for the exit. One down, nine to go.

"Where to next?" Chase asked.

"Chubbys Sports Bar is just around the corner. Topless waitresses, beer, and all the big games on a giant screen. The girls dance on the bar at halftime."

"Does Chubbys refer to the bar's owner or the employees' attributes?"

"I couldn't work that out. If Chubby owned the place, wouldn't you need an apostrophe?"

English hadn't been my best subject at school, but I'd learned the basics.

"Yes, but if it's referring to multiple plus-sized performers, then I'd spell it with I-E-S at the end."

"I guess we'll just have to go and find out."

By the end of the evening, we were still no further forward, not with our search for Erin or in identifying the origin of the name Chubbys. None of the girls who worked there was more than a size six, and the owner was a rail-thin prick named Donnie who sat at the end of the bar all night, drinking the profits and complaining about the girls' outfits. Erin didn't work there, and neither was she employed at Blue Moon or Sunset Strip. By five a.m., I'd listened to more Beyoncé songs than I could count, seen enough towering heels that my feet hurt in sympathy, and tucked several of Chase's hundred-dollar bills into the thong of a dead-eyed blonde who'd looked so miserable that I just wanted to wipe the glitter off her face and give her a hug.

I'd also learned a little more about Chase. Not his background or his surname or anything juicy like that, but I understood why Alexa kept him around. He was a real gentleman. Sure, he'd step in and out of character in the clubs as required, but when we were alone, he was kind and easygoing. Secretive, but not sleazy at all.

I liked him.

Not in the way I liked Zach—I'd never feel that way about any man again—but I couldn't have asked for a better partner tonight.

"Where are you staying?" I asked after we'd finished the night shift, and he just smiled, enigmatic this time. He had his own vehicle, another rental, a Mercedes the twin of mine.

"I'll meet you at Scores this evening. Eight o'clock?"

I nodded my agreement. "The steakhouse seems reasonable. Want to eat there before we head to Venus and Secrets?"

"It's been a while since I had a good rib-eye."

"Alexa doesn't do steak?"

"Alexa does filet mignon."

Expensive tastes, but that didn't surprise me. Everything about Alexa screamed "low-key wealth." The Mercedes "company cars" that Chase and I drove. Her constant under-the-radar travels. Chase himself. He wore good-quality, well-tailored clothes and shoes, but no flashy designer labels.

A real enigma.

Being the gentleman that he was, he insisted on seeing me back to my hotel, and when he departed from the parking lot, I considered following him. There was a possibility that Alexa was somewhere nearby. But as I sat in my car, drumming my fingers on the steering wheel, I decided to stay put. Alexa had put her trust in me, and invading her carefully guarded privacy would be a breach of that trust.

If she ever wanted to reveal herself, it was her choice to make.

In the meantime, I'd be grateful for the chance she'd given me to help Zach, and I'd damn well make sure he stayed safe.

CHAPTER 45
ZACH

"How are we feeling about strip clubs?"

Zach groaned and slumped across the breakfast bar in the rented Hawaiian villa. This was the problem with Tyler—he hated to spend a night alone. Maya kidded that he was like a dog with separation anxiety—the man had some kind of genetic need for company.

"Strip clubs? I'm feeling that I don't want to go to one."

This past Tuesday in Seagrass Point, they'd decided on a cookout, just the four of them—Zach, Kai, Tyler, and Maya. But on the way up the driveway at Zach's place, Tyler had rounded up the seven groupies waiting outside and invited them in for dinner. Maya hadn't been happy at all, and Zach had ended up calling cabs at eleven p.m. in a not-so-subtle hint to get the girls to skedaddle. Worse, word had gotten around, and by the time he, Kai, and Tyler left for Oahu, there were twenty women lolling around outside the gates.

And now that they were overseas, Tyler was determined to continue where he'd left off.

"Aw, c'mon. Three single guys on vacation, we gotta have fun."

Kai glanced up from his book. "I *am* having fun. And what happened to keeping a low profile?"

Tyler made another attempt at persuasion. "For once, we don't have Maya here to cramp our style. We should make the most of it."

Wait, what?

"You think Maya 'cramps our style'? That's my sister you're talking about. Do you have any idea how much she does for us? Right now, she's at home, running the office and waiting on our new shorts and leashes to be delivered so we could come here and surf."

Tyler must have picked up on the warning in Zach's tone. "Hey, man, it was only a figure of speech. I just meant that we wouldn't take her to a strip club."

"I'm not spending the evening in a fucking strip club. If you want to go, you know where the door is."

"You need to loosen up."

"Just because I don't want to watch girls shaking their tits in front of me doesn't mean I have to loosen up."

"You're in danger of getting stuck in some weird, self-induced celibacy cycle."

"So?"

"So, there's plenty more fish in the sea. Ari was just one woman."

Not for the first time, Zach wished he'd stayed at home. The waves were breaking all along the North Shore, but his heart wasn't in surfing this week. And Tyler was asking to get his damn nose broken.

"Shut the fuck up. Ari was *the* woman, not *a* woman."

"Bullshit. She lied to you. Whatever you built her up to be in your head, she wasn't it."

"Stop! Just fucking *stop*. You call yourself a friend?"

"Yeah, because a friend tells you the truth, even if that truth hurts."

Kai put the book down and stood, hands out like a referee.

"Both of you need to stop. Remember the old days? When we had to decide between food or surf wax? We survived because we stuck together, and now we're here on this beautiful island with great swells and time to enjoy them. We've bought our own homes. We're financially secure. We're healthy, and we're still young. Let's be thankful for what we have rather than chasing what we don't."

Zach stomped over to the refrigerator and grabbed a beer. Out of habit, he checked that the top was securely in place before he flipped it off with the shark-shaped bottle opener attached to his keys. Ari had bought him that key ring, just a little gift for no reason other than she'd seen it and thought it might make him smile.

But his friends were right. Even Tyler, although he hated to admit it. Arizona wasn't his dream woman, and he needed to accept that fact. He was pining for something he'd never truly had. Kai, Tyler, and Maya had supported him before Ari appeared on the scene, and they were still here. Yes, Baylee had tried to corrupt Tyler, but he'd seen the light. Now Zach had to do the same.

He had to move on.

Maybe Ari had been right about Baylee, but now she'd served her purpose. She'd done the job she was paid to do, and although her betrayal hurt, he had to be grateful that she'd briefly fought in his corner. As time passed and the pain began to fade, he saw that. He also saw that she hadn't known his friends the way he did. Ari had suspected Maya, for crying out loud, and for a moment, she'd planted seeds of doubt in Zach's head too.

Yeah, she'd done a real number on him.

But removed from the source of the problem, he could begin to heal. He had to. What were the other options? Working out his anger in the army like Dawson? Dropping off the face of the earth like Jerry? Fucking anything that moved like Tyler? Turning into a paranoid recluse like Alexa?

Alexa... Now, there was a woman who'd give Ari a run for her money in the twisted stakes. Alexa's moral compass didn't just point in a different direction, it resided on a whole other planet where the normal rules of physics didn't apply.

He still remembered the day she'd come to live in Blackstone House. Dawson had brought her home, a skinny waif he'd found living in a crypt, of all places. She'd claimed to be sixteen, but she looked more like twelve. After some back and forth, they'd settled on fifteen, and Greyson wanted to call Child Protective Services. Alexa said she'd just run away again, and nobody doubted that was true. In those days, Levi had seemed like a good guy, and he'd agreed to her renting the empty storage room in the basement, a dark little hole where the only light came from a narrow window near the ceiling. But Alexa was happy with the arrangement. The rent was fifty bucks a week, and she got a job moderating chat rooms to pay for it. Or so she'd claimed. In Blackstone House, it had been an open secret that Alexa was a hacker, although nobody had realised quite how good of a hacker until after Ruby died. White hat, black hat, and everything in between. There was a standing joke among the housemates— never click on an email attachment from Alexa.

Anyhow, for the most part, they'd barely noticed Alexa was there. She rarely emerged from her basement hideaway, although she'd contributed to the renovation in a big way by designing and acquiring the security system. Jerry, Justin, and Dawson had helped her to install it. Out of all the Blackstone housemates, Ruby had made the most effort to befriend her, always checking in and making sure she ate. And Alexa had shown a weird affinity for Nolan, probably because he did most of the cooking. She'd graduated from living on crackers to ordering gourmet ingredients from every corner of the planet, and Nolan was always happy to prepare the dishes.

World domination undoubtedly took a lot of energy.

That Alexa broke the law was in no doubt. That she was a

genius was in no doubt. That she loved fancy food was in no doubt. But beyond that, none of the Blackstone crew knew much about her, even after living with her for two years. Greyson, who liked to understand everything, was convinced she was on the spectrum. Asperger's, he said. Zach had done some reading and thought that maybe he was right, but Ruby said that they shouldn't try to pigeonhole people with labels. Alexa was just Alexa.

And Ari was just Ari.

A beautiful, smart, courageous, sweet illusion.

"I'm sorry I snapped," Zach said. "It's been a difficult month, that's all, and I know it hasn't been easy for you guys either."

Tyler offered a grin. "No problem. Does that mean—"

"We're still not going to a strip club."

"How about nachos and baseball?"

That was a compromise Zach could live with. He took another bottle of beer and a soda from the refrigerator, passed them to his friends.

"Who's playing?"

CHAPTER 46
ARI

"Well, that's a bust."

Chase tilted his head critically and eyed the woman gyrating ten feet away. "I'd give it an eight."

"Eight? Why only an eight?"

"It's out of proportion, and the bikini doesn't suit her skin tone."

After visiting eight strip clubs and seeing boobs in every size, shape, and colour possible, I had to concede that he'd become something of an expert, although not once had he tried to touch.

"I guess I can see where you're coming from. But that wasn't what I meant."

"No Erin?"

"We've been here for two hours, and I can't see her."

Our server in Cheetahs was working her first day, and she hadn't been as helpful as Misty at Nip and Tuck. We'd been forced to order several rounds of drinks and watch the endless parade of skin on the club's main stage as I surreptitiously checked out the other staff. San Jose had been a total washout, and tonight, we'd moved on to Santa Maria. I was hoping the four-hour drive would be worth it.

"What's next on the list?"

"Sin City."

Which was the closest I'd get to home for a few more days at least.

Visiting gentlemen's clubs on a Saturday night had both pros and cons. The advantage was that more staff worked when the places were busy, giving us a better opportunity to spot Erin. The disadvantage? Every club was packed with rowdy customers, most of them drunk.

Sin City had a sign fashioned after the famous one on the Strip. *Welcome to Fabulous Sin City.* Although online reviewers rated it slightly higher than Cheetahs, I had to dispute the "fabulous" part. My feet stuck to the floor as soon as we crossed the threshold. Hadn't these people ever heard of a mop?

Chase's faint grimace echoed my own feelings. I'd gotten to know him a little better over the past several days, and he didn't tend to show much emotion. The big smiles were all fake. He'd been a model once, he'd confessed over lunch yesterday—magazines, not runway—which was possibly where he'd learned to turn his expressions on and off at will. Yes, we'd eaten lunch together. I'd been surprised to find him in the hotel dining room, his hair still damp from the shower.

"What are you doing here?" I'd asked. "I thought you were staying somewhere else?"

Maybe the four-star hotel with the ocean view rather than the redwoods?

Chase gifted me a small smile, one of the rare genuine ones.

"Alexa wanted to see if you'd try to tail me this morning."

Damn, that had been a test? I'd almost failed it.

"What would have happened if I had?"

"She would have been irritated."

"Would she have fired me?"

Chase considered the question for a moment before finally shaking his head. "I don't think so. Probably because in your position, she'd definitely have followed. But she'd have considered it a breach of trust, and that would have made us both warier. I wouldn't be having lunch with you now."

Well, that had settled the question of whether I should take the other seat at his table. We'd eaten lunch together today as well, and I was beginning to understand how Alexa worked. If you gained her trust, she'd give you little pieces of herself. In this case, she'd sent Chase, and because I'd respected their privacy, I was allowed to spend more time with him. From Alexa, that was a gift. She wasn't in the hotel herself—I'd gleaned that much. No, Chase had stashed her somewhere else.

Alexa and I did speak over the messenger app, discussions about strategy after I updated her on our limited progress. In an ideal world, we'd find Erin and observe her covertly, track her to see where she went and who she spoke with. But this wasn't an ideal world, and time—or rather, the lack of it—was the critical factor. If we didn't identify our nemesis by the end of the Hawaiian round, our chances of catching them would decrease markedly. If they cut their losses, the trail would go cold, and if they doubled down and carried on with their sick plan, we'd go through all this again next season.

Which was why, when I spotted Erin carrying a tray toward a group of sweaty businessmen, I didn't turn around and leave. No, I just squeezed Chase's arm in a prearranged signal and nodded in her direction. He didn't react, merely thanked the hostess as she seated us at a small table near the main stage.

"Erin will be looking after you tonight."

I blew out a breath as the hostess walked away.

"This should be interesting," Chase murmured, then grimaced faintly. "My seat is damp."

Gross. "I definitely don't want to see this place with the lights on."

And then she was there, larger than life and twice as vibrant, thanks to the neon stripes in her hair.

"Hey, folks. What can I get ya?"

It was a line more suited to a diner than a gentlemen's club, but she was perky enough to pull it off. Then she leaned forward and squinted.

"Ari? Non-surfer chick? Is that you?" She didn't wait for an answer before focusing on Chase. "Wait, wait, wait. You are *not* Zach." Her mouth dropped open. "Ohmigosh! You're cheating on *Zach Torres*?"

Her voice had risen high enough that the guy at the next table took his eyes off the brunette grinding on his lap to stare. Crap, this was even more awkward than I'd expected.

"I'm not cheating on Zach."

"The hell you aren't. No guy brings a girl here if they're just friends, believe me, and Zach totally doesn't deserve this."

Okay, I didn't have "getting chewed out by the server" on my list of things to do in a strip club. When I glanced at Chase, his lips were twitching. Well, I was glad one of us was having fun.

"You don't understand; we broke up."

"What? Did you lose your mind? I mean, this dude's pretty 'n' all, but you had *Zach Torres*."

"Actually, it was him who dumped me."

"Oh. I guess that makes more sense."

"Do you find you get better tips if you insult your customers?"

"Shit! Uh, sorry?"

The guy beside us decided to join the conversation. "Can you keep it down? You're ruinin' the ambience."

Ambience? Sheesh. But I held back my retort when I saw the woman on his lap trying to move away. He held her in place with hairy paws that would have put Bigfoot to shame.

"We're not done, darlin'."

Erin stepped forward. "Hey, you're not allowed to touch the dancers."

"I paid for her, so I'll do whatever I damn well want."

The woman tried to remove his hand from her thigh, but he clamped it tight while the other moved up to squeeze her breast. Erin looked around frantically, presumably for security, but there were no bouncers in sight. I considered pulling out my pepper spray. No, not indoors. My stun gun? That might work. But before I could reach for my purse, Erin grabbed a pitcher of water from a nearby table and upended it over the asshole's head.

With a roar, he threw the dancer to the side, and I mean *threw*. She landed with a yelp, a heap of tan skin and spangled Lycra. Then he went for Erin. He hooked an arm around her waist and grabbed her face with the other, twisting her neck at an unnatural angle as he forced her to look at him.

"You think you can throw water at me, little girl?"

Fuck, where was the damn stun gun?

Heart thumping, I took my eyes off the two of them for a second to rummage in my purse. I really needed to get a new one, something with internal pockets so my stuff didn't get all jumbled up. At least I knew the batteries in the stunner were fresh—I'd replaced them after I fried Jankowski's family jewels.

But before I managed to get my hands on my weapon, I heard a grunt, followed by the sound of splintering wood. What the...?

Chase had Bigfoot on the floor, one meaty arm forced behind his back. When the asshole tried to rise, Chase applied more pressure, and the giant's yelp put the stripper's to shame. Wow. I was breathing harder than Chase, and I hadn't even done anything.

"Are you okay?" I asked Erin.

She nodded, and I dropped to my knees beside the dancer. She'd rolled to her knees now, groaning, and every head in the club had turned to look at us. In the background, Beyoncé sang away.

"Did he hurt you?"

"My…my ankle."

That wasn't a surprise. Her heels had to be six inches high.

"Can you get up? Here, take my arm."

She made it to her feet just as security finally showed up, hovering like besuited robots behind a short guy with a moonish face and a comb-over. Chase allowed his prisoner to stand as well, presumably with the intention of turning him over to Terminator and RoboCop.

"What's going on here?" Moonface demanded.

I was about to tell him that his security team had been asleep on the job, but the asshole got in first.

"That crazy bitch threw water over me."

A slice of lemon too—it was wedged in the neck of his shirt.

"Which bitch are we talking about, sir?"

Sir?

He pointed at Erin. "That one. Bad hair, bad attitude."

Now wait a minute… "He was molesting the dancer."

Moonface turned to the nearly naked woman. "Crystal, is this true?"

"It was just a misunderstanding."

Chase tried to help. "He had his hands all over her."

But Moonface was already shaking his head. "You…" He jerked a thumb at Erin. "You're done here."

Seriously? He was firing her? "But—"

"Do you know who this is? This is State Senator Adams's

son. If Crystal says it was a misunderstanding, then it was a misunderstanding."

The robots closed in, and the asshole smirked as they herded us out of Sin City. I wasn't sorry to see the back of the place, but anger simmered inside me. Moonface was a world-class jerk. If Erin was involved in the plot against Zach, then losing her job would be karma, but the more time we'd spent visiting strip clubs, the more trouble I had believing that she was in cahoots with Kai. Because Kai had money, not as much as Zach, but he was still well-off. Would he really let his sister work in a dump like Sin City rather than giving her a helping hand the way Zach did with Maya?

My job was to find out.

When we got outside, Erin walked over to a white Cadillac parked beside the entrance and kicked it.

"Jackass."

I'd hazard a guess that the Caddy belonged to Moonface. Chase's expression didn't change, but he did pull out his phone and snap a picture of the licence plate as I offered comfort to Erin.

"I'm sorry you lost your job."

"It was a crappy job, but I still need to make the rent. Damn politicians." A tear rolled down her cheek, glistening in the light from the neon sign. "I can't help having short hair."

"The cut suits you."

"You think so?"

"It's cute."

"I was going for edgy."

"Edgy-cute. Do you have a ride home?"

"I usually take the bus."

"Does the bus run at this time?"

"I catch the first one in the morning."

"But it's ten minutes after midnight."

"I live nearly an hour away, and I gotta get my stuff back

anyway." She glanced at the squat grey building that housed Sin City. "My purse is in my locker. My sneakers too."

"We'll give you a ride wherever you need to go. Will you be able to get to your locker?"

"There's a door at the side. The dickwad won't even notice. You'll really give me a ride?"

"We'll be waiting here when you get back."

Erin strode off, shoulders set, and Chase watched her go.

"Think she'll be okay?" he asked.

"Physically? I don't think anyone's gonna stop her from emptying her locker." Then I nudged him. "You're a dark horse, aren't you? Did I get it wrong? You're Alexa's bodyguard?"

He barked out a laugh. "The aikido? That's just the fruits of a misspent youth."

"Do you have any other special skills?"

"Maybe."

"Are you gonna tell me what they are?"

"No."

My turn to laugh. I wouldn't have expected him to say anything else.

"So, how are we planning to do this? I don't want to corner Erin in the car. That's just low."

"Let's give her a ride as you promised. That way, we'll know where she lives, and we can ask her a few questions before she goes inside her home."

The drive to the two-bedroom apartment Erin shared with five others was…harrowing. She didn't mean it to be. In fact, she was more upbeat than I could ever have been in her position. She apologised for being tearful—apologised—and confessed that the asshole had struck a nerve with his "bad hair" insult. The pixie cut was a necessity after a bout of stress-induced alopecia, the third time in her life that she'd lost most of her hair. She was one hundred and thirty bucks short for the rent at the end of the month, and that was if she didn't buy any more food. But there was always ramen, right? And she actually asked if *I* was okay.

"You and Zach were so perfect for each other. I followed the story online. Not like a stalker or anything, honest, but who doesn't check out his Insta? And he looked so happy. Like, smilier."

"We had some differences that couldn't be resolved."

"That's super sad. His Twitter fan club gave you one of those couple names, did you know that? Zari. Zach and Ari."

"No, I didn't know that."

And the more she spoke, the less I thought she was involved. If she and Kai were working together, why couldn't *he* give her a hundred and thirty bucks? I'd helped Maya with his admin. I knew how much he spent on surf wax and guitar picks and organic smoothies. By the time we reached the sorry-looking building his sister called home, I wanted to pay the rent myself. I'd always thought my life had been hard, but Erin's had been ten times harder. She'd survived a cult, only to live hand to mouth in a sweltering apartment—the landlord refused to fix the AC—with one creep who scared her and four other roommates she merely disliked.

I hated to hurt her further.

But I had to.

I had to be sure.

As Chase brought the car to a halt, I twisted in my seat.

"Why are you here in California, Joy?"

In all my years in the investigative business, I'd never seen such a look of shock, even when, on one memorable job, I'd watched a man and his mistress get surprised in a seedy motel room by his other mistress, who was carrying a baseball bat. The wife who hired us had been devastated by the betrayal, but after the divorce settlement, she'd sent me a box of candy and a thank-you card.

Erin turned white and clutched at her chest, and I really

hoped that one of Chase's secret skills involved medical training. Then she scrabbled for the door handle.

"Don't take me back there! Don't! I'd rather die."

She threw open the door and tried to run, but she'd forgotten to unclip her seat belt, so instead she just hung there, hyperventilating as I leapt out to assist.

"Get away from me!"

"We're not taking you anywhere. We brought you home."

"Who are you people? Did the Prophet send you? I haven't said a word to anyone, I swear."

A word about what?

"Let me help you."

She began crying, great racking sobs that didn't help with the seat-belt situation. I'd wanted to provoke a reaction, but not this one. Not sheer terror. Chase took her weight while I untangled her, and now she looked at us with fear rather than friendliness. In that moment, I hated myself. Why was *I* here in California? To break people. First, I'd hurt Zach, and now I'd done the same to Erin.

"Just answer me one question: are you working with Kai?"

"Kai? I...I haven't s-s-spoken to Kai in n-n-nearly ten years."

I believed her. Nobody could fake this kind of emotion, not even Violet Miller. Which meant we'd exhausted another lead in the case, but we were left with a woman whose life we'd just turned upside down. Erin slumped to the ground, leaning against the car's rear wheel as she wept.

"Hey, it's okay. We're not from People's Promise."

"Then w-w-why are you here?"

"It's a long story. The short version is that someone's been trying to harm Zach, and we thought you might be involved."

"Huh? I'd never hurt Zach."

"Even if it helped your brother?"

Fear turned to confusion, which was a marginal improvement.

"I don't understand? Kai and Zach are friends. Hurting a friend wouldn't help Kai, it would destroy him."

"But Kai might have done something similar in the past. Someone's been tampering with Zach's drinks, and there was an incident with your father..." Aaaaaand the tears were back. "I'm sorry for your loss."

Chase leaned down with a handkerchief, but instead of wiping away her tears, Erin twisted the pristine white cotton in her hands, biting her lip so hard she drew blood. How I wished we could turn back the clock. I'd been ninety percent certain she wasn't involved, but I'd just had to push it for that last ten, hadn't I?

"I understand how hard it is to lose a father."

"Do you? Did your father die too?"

"No, but he went to jail when I was very young."

"Then you were one of the lucky ones."

What? What did she mean by that? I recalled Jake Smith's comment about the bruises. Had Manu Kealoha harmed his daughter as well as his wife?

"Your father abused you?"

Instead of answering the question, she looked me in the eye with surprising ferocity.

"Whatever you think Kai did, he didn't do it. My brother has a good heart. He saved me. Do you understand that? He saved me."

Was Erin saying what I thought she was saying? That Kai had laced their father's Kool-Aid with ethylene glycol to free his sister from the man's evil clutches? Fuck? The information was dynamite, but what was I meant to do with it?

The answer?

Nothing, not right now. Not when I had a devastated woman to take care of. Gone was the upbeat Erin that I'd met at Pleasure Point. I'd torn open old wounds, leaving her raw in the dirt, pain bleeding out.

"What can I do to help?"

The question was directed at Erin, but Chase was the one who answered, calm as always.

"We can do whatever Erin needs."

When he lifted her back into the car, she didn't protest, and I sat on the door sill holding her limp hand in mine until the tears subsided. Chase stood guard, ever vigilant, and when a trio of teenagers approached, he stared them down. They kept walking.

Finally, Erin's tears turned into sniffles.

"You want us to walk you inside?" I asked. "I'll pay your rent this month, okay? You don't need to worry about that."

She shook her head. "The creep's there, but he leaves for work at six. I'll go back after that."

"You can't stay outside all night."

"There's a twenty-four-hour diner two blocks away. If I buy a coffee, the waitress lets me sit there for as long as I want."

"We can wait with you. Buy you dinner. Well, breakfast."

Chase sidled away, and I heard him speaking on the phone, too softly for me to make out the words. Who was he calling? Alexa? Was he telling her that I'd screwed up and set off a chain reaction that had resulted in a young woman's breakdown?

"You don't have to wait. I'll survive. I always do."

"I'm sure that's true, but I don't like leaving you. And I'm sorry about earlier. The fight, and also that I misrepresented myself. My goal is to keep Zach safe, and there's a fine balance between being mindful of people's feelings and acting fast enough to prevent another incident. Sometimes I wobble."

"Is that why you and Zach broke up? Or was that some fake-dating scheme? Were you ever really together?"

"Yes, we were together, but only for a few days. Then he found out I was a private investigator who'd been hired to spy on him, and I'm sure you can imagine how that went."

"And someone tried to put antifreeze in his drink?"

"Not antifreeze, but other things."

"That sucks. He seems like a nice guy."

"Are you really his biggest fan? Because that would be a weird coincidence."

"If I say up front that I'm a Zach Torres fan, nobody ever asks more questions. Most people just figure I'm like one of those crazies that hang around outside his house, and then they avoid me."

"But you're actually there for Kai?" I guessed.

There was no mistaking the sadness in her tone. "It's the only chance I get to see him."

"The two of you don't speak anymore?"

"After everything that happened, he left the Promised Land. You know what that is?"

I nodded.

"He left, and that was it. Poof. He was gone, and he never tried to get in touch. Not that I can blame him for that. But I always missed him. I thought I'd never see him again, but two years after I escaped, there he was on the TV."

"You escaped?"

"Yup. It's not like summer camp. You can't just quit if you're not having a good time. I snuck out in the night with thirty bucks, half a loaf of bread, and a kitchen knife in case that motherfucker tried to come after me."

"Which motherfucker? Did your mom remarry? I heard she was having an affair with the neighbour."

"Oh, yeah, she married him, like, three weeks after the burial. But I was talking about my husband."

With every sentence Erin uttered, this got worse and worse. At least she'd stopped crying now, but I feared the next tears would be mine.

"You were married?"

"To the Prophet's brother. Wife number five."

"He had five wives?"

"You'd think it wouldn't be so bad if he lost one, right? But I've seen girls run away and get brought back before, and boy, do they suffer for their disobedience. I'm *not* going to spend the rest of my life cleaning out pigs."

"And you figured that's why Chase and I came here? To take you back?"

"After seven years, I'd started to let my guard down."

"Seven years?" According to Jake Smith, Erin was only twenty-two now. "You left when you were fifteen?"

Her words gradually sank in. She'd been *married* at fifteen? Holy shit.

"I'd just had a miscarriage, and I knew that if I didn't leave then, I'd be trapped there forever."

Her matter-of-fact tone gave me chills. As if she'd grown so used to the grocery list of horrors, they no longer had the power to shock.

"Did you call the police? I mean, isn't that statutory rape?"

I wasn't totally up to speed on the rules for marriage in California, but married and pregnant against her will at the age of fifteen? That had to be illegal, right?

"The police don't help people like me."

"But—"

"Did you get what you want yet? Or do you need to keep squeezing for that last drop of blood? I don't need people telling me how to live my life."

Chase cleared his throat from behind us. "Then this could get slightly awkward."

We both turned to face him.

"Erin, you're not staying here."

"The hell I'm not. I don't have anywhere else to go."

"Nobody should have to sleep in a place where they feel unsafe."

"Now you sound like the freaking Prophet. He spewed that bullshit. Everyone should live in utopia, a land of love, abundant food, free homes for everyone, blah, blah, blah. And yeah, the People's Council provided housing, but we paid for that. Not in money, but with our damn sanity."

"This world is far from utopian; we can agree on that."

"So what's your point?"

"The point is that we're going to rent you a new apartment so you can get back on your feet."

"If you're gonna lie, you could at least try to be convincing."

"I'm not lying. A friend of ours understands what it's like to be homeless at a young age, and they've offered to sponsor you for a year."

"That's a pile of crap."

"Do you have anything you want to bring with you?"

"What are you gonna do if I tell you to get lost? Kidnap me?"

"No, but we'll have to remove the creep, which could get messy, and that would still leave you living in an apartment that's only one phone call away from being condemned."

"You people are assholes, did anyone ever tell you that?"

"Once or twice," Chase said.

"Way more times than that," I added. "Although 'bitch' is more common."

In the end, Erin acquiesced. Chase didn't leave her with much choice. In today's society, money equalled power, and he was being bankrolled by Alexa. The creep wasn't happy about being woken in the middle of the night, but Chase was two inches taller than him and forty pounds heavier, so he just stood in the corner of the kitchen whining about the noise while I helped Erin to pack up her things. She didn't have much, just a few items of clothing, a plastic bag full of toiletries, and the world's tiniest wooden surfboard.

By two thirty, we were in the car and heading back to the hotel, exhausted. And I had no idea what tomorrow would bring.

CHAPTER 47
ARI

One big advantage of the Forest Lodge Hotel and Spa? The room service menu offered eight different kinds of coffee. I ordered three of them on Sunday morning because, boy, did I need the caffeine.

Five a.m. had come and gone by the time I crawled into bed last night, and even though it was ten o'clock now, I'd barely slept. I'd been worrying for days about how to approach Erin, but the showdown at Sin City had gone worse than I'd ever imagined.

And we still had the fallout to deal with.

Plus a case to solve.

And when I said "we," I meant "me" because I had no idea how long Chase planned to stick around now that we'd finished the strip club assignment. I drained the espresso, then picked up coffees number two and three and headed for Erin's room along the hallway. Chase had sweet-talked the hotel's night manager, and he'd had the key waiting for us when we arrived back.

As I knocked, I wondered if Erin might have done a vanishing act, but after a long minute, the chain on the inside of the door rattled.

"Did I wake you?"

"I couldn't sleep. Do you know if the breakfast here is free?"

"It's included in the room rate. Can I come in for a moment?"

She opened the door wide enough for me to slip through. "I guess. Is that guy for real? The Ken-doll guy? He said someone would sponsor me."

"He's for real."

"What does 'sponsor' even mean? Because I don't do the sugar daddy thing. I tried it for, like, three weeks, and the guy wanted me to shave my bits and dress up as a little girl."

"Your sponsor is female. And I guess she'll help out with your rent and maybe your living expenses."

"I don't do women either."

"She's not expecting sexual favours."

"Then what's the catch?"

"Honestly? I'm not sure. I don't think there is one, although if you can shed any light on Kai's background, we'd be grateful."

"Whoa, whoa, whoa. I'm not gonna give you dirt on my brother, no matter how much you pay me."

"Nobody's asking you for dirt. But we don't have much time left to narrow down the suspect list, so any information you could offer would be useful. Kai's such a private person, and we really don't know him well."

"I still don't understand what's going on, and Kai keeps quiet for a reason. You're not a reporter, are you?"

"I already told you that I'm a PI."

"What if you're lying?" Erin took a step back. "What if you're a sex trafficker? One of the dancers at Sin City, she nearly got kidnapped by some psycho who drugged her and drove her to Salt Lake City."

"I don't think sex traffickers shell out four hundred bucks for a hotel room."

Erin stared around the room with newfound appreciation. "Four hundred bucks? That's nearly a month's rent. The little bottles in the bathroom—are we allowed to keep those?"

"Yes, and the cookies in the basket by the TV."

"What will happen tonight? Where am I meant to go?"

"We'll probably stay here again."

"Another four hundred bucks? You people are crazy."

"Believe me, I understand where you're coming from."

"Do you? I bet you never had to build a cardboard wall around your bed because your roommate likes to watch you as you sleep."

"No, but when I'm not sleeping in a four-hundred-dollar-a-night hotel room, I share a one-bedroom apartment with my nana and my daughter, and that's where I'll go back to when this is over."

Now Erin eyed me curiously. "You have a daughter? How old is she?"

"She just turned nine."

Her voice dropped to a whisper. "I was so scared when I was pregnant. Mama told me that it was normal, that everyone had kids, but Kai told me she nearly bled out when I was born, which is why there were only two of us."

"You and Kai were close?"

A nod. "He's five years older than me, but we always looked out for each other."

"Have you tried to contact him in recent years?"

A shake of the head.

"Why not?"

A shrug. "Things were kind of awkward between us when he left. I guess... I guess I'd rather imagine that maybe he doesn't hate me than speak to him and find out he does."

Kai didn't strike me as a hateful person, but who knew what a place like the Promised Land did to a man's psyche? Erin surely understood her brother better than I did. They'd both lived the experience, every awful day of it.

"But you watch him surfing? Isn't that a risk?"

"Not really. He gets into this zone, and he doesn't see anything but the waves. Zach too—haven't you noticed? I only go if there's a crowd, and I always leave before Kai finishes the session."

Erin was calmer this morning. Less hostile. Still a far cry from the bubbly girl I'd met at Pleasure Point, but I'd take what I could get.

"Do you surf much yourself?"

"No, but I skimboard every chance I get."

"That's what the tiny board is?"

"I can't take a surfboard on the bus."

"Have you ever learned to drive?"

"I don't have a licence. And even if I did, I couldn't afford to run a car, so what's the point? Did Zach teach you to surf?"

"The one time I ended up in the ocean, he had to rescue me. But he taught me to swim."

"Kai taught me. There was a swimming hole at the ranch, and in the summer, we used to sneak off there at dawn before anyone else woke up. At least, we did until one of the elders caught me there in my underwear."

"Underwear? With Kai?"

"It wasn't, like, incest or anything. We just weren't allowed bathing suits. The choices were fully clothed, underwear, or naked. Did you see those stupid baggy pants we had to wear? They dragged you under. Plus I had to find a way of drying them afterward without anyone noticing. Are you honestly a private investigator?"

She seemed real hung up on that part.

"You can verify my licence on the State of Nevada website if you want."

"My phone ran out of data."

"You want to use—"

A knock at the door interrupted me, and when Erin made

no move to open it, I did so myself. Chase looked good considering the amount of sleep he hadn't had. No dark shadows under his eyes, hair neatly combed, clothes without a single wrinkle. Me? I'd slept in my leggings, and I felt a deep sense of shame that I hadn't changed my underwear today.

"Good morning."

"Is it?" Erin asked.

"You're not a glass-half-full person, are you?"

"Can you blame me? Have you guys had breakfast yet? I'm super hungry."

There was that lip twitch again. "I rarely eat breakfast."

"It's the most important meal of the day, didn't anyone ever tell you that?" Erin paused for a moment, lips scrunched as she pondered. "Actually, that's dumb. All meals are important."

The twitch turned into a smile. "You sound like Alexa."

"Who's Alexa?"

"The person who's offered to pay your rent for the next year."

"With no sexual favours involved," I added.

Chase looked at me funny. "What?"

"Just a joke."

His gaze switched between us, but finally, he shrugged. "We should discuss the logistics, and we can do that over breakfast if you like. Should I order pain au chocolat?"

"Pain au chocolat? What, are we French now?"

"You'd prefer pancakes?"

Erin considered the question. "I'd prefer both."

A half hour later, we sat down to a feast. Chase had made the mistake of allowing Erin to look at the room service menu, and pain au chocolat and pancakes had become one of everything. As we waited, he'd laid out the plan: Alexa would pay for rent on an "average" one-bedroom apartment as well as covering the damage deposit, utility costs, and medical insurance, and she'd also provide a weekly allowance of two hundred dollars. Damn, I could have done with a Guardian Alexa myself when I was younger.

Now we were looking at apartments online while we ate, a brief respite before I spoke with our esteemed leader to brainstorm the next move. Less than a week until Zach took to the water in Hawaii, and we still had no definite suspect. Baylee was off the table. Erin flatly denied that Kai would risk harming a friend, and Alexa didn't think Maya was involved, although there was still a huge question mark over her dalliance with Zed Nelson. Which left Tyler and Gloria, neither of whom had a great motive. Gloria's husband, Alvaro, had health issues, and Tyler was looking to buy a surf store, both of which would require money. Jankowski had mentioned medical debt, but Alvaro held a managerial position, and his employer offered insurance for comparable roles—I'd checked the details on the careers section of the company's website. Had Jankowski made a mistake? Or perhaps Alvaro was being crippled by copays? And Memphis had said that Tyler was seeking bank funding. Why would he do that if he had several years' worth of kickbacks tucked away?

Nothing made sense. Somehow, I had to unravel all of those loose threads, and I had to do it fast.

But after waffles and bacon.

"What do you think of this one?" Erin asked.

Chase checked out the listing—Erin had borrowed his laptop. "Where is it?"

"Santa Cruz. It has a communal pool, and a laundry room, and an elevator, and a balcony, and it's, like, five minutes from the grocery store." Her enthusiasm waned. "But none of that stuff is essential. It's too expensive, right?"

"No, it's fine."

"Really? I'll totally pay you back for this. I mean, I don't have any money right now, but I'll get a job, and in a few years… Okay, maybe a few decades… Anyhow, I'm totally your bitch this week."

"That's not necessary."

"It's no trouble, honest. I read loads of Nancy Drew books when I was younger—at least, I did until the Prophet banned them—and I always wanted to be a detective. Plus I have inside knowledge."

"You do?" I asked.

"Yeah, duh. I know Kai wasn't involved in this, and I'm definitely better at surfing than you are."

Oh, this had "recipe for disaster" written all over it.

"You'll be busy with apartment hunting."

"I can totally multitask. One time, I babysat this shih-tzu for a month while some rich jackass went on vacay to the Caribbean, and I got a gig delivering flyers at the same time, so me and the pooch walked around half of Fort Lauderdale."

Chase tried the diplomatic approach. "Alexa should have the final say. She's in charge of this operation."

Smooth. Pushing the decision onto the person controlling the purse strings meant Erin wouldn't be able to complain about an answer she didn't like.

A real smart move.

Or not.

"Yeah, we might need extra eyes this week." Alexa's avatar was wearing a black hat today. "This is crunch time."

Uh-oh. "But Erin has no experience with this kind of work."

"Not formal experience, but she has experience with life."

Cartoon Alexa turned. "You've lived off-grid for seven years, yes?"

Erin nodded. "Seven and a quarter."

"That's not easy to do. Trust me, I know. You've gotta be good at sneaking around, have eyes in the back of your head, and learn to size people up at ten paces because thirty percent of people are assholes."

"Is that an official statistic?" I asked.

"There are lies, damn lies, and statistics. But in my experience, thirty percent is about right."

I considered her assertion and realised it wasn't a bad estimate. Thirty percent of Morty's clients had been dicks, same with thirty percent of the boys in high school and thirty percent of my own family. Many jerks could be avoided, but a handful always stuck around to ruin your day.

"I'm used to working alone or with an experienced partner."

"So was I, once. But then I realised teamwork wasn't as terrible as I thought it would be. Speaking of which, I need Chase back."

My heart sank. I'd known he wouldn't be around forever, but I'd miss having reasonably competent backup. Erin struck me as something of a loose cannon. Interesting that Alexa had mentioned teamwork, though. Did she work with others besides Chase? Initially, I'd pegged her as a lone wolf, probably because Zach had given the impression that she didn't play nice with others.

I had one last try. "Erin doesn't have a driver's licence."

"As in, she can't drive at all?"

Erin chipped in. "I spent three months working at a real busy off-airport parking lot. I'm great at moving vehicles around, but I haven't spent much time driving on actual roads."

Was she serious? "They let you drive cars without a licence?"

"It was a low-budget operation. But then the DEA raided the place, and I lost my job."

"Why did the DEA raid a parking lot?"

"So it turned out the owner used to tape packages of drugs to the underside of the vehicles, and then when the owners drove them home, someone would retrieve the merchandise at the other end. Like, they were unwitting drug mules travelling all over Florida. A clever idea, don't you think?" She must have caught my incredulous look. "Uh, and totally illegal, obviously."

"Plus he got caught."

"Yeah, one of my ex-colleagues was an undercover DEA agent. Charlie, that was his fake name, and I totally believed the story about his girlfriend kicking him out after she cheated with their dog groomer."

Cartoon Alexa was smiling. "Who got custody of the dog?"

"The girlfriend. What a bitch, right?"

"Nice touch."

"Charlie was an okay guy. Always used to give me his potato chips when I couldn't afford lunch."

"He probably expensed those. Speaking of fake names, what name do you want on your driver's licence?"

"Don't I have to take a test for that?"

"Technically."

Wait, wait, wait… "Erin just said she doesn't know how to drive on the highway."

"Relax, we'll give her a crash course."

Give me strength. "There will be no crashing. And who's 'we'?"

"Chase can find someone. The name? Erin? Joy? Something different?"

She shuddered. "Not Joy. I hate that name."

"Where did Erin come from?" I asked.

"From a movie. *Erin Brockovich*. Have you seen it?"

I shook my head.

"It was the first movie I ever watched. In the Promised Land, TV isn't really a thing, although I bet the Prophet has a fifty-inch flat screen stashed in his basement. Anyhow, Erin Brockovich beat the system and won, and that's what I wanted to do. Beat the Prophet and prove that I could make a life for myself. Nobody was going to fight for me in that place. Well, Kai did, but when he got kicked out, I was left on my own."

"Kai got kicked out of the Promised Land? He didn't leave of his own accord?"

Erin's eyes widened as she realised she'd said too much. "He just went, okay? One day he was there, and the next, he wasn't."

I wanted to push for more, but Alexa stopped me.

"You want to keep the name Erin?"

"Yes."

"Surname?"

"I...I don't know. I started out with Kealoha, the same as Kai, but then Mom got married again and it changed to Hodges. But I hated both of my fathers. And when I left, I used the name Johnson because there's loads of Johnsons, and it didn't stand out."

"So, are we going with Johnson?"

"Can I think about it?"

"For five minutes. We're working with a time limit here."

"Smith? Williams? Brown?" Chase suggested. "Those are all common names too."

Suddenly, inspiration struck. "How about Prince?"

Erin tilted her head to one side. "Prince?"

"Wonder Woman's surname. You like movie names, don't you? And you've shown great strength over the past several years, escaping from a cult and learning to reverse park."

"I kind of like it."

"Good, that's settled," Alexa said. "Erin Prince. Do you need anything else? Social security number? Passport?"

"I need everything. I mean, I guess I have a social security number, but I never found out what it was, and even if I knew, I wouldn't dare to use it in case the Prophet's enforcers tracked me down."

"Hold on, is this legal?" I asked.

Alexa snorted. "In my experience, the right thing to do and the legal thing to do don't always correlate. I'll move your date of birth by a week, okay?"

Chase remained silent on the issue, and I wondered whether he'd known all along what our diabolical boss would say. Earlier, I assumed he'd played the Alexa card to stop Erin arguing, but had it been me he wanted to keep quiet?

Either way, now it seemed as if I didn't have a choice in the matter. *Stay calm, Ari.* I could keep Erin out of the way by having her conduct meaningless surveillance—*not* in a vehicle—or send her to follow up on a red herring. No big deal.

"Okay, fine. We'll include Erin on the team."

"Excellent. And I have a new lead for you. Rumour says that Alvaro Sanchez lost his job recently."

Gloria's husband? "How recently are we talking?"

"Seven weeks."

Why had she kept it quiet? At Haven's Rest, we'd spoken almost every day.

"Weird that she didn't mention it."

"You know what's weirder? Three years ago, Alvaro was making six figures as a psychiatrist before he quit to go manage strawberries."

"Are you certain?"

Why would he make such a drastic change?

"Yup. Before that, Gloria didn't work."

"How did you find out?"

"Trade secret."

I blew out a breath. Was Alexa wondering why I hadn't ferreted out that information? I was meant to be the PI, after all. But, like Kai, Gloria hadn't talked much about herself. And three years… The timeline fit. Soon after that, Zach had been drugged for the first time. But for Gloria to do the deed, it would have taken a lot of luck. Yes, she packed his food and drink, but how had she guaranteed that he would ingest it at the right time?

Wait… Her husband was a psychiatrist. A doctor. Baylee worked at the hospital—could they have planned this together?

"I don't suppose you found any link between Alvaro and Baylee?"

"Nothing definitive. They both worked at Santa Cruz Medical Center, but not at the same time. Alvaro left before Baylee got the job there, although Baylee's aunt heads up the finance department, which is probably why she was able to take so much time off to travel with Tyler. I'll keep looking."

"Another loose end: when I was in Huntington Beach, I spoke with the owner of the surf store that Tyler wants to buy, and he said Tyler's looking for bank financing. But at such a preliminary stage, I don't have any way to verify whether that's true. Maybe Erin could try calling the banks? They won't give out any information without security checks, but if they get as far as asking the questions, then at least we'd know Peralta was a client."

"I can handle that one to start off with."

Really? I'd thought making endless, fruitless phone calls would be beneath Alexa's pay grade.

"Okay, as long as you're sure?"

"I am."

"In that case, I'll focus on Gloria. At this stage, I think the best approach is to try talking with her. See if anything shakes loose. She might get hostile, and usually I don't like to burn bridges, but with so little time left until Zach competes at Pipeline…"

"Are we gonna play 'good cop, bad cop'?" Erin asked. "Can I be the bad cop?"

"No, I'm going to be the good cop, and you're going to wait in the car."

"Awwww."

This promised to be a long, long week.

CHAPTER 48
ARI

Gloria and her family lived in a small but tidy duplex between Santa Cruz and Watsonville. Not so convenient for Gloria to get to Seagrass Point, but until he lost his job, her husband had worked at a strawberry farm nearby. Although "farm" was something of a misnomer. It was a vast expanse of land owned by an international farming conglomerate, not a sweet little family-run place.

At least I'd solved the mystery of why he'd switched career—after leaving medicine, Alvaro Sanchez had penned several articles on the dangers of professional burnout. Too late for him, but perhaps the information would help somebody else?

A moment after I knocked on the door, footsteps approached, flip-flops on tile, and I heard the rattle of a chain. The *click* of a lock. After waiting most of Monday for Gloria to leave Zach's place, I'd be beyond frustrated if she slammed the door in my face.

"Ari?" Gloria's eyes narrowed as she peered through the gap.

"Do you have a moment to talk?"

"I thought you moved away? Maya said you went back to Las Vegas."

Maya, not Zach. How much had they told Gloria about my departure? Not much, as it turned out, but she'd filled in the blanks herself.

"At the moment, I'm still in the area."

"Well, maybe it's not my place to say, but you hurt Zach when you left. Couldn't you have stayed to talk things through?"

"He didn't want me to do that."

"All couples have fights, and when an argument gets heated, people often say words they don't mean."

"Zach definitely meant it."

"Sometimes men are wrong." Gloria sighed, and I sensed a little of the hostility ebbing away. "People talk about chemistry, but understanding, compromise, and patience are just as important in a relationship." And now that she'd said her piece, puzzlement crept in. "Why did you come here?"

At least she hadn't asked how I'd gotten her address.

"I'm hoping you might do me a favour."

"What kind of a favour?"

"When I unpacked in my new place, I realised I'd left my ring behind. You know the rose gold one with the ruby that I used to wear?"

Gloria nodded. "*Sí, sí*, I remember."

"It was a gift from my grandma." That was true—she'd won it in a card game—but the part about losing it wasn't. The ring was tucked up in the safe at the Forest Lodge Hotel. "If you see it at Haven's Rest, would you be able to pick it up for me?"

"I guess I could do that, although I haven't noticed it lying around. And I'm not searching through Zach's things." A pause. "Do you want coffee?"

I'd already over-caffeinated today, but I did want more time with Gloria. *That* was the true reason for my visit. But now I had to try and steer the conversation around to the topics I needed to discuss. Judging by what Gloria had said so far, I suspected she had an ulterior motive for offering hospitality—she wanted to encourage me to talk with Zach, something I'd do in a heartbeat if he agreed.

"Do you have decaf?"

Gloria nodded. "My husband drinks it."

Perfect. "How is he doing?"

"He… It's been difficult." Gloria glanced toward the stairs as we passed, and I wondered if Alvaro was resting in bed. The sound of the TV drifted through from the living room, a cartoon by the sound of it, so Gloria's sons were most likely in there.

She led me into a small kitchen, not untidy, but definitely lived in. Children's drawings were stuck to the refrigerator, and a corkboard was filled with postcards and notes and messages and a calendar. As Gloria ushered me over to the table, I caught sight of the entry for tomorrow—*Alvaro chemo*.

Oh, hell. They had a diagnosis now, and it was one of the worst.

"Do you need help with anything?"

"No, no, the kettle just boiled."

"I meant while your husband is sick. My schedule's packed this week, but over the next month, I might have a few days to spare."

If I was in California, I might as well make myself useful in my downtime. Haven would understand, especially if I made it back for the weekends.

"I think we'll be okay. Everyone offered to help—Zach, Tyler, Kai, Maya—and all Alvaro really wants to do is sleep. Zach said I could take as much time off as I need."

"If you're sure, but just call me if you need a hand. I'll give you my new number."

"You have a good heart, Ari. Not like that other one."

"Other one?"

Gloria's lip curled up in disgust. "Baylee. I shouldn't speak ill of people, but I can't say I was disappointed when Tyler finally came to his senses."

"The two of you didn't get along? Around the house, I always thought…" I trailed off, hoping Gloria would fill in the blanks.

"Oh, I understand when to keep my mouth closed. If I'd complained, she'd have made life difficult, I'm sure of that. But she's a nasty piece of work, only out for what she can get. A user. After… Well, we fell behind on Alvaro's medical bills. He lost his job…" Gloria wiped an eye. "We couldn't keep up, and she called to chase the payment. And she was just so *cold.*" A sniffle. "*I'm sorry, Mrs. Sanchez, but it's hospital policy. If you don't make a payment, we can't continue with treatment.* I spent months cleaning up after her and cooking for her fad diets, and she couldn't even use my first name."

That didn't surprise me one bit. Working in credit control was probably Baylee's dream job because she got to be a bitch to everyone.

"I'm so sorry she behaved that way. I don't have much spare money, but if you need to borrow a little…"

Thanks to Alexa's twenty thousand, I was off the breadline now. And Gloria was a friend. Nana always said you should help your friends, and what sort of example would I be setting to my daughter if I turned my back?

Gloria put down the coffee canister and squeezed my hand. "I really do appreciate that, but Zach and Kai are helping out. I had a bad moment at work last week—you know how you keep everything bottled up, and suddenly it all comes rushing out? Anyhow, Zach made me tell him the details, and he said they'd take care of everything. Honestly, I have no idea how I'll ever repay them, but I couldn't afford to say no, not when Alvaro is so sick."

Zach and Kai were paying the medical bills? That didn't shock me—Zach had a generous streak a mile wide and two miles deep—but it did eliminate the tenuous motive I'd assigned to Gloria. Plus her animosity toward Baylee was clear. No way would they be working together.

"Tyler didn't chip in too?"

"That boy's terrible with money." Gloria set a mug of milky coffee in front of me. "Every woman he ever dates takes advantage of him, and what they don't spend, his brother scrounges."

"His brother?" I frantically tried to recall Alexa's dossier. Tyler and Troy, with Troy the older by over a decade. Last known address: Victorville, California. Employed at All-in-One Financial Solutions. "He's a CPA, right? Don't they earn good money?"

"What's the old saying? *Those who can't, teach.* I don't suppose that holds true in most cases, but Troy's a rare exception. He spends his days taking care of other people's money, but he can't manage his own."

Now this, *this* was interesting.

"Does he spend much time with Tyler?"

"Not really. Maya told me they had a fight a few years back. Troy ended up in rehab, and Zach convinced Tyler not to bail him out every five minutes or he'd never learn to stand on his own two feet."

Troy Peralta. Had a new suspect just thrown his hat into the ring? Perhaps he had a motive, two even. A desire for money, and possibly revenge if he knew Zach had encouraged his brother to cut him off. But wait a second... Troy would have to be working with Tyler. And from what Gloria had said, they didn't see eye to eye anymore.

But it was something. Another loose end that needed to be tied up. I took a sip of my coffee, thinking things through. Gloria had given me a whole lot of information without even realising it.

"Hearing stories like that makes me glad I don't have siblings."

"Don't let one fool colour your views. My own brother's always been real supportive, although he lives in New York now. When Alvaro has his operation, Nicolas is going to come and stay for a month to help with the heavy jobs. And look at Maya—she'll do anything for Zach. Some days, I don't know how he'd manage without her."

"I guess. Does Kai have any brothers or sisters?"

"No, I don't think so. Not that he's ever mentioned, anyway."

Ouch. Poor Erin. Like Maya with Zach, I sensed she'd do anything to help Kai, but he didn't even acknowledge her existence.

A voice crackled behind me, dry and raspy. "Gloria?"

When I looked around, nobody was there, but I spotted what looked like a baby monitor on the counter. Gloria followed my gaze.

"We bought that so Alvaro could talk to me from upstairs. Uh, could you excuse me?"

I drained the last of my coffee. "I should go anyway. But if you could keep an eye out for the ring, I'd be so grateful."

"I'll do that. And will you talk to Zach? He's in Hawaii right now, but when he comes back, he'll have had enough time to cool off from whatever that fight was about."

"Maybe."

"Trust me, what you two have is too good to throw away." Gloria's eyes glistened. "I understand just how short life can be."

"If he wants to speak with me, I'm available."

"Sometimes, a woman has to take the initiative. And Zach's been moping around the whole time you've been gone."

He had?

Dammit, she was right. I had tremendous doubts that Zach would want to see me, but if I didn't at least make an attempt to speak with him, I'd regret it forever. I loved him still. I'd always love him.

"Okay, I'll try. When he comes back, I'll try."

Gloria's half-smile didn't erase the sadness from her eyes. "You won't regret it."

CHAPTER 49
ARI

"I made you coffee. Okay, so I totally ordered it from room service, but here you go."

Why had I opened the freaking door? And how did Erin look so damn perky at this time in the morning?

"It's five thirty a.m."

"I know, I had a lie-in."

"A what?"

"You know, a lie-in? When you stay in bed later than you should? My body clock starts ticking at five. That job at Sin City totally messed with my head—I had to go to sleep at the time when I'd usually get up. Do you want croissants? I thought they'd suck, but they're actually okay, except you need ten of them to fill you up, and that costs, like, thirty bucks. I googled the recipe, and it's basically flour and butter, but you gotta roll it out a hundred times."

"It's too early for this."

"Alexa emailed, by the way. She said Tyler Peralta applied for business financing with California Savings & Loan. Two hundred and fifty thousand bucks, which is crazy money, but it'll probably go through."

"She said that?"

"Boy, you really aren't a morning person, are you?"

"Banks don't normally give out that kind of confidential information."

"Alexa's, like, a wizard. Hey, do you think she's even a real person? I saw this movie once, and the bad guy turned out to be this sentient computer whose AI went loopy or whatever."

The more likely scenario was that Alexa had paid somebody off. I'd done the same thing myself once, although it had taken me a month to identify a suitable candidate for bribery and two more weeks to convince him that he wanted to help me. Alexa had taken less than two days, so maybe Erin was right? Maybe Alexa truly did have supernatural powers?

"She's flesh and blood. Zach knows her from way back. Wait, why did she email you about Peralta?"

"Because I'm your assistant." Erin put the tray with the coffee down on the desk-slash-dressing table and snapped her fingers in my face. "Wake up, sleepyhead."

If only I could. This was like a bad dream. I'd kept her busy yesterday by having her track Zach online, but still she managed to nose around the case. Zach had gone more or less dark—no posts to any of his social media accounts—but the odd sighting had cropped up, pictures and videos taken by fans. Yesterday, he'd been practising aerial at Sunset Beach, staying out on the water with Kai and Tyler rather than interacting with anyone on the shore. Erin had whooped every time she found a new update, and I'd been forced to look at every single one. At least Zach appeared healthy.

"Why don't you try apartment hunting?"

"Because we have work to do. What's the plan, boss?"

"The plan is that I go back to sleep until my alarm goes off at seven."

"I already checked the social media sites. No sightings yet. Should I get pancakes again? Waffles?"

I was only twenty-seven, but at times like this, I felt so much older. Perhaps it was something to do with being constantly tired? I hadn't slept much. All night, I tossed and turned, worrying about Zach and the upcoming contest and replaying Haven's "I miss you, Momma" over and over.

One more week. One more week of full steam ahead. If nothing shook out, then I'd keep working the case for Alexa, but I'd spend some time back in Vegas while I dug deeper into the remaining leads, one of those being Kai.

On the plus side, at least Erin was back to her usual self. Slightly annoying, yes, but this never-ending perkiness was better than tears.

"It's too early for food. I want to take a look at Tyler's brother, and also Zed Nelson. The affair with Maya still bothers me."

"He's a sleaze. A predator."

Another Jankowski? Yes, I could see that. And there was something about the way she said it...

"Do you know much about him?"

"About *him*? No. About men *like* him. *Way* too much." Erin bent to pour coffee from the French press into the two cups on the tray, ending with a flourish. "I used to be a waitress, did you know that? Anyhow, last year at the Huntington Classic, or maybe it was Surf 365, I can't remember, I was hanging with a bunch of girls from Long Beach—they were a real hoot—and one of them, she hooked up with Zed Nelson after some TV shindig in LA, and she said he was real pushy. Like, he wanted her to bend over and take it up the—"

"Okay, I get the picture."

"My stepfather used to act the same, except he liked it the other way too, which was how I ended up pregnant."

Holy fuck.

"I thought you were married," I said hollowly.

"Oh, yeah, I was. But my husband had problems in that

department, thank the stars. I think because his mom was also his sister, something got wired up wrong down there."

I blew out a long breath, the warmth of the room replaced with cold horror.

"How can you talk about this so...so...calmly?"

A shrug. "I used to cry a lot. And sometimes I still do, but talking helps too. What I really want to do is take out an ad in the *LA Times* to tell everyone what those sick freaks at the Promised Land do, but I can't."

"Too expensive? What about dishing the dirt online? Or going to the police? If there's incest going on, or forced marriage..."

"No, no, no." Erin took a step back. "A thousand times no."

"You could ask to stay anonymous. Didn't the authorities raid another cult recently? Over near Bakersfield? I saw it on TV."

"Even if my name stayed out of the papers, the cops would still know who I was. And if they started digging into my family... Just no."

Was she trying to protect Kai?

"Is this about what happened to your father? Because I spoke to the detective who investigated, and he said they couldn't prove who did it."

"The Prophet is vindictive like you wouldn't believe. It's weird—when you live there, you just don't see it. All the lies, all the manipulation. And the hypocrisy. Don't get me started on the hypocrisy. But if you leave and open your mind, see and experience things for yourself rather than relying on what other people tell you, everything changes. We had lessons each morning, and most of what they taught us was bullshit. I mean, sheesh, I spent half my life thinking the earth was flat, and it's really hard to unlearn that. The first time Kai announced on Insta that he was flying to Hawaii, I couldn't sleep for a whole week because I was scared he'd fall off the edge. Logically, I understand now that the earth is round, but deep down… I can't get rid of the fear. It lessens with every passing month, but it'll never go away completely."

"You never learned about space? About the universe?"

"Swear on my life, the Prophet must've gotten high and watched *The Matrix*, then woken up the next morning and thought, 'I know, I'll start my own religion.' Okay, so *The Matrix* hadn't been released when he came up with the plan, but I guess he was just ahead of his time. He said most of the outside world was an artificial construct designed to control us. If we ever left the Promised Land, we had to wear these little amulets with vials of his blood around our necks. His *sacrifice*. They were meant to protect us from corrupting influences. Once a month, there'd be a ceremony where he filled up fresh amulets and we all had to kneel and watch." Erin snorted and moved over to the window with its view of the forest. "And we thought that was *normal*."

"Wow."

"Sucks ass, right? I wasted so much of my life."

It absolutely did. But I saw now that despite the occasional blip, Erin was strong. Stronger than I'd ever been. And Chase said Alexa saw herself in Erin, which figured. She'd achieved so much as well.

"Why did you quit? I know you were pregnant, but if that was considered to be normal, what made you finally break free?"

"Kai did."

"But he left when he was seventeen. You stayed for three more years."

"He was the only person who asked questions, who didn't take the Prophet's word as the absolute truth, and that made me start asking questions too. Okay, not actually asking them, because that would've gotten me remedial lessons and zero freedom, but I started to look beyond what we were being told. The elders were total bullshitters. Remember how I said

I was married to the Prophet's brother? Well, one time, they said they were making a pilgrimage to the mountains in Colorado—did you know there's another People's Promise ranch there?—and when they came back, they started saying all this stuff that the supreme being had supposedly told them. But I overheard them talking in the kitchen late one night, and do you know where they went?"

"Where?"

"Wonder World."

"The theme park? Are you serious?"

"Couldn't make it up."

Erin's story was a dystopian nightmare. At first when Alexa had offered to sponsor her, I'd admit to feeling a tiny bit jealous. She'd get a whole year of living expenses handed to her on a plate, while I'd had to struggle for every cent when I was her age. But now I understood. The whole damn world owed her reparations. The Prophet was a monster using religion as a mask, and the Promised Land was hell on earth.

"I know it's hard, but you really should consider speaking with the authorities. What if there are other girls like you stuck at the ranch, and in Colorado too? If we found a sympathetic FBI agent…"

"No!"

"Don't you want to help?"

"Yes, but don't you get it? If the Prophet thought I'd betrayed him, he'd make sure Kai went to prison."

"For your father's death? But I thought you said Kai didn't do it?"

"He didn't, but he said he did. That's why they made him leave. There was this…this understanding. That if nobody talked, it would all just go away."

"How can you be sure he wasn't responsible? If he confessed…"

"Because I know, okay?"

And just like that, I knew too. I saw the fear in Erin's eyes. Kai hadn't poisoned their father; *she* had. Erin had laced the Kool-Aid with antifreeze, and a man had died.

Shit.

Shit, shit, shit.

What the hell was I meant to do? I mean, I couldn't prove anything. If I went to Jake Smith with what I suspected, her life would be torn apart again, probably Kai's too. And for what? One of Satan's disciples had breathed his last, hopefully choking a little along the way, and I couldn't be too upset about that.

But I had to understand.

"Why did you do it?" I asked.

Every tinge of colour drained from Erin's face. No wonder she'd never tried to contact Kai—she'd murdered their father, and he'd taken the fall for her. Kai had been kicked to the kerb with nothing, left to rebuild his life from scratch.

"Do what?"

"If we're going to work together, I need to know. Or do Zach and I both need to watch what we drink from now on?"

"What? *No.*" There was the longest pause, and Erin glanced toward the door, a cornered animal. But finally, she spoke in a whisper. "He wasn't meant to die."

"What happened?"

"I overheard him and Mama talking. He was going to take me to Colorado to get married to this guy...this guy who made my skin crawl. I met him once, and he had a way of looking at me... Like he was imagining all the things he wanted to do once I was his. And I...I guess I just panicked. I'd seen the bottle on the shelf in the garage. My father used to pour more into the truck engine before he drove to Manitou Springs in winter, and it had that little warning on it —poisonous, do not ingest—and I figured that if I tipped some into his drink, he'd get sick, and while he was sick, I could escape. Will I go to prison now? Because Kai had nothing to do with it."

What a decision…

Nearly a decade ago, when Morty Coulson had asked me why I wanted to become a PI, I'd made a noble speech about justice and integrity. Whereupon he'd laughed and said that wasn't how the world worked. Justice didn't pay the bills. And while I'd tried to avoid clients whose morals I'd fundamentally disagreed with, there were times when I'd had to take a case for financial reasons and then hated myself afterward.

If I told Alexa about Erin's confession, what would she do? I might not have known her for long, but I very much suspected that she'd say "good for her." And let's be honest, those words were running through my mind as well. I didn't want Erin to get punished for achieving the only justice possible under terrible circumstances.

"If everything you've said is true, then you're not going to prison. This conversation didn't happen."

"Really?" Her voice was tight. "I…I don't even know why I told you."

"Because sometimes, it helps to get things off your chest."

It was compulsion as old as time—look at all the Catholics who went to confession. And a cop acquaintance of mine in Vegas once told me that fifty percent of murderers got caught because they couldn't keep their mouths shut. Out of stupidity, arrogance, guilt… Guilt could tear people up inside. Several years ago, I'd been hired to find evidence of a husband's infidelity, and I'd followed him from his mistress's apartment all the way home, where he'd dropped to his knees on the porch and begged his wife for forgiveness.

Erin's confession put another check in the "no" column for her brother as well. He still had the motive and the opportunity to poison Zach, but not necessarily the means.

He was no killer. Which left Tyler and Maya. Tyler and Maya, Tyler and Maya, Tyler and Maya…

I hadn't realised I was speaking out loud until Erin said, "Tyler."

"I'm inclined to agree with you, but the Zed Nelson thing is a loose end."

"So go ask Maya about it."

At first, I thought Erin was joking, but her indignant expression when I laughed quickly told me she wasn't.

"Why is it such a bad idea?" she asked. "You just said that people like to get things off their chests."

"Guilty secrets, not their current involvement in gambling fraud."

"Is Maya Torres dumb?"

"No, not at all."

"Then trust me, she's not hooking up with the sleaze because he's hot."

"But he's rich, and he's powerful. That combination can override common sense."

Erin regarded me curiously, head tilted to one side.

"What?" I asked.

"You did that, didn't you? Got down and dirty with a rich sleaze?"

I figured I might as well answer—my burning cheeks gave the game away in any case.

"I was young, okay? Young and stupid."

"Was he just a jerk, or was he a full-on jackass?"

"Full-on jackass."

"And you think that because you made a mistake, then Maya might have done the same."

A part of me hated having such a perceptive assistant because, damn, being called out on my past screw-ups was embarrassing. But I also began to realise what Alexa saw in Erin. Kai's sister was no fool.

"That might be true," I admitted grudgingly.

"Then go talk to her. Coerce her into spilling the beans so you can rule her out once and for all."

"Or not."

Erin shrugged. "Or not."

With a heavy heart, I realised she was right. In order to save Zach's career and possibly his life, I'd have to make his sister very uncomfortable. Myself too, because I'd always considered Maya a friend. But left unchecked, whoever had targeted Zach could strike again, and next time, the man I loved could be injured or worse.

"I'll need to go see Maya this morning. Alexa said that she's flying to Hawaii tonight."

"You want me to come?"

"No, I need to do this alone."

Erin grinned and flumped onto my couch. "Suit yourself. I'll just stay here and stalk Zach on Insta."

CHAPTER 50
ARI

"What are you doing here?" During the drive to Haven's Rest, I'd worked hard to convince myself that Maya wouldn't be angry to see me. That she'd invite me in, perhaps reluctantly, and offer me a drink I wouldn't take. But the effort had been for nothing. Hostility was written all over her face in block capitals.

"I need to talk with you."

"Why? Haven't you hurt my family enough already?"

Clearly, I hadn't. Maya didn't open the door more than a foot, blocking the way with her body.

"My goal is to keep Zach safe."

"He made his feelings clear; he doesn't want you anywhere near him, and neither do I. *I'll* keep him safe this weekend. I'm gonna monitor everything he eats and drinks, so you can go back to Las Vegas and leave us alone."

Was Maya playing food and beverage manager this weekend a good thing or a bad thing? The jury was still out.

"Just because we're not personally involved anymore doesn't mean my client will let me quit."

"Who's your client?"

"I can't divulge that information."

"So someone's paying you to meddle in our lives, and you won't even tell us who?"

"I signed a non-disclosure agreement."

Maya huffed out a breath. "I thought we were friends."

"We were. We still can be if you want that."

Oh, that was the wrong thing to say.

"How dare you even suggest that after the lies you told?" Maya began to close the door. "Whatever you need to do, you can do it someplace else."

"I know about you and Zed Nelson."

She froze. She froze, and for the second time in as many days, I got to watch all the blood drain out of a person's face. Maya didn't go as pale as Erin, but she made up for it by swaying and clutching at the doorjamb.

"Are you okay?"

Her mouth goldfished, but no sound came out.

"I wouldn't put it past Nelson to mess with Zach's performance for ratings, and you keep sneaking off to see him. Tell me what I'm supposed to think, Maya."

"I...I... It's none of your business."

"Where does your loyalty lie? If it's with Zach, then why the secrecy?"

"You seriously think I would hurt my own brother? Are you crazy?"

"It's hard not to think the worst when you keep evading the question."

"It's not what you think."

At least she wasn't trying to deny it anymore.

"So enlighten me."

The anger came back. "What did you do, follow me? Eavesdrop? Snoop through my phone?"

"I followed you. It was my job."

"Then your job is immoral. Did you get a thrill out of it?

Out of worming yourself into our lives and lying to us for months? Zach's devastated, do you realise that?"

"I never meant for that to happen. The lines between work and…everything else got blurred. I love your brother. I'll always love him. Do you think I want to be here, digging into the dark parts of your lives? Because I don't. But I believe Zach could still be in danger, and I'll do everything I can to stop him from getting hurt. Which brings us back to Zed Nelson. What the hell is going on, Maya? He's bad news. I've even heard him described as a predator."

Predator. That single word changed Maya's demeanour. The prickliness faded away, replaced by the wide-eyed fear of a cornered animal.

"H-h-he's not tampering with Zach's drinks."

"Then how is he involved?"

"He isn't!"

"So why are you with him? Because I don't believe for a minute that you and Zed Nelson are soulmates."

"How could we be?" she snapped. "He doesn't even have a soul."

"Just tell me what's happening. I only need enough to rule you out of the investigation."

Maya opened the door wider, but instead of inviting me in, she leaned against the wall and sank to the floor, hugging her knees as tears rolled down her cheeks. I longed to comfort her, but I didn't think touching her was a good idea. Not when she still bore so much animosity toward me.

"He's blackmailing me, okay? That pig is blackmailing me."

"Blackmailing you? Over what?"

"Over Zach."

"I don't understand."

"Last year, Zach punched a guy at a WST event. A sponsor's son."

"You told me about that before."

"I didn't tell you that Zed almost kicked him off the tour. The guy wanted to sue, and the sponsor withdrew, and Zed was furious that Zach had lost his temper again, especially so soon after the Scottie Stenson incident. I begged Zed to let Zach stay. Said I'd do anything. *Anything.*"

Fuck, Nelson was forcing Maya to suck his dick—and maybe more—in order for Zach to keep his place on the tour?

"But Zach's at the top of the leaderboard. He powers the ratings. Would Nelson really fire his star?"

"He said there're a thousand more wannabes waiting in the wings. Pretty boys with better temperaments who won't kick up a fuss about showing a bit of flesh—his words, not mine. And every time Zach acts out, Zed wants more, more, more."

"Zach would have quit on the spot if he thought Zed was taking advantage of you."

"You think I don't know that? But I want Zach to win. He's too talented to be an also-ran, and having 'champion' on his résumé would open up so many doors. Waterside Films wants to make a documentary series starring this year's winner—that contract alone is worth a hundred thousand bucks."

"I don't think Zach cares about doors, or documentaries, or cash."

"*I* care about doors. Do you realise how hard it is to make it as a pro surfer? Our parents struggled with money their whole life, and after they died, things only got worse. There's a mortgage on this place, did Zach tell you that? I just want security. I want to wake up in the mornings knowing that nobody can take our home away from us, and if that means agreeing to Zed's demands, then I have to do it."

That vile bastard. If Maya was telling the truth, and I suspected she was because Zed was a slimeball, then she moved so far down the suspect list that her name was at the bottom of the Mariana Trench.

"Nelson's sick."

"I dream of pushing him off a cliff and watching him hit every rock on the way to the ground. The first time he summoned me, I spent the whole night puking afterward." Her voice hardened. "So whatever dumb idea you have in your head about me spiking my brother's drink, you can forget it. I'll do whatever it takes to see him win."

"I didn't realise…"

"Now get out of our home."

"But—"

"I never want to see you again! My private life is nothing to do with your stupid case, and if you ever breathe a word of this to Zach…"

"I won't, I swear."

Maya lurched to her feet, her cheeks still damp, and began pushing me along the terrace. This part, I understood. She was upset, still angry, and mortified that she'd spilled her darkest secret.

"Get out! Get out!"

"I'm leaving. Just make sure you watch Zach's back."

"I've been doing that for longer than you've known him."

"It's Kai or Tyler who's doing this."

A tiny pause, then a whisper. "That's insane. They're his best friends."

"Those are the only suspects left."

"What about Baylee? She was always hanging around like a wasp with a shoe fetish."

"We ruled her out. Trust me, it's Kai or Tyler. I've been working on this for months, and if you're not involved, there are no other possibilities left."

"Which one?" A hint of panic crept in. "We're meant to be sharing a house in Hawaii. How do I know which one?"

"I can't say for sure, not yet."

"You must have a clue. Otherwise, what have you even

been doing all these months? Aren't you meant to be a detective?"

Morty Coulson used to do this. Ask me to give an opinion based on my gut before all the facts were revealed. I always hated having to commit, hated the thought that I might be wrong, not only due to my pride but because bias might lead me to focus my investigative efforts in the wrong direction. I preferred to apply logic and follow the evidence. But still he'd made me guess, and not long before he died, we'd been watching an impromptu press conference together on TV, a husband begging for his missing wife's safe return.

"Did he do it?" Morty had asked. "The husband?"

"How would I know?"

"Just watch him."

So I did. I watched the way he wiped his eyes without any actual tears falling. I studied his body language and his demeanour, fidgety, arms folded, his words a little too smooth, glib almost, before he remembered where he was and sobbed again. He looked at the cameras, but he didn't make eye contact with the cops asking him questions. Some answers—those that dealt with the timeline—were hesitant, while others came more easily.

Finally, I'd nodded. "Yes, I think he's guilty."

Less than a week later, the man had been arrested for the murder of his wife and four-year-old daughter. The cops had picked him up at the airport with his mistress.

"Right again," Morty said when we heard the news. "You need to trust your instincts."

"I only trust hard facts."

"Your batting average is eighty-three percent. That's not bad."

"You've been keeping score?"

Morty had been a baseball fan. His happy place was cheering on the Aviators at the Las Vegas Ballpark.

"You like facts; I like statistics. But there are times in this business when we have to go with a hunch."

A hunch… What was my gut telling me now? Alexa had been right about Maya, and Erin was equally adamant that Kai wasn't involved. Going on intuition alone, I had to agree.

"Watch Tyler closely. Don't leave him alone with Zach, and don't tip him off that we're investigating."

"I won't," Maya promised, and then her eyes narrowed. "Now get the hell away from me. I never want to speak to you again."

Staying would serve no purpose in any case. I'd gotten the information I'd come for, and Maya needed time to cool off. It was as much as I could hope for under the circumstances.

So I turned and walked away.

My cell rang at five past twelve. The in-car screen lit up with an unknown number, and when I answered, Lila whispered through the phone.

"It's happening again."

There was only one "it" she could be talking about.

"Betting against Zach?"

"Yes, and much bigger than before. I have to go."

My turn to lose colour. I felt it drain from my cheeks. Shit. Usually, I liked being right, but not this time. Whoever was manipulating Zach's results, they were doubling down. They wanted their money back. Which meant two things: that they had deep pockets, and that Zach was in more danger than ever. Our culprit wouldn't want to lose again.

I tried calling Alexa, but for the first time since I'd begun working with her, she didn't answer, and neither did Chase. Instead, I got bounced to what sounded like a corporate switchboard.

"Good afternoon, you've reached the Church Group," a perky woman said. I imagined a perfectly coiffed brunette sitting at a minimalistic desk in some huge glass skyscraper. A clone of Rennick's minions. "How may I help you?"

"Uh…" I hadn't been expecting this. "Uh, I'm trying to get ahold of Alexa. I don't have a surname."

Her tone didn't change. "I'm afraid Alexa is unavailable at this time. Can I take a message?"

"Could you ask her to call Ari when she's free?"

"I'll certainly do that."

Of course, because Alexa was Alexa, the call came at five thirty in the morning, roughly two minutes after Erin knocked on my door with coffee, poached eggs and avocado on toast, and a platter of fresh pineapple. What was wrong with her? Not only was being up at this hour unnatural, but avocado was also gross.

Since I'd spent most of yesterday afternoon and the whole of the evening alternately pacing my hotel room and running searches on Tyler Peralta, I wasn't entirely awake, and no amount of caffeine would help. According to Erin, Zach had spent the day on the beach with Kai and Tyler before the three of them headed to a bar. There were women everywhere, and looking at the pictures made me feel a tiny bit sick. I hadn't been lying to Maya—I did still love her brother, so much it physically hurt.

"Church Group?" I asked Alexa.

Do you have any idea how many hits you get if you google "Church Group"? Thousands. Not only companies with similar names, but a seemingly infinite number of religious institutions.

"It's just a name." Alexa dodged the personal question, as usual. "What's up?"

I explained. First, I recounted what Maya had said and the implications for the investigation.

"So, Maya's out as a suspect, which leaves us with Tyler

and Kai. If the culprit stays true to form and takes Zach out in the final, we have four days to expose him."

"Maya and Zed? That's fucked up."

"Tell me about it. I know she instructed me to butt out, but I really want to take a power sander to his genitals."

"That's an interesting idea. I know someone who might be able to help."

The way Alexa said it, I almost thought she might be serious.

"I don't want to get arrested for conspiracy to castrate a man."

"I promise that won't happen."

Phew.

Alexa didn't seem shocked by the news from Lila, but her total lack of alarm was unnerving.

"So they're still in the game? Good. That's good."

"Good? I'm not sure I'd describe it that way. Should I book a ticket to Hawaii?"

"Not yet."

"But—"

"I have another avenue I'm exploring right now, and I need you on hand to run it down. And it *is* good because it gives our guy an opportunity to make a mistake. One we can exploit. I'll warn Zach to be careful."

Oh, how I wished I shared her nonchalance.

"Maya's looking out for him, but maybe a reminder not to tip anyone off would be beneficial?"

Even with Maya on board, I still felt twitchy.

"Sure, I'll mention it."

"Both of our suspects are already in Oahu. If there's a problem, I can't help from here." Did that pause mean Alexa was reconsidering? I gave her another nudge. "Surveillance might be needed, and that needs to be done in person."

"That's so old-school."

"I'm sorry?"

"Remote surveillance is entirely possible. Ever heard of cameras?"

"Someone still needs to set those up."

"We'll see." What did that mean? "But I guess having boots on the ground could be useful."

"I'm glad you—"

"Erin can go."

I spluttered the mouthful of coffee I'd just taken. "But Erin has no real experience with surveillance."

"She's been spying on her brother for years. I'd say that counts."

"What if he spots her?"

"He totally won't," Erin said from her spot on the velvet couch, and I immediately regretted putting the phone on speaker. "I'm excellent at sneaking around, and Kai's hopeless with faces. Plus I have three different wigs, four pairs of sunglasses, and a bunch of hats."

"Do you even have a passport yet?"

She grinned. "Some guy delivered it this morning. He looked like a Mafia foot soldier. I mean, he had an Italian accent and everything."

"Alexa, tell me you're not involved with organised crime?"

"Not this week."

"Is that meant to be comforting?"

"Leonardo's a graphic designer from San Francisco, okay? The IDs are a sideline. Do you know how much rent has gone up in the Bay Area? I'll get Chase to book a plane ticket and accommodation."

"What about me? What am I supposed to do?"

"I hear the spa is nice."

"The freaking spa?"

"Maybe you could drive Erin to the airport as well? I've got stuff to do—speak later."

And once again, she was gone.

CHAPTER 51
ARI

Use the spa, Alexa had said.

Yeah, right.

Chase had called a little after ten this morning with Erin's travel itinerary and an instruction for me to return to the Forest Lodge Hotel after I'd dropped her off at San Francisco International. Alexa was busy working, apparently, and she'd call me later with an update, but how much later, Chase hadn't specified.

So, here I was.

Waiting.

Earlier, I'd dug out my sneakers and gone for a run, pounding along the trails near the hotel until my lungs burned and my legs ached. When Morty was alive, I'd gone to the gym religiously three times a week, sometimes four, but during my months in California, exercise had fallen by the wayside. With Zach, I'd gotten used to leisurely days chilling on the beach while he did all the hard work, and carrying out surveillance for Alexa hadn't improved matters. Boy, was I unfit.

After I'd scrubbed off the sweat in the shower, I figured

I'd take over Zach-watch since Erin was on an airplane, but when I logged into my laptop, I found that she was flying business class with a lie-flat bed, free Wi-Fi, and all the snacks she could eat. She'd emailed a picture of herself in the complimentary pyjamas along with seventeen links to Zach sightings and an assurance that she wasn't slacking.

No, it was me who felt like a spare part.

I checked every photo and video and post, and then began reviewing my files. Even though I'd told Maya that Tyler was the man to watch, I still wasn't sure why. We were missing a piece. On paper, Kai had the stronger motive, but maybe I'd been swayed by the fact that he wasn't materialistic at all—his favourite shoes had holes in them, for crying out loud—and also by Erin's unshakeable confidence in her brother's innocence. If Tyler and Baylee hadn't broken up, I'd have suspected they were working together, but their relationship was over and she'd moved on.

What about Tyler and his brother? Gloria had mentioned they didn't get along, but how deep did the animosity run? Out of curiosity, I checked All-in-One's company website. *Say goodbye to accounting headaches! Let us handle your books while you get the job done.* The "Meet Our Team" page showed a slim man in a suit, his serious expression the opposite of Tyler's relaxed mischief. Worry lines crossed his brow, but the corners of his eyes and mouth were smooth. This was a man who frowned a lot but didn't smile.

As I'd done with Gloria's husband, I checked for any legal issues—court cases, bad publicity, malpractice suits—but there was nothing in either his personal or private life. Quite the opposite, in fact—the testimonials on the All-in-One website were positively glowing. Troy went above and beyond to help his clients. Nothing was too much trouble.

His home was modest, a Craftsman bungalow on a small lot, and he wasn't married. Possibly because he was a bit of a whiner. On the neighbourhood internet forum, he always found something to complain about—stray dogs, loud cars, louder kids, trash pickup, substandard mail delivery, cat poop, teenagers on bicycles, lousy parking, overhanging trees, lawn sprinklers, the list went on—but that was hardly criminal. Although it might have explained why the two brothers weren't close. Troy was as uptight as Tyler was easygoing.

With no obvious source of wealth, I considered it unlikely that Troy was the money man in the AnyBet scam, but I couldn't rule out his involvement. A CPA would be good with spreadsheets, wouldn't he? And perhaps he was the one who'd found the backer? Did he have wealthy friends? Or clients? From the company website, it seemed as if All-in-One catered more to the lower end of the market, small businesses and middle-income families, but Troy hadn't worked there his whole life. He'd spent time in New York and Chicago before he moved to California.

Between running and pacing, I'd burned an entire day's calories by the time Alexa called in the late afternoon. I pushed away the salad I wasn't eating anyway and answered.

"Tell me you have news."

She did, I was certain. Cartoon Alexa was grinning like a lunatic under her black fedora.

"Pack your bags—you're going to Victorville."

I freaking knew it!

"Tyler's brother. It's his brother, right?"

"I can't say that for sure, but it's interesting that he lives in the same place, don't you think?"

"The same place as what?"

"As the people funding the betting accounts."

"Hey, back up, back up. What are you talking about?"

"While you've been following people, I've been following the money."

"But a...well, I guess you could call him a colleague, he

already checked out the account holders. None of them exist. They're just made-up names at real addresses."

"Not quite. The names are real too."

"You're gonna have to start from the beginning."

A blue cartoon couch appeared on the screen, the colour perfectly matched to Alexa's eyes, and she settled back into the cushions, hands in her lap. It was story time. Perhaps I should have sat down too, but with the clock ticking in the background, I was too wound up to relax.

"Okay, so the way AnyBet and its various subsidiaries work is that you don't need to provide proof of address to open an account, just proof of identity, but if you want to withdraw any funds you pay in, they have to be sent back using the original payment method. So if you use a credit card, the money gets refunded to that same card, and if you use a digital wallet, the money gets returned there. The name on the AnyBet account and the payment method have to match, by the way. Are you following?"

"Uh, yes?"

"Good. So any winnings from this betting-against-Zach scheme get sent back to the digital wallets they came from, but to withdraw *those* funds, an ID showing an address is required. And the fun part is the addresses used to open the digital wallets don't match those on the betting accounts. Same names, totally different addresses."

"Are you saying the addresses on the digital wallets are the right ones? And they're all in Victorville?"

"You got it. In or nearby."

Holy shit. Someone—Troy Peralta?—had found a loophole in AnyBet's system and exploited it to cover their tracks. That still didn't tell us where the seed money originally came from, but it explained how the fraud had occurred. Was he running a syndicate? Did a bunch of his friends and neighbours chip in cash with the promise of big returns?

Then it hit me.

Alexa had found a loophole in AnyBet's system.

But I'd never told her that AnyBet was my client. In fact, I'd gone out of my way to maintain client confidentiality, firstly because of ethics, and secondly because I didn't want to get sued for breaching Rennick's NDA. And yet here was Alexa, casually dropping the sportsbook's name into the conversation.

"How…?" It came out as a whisper. "How did you know about AnyBet?"

"Oh, I read your reports."

"What reports?"

"The ones you wrote for Digby Rennick."

"But…but I never sent those to you."

I began to second-guess myself, questioning whether I'd accidentally attached the wrong file to an email. But no, I was always so careful about that.

"You didn't have to."

The hits kept on coming.

"Wait, you hacked into my email?"

"Not just your email, your whole computer."

She'd *what*? Now I realised why Alexa stayed hidden away on the other side of the world, because if she'd been standing next to me at this moment, I'd quite cheerfully have strangled her.

"You…you… Don't you have any morals whatsoever?"

"Apparently not."

Even though I wasn't touching the mouse, a window opened on my screen, a spreadsheet with a dozen addresses. I slammed the laptop closed, seething, but whatever she'd done to it, the speakers were still working.

"I don't know why you're so upset. Didn't you dig through Zach's files for information?"

Thanks to the reports, she knew full well that I had.

"That was different. He gave me permission to use his computer."

"I doubt he expected you to go through his personal emails, his tax returns, his bank accounts…"

"Shut up!" A long second passed. "How did you break into my computer anyway? I run antivirus software. A firewall. And I never click on unknown attachments."

"Do you want me to talk or don't you?"

"Just answer the question," I snapped.

"Your security software is mediocre at best. I could have gotten around it in an hour or two, but time is money, and it was more cost-effective to send you the executable and pay you to open it."

A groan escaped from my lips, unbidden. "The contract? You embedded some kind of Trojan horse in the contract when you returned it?"

"You were never gonna turn down twenty grand, amirite?"

Everything began to make sense. The quick offer, the lack of a coherent plan in the beginning, this morning's instruction to go to the spa. I felt it now. The same gut-wrenching sense of betrayal that Zach—and Maya—must have experienced when they found out why I'd moved to Seagrass Point. The dawning horror that I'd been used, and by someone I'd considered a friend. Was that the point? Had Zach put Alexa up to this?

"Is that why you hired me? To hurt me the same way I hurt Zach and Maya?"

"Of course not. I'm merely pointing out that you're a hypocrite. If I wanted revenge, I'd have sold your identity to a Russian extortion gang."

Boy, that was comforting.

"But you didn't care about my investigative skills; you just wanted to know what I knew."

"Mostly, at first. I figured you might be useful in some capacity, but you turned out to be surprisingly competent."

Surprisingly competent. Gee, thanks for the vote of

confidence. If I hadn't wanted to crawl down a hole already, that little revelation would have squashed me into the dirt. And now I understood why Zach and Maya wanted nothing to do with me anymore. I deserved their animosity.

"Well, good luck finding Troy Peralta." I turned the laptop over, trying to work out how to remove the battery. A simple clip, it appeared.

"I already have his address. You need to—"

Click. Alexa disappeared, and I closed my eyes for a long minute, focusing on my breathing as I willed myself not to scream or throw the no-doubt expensive table lamp across the room. *Relax. Just relax. Don't do anything you'll regret. Rejoice in the knowledge that you've earned twenty thousand bucks.* Since Alexa had basically admitted that the money was payment for clicking on her malicious little file, I felt entitled to keep every last cent.

Although that did leave the problem of how to retrieve my files. I'd have to spend a chunk of my hard-earned money on a new laptop, disconnect the old one from the internet, and transfer what I needed on a flash drive. Thank goodness I'd encrypted the footage of Maya and Zed Nelson. At least Alexa couldn't have watched that in graphic detail.

My stomach dropped to my feet as I realised that even without the video evidence, Alexa still knew about Maya and Zed. She wouldn't say anything to Zach, would she? At the time when I'd told her, I'd trusted her to keep quiet, but that trust had been built on a foundation of quicksand.

The whole house of cards was tumbling down.

My cell rang, and even though the number was withheld, I knew exactly who was calling. I turned it off, and when the phone on the nightstand trilled, I unplugged it from the wall. Damn, this woman was persistent.

I had to pack. Seeing as I'd quit, Alexa wouldn't keep paying for the room, but I was darn well going to drive the

Mercedes back to Las Vegas. Alexa was the one who'd sent me here, so she could provide my transport home.

The tears came as I stuffed clothes into my suitcase. Tears and a mess of muddled emotions that I couldn't begin to untangle. I'd always been aware that my job involved invading people's privacy, but I'd somehow convinced myself it was okay if my goal involved a greater good. Yes, I'd photographed men with their mistresses, but I'd helped their wives to achieve closure. I might have gathered evidence of insurance fraud, but those cheats pushed up premiums for everyone. Sure, I'd stabbed Zach in the back, but I'd been trying to save his career. Okay, not at the beginning, but back then, I'd thought he was stealing from Rennick, and I'd been trying to help *him*. And also my daughter. Money really was the root of all evil.

Someone knocked smartly on the door, and I clunked my head on the dressing table as I straightened.

"Who is it?"

"The concierge, ma'am."

Great, had Alexa sent him to evict me? Because I was leaving anyway.

I hurried to the door and yanked it open.

"I've almost finished packing, okay? I—"

Why was he holding a cell phone on a silver platter?

"Your nana is trying to reach you, ma'am."

My heart leapt from my chest to my throat. What was wrong? Nana would never call the hotel unless there was an emergency. Had something happened to Haven?

I snatched up the device and pressed it to my ear. "Is everything okay?"

"It's rude to hang up on people."

Alexa.

"Do you ever tell the truth?"

"Occasionally, if it's advantageous."

"Give me one good reason why I shouldn't hang up on you again."

"Because I'll ask the concierge to stand in the hallway and yell my half of our conversation through the door?"

"I really hate you right now." Seething, I attempted a half-smile for the concierge and retreated into the hotel room. "I was already raw after the fight with Zach. You took advantage while I was vulnerable."

"Yeah, I get that. Look, we're both just doing our jobs, and we have the same goal: to keep Zach safe."

"Then why lie?"

"Because I needed the information, and I couldn't take the chance of you getting all ethical on me. And the twenty thousand was a nice touch, right?"

"How much money do you have that you can afford to throw it around like that?"

"Do you honestly expect me to tell you?"

"No, I guess not."

A long silence followed, and I wondered if she'd been the one to hang up this time. But finally, she spoke.

"I have enough." Her voice was softer now. "I've never added it up, and share prices fluctuate every day." Another pause. "I made my first million when I was seventeen."

"How?"

"It was mostly legal. Companies offer bounties if you discover a bug in their software, and I'm good at that."

"Is that how you found the Victorville addresses? You broke into AnyBet's system?"

"And the digital wallets." Sheesh. Alexa's revelations were enough to make me close my bank account and stuff all the cash into a big ol' mattress. "I still need to trace the funds back to their source, and I only have two days to do it, so you need to get to Victorville and play your part."

"Seriously? You expect me to keep working with you after this…this massive invasion of privacy?"

"Yes, because you still love Zach. Don't you?"

She had me there.

"I do."

And of course, she already knew that.

"Call me when you get to Victorville. Chase will book you a hotel room."

Once again, Alexa disappeared without so much as a goodbye.

CHAPTER 52
ARI

Three times on the way to Victorville, I broke down and cried at the side of the road. Until today, I'd harboured a stupid notion that if I could just solve the case, Zach would forgive me, but now that I'd felt the same pain for myself, I realised how much I was asking.

Worse, Erin was still sending through links of the guys surfing, and I had to watch the three of them cresting waves without a care in the world, two good men with a traitor lurking among them.

As I neared Paso Robles, Chase sent a message. I'd be staying in a three-star hotel, a development that seemed to embarrass him more than the fact that his boss was a scheming liar. He'd kept me in the dark too, but I couldn't accuse him of lying outright because he'd barely said a thing about Alexa in the whole of our time together. How much did that kind of loyalty cost? If she'd pay twenty thousand for the contents of my hard drive, he had to be on a substantial salary.

By Bakersfield, some of the hurt had turned to anger. At Alexa, at Chase, but most of all at Tyler Peralta for putting me in this position. Several times, I nearly turned around and headed for the airport because I itched to knock his damn teeth out.

But in order for the dirt to stick, I needed proof, and that meant carrying on to Victorville.

The city was twice the size of Santa Cruz, clinging to the edge of the Mojave Desert just north of the San Bernardino Mountains. Even at this time of year, the days were hot and dry, not so different from Las Vegas, really.

Before I checked into the hotel, I drove past Troy Peralta's home on Pine Avenue. The place was neat and tidy, but on first impressions, soulless. No pine trees in sight. The plants in pots on either side of the front door were too perfect to be real, the same with the square of bright green grass. The rest of the driveway was paved and empty, the windows dark, the drapes open. According to Alexa, Troy drove a silver Lexus. Where was he? Still at work? Having dinner with a girlfriend? Hanging out in a sports bar? On a Tinder date? Scratch the last one—the man wore a pocket protector. He didn't seem like the type to take risks.

Although he had bet—and lost—thousands in his dealings with AnyBet. Maybe he used Tinder after all?

I made another circuit and pulled over, trying to get a feel for the neighbourhood. At nine in the evening, it was quiet apart from the raised voices of an argument coming from a nearby home. Light from TV screens flickered in the windows, and a raccoon ambled across the road in front of my car. Troy's neighbours both had kids. A scooter had been abandoned in the front yard of the home to the left, and to the right, a minivan with two car seats occupied the weed-dotted driveway.

A sign in Troy's yard boasted of a home security system, and I didn't want to take a closer look in case there were cameras. There was nothing more I could do here tonight. Tomorrow, I'd come back and start intruding into yet another person's life.

"Could I make an appointment to see Troy Peralta?"

"Are you an existing customer?"

"No, I actually just moved to the area."

When Troy hadn't shown up by morning, I tried calling the number listed on the All-in-One website, but instead of speaking to my suspect, I'd been put through to the efficient-sounding Samantha, who assured me she was there to help.

"What type of services are you looking for?"

"Everything for a small business. I almost lost my mind trying to do my taxes last year, and I'm sure I'm not taking all the deductions allowable."

"We can definitely assist you—reducing the tax burden for everyday Americans is our passion. I'm afraid Mr. Peralta is on vacation this week, but if you don't want to wait, we have a team of excellent CPAs who would be only too happy to meet with you."

On vacation? Could he be in Hawaii?

"I hope he's gone somewhere nice."

"So do I—he's a real hard worker. Should I set up a meeting with one of our other advisors?"

"I'd rather wait to speak with Mr. Peralta. My neighbour recommended him specifically."

"Really? Who's your neighbour? We always like to thank any client who makes a recommendation."

I'd anticipated this question, and now I had a choice. Should I play it safe and go with Rob Griffin, who'd penned a five-star Yelp review that mentioned Troy specifically? Or should I take a risk?

Decisions, decisions…

"Michael Cooling. My AC broke two days after I moved in, and he came to the rescue."

"Mike's been with us for years. A great guy. With that name, he was born to be an AC tech, don't you think?"

I felt like punching the air, but I fought to keep the elation out of my voice. Samantha had just confirmed that the first name on Alexa's list of digital wallet holders was an All-in-One client, and I'd put money on the others using Troy's services too.

"You bet. Do you know when Mr. Peralta will be back in the office?"

"Wait one moment while I check his calendar. Uh… Okay, he'll be back next Wednesday, but he doesn't have any free slots until the following Monday. Would that work for you?"

"Sure, that's fine."

"Ten thirty? What sort of business do you run?"

"I make customised dog tags."

"You mean, like, for soldiers?"

"No, for dog collars."

"Oh, wow. Do you have a website? My sister just got a puppy."

"How about I bring some samples when I come in?"

Who didn't like free stuff?

"That would be wonderful."

I used my phone to email Alexa. At least I didn't have to face her now that she knew all my secrets. My laptop held so many little details I'd wanted to keep confidential—a spreadsheet showing the dire state of my finances, notes on past clients, private emails between me and Morty, who at times had acted more like the father I'd never had than my boss. Legal documents from my battle for Haven's child support, the results of her paternity test, the timeline of my shitty relationship with Maxwell and his accusations of cheating. Hell, notes on the case I'd built to send him to prison. He didn't realise it was me who'd ferreted out the evidence and passed it to his clients. Sure, the child support paperwork had said I'd become a private investigator, but in his head, I was still the dumb waitress who'd fallen for his dubious charms.

But Alexa knew.

She knew everything.

Beside her, I was the kid in remedial classes, constantly playing catch up.

But I had gleaned a little information this morning, and I needed to call Erin. She answered on the first ring, slightly breathless.

"OMG! Hawaii is *amazeballs*. When I checked into the hotel, they gave me one of those flower necklaces, and the swimming pool's so big it has an island in the middle. And now I'm in a beach bar, drinking a cocktail out of a coconut."

"You realise this is a work trip?"

"Oh, totally. I'm multitasking. I gave the waiter twenty bucks, and he seated me at a table overlooking the ocean. This expense account thing is so cool. I mean, I'm spending someone else's money to have fun. Maya's here, by the way."

"Alexa said she was flying out yesterday."

She'd probably hacked into the airline's database to find out.

"No, I mean she's surfing. I've never seen her surf before. She's really good."

I'd never seen her surf before either. So much had changed this week. But at least she was staying close to Zach as she'd promised, and for that, I had to be grateful.

"I'm going to send you a picture. It's Tyler's brother, and if you see him, I need you to call me."

"Is he, like, definitely involved?"

"Yes, there's no doubt now."

"Wow. I mean, I'll absolutely watch for him."

I considered telling Erin about Alexa, but now wasn't the time. Erin needed to stay focused.

"Those cocktails better be non-alcoholic."

"They're pineapple and coconut."

"Let me know when you have news."

Ten minutes after I penned my update to Alexa, I received a note from Chase. *Alexa has her head down and can't be disturbed. Will pass on the message when I can.* Was she still following the money? Or hunting for bugs? Or tearing somebody else's life apart? I headed back to the hotel, ordered coffee, and set about calling the rest of the names on Alexa's list. By posing as a customer service liaison from All-in-One, I confirmed that every single person was on Troy's client roster. The remaining question? Were they involved in the scam, or had they simply been unwitting pawns in his game?

Alexa had given me sixteen names, and I didn't even know if that was all of them. Rennick had said the first incident netted the scammers fifty thousand, and fifty thousand split sixteen ways, plus a share to Troy, wouldn't have gained an individual a huge amount. Would a person risk their reputation for under three thousand bucks? They'd have to be desperate, but Troy was in a position to understand their finances. He'd know who to target. But what if one of the clients he approached had more ethics than greed? His little scheme would have been blown out of the water.

On balance, I believed the clients were innocent. Troy was using their identities and possibly even their legitimate bank accounts to launder his ill-gotten gains. But where had the capital come from?

With no news from Alexa, I fired off a brief report and headed back to Pine Avenue to talk with the neighbours. If I could get proof that Troy had indeed flown to Hawaii, it would make my decision whether to hop on a plane or not so much easier.

Thursday morning, and the street had come alive. A grey-haired man was painting a picket fence eggshell-blue, a peppy blonde jogged past with a panting dog on a leash, and two women chatted at the end of a driveway. In daylight, I could see the video doorbell mounted beside Troy's front door, and I pulled on the ball cap I kept for such occasions.

Okay, here goes.

Spinning a story meant making it believable, so I pulled to a smooth stop near the house, close but out of camera range. Head down and purse in hand, I ambled up to his front porch and rang the bell. The chimes echoed inside the house. As expected, nobody came, but I had to go through the charade. Was two-way talk enabled? If it was, I'd pretend to have the wrong house, but the intercom remained silent. If Troy checked the video log, he'd know I was a Yankees fan and not much else. After an appropriate length of time, I backed up and returned to the sidewalk, making a beeline for the two women.

"Say, I don't suppose Troy mentioned when he'd be back? I called him at work, but they said he took the day off."

The taller of the two, a bespectacled brunette, looked me up and down.

"Did you try his cell?"

"It went to voicemail."

"Are you a friend of his?"

"We met at an accounting seminar last month. He said I should drop by if I was in the area."

"He went on vacation," her friend offered. "Marie's feeding his cat again."

"Oh, boy." Disappointed face. "I guess I had a wasted journey. I hope he's gone someplace nice."

The brunette spoke once more. "He probably went to visit his girlfriend."

Really? This was the first hint that I'd gotten of a relationship.

"A girlfriend?" Shocked expression.

"He didn't tell you, huh? Take my advice and give this one a miss. Troy Peralta has a girlfriend and a drinking problem. If you saw how many empty wine bottles he puts out with his trash, you'd run a mile."

"Marie thinks he has a gambling problem too," the friend added. "All those trips to Vegas."

Whoa, whoa, whoa. Vegas?

"I can't believe this. He said he was single."

"Men lie all the time, hun. You had a lucky escape."

"I still kind of wish I could find him. He deserves a kick in the balls."

"Try the slot machines at Caesars. Or better yet, forget him and find a man who won't break your heart."

I'd already done that, and then I'd ruined everything.

CHAPTER 53
ARI

"Time to pack your bags. Guess where you're going next?"

Alexa had finally called, and this time, her avatar was drinking a cocktail. Had she been speaking with Erin? Whatever, I'd anticipated the request, and my suitcase was waiting by the hotel room door.

"Vegas?"

"Awww." Good. I'd taken some of the wind out of her sails. "How did you know?"

"Because I heard a rumour that Troy Peralta might be there."

"Oh yeah? Now that's interesting."

Alexa wasn't aware of Troy's gambling habit? Then why was she sending me to Vegas?

"What did you find?"

"The money. Are you ready for this? Because it's absolutely fucked up."

"Just tell me."

"Okay, okay, so all the cash in these digital wallets, all the money flowing into the accounts opened in Troy's clients' names, it's coming from an AnyBet corporate account. Every last dollar."

"What the hell?"

"Exactly."

"I...I don't understand."

"It probably goes something like this... On designated weekends, Troy and his accomplice borrow a bunch of money from the company and use it to place bets. Tyler rigs the contest and they collect the winnings, then they repay the capital and keep the profit. Quite a clever scheme in theory."

"In theory. They lost all the money last time. There must be a massive hole in the accounts somewhere."

"Yeah, that's the flaw. I bet they're panicking now."

"How could this happen?"

"Well, there are two possibilities. Either Rennick hired you to do a sham investigation as a cover-up, or he doesn't know that one or more of his staff is stealing from him."

Could it be true? Had Rennick lied as well? All those times Maxwell had called me stupid... But no, Rennick had hired Jankowski too, and even though my former boss wasn't as smart as he liked to make out, most people believed he was competent. If Rennick had only wanted an investigator to take a cursory glance at the situation, he wouldn't have contracted with both of us. Jankowski was more than capable of screwing things up on his own. Plus, Rennick owned the company. He'd only be stealing from himself.

"He doesn't know. Rennick doesn't know. I need to speak with him. Troy Peralta's conspiring with someone on the AnyBet payroll."

"I'll send you a list, but there are seven hundred and twenty-nine employees."

"You hacked the HR system?"

"They should learn to secure their database better."

I recalled a moment with Dawson months ago, at the restaurant in Huntington Beach. His quiet mutter of, "Fuckin'

Alexa." Now I understood exactly where that sentiment had come from. She had the morals of an alley cat.

"We can narrow this down. Whoever Troy's working with, they'd need access to the finance system. Are you able to filter on the accounting department?"

"Seventeen people."

"It's a woman. I just found out he has a girlfriend in Vegas."

"That leaves eleven."

"Do you have their birth dates?"

"Of course."

"Troy Peralta is forty-one. Give me everyone between the ages of thirty and fifty."

"Make it twenty-five and forty-five. Men are more likely to go younger."

True. Maxwell had been thirty when we met, while I'd been young and naive. Never again would I date a much older man.

"How many does that give?" I asked after a moment.

"Six."

"Send me the names. Although I have no idea how to explain this to Rennick. I can't tell him I met an ethically challenged hacker who broke every privacy law known to man."

"Just hint at the truth and let him connect the dots. Tell him you heard that Troy's dating one of AnyBet's accounting staff."

That might work. I'd have to contact Lila first and explain the basics, then hope Rennick would agree to see me. If I came bearing gifts, he'd be crazy not to. I wasn't even charging him for my time. All I wanted was for this nightmare to stop so Zach could get on with his life in safety.

"I'm leaving for Vegas right away."

The Mercedes came with every option available, so I programmed the cruise control and set about making some calls as I drove, hands-free, of course. The first went to Rennick's private number, which wasn't truly his, but Lila's. She'd once told me that he didn't carry a phone, unfathomable for a man who'd made his fortune on the back of technology. Apparently—and I quote—he liked the freedom of being untethered in a connected world.

"Good morning, Mr. Rennick's office."

But it wasn't Lila who answered.

"Could I speak with Lila?"

"I'm afraid Lila is off sick today. This is Meryl—can I help?"

"My name is Arizona Danner, and I need to meet with Mr. Rennick. It's urgent."

"One moment, please." Then, "I'm afraid you're not on the list of approved visitors."

"I know that. I used to be, but—"

"Mr. Rennick is very strict about who he sees. His time is extremely valuable."

If I hadn't met Meryl in person, I'd swear she was a robot. She'd perfected that false sincerity.

"I understand, but this is about a job he hired me to do, and—"

"One moment, please." The pause was longer this time. "You're not on the list of approved contractors either."

"Not at this time, no, but I was until recently. We met in his office—do you remember?"

"Sorry, but I can't help you. If you were removed from the list, there was a reason for that, and I can't upset Mr. Rennick by making exceptions." Her voice softened. "If you want to leave a message, I can add it to his Monday morning briefing."

"Is there a Friday morning briefing? I really need to get this information to him as soon as possible."

"Mr. Rennick has quiet time on Fridays. Do you want to leave a message? Otherwise, I can transfer you back to the main switchboard."

"Could you just tell him there's been an unexpected development, and I have news he'll want to hear? He already has my number."

"If you've been taken off the list, he probably erased it. Mr. Rennick doesn't like superfluous information. You should leave it again."

I read out the digits and then hung up. Dammit. Now what was I meant to do? Stake out the building? Actually, that wasn't a bad idea, but would he come out of the main entrance or the parking garage? Did he have a chauffeur? Undoubtedly. The guy delegated almost everything—why should he drive himself? Exiting through the garage would offer additional anonymity, but leaving via the lobby would save precious time. Which option would Rennick choose? Maybe it would be better to visit him at home?

My next call was to Alexa. I was still mad at her, but right now, solving the mystery came first. Zach came first. Later, after the Peralta brothers were safely out of the picture, I could tell her exactly what I thought of her.

"Could you find me two addresses?"

"There's a high likelihood that I can. Whose?"

"Digby Rennick and Lila Margot."

"Lila? That's the assistant, yes?"

"One of them. She's off sick. I spoke to the other, and she won't put me through because my name isn't on the official list."

"Where's the list? Is it a spreadsheet or something? If it's inside the system, I could add you."

"It's too late for that. She'll recognise my name. But Lila is more flexible, and if I can find her and explain the situation, I'm ninety percent sure she'll help me."

"Can't you just send him an email?"

"It won't reach him. They all get screened."

"How can he work like that?"

"Do you read every single one of your emails? Or does Chase help?"

"He helps, but we don't have some dumb list of people. He's allowed to use his brain."

"Well, Rennick's a control freak, and Meryl's a sycophant. I need to either get to Rennick in person or speak with Lila tomorrow, assuming she goes to work. She probably won't be in the office over the weekend."

"Get to Vegas. I'll have the information by the time you arrive."

"Mommy!"

Haven leapt up, and I braced for impact. Two seconds later, she barrelled into me, and I tipped back against the living room wall. Well, at least someone was happy to see me. I wrapped my arms around my daughter and squeezed her tight, breathing in the strawberry scent of her shampoo. I could almost rest my chin on the top of her head now. She'd grown an inch since I started the Torres investigation, and I'd always regret missing out on so much time with her this year. Whoever said money was a necessary evil had been absolutely correct.

By rights, I should have been thrilled to spend the night back home, but even as I hugged Haven, I couldn't stop worrying about what was going on in Hawaii. Or about what Alexa was doing.

"Hey, sweetie. How was school?"

"It sucked."

"It sucked?" My stomach clenched. "Were the other kids mean to you again?"

"Everyone else's mom came to watch our play this morning, and you weren't there. And Kelly told people you left the way Sophia's mom did."

Sophia's mom had run off with the school guidance counsellor last year—quite the scandal. At first, Sophia's father pretended his wife had taken a job in Ohio, but as the split grew ever more acrimonious, Sophia's mom had spilled the tea in the parents' WhatsApp group, in a post entitled "Spencer sucks, but not very well." The poor guy hadn't been able to look anyone in the eye since.

"Work just got busy again, munchkin, but I'll be able to spend more time with you soon."

"You said that the last time, and then you got a new boss."

"The case is almost over, I promise."

Her roll of the eyes said she didn't believe me. "Can we go out for pizza tonight?"

Okay, she was right to have doubts. "Not tonight. Momma has to pay a quick visit to her old boss."

Haven huffed and tried to pull away, but I tightened the hug, running my fingers through her silken hair. I hated to let her down, but I had to solve this mystery.

"Nana said he fired you."

"That's true, but I still need to speak with him."

"Why? If someone fired me, I wouldn't want to be their friend. I'd go for pizza instead."

Nice try. But I could tell Haven was disappointed, and I'd disappointed her often enough.

"How would you like to help Momma with surveillance?"

I was only going to take a quick look at Rennick's place. Alexa had sent me the address, several satellite photos—one of which had come from Google Earth and two more in higher resolution; I didn't even want to think about where she'd gotten those from—plus a floor plan for his mansion and a list of employees. Housekeeper, chef, gardener, driver... No bodyguard, although the driver could have been multifunctional. He had a top-of-the-line home security system, and Alexa had marked the locations of the cameras with red Xs. Again, I didn't want to know.

Rennick lived in Granite Ridge, a new gated community where lots were large, homes were luxurious, and even the smallest property cost millions. According to the realtor listings in the area, the enclave boasted twenty-four-seven security with a manned gatehouse and regular patrols. Getting near the residence would be a challenge. But I'd take a look, and if anyone happened to spot me checking the place out, having a child along for the ride would remove any suspicion.

As soon as I'd had that thought, I wanted to take it back.

Haven wasn't a cover story. She was my daughter.

"Really?" Haven asked.

"We can pick up a pizza on the way back."

"And ice cream?"

"You know you can't have both together."

In the background, Nana's folded arms told me that her patience was wearing thin. On the plus side, we could afford pizza now, but this case had to end, and it had to end soon.

CHAPTER 54
ARI

Eleven a.m. on Friday found me in a diner not too far from AnyBet's corporate headquarters, sipping my fourth coffee of the morning as I skulked behind my laptop. Yes, I'd given up and turned it back on. Alexa already had all my files; there was nothing left for me to hide. And at some point, I'd have to swap to decaf. Lila was still off sick—I'd called the main switchboard to check—and as yet, there was no sign of Rennick.

The diner lay on the route Rennick would take if he drove to the office from his fancy-schmancy mansion in fancy-schmancy Granite Ridge. Paying him a visit at home would be almost impossible. Even though Alexa had somehow gotten my name on the development's visitor list, that only got me through the front gate. Yesterday evening, I'd paused near Rennick's place for under five minutes before one of the advertised patrols showed up. The guard had been polite when I told him I'd just pulled over to reply to an email, and he'd smiled when he saw Haven in the back seat, but he'd also hung around to make sure I left afterward. Earning his money.

Hence the vigil at AnyBet.

Alexa had provided me with a list of Rennick's vehicles—he had three of them. A Mercedes town car, a Porsche 911 Turbo, and a Ford Fusion plug-in hybrid. If I saw him drive past, I could stuff my laptop into my purse, sprint out the diner door, cut through the alley that ran alongside the AnyBet building, and meet Rennick at either the entrance to the lobby or the roller door that secured the parking garage. I'd look like a lunatic when I threw myself in front of him, but that was a small price to pay to grab his attention.

And if Rennick didn't show up, I'd visit Lila this evening. Working for Rennick must pay well because she lived in a swanky apartment with a concierge, which was another reason I'd decided to try catching her boss first. Speaking to her wouldn't be easy. Alexa had found me a personal phone number, but it kept going straight to voicemail, and although I'd left a message begging her to call me, so far, there'd been radio silence.

Alexa had also sent me a link.

And when I clicked on it, there was Zach.

My heart lurched as he ambled across an unfamiliar kitchen, heading for the refrigerator. The place had a rustic vibe with exposed wooden beams, cream painted cabinets, and a stone butler sink. A large window above the sink looked out on a yard full of tropical plants, and a wooden plaque on the wall said *Live your life while the sun is still shining*. Then I heard Maya's voice.

"Only the cans, remember?"

It took me a moment to process what I was seeing, but once I understood, I wanted to murder Alexa all over again. And also kiss her feet.

ME

You hacked Maya's webcam?????

ALEXA

Zach's too. Just click on the menu at the
side.

ME

Don't you have any respect for privacy?

ALEXA

Enjoy.

I clicked to close the window, cursing under my breath.
Spying on people was so…so *rude*. But half a minute later, I
accessed the link again, just to check that Zach was indeed
drinking from a can. He was. Then Tyler appeared, and my
head began to throb as I watched him pour a glass of orange
juice. I understood that in America, a man was innocent until
proven guilty, and also that Tyler was supposedly one of
Zach's best friends, but the *gall* of the man. He acted as if
nothing was wrong.

ME

Can you hack Tyler's webcam?

ALEXA

His laptop's turned off, and there's nothing
interesting on it anyway.

Tyler opened a cupboard, and I zoomed in to take a look.
That was the moment when I realised I'd joined Alexa on the
dark side. This was the point of no return. The moment where
I chose between white-hat Ari, the woman I'd once pretended
to be, or black-hat Ari.

If I'd learned one thing in the last decade, it was that
justice didn't exist, not the way it did in the movies. No
matter how noble your intentions, someone always got hurt.
The road to happiness was paved with bear traps. And
happiness itself was a relative concept—often, it meant

settling for the least awful option rather than pure unmitigated joy.

And in the last month, I'd also learned more about myself. The righteous part of me might have hated Alexa's complete disregard for the rules, but deep down inside, I envied her ability to give societal norms the finger with no qualms whatsoever.

I needed to buy myself a black fedora.

ME

Keep looking.

"Hi, I'm a friend of Lila. She's not answering her phone, and I'm a little worried."

The concierge was a young Black guy, barely out of high school by the look of him. The uniform he wore was a size too big, and he fiddled with the shiny gold buttons on the jacket cuff as he struggled to maintain eye contact. His badge said "Jerome," and his nervousness said he was new to the job.

"You're a friend of Miss Lila?"

"That's right. We work together."

"I ain't seen you here before."

Uh-oh. He was observant. I held up the paper bag I was carrying, the name of a local deli emblazoned on the side.

"She called in sick for the last two days, so I thought I'd bring her dinner in case she's not feeling well enough to cook."

"We're not meant to let unannounced visitors through. But if you want to leave the food here, I can let her know."

I'd thought that might happen, which was why I'd left a note in the bag. But if Lila didn't feel like eating and just put the food in the refrigerator—or worse, the trash—that would only lead to more delays.

"Could you try calling her now? The soup's hot."

Jerome shrugged, probably running through the rules in his head for any possible violations but not finding any.

"I guess I can do that."

Okay, this was progress. Now the odds were fifty-fifty—either Lila would consent to hearing my story, or she'd blow me off. But as Jerome punched the buttons and listened, and listened, and listened, apprehension began to needle at me. I'd been calling on Lila's mobile, and the concierge was using the internal intercom. She wasn't answering that either.

"Maybe she went out?" he said.

I could understand Lila avoiding me. I could understand her not answering a call from a withheld number. But no way would she ignore the concierge, not unless she wasn't physically able to pick up. Yes, it was possible she'd gone to the drugstore, but what if there was another explanation?

What if…? How much access did Lila have to AnyBet's corporate accounts?

"Have you seen Lila today?"

Jerome shook his head. "But my shift only started an hour ago."

I needed to find out whether she was in the building.

"I'm getting really concerned about her. When I spoke with her yesterday, she sounded so sick, and… Do you have a key to her apartment?"

"Only for emergencies."

"This might be an emergency. A medical emergency."

"They never covered that in the training. They said a water leak or a fire."

"What if she's lying in bed, unable to come to the door? Do you want to be responsible if she dies?"

Okay, I was laying it on a bit thick, but it had the right effect. Jerome swallowed hard.

"I'd have to call my supervisor."

"I'll try Lila again while you do that."

No answer, not that I'd truly expected one. I sent a quick message to Alexa, updating her on the situation and my thoughts, and then Jerome pushed a paper ledger across the counter toward me.

"You'll have to sign the visitor book. My boss says we can open the door and take a quick look around, but we're not permitted to touch anything."

"I appreciate your help."

"Did you park in the visitors' lot by the front door?"

"Yes."

"Then you need to add your registration too."

Hmm, I wasn't Lila's only visitor today. At seventeen minutes past one, someone had signed in against apartment 704, but the name was illegible and the registration was missing. Presumably a person she knew, though, seeing as they'd been allowed past the front desk.

The elevator rose smoothly to the seventh floor, and I began to wonder how much Rennick's assistants got paid. A heck of a lot more than I did, that was for sure. Maybe I could ask Alexa? No, no, *no*. Sheesh. I couldn't condone hacking.

Outside 704, Jerome knocked on the smooth white wooden door, then waited. Knocked again. He really didn't want to go inside, did he? Me? I was itching to get a look at Lila's home. At work, she never had a hair out of place, and I was curious whether her apartment would be neat as a pin or chaotic or somewhere in between. Was the quiet perfection an act or her true personality?

After what Jerome considered to be an appropriate amount of time, he inserted the key into the lock, and the door swung open on silent hinges.

"Don't touch anything," he reminded me.

The first thing that hit me was the smell. It turned out that Lila brought her work persona home with her, or vice versa, and the stench of stale vomit was totally at odds with the monochromatic, minimalist aesthetic. Jerome stared at me, eyes wide, and I cursed under my breath.

Where was Lila?

A quiet groan came from my left, and I hurried toward the source of the sound with Jerome trailing behind. Oh, hell. In truth, I'd expected to find the apartment empty, but Lila was lying in bed, eyes closed, surrounded by wadded-up tissues. The stink was coming from a bowl on the floor beside her, except she hadn't been too accurate when she puked, and splotches of vomit dotted the white tile. A bottle of painkillers lay on its side on the nightstand beside a half-empty glass of water, and when Lila turned her head toward me, her eyes were bloodshot.

"I…I…" She squinted, wincing as she did so. "Who…are you?"

Aw, shit.

I rushed forward, desperately trying to remember the basics from the first-aid course Morty had made me attend.

"Lila, it's Ari. What happened?"

"Everything…hurts." The words came out as a croak, and then she retched over the side of the bed. I jumped back, but there was nothing left to come out. "Head…hurts."

I laid a hand on her forehead—she was burning up. There were streaks of blood in the vomit, and her gaze was wandering everywhere. I glanced back at Jerome, who'd frozen in horror in the doorway.

"Call an ambulance. Now!"

"Yes, ma'am."

"Lila? Is everything all right?" Rennick asked.

Jerome hadn't said a word as I'd searched Lila's apartment

for her phone. In fact, he'd helped me once I told him what I was looking for. I'd finally found it under a cushion on the couch, set to silent and low on juice. She'd been delirious on the way to the ambulance, asking for someone named Melissa as the EMTs inserted a line to give her fluids. I'd used Face ID to unlock the phone, then set the auto-lock feature to "never" before running to my car. I'd follow her to Hillview Medical Center in the north of the city.

Fortunately, I had a charger with me, and I thumbed through her contacts looking for next of kin, my palms sweating. Mom, Dad, the mysterious Melissa… None were listed. I checked her recents list, and, sheesh, the poor woman didn't have much of a life. Mr. R, Mr. R, Mr. R, Mr. R, Meryl, Mr. R, Mr. R, Mario's Italian, Mr. R, Mr. R, Meryl, Mr. R. Screw it. Rennick should know how to contact his executive assistant's family.

"It's Ari Danner, and no, everything is far from all right."

In a heartbeat, Rennick's voice turned from friendly—almost affectionate—to hostile.

"Why do you have Lila's phone?"

"A long story, but the upshot is that she's sick. We're on our way to the hospital."

"Sick? What kind of sick? When I spoke to her earlier, she said she was doing better."

"I don't freaking know!" When she tried to punch one of the EMTs, I'd heard them muttering about substance abuse, then ataxia, then dehydration. She'd quickly quietened down, and that had been just as scary. "She was puking everywhere and acting crazy. Do you have contact details for her parents?"

"Her mom passed away."

"Her father?"

"He was never on the scene."

"Who's Melissa? Lila was asking for her."

"Her sister. She died in the same car wreck as their mom.

Fuck." The curse represented a rare loss of control for Rennick. "Which hospital? I'll meet you there."

"They're taking her to Hillview. Does she have insurance?"

"Of course she has insurance. Anything that isn't covered, I'll pay for. Make sure they know that."

He might have been weird, but at least he was generous.

"Okay, I'll tell them."

CHAPTER 55
ARI

"How is she?" Rennick asked.

"Are you Ms. Margot's next of kin?"

The doctor couldn't have been much older than me, but his eyes were already jaded. He stifled a yawn, and his five o'clock shadow suggested he was fourteen hours into a twelve-hour shift. I opened my mouth to explain the situation, but Rennick got in first.

"Yes, I'm her next of kin."

Said without a hint of guilt. Okay, he'd get along great with Alexa.

"Ms. Margot's condition is serious. She had a convulsion soon after she arrived, and then there are the gastrointestinal issues, plus she's suffering from extreme confusion."

"What's wrong with her? I mean, what's the cause?"

"We're still running tests."

I'd been at the hospital for almost four hours now, and Rennick had arrived right after I did. He'd spent most of the time filling in forms and dealing with bean counters who wanted to be absolutely certain they were going to be paid before they offered so much as an aspirin. One pedantic brunette acted as if she were Baylee's sister from another mister, and I almost cheered when Rennick finally lost his patience and told her to go screw herself in triplicate. The carefully controlled facade was gone now, and when he wasn't dealing with bureaucracy, he mostly paced the tiny room they'd put us in. *Back and forth, back and forth, back and forth.* At the two-hour mark, he made a brief attempt to meditate cross-legged, but that lasted less than ten minutes before he got to his feet, muttered something about "fucking therapists," and carried on pacing. This was the first time a doctor had come to speak with us, despite Rennick asking every member of staff he saw whether there was any news.

"Then run them faster. Money is no object."

"Sir, it's not possible to get the results any quicker."

"She'll be okay, though? She has to be."

The doctor avoided giving an answer. "I need to ask you some questions about her medical history." Uh-oh. Would Rennick be able to help? "Has she suffered from convulsions before?"

"No, never."

"Is there any family history of epilepsy?"

"No."

"How about Guillain-Barré syndrome?"

"What's that?"

"It's a rare disorder where a person's immune system attacks their nerves."

"No, no, nothing like that. Can I see her?"

The doctor glanced at his watch. "The nurses are still with her right now, but hopefully in an hour or so. Do you know what Ms. Margot might have eaten in the past few days? We could be looking at some kind of food poisoning here."

"On Monday, we had a sandwich lunch in the office and dinner delivered from Mario's. Tuesday, we visited my sports bar downtown and she ordered nachos. In the evening… I don't know what she ate in the evening."

The panic in his voice sent a wave of sympathy through

me. "If she didn't throw the trash out, I could go to her apartment and take a look."

"I'll come back to you if that's necessary," the doctor said, writing notes on a clipboard. "Anything else you can remember?"

Rennick carried on. "She rarely eats breakfast. And she drinks a lot of coffee. But she first mentioned stomach pains a couple of weeks ago, so should we go back further?"

The doctor looked at him sharply. "This has been building up for weeks?"

"Possibly? I overheard her asking Meryl for acetaminophen, and when Meryl asked if she was okay, she said it was probably just that time of the month." Rennick's cheeks reddened. Did he make a habit of eavesdropping on his staff? "And last week, she skipped lunch one day because she had a stomachache. Wednesday or Thursday, I'm not sure which, but I can ask Li—" He paused and pinched the bridge of his nose. "I can ask Meryl to check my schedule. And on Monday, Lila had a headache. Tuesday too, but she insisted on staying at work. She's going to recover, isn't she? You must have medication for whatever this is."

"We need to get a diagnosis first. That's proving to be a challenge, but Ms. Margot is resting at the moment. We've given her pain relief and a mild sedative."

"Do you need to get a specialist in? I can cover the cost."

"Money isn't the issue, sir. We're consulting with specialists already." The doctor made another note. "Can I ask what your relationship is to Ms. Margot?"

"I'm her employer." Rennick glanced in my direction and gave a heavy sigh. "And also her father, technically." What the actual fuck? Her *father*? Nowhere in my research had that little snippet of information popped up, and every one of Rennick's online bios said he was single and childless. "But she's not aware of that last part, so I'd appreciate you keeping it confidential."

Oh boy.

The doctor's pen had paused mid-note, and suddenly he seemed more awake. Probably it wasn't every day that a patient's representative confessed to a deep, dark family secret.

"This is unusual," he managed.

"Her mother and I weren't close. I'm not certain how much Ellie told Lila about me, but I expect little to nothing at all."

"Are you in touch with Ms. Margot's mother?"

"She passed away seven years ago. Lila doesn't have any other family that I'm aware of. But I know a reasonable amount about her history, and obviously I'm aware of my own health status, so if you have any further medical questions, I can assist with those. The short answer is that she doesn't have any pre-existing conditions, and I'm not aware of any genetic factors that could produce the symptoms she has."

"Right." The doctor had given up on the notes. "Okay."

"You'll update us when the test results come back?"

"Sir, I'll be honest—I'm not sure of the ethics of your… situation. I'll need to consult with our legal department."

And Rennick would no doubt call his own attorney, and two high-priced men in suits would spend the night slugging out the details while Lila lay in a hospital bed. I was more concerned with her.

"Could I make a suggestion?" I asked. Rennick and the doctor both turned to me. "When you run your tests, you might want to screen for poisons."

The Peralta brothers had been tampering with Zach's food and drink for years, so why not Lila's as well? Sure, there could have been an innocent explanation—food poisoning, for example—but the timing was remarkably convenient.

"Why do you say that?" the doctor asked.

"I'm a private investigator working for Mr. Rennick, and

there have been several instances of suspected poisoning in the case I'm working on. Lila was only involved on the periphery, but it's possible that somebody tampered with her food."

"Order every single test," Rennick told him.

The doctor's shake of the head as he left said he didn't get paid enough for this.

"Let me get this straight… Lila has been working for you for nearly four years, she knows how you take your coffee, your shoe size, and the name of your favourite hotel, but she has no idea you're related?"

Rennick sighed. "I've never worked out a good way to tell her."

I wasn't certain that while she was lying sick in the hospital was the right moment either, but the doctor had been sworn to secrecy. For now. Surely Rennick would have to confess at some point? His lawyer had arrived within the hour, and I wasn't privy to those conversations.

"How did you even find her? I thought there were rules about confidentiality?"

I only knew part of the story so far. Digby Rennick hadn't always been rich, and twenty-six years ago when he was a lowly student at Harvard, he'd decided to supplement his meagre income by donating to a sperm bank. Fast-forward a decade, and not only had he made his first few million, but he'd also grown curious about any offspring he might have sired.

"The receptionist at the clinic had three kids in college. And I swear I didn't mean to contact any of my children." Sheesh, there was more than one? "I just wanted to see how they were doing."

"How many are there?"

Another sigh. "Five. Three girls, two boys. Lila fell into difficulties after her mother and sister died. She didn't have anyone else, and people were taking advantage of her. It all came to a head one night when the police found her on the French King Bridge."

"She wasn't going to…?"

He nodded. "And it would have been such a waste. She's highly intelligent, kind, and empathetic too. Empathy is something I've always struggled with, or so my therapist says."

"I'd noticed."

Rennick gave a rueful smile, and I realised that perhaps he was human after all. Weird, but human. And smart enough to seek professional help.

"She must have inherited that particular trait from her mother," he said.

"Did you ever meet Ellie Margot?"

"Once. She was a real estate agent in Massachusetts, but after the market downturn, she began waiting tables. I left her a five-hundred-dollar tip. Maybe I should have done more, but I didn't want to interfere. Lila seemed happy back then."

"How did you find out that things had changed?"

"Twice a year, I had a local investigator write a brief report. I realise what you must think of me, but I'm not a stalker. I didn't ask for many details. I simply wanted to ensure that the young people I'd helped to bring into the world didn't suffer as I—" Rennick paused to compose himself. "I didn't want them to suffer. And one day, I found out that Lila was having a hard time, and I couldn't leave her to face the challenges alone. Nor could I waltz into her life and announce I was her long-lost sperm donor. So I reached out to a local organisation and had them provide assistance."

"A local organisation?"

"A suicide prevention centre. Obviously, I couldn't single

out Lila, but there was a waiting list for therapists, so I funded the entire program for a year. And after that, I found out she was looking for an administrative role, so I made sure that details of the position at AnyBet appeared on her radar. Her predecessor had just moved back to Japan, and there was too much work for Meryl to handle alone. It seemed like fate. But now here we are…" Rennick waved a hand. "The half-truths are coming back to haunt me."

"Boy, I know that feeling."

"Ah, yes, the issue with Zach Torres." For the first time, Rennick really looked at me. "Why were you with Lila this evening? I didn't realise the two of you had become friends."

"We haven't. I was actually trying to get ahold of you." Rennick wasn't my client anymore, and he'd made my life far more difficult than it needed to be, so I channelled Alexa. "But you took me off your dumb-ass contact list, so I was forced to find a workaround. And I suppose it's a good thing I did because Lila was in bad shape when I convinced the concierge to let me into her apartment."

Rennick's mouth dropped open, then closed again. How long since somebody had been so blunt with him?

"The list is a necessity. Before I implemented the system, I was getting calls every five minutes. Focusing on anything was impossible." A pause. "Why were you trying to speak with me?"

"Because the Torres mystery is ninety percent resolved. We're just missing one culprit and possibly part of the motive."

"You kept working on that? But I…"

"Fired me? Yes, you did." A hint of bitterness crept into my voice, and I didn't try to hide it. "But another party with an interest in the case hired me, and I've been working on it ever since."

"Who else would be interested? It's my money that's getting stolen."

Rennick's attitude was beginning to grate, as was his endless pacing. I was tired just from watching him.

"I realise this might be a difficult concept for you to understand, but life isn't always about the money," I said. His hands balled into fists, and I took in the dark circles under his eyes. Okay, he did genuinely care about Lila. "Sorry, that came out harsher than I intended, but some people are concerned about Zach's health and well-being, me included. I hate him being treated as a pawn in somebody else's game. Left unchecked, it would only have been a matter of time before he got physically hurt, either through whatever Tyler put in his food directly, or by falling off his surfboard while he was under the influence."

Now I had Rennick's attention. "Tyler? Tyler Peralta? You know that for certain?"

"I'm as sure as I can be, but he isn't working alone. He has an older brother who's involved, plus there's an insider at AnyBet."

"An insider?" Rennick's gaze lasered into me. "Who?"

"I'm not sure yet. That's why I was trying to speak with you."

"Why would they need an insider? Apart from the need to affect Torres's performance, the scheme is elegant in its simplicity. There's no need to access our internal systems."

"Oh, but there is. They needed capital to make the bets, and where do you think they're getting it?"

"I assume they have a rich backer."

"They do. You."

Rennick bristled. "Are you accusing me of being complicit in this scheme?"

"No, I'm saying that someone who works for you is borrowing money from your company accounts to place the bets, creaming off the profits, then putting the stolen money back afterward. Except last time, they couldn't. So now they're doubling down in order to fill the hole."

"How do you know that?"

"Lila called me. I'd asked her to tell me if more suspicious bets were placed, and now I'm wondering..." Nervously, I glanced toward the ER. "I'm wondering if she dug around and noticed something she shouldn't have."

"You honestly think somebody did this to her? On purpose?"

"She got sick at work, didn't she?"

"This...this is insane. I thought we were dealing with a simple case of financial fraud. Wait a second..." Rennick continued to process what I'd just told him. "How could you know that the stakes came from AnyBet? You don't have access to our financial information."

I was walking a narrow tightrope here, one that didn't come with a safety net.

"I'm not the only person working for my new client. A cyber specialist has been following the money, and while I can't pretend to know everything that's being done, I understand there's a security flaw in one or more of the digital wallets the culprits are utilising."

"I thought for a moment that you were going to tell me AnyBet's system had been hacked."

Don't fall, Ari.

"I can't comment on your network, but if you haven't had a cybersecurity audit recently, then it's probably a good idea. I mean, someone *has* stolen a large sum of money from your company. Well, kind of. Technically, you have it back for now, but if Zach loses the Pipeline Special, you'll be expected to pay it out again."

"The hell we will."

"You have a list of accounts you believe are suspect based upon betting characteristics—the size of the wager, the date placed, and the payment method. But what if an innocent client gets caught up in the sweep? You risk reputational damage."

"Some risks are worth taking. My daughter's lying in the emergency room, and as you pointed out, Zach Torres is in danger too."

"There might actually be a better way to handle this. Nobody can harm Lila further this weekend, and Zach has people looking out for him. We need to find the mole in your company before they realise we're onto them and burrow deep underground."

"And how are we meant to do that?"

"Your chief financial officer is a man, isn't he?"

"Yes, but AnyBet is an equal opportunities employer. He just happened to be the best person for the job."

I ignored the corporate defensiveness. "We suspect the accomplice is a woman, most likely aged between twenty-five and forty-five. Your CFO—him personally, no delegation— needs to find out which of your bank accounts are involved and compile a list of everyone with access who fits the profile. Then we watch them. Sooner or later, the suspect's going to meet with Troy Peralta, and we need to get evidence of that connection. You still have Jankowski on retainer?"

"Yes, although if your assertions are proven correct, then I'll be reconsidering that partnership. Dale didn't find any of these issues."

"No, he didn't. I can't pretend there isn't bad blood between Jankowski and me, but I'm being honest when I say you could do better than Twilight. If you're looking to hire a new firm for your investigative work, I hear Blackwood's good."

"I'll bear that in mind."

CHAPTER 56
ARI

When I was a little girl—after I'd ruled out moving to Hollywood—I'd dreamed of joining the circus. Nana used to take me to the free show on the Strip, and I'd giggled at the clowns, watched in awe as the trapeze artists flew through the air, and *ooh*ed and *aah*ed at the performer on the German wheel. And now? Now I could juggle, and that was it. But twenty-four hours on from Lila's admission to the hospital, I found myself stuck in the middle of an investigative circus, and everybody wanted to be the ringmaster.

It turned out the "next of kin" discussion had just been the warmup act. After the doctors found thallium in Lila's urine, they'd called the police, and now I'd been stuck in a windowless room answering questions for hours. Rennick had insisted on providing me with legal representation "just in case," although I hadn't done anything wrong. I'd been the one to suggest the additional tests, hadn't I? Until the results came back, I hadn't truly believed that someone was trying to kill Lila, but the doctor said thallium poisoning could be deadly if it wasn't caught in time.

Earlier this morning, they'd performed intestinal lavage,

which basically involved washing out her gut with saltwater, and now she was being treated with Prussian blue given orally, plus a whole variety of injections to try and clean the heavy metal out of her body. We'd been allowed to see her briefly, and hell... If I ever got my hands on Troy Peralta's accomplice, I'd wring her freaking neck. Lila had been miserable, her cheeks stained with tears, freaked out more by the injections than the intestinal lavage or even the poisoning because she was needle phobic and the doctors had turned her into a pincushion.

And while Rennick could be a dick at times, I'd been surprised to see the affection between him and Lila outside of the office. It was clear he cared for her, and she felt comfortable in his presence. Comfortable enough to cry and accept a hug, although she also apologised for taking so much time off work. She had no idea who might have poisoned her, although she did mention that she played volleyball with several members of the accounting team every Saturday morning. And two weeks ago, she'd found a cupcake in a fancy box on her desk, no note, but she'd assumed it was from Rennick. Apparently, he often left her little surprises like that—who'd have thought it? Same with a box of chocolates last week.

But neither gift had been from him. Sadly, the packaging was long gone, although she recalled that the chocolates had come from a boutique chocolatier downtown. The police would look into that lead, right?

At least, I hoped so.

Their investigation had hit a snag ten minutes into my interview when the third attorney showed up.

"Don Kessler, representing 1812 Enterprises."

Ah, crap.

"What's 1812 Enterprises, and why is it relevant?" one of the two detectives asked.

"I represent Ms. Danner's client."

Rennick's attorney looked puzzled. "But I'm here to represent Ms. Danner's client."

"As I understand it, you represent her former client. After he fired her, my client hired her."

Kessler had shut down every line of questioning that didn't directly relate to Lila or the thallium, turning me into a spare part in my own interview. I wasn't allowed to mention the Peralta brothers, or Zach, or digital wallets. I understood why—Alexa didn't want to answer questions about her illegal hacking—but that didn't mean I was happy with the state of affairs. The only reason I put up with Kessler's heavy-handed approach was because I knew Zach was okay. Not only was Maya carefully controlling everything he ingested, but she'd also joined him in the water. Erin had sent me the link: *Guess who's out on a jet ski?????!!!!!!* I'd been on a call with Alexa when I'd clicked on it, and I'd nearly choked.

"What?" Alexa asked. "Are you sick as well now?"

"Have you seen this? Maya's on a jet ski, and the waves are enormous."

"Oh, yeah. Keep watching—every couple of minutes, she glares at Tyler. If looks could kill, he'd be a dead man."

"She's meant to be keeping Zach safe, not putting herself in danger."

"You think Maya can't look after herself?"

"She hardly ever goes in the water, and now she's joined Sal's Army? I mean, I know she helps out with admin, but..."

"Joined it? She started it."

"Huh? Then who's Sal?"

"Salacia, goddess of the sea. Zach came up with the name."

Was Alexa joking? She sounded serious, but I'd researched Maya extensively. Nowhere had I heard of her having a more practical role on the team.

"There's no mention of that online."

"No, and do you have any clue how long it took me to scrub every reference? Months. It took months."

"Why would you do that?"

"Zach never mentioned the bullying?"

"What bullying?"

Thanks to Alexa, I was learning precisely how much I didn't know about the Torres family. Maybe the old saying really was true—ignorance had been bliss.

"Huh. Guess that's a no, then."

"Will you just tell me what happened?"

"Ever hear of an asshole named Scottie Stenson?"

"Sure, he's on the WST. I also heard that Zach gave him a black eye a couple of years ago."

"Not black enough. The guy's asking to be punched every time he opens his mouth. Anyhow, he made a comment about Maya's weight that Zach didn't appreciate, and after the black-eye incident, it escalated. His fans got involved, and they tore Maya to shreds online. Memes, catty comments, even a bunch of deepfake porn videos. She couldn't handle it and dropped out of sight."

"That's…that's… Why didn't she tell me? I could have accidentally-on-purpose kneed Scottie in the balls."

"Better not to do that. Zach doesn't need any more blowback."

"I can't believe I'm going to ask this, but what are the chances of you finding his social media passwords?"

"You think I don't already have them?"

I guess that had been a dumb question. If Alexa could breach AnyBet's system, she could crack Scottie's Twitter account.

"Have you used them?"

First, she hummed the opening bars from "Every Breath You Take," and when she spoke, I heard the smile in her voice.

"Sometimes, revenge is a dish best served ice cold."

And sometimes, that woman made me very nervous.

"Aren't you meant to be speaking with the police?" Lila asked.

Her private room was on the third floor, and luckily, visiting hours didn't seem to be a problem when a man like Rennick was involved. The windowsill was filled with flowers. Since she had no family—that she was aware of—and news of her hospitalisation had been kept quiet, I had to assume he'd found the phone number of a local florist. Since it was nearly nine p.m., I'd thought she might be asleep, but her eyes were open, the head of the bed raised so she could watch TV. And what was she watching? A replay of today's WST heats. I recognised Scottie Stenson wiping out and gave a silent cheer.

"I told them everything I could. The cops and lawyers are so busy slinging words at each other, I'm not even sure they noticed when I left. How are you feeling?"

Her bottom lip quivered. "Honestly? I'm scared. Mr. Rennick says the best doctors are treating me, but nobody will give me a straight answer about anything, and they took my phone away so I can't even google."

That was probably a smart idea. I'd googled extensively myself, and thallium poisoning wasn't pretty. Did she realise that she'd start losing her hair soon? I spotted a few loose strands on the pillow and a lump came into my throat. If nobody had told her, she'd work it out soon. Should I mention it? If it only thinned a little, then I might worry her for nothing.

"At least you have a diagnosis now."

She managed a wan smile. "I really wish I had food poisoning instead. That's what I thought it was. Or an intolerance. Shona in accounting ate bread her whole life, and then she woke up one morning and found she was allergic to gluten. Do you think I can still eat bread? They didn't say I couldn't, but all they bring me is soup."

Like Rennick, Lila had become more human when faced with difficulty. The primness had fallen away, replaced with vulnerability.

"Want me to find out? If you're allowed other food, I could sneak in a pastry for breakfast."

Or maybe a dozen. If I mentioned the issue to Rennick, he'd buy her a whole patisserie. And that wouldn't be a bad thing—Lila had always been slender, but now she looked gaunt, her cheeks sunken.

"I'd love a Danish."

"Do you need anything else? Slippers? Magazines? A toothbrush?"

"Mr. Rennick had toiletries delivered, and I don't want to put you to any trouble."

"It's no trouble."

"Really?" She bit her lip. "If you're near my apartment, could you pick up some books? There's a stack on my nightstand. I'm not sure what happened to my key, but there's a spare in my desk drawer at work. Mr. Rennick might be able to give you access?"

Was AnyBet headquarters open on a Sunday? "Or you could call the concierge in your apartment building and ask them to let me in?"

"Yes, I could do that. But why are you here? I thought you'd travel to Hawaii to watch Zach this weekend."

"All the action seems to be in Vegas. And things between Zach and me…they're not good."

Lila reached out a hand and squeezed mine. This was all wrong—I was supposed to be the one comforting *her*. She was sick; I was healthy. And if her poisoning was connected to the Torres case, then I'd failed in the worst possible way. Lila should never have become collateral damage. I should have foreseen this. Worked harder. Joined the dots faster.

"I'm so sorry for that," she said. "But it'll be okay. My mom, she was a great believer in fate. I had some real dark days in the past, and one time, I almost got overwhelmed, but it turned out that the universe had a different plan for me." Or her meddling father did. "If you keep the faith, everything will resolve itself."

"I prefer to take a more hands-on approach. I have several leads to follow up after breakfast tomorrow."

Rennick had eventually managed to reach his CFO on the golf course, and the man was on his way back to Las Vegas. He'd promised to provide a list of names by first thing tomorrow. Thankfully, Alexa was ahead of the game—although we couldn't admit as much—and I'd start taking a look at the new suspects in the morning. One of the women— Riley Morrow—hailed from Chicago, which suggested a possible connection to Troy, plus she played on the AnyBet volleyball team with Lila. Riley was first on my list to visit. Alexa had promised to send through all the information she'd compiled, but she'd gone AWOL again. The lady who answered the phone at Church Group had taken a message.

"Following leads is more important than my books." Lila glanced at the screen. "Oh, wow. Zach Torres really is phenomenal. I don't understand most of what the commentator says, but that part where he ends up in the middle of a wave and then pops out of the end is spectacular." Her cheeks reddened. "You probably already know that."

"It's called 'getting barrelled.'" I took a seat in the visitor chair for the slow-motion replay. "Where is he on the leaderboard?"

"First place. Shane Lotter is second, and Kai Kealoha is third. Bad news for the people trying to steal from Mr. Rennick."

Yes, it was. When the camera panned, I spotted Maya on the jet ski, and yes, I saw what Alexa meant about the evil looks. Maya wasn't happy with the situation, not one bit, and I noted she was keeping herself between Tyler and Zach. Good.

"I can wake up early and grab your books."

Something told me I wouldn't be getting much sleep tonight.

CHAPTER 57
ARI

"You can't keep the police out of this investigation," I told Alexa. "Thallium is on a whole other level compared to replacing Zach's oat milk with the cow version."

A yawn crept up on me. Sleep hadn't come easy last night. Haven and Nana had already gone to bed when I got home, and with nothing to distract me, I'd logged on to Alexa's portal to watch Zach in Hawaii. Although I'd spent most of the time monitoring Tyler, gritting my teeth as I did so. Maya's laptop had been moved to the counter, giving me a slightly better angle to watch as he set Zach's board on the kitchen table, donned a pair of gloves to strip off the old wax with a heat gun followed by solvent, and then methodically reapplied fresh wax until the surface was covered in tiny bumps. From the stilted conversation Tyler had with Maya, I understood that Zach and Kai were out at a meet-and-greet, probably under duress.

When she opened the refrigerator, I was pleased to note the minimal contents, and the only drinks were in cans rather than bottles or cartons. According to Alexa, Maya was buying food right before each meal, either from a local grocery store or from one of the WST food vendors. When Tyler had questioned the arrangement, she'd told him they should all make an effort to eat fresher food.

Yes, Maya was playing her part; now I had to do the same.

I cradled the phone against my shoulder while I opened Lila's refrigerator. As expected, the police had removed everything edible from her apartment, but they'd left the place surprisingly tidy after their search. I'd seen apartments turned upside down in the past, but I guess the cops made more of an effort when the home belonged to a victim rather than a suspect.

"I'm not trying to keep the police out entirely, just stall them," Alexa said.

"Why? Why would you want to do that?"

She'd finally called back, although she didn't apologise for going AWOL at a critical moment, and now she was throwing up roadblock after roadblock.

"Because we're doing fine on our own, aren't we? What can they do that we can't?"

"Arrest people?"

Alexa fell silent. Suspiciously silent.

"That was always the endgame, right? To gather enough evidence to prove that a crime had taken place?"

Although I realised now that we'd never actually discussed what would happen after we identified the culprits. I'd just assumed we'd involve the authorities because that was what normal people did, wasn't it? Except too late, I'd realised that Alexa was far from normal. Say, if normal was downtown Vegas, then Alexa was the dark side of the moon.

"Justice doesn't always come through the legal system," she muttered.

Oh, you've got to be kidding me.

"I'm not some vigilante. What were you planning to do? Send a heavy over to break their legs?"

I abandoned Lila's kitchen and headed through to the

bedroom. The smell of vomit still permeated the air, although someone had cleaned up the floor now. The bed had been stripped too. For evidence? Or had the linen been laundered? I'd brought a tote bag for the books, half a dozen of them, all detective stories. Bet Lila hadn't expected to become embroiled in her own mystery.

I'd already driven past Riley Morrow's place, a neat ranch-style home in the suburbs. The windows had been dark, the drapes closed. The two vehicles in the driveway—a minivan and a pickup that had never seen dirt in its life—suggested she was a later riser rather than on the run. After I'd swung by the grocery store for Lila's pastries and dropped them off at the hospital, I'd pay another visit to the Morrow home. People parked on the street around there, so I could watch from the car for a while without a concerned neighbour filing a report.

"Ugh. Breaking legs is so Mafia," Alexa said. "There are far better ways to send a message."

I'd probably regret asking, but… "Such as?"

"They're in this for the money, right? So ruining them financially would be a good start."

The way she said that, I absolutely knew she'd done it before. Shit. Once again, I felt as if I was walking on eggshells around Alexa. What if she decided I was persona non grata? Would she ruin me? Although I wasn't exactly swimming in cash, so she'd have to get creative.

"You don't think jail would be enough of a punishment?"

"It's so cute that you trust the cops to do their job."

"You don't?"

"You know who they protect and serve? Themselves."

Fuck.

I froze, and not because of Alexa's attitude toward law enforcement. No, I froze because I'd just heard a knock, and I had no idea who was on the other side of the door. Jerome? No, his shift was over now—he'd been about to go home when I arrived. Or Rennick? No, I'd messaged him to say I was coming to get the books, and he'd have mentioned it if he planned to meet me here. After my comment about his stupid list, he'd found a phone from somewhere and given me the number.

"There's somebody here," I whispered.

"Who?"

"I don't freaking know. If I could see through walls, I'd have said their name."

"Maybe it's a friend. Or a neighbour with cookies."

"Or maybe it's someone with darker intentions."

"Do you have a gun?"

"No."

"Why not? You should get one."

"Now isn't the time for this discussion," I said through gritted teeth, right before I heard the telltale scrape of a key in the lock. "They're coming in."

"Stay on the line. If it turns out to be an axe-wielding psychopath, I'll call nine-one-one and the cops can come and rescue you. Will that make you happy?"

"Delirious. Shh."

The door swung open as I tucked the phone into my pocket, and for a brief second, I was tempted to hide. But I was entitled to be here, and I had dubious backup in the form of Alexa.

"Lila?" the newcomer called. A woman. "Are you okay?"

I stepped out of the bedroom. "She's not here."

Meryl's eyes widened when she saw me, and her grip on the paper carrier bag she was holding tightened. It took me a second to recognise her—gone were the sleek shift dress and perfect chignon, replaced by yoga pants and a messy bun. She'd swapped her glasses for contacts, too.

"Who are you? Wait a second... I've seen you before. In the office?"

"I'm a friend of Lila's."

"Where is she? Is she still sick? I tried to call her, but she's not answering her phone."

"Didn't the guy at the front desk tell you?"

"Seth? He just waved me through. Tell me what? Why are you in her apartment?"

"Lila's in the hospital."

"The *hospital*? Because of a stomachache?"

How much should I tell Meryl? There was every chance she was simply a concerned friend, but beyond Zach, Nana, and Haven, I didn't trust anyone, not now.

"They're running tests."

"My gosh, is it serious?"

"The EMTs seemed concerned. When I see her, I'll tell her you dropped by." Then I got curious. "You have a key to her apartment?"

"She leaves it in her desk drawer. I water her plants when she travels with Mr. Rennick. Did you water the plants? The fern in the bathroom gets very thirsty."

"I haven't, not yet."

"Want me to do it while I'm here? And is there anything else Lila needs? I could run to the store after my yoga class." She held up the carrier bag. "Are you hungry? I brought Lila breakfast from Franco's—she loves Franco's—and it'll go to waste otherwise."

"I'm actually going to visit her in the hospital. Want me to take it? She's sick of eating soup."

"That's kind of you." Meryl put the bag on the counter. "And let me give you my number. If she needs any help, just call. I'll let Mr. Rennick know as well. Do you have any idea when she'll be back at work?" A giggle. "I realise that sounds callous, but it's the first question he'll ask."

I nearly told her that he was aware of the situation already, but then I figured I'd let him handle it. Right now, information was being given out on a need-to-know basis, and Meryl didn't need the details.

"Sorry, but I don't have that information."

"Are you taking her something to read? She's a real bookworm."

"That's why I'm here—she asked me to pick up her books."

"Good, good. I'll just water the fern, and then I'll get out of your way." She checked her phone screen. "My class starts in thirty minutes."

I watched as she found a watering can and a bottle of plant food in the cupboard under the sink, replaying the conversation in my mind. Was Meryl simply checking on a sick colleague? Or did she have an ulterior motive for being here? This case had turned me paranoid. But was it really paranoia when someone was running around with thallium? Zach had already been betrayed by one of his close friends, hadn't he? I quickly stuffed the books into the tote bag, picked up the bag of goodies from Franco's, and met Meryl at the door.

"Stairs or elevator?" she asked. "I always take the stairs. With a desk job, I need to fit in exercise when I can."

"The stairs are fine." Although I had visions of being shoved down them and landing in a broken heap at the bottom. "After you."

"Tell Lila that I hope she feels better soon? She can call me any time."

"I'll pass on the message."

"And let her know I'll water the plants for as long as she needs."

Mental note: get those locks changed. If Meryl had borrowed the key from Lila's drawer, who else could have gotten ahold of it? They wouldn't even have to keep it—I could name half a dozen locksmiths who'd cut a spare, no questions asked, even if the key was marked "do not duplicate."

Meryl waved to the grey-haired man who'd replaced Jerome at the front desk, and we exited into bright sunlight.

"See you soon," she said, heading toward a silver Lexus.

Wait.

A silver Lexus?

I frantically searched my sleep-deprived brain for the registration I'd memorised last week. Holy shit, it matched. I knew who that car belonged to, and it wasn't Meryl Krieger.

Oh yeah, I'd be seeing her *very* soon.

CHAPTER 58
ARI

"I have to take this to the police."

The breakfast Meryl had brought for Lila was sitting on my passenger seat. A smoothie, a tub of chopped fruit, and some kind of Danish in a grease-spotted paper bag. I'd been careful not to touch any of the contents. The question we now had to answer was, did any of them contain thallium? If she was cold enough to sit at her desk every day, poisoning the woman she pretended to care about and stealing from her boss, I honestly wouldn't have put it past her to serve up a poisonous pastry.

"We can run lab tests privately," Alexa told me.

"That won't be admissible in court."

"Who cares about court?"

"Meryl Krieger committed a crime. There's a process we have to go through. Laws we have to follow."

"Laws, schmaws."

"Would you prefer anarchy?"

"You think the cops follow their own rules?"

"As in any profession, there are some who don't, but plenty who do. We need to turn this evidence over to them."

"No."

"No? That's it? No? Stating the obvious, how are you going to stop me?"

"I'll find a way."

"From Norway or Japan or the Bahamas or wherever the hell you are?"

"I'm in Las Vegas."

Really? Well, wasn't that interesting?

"So? It's a big city. What's to prevent me from driving straight to the nearest police station?"

"The delivery truck parked in front of your car."

Oh, that little… Was Alexa here? Actually here? I flung the door open, leapt out, and ran around the truck, vaguely aware of her laughing through the phone as I stared wildly around. Then I spotted the beady eye of a traffic camera high up on the pole and growled in frustration.

"You hacked the city's camera network?"

"Of course."

"Well, that changes nothing. In five minutes, the truck will be gone, and I can drive wherever I want with Lila's breakfast."

"We have a contract. I'm the client."

"What are you gonna do if I breach it? Take me to court? Drain my bank account?"

"Look, you just have to trust me. I know what I'm doing."

That was debatable. Alexa was a loose cannon.

"Trust you? Why should I trust you? You hacked my laptop, screwed with my mind, and now you're spying on me. Why can't you trust me when I say we should go to the cops?"

"Because my uncle was a police captain. He was also the man who abused me for six years while his buddies looked the other way. Cops are scum."

Alexa stopped abruptly, and I sensed she hadn't meant to say so much. That was the first truly personal thing she'd ever told me, and boy, was it a humdinger of a revelation.

"I'm so sorry you went through that."

"I don't need your damn sympathy. I need justice for Zach, and a woman like Meryl Krieger would shed a few tears in front of the jury and get six months in minimum security. Troy Peralta would get zip for the sportsbook scam. The two of them have a history of putting the money back, and the Clark County DA is notoriously soft on white-collar criminals."

A part of me feared that Alexa was right. And I also knew there was no direct link to Tyler's involvement in spiking Zach's drinks, just a bunch of circumstantial evidence and the assumptions that had led us to Meryl today. He'd get off scot-free, and I hated that.

But ultimately, Zach had escaped relatively unscathed. Lila was the one lying in the hospital.

"I also want them to pay—Meryl, Troy, and Tyler—but right now, the person I'm most concerned about is Lila. She needs to be involved in the process too. Yes, Meryl's sentence might be lighter than you or I would like, but at least Lila would get closure. If you dispense some alternative brand of justice in secret, she'll always be looking over her shoulder, wondering if the person who tried to kill her is still out there, waiting." I climbed back into the car and closed my eyes, blocking out the carrier bag on the passenger seat as I combed through what little I knew about the most difficult client I'd ever worked with. "How would your life be different if your uncle had been arrested and jailed? If, instead of covering for him, his colleagues had done as they were supposed to do and sided with you? Would you sleep easier at night? Would you go out in public instead of hiding away from the world? Would you stay in one place instead of constantly running?"

"Stop."

"Would you have a home? A boyfriend? A puppy you took to the dog park?"

"Just stop!"

"Would you answer questions instead of avoiding them?"

"Fuck you."

Alexa hung up, and I let out a long breath as I stared through the windshield, vaguely aware of the delivery truck backing away and turning out of the visitors' lot. Hot damn, I hadn't just touched a nerve with Alexa, I'd jump-started a whole freaking bunch of them. She'd never been anything but cool and snarky before.

Now what was I meant to do? Should I call back? Apologise? I did see her point about the court system, and the current DA had been a disappointment ever since he was elected. He'd run on a platform of anti-corruption, which turned out to be bullshit. Only after he took office had rumours of him accepting bribes as a prosecutor begun to swirl.

But Morty had been a detective with the LVMPD, and I'd crossed paths with plenty of good cops during my years as an investigator. I could see both sides of the story. Alexa only saw one, and now I understood why.

Sighing, I called her again.

No answer.

But I wasn't giving up. I knew she was there, and she was probably hurting too.

"Leave me alone," she snapped on the fifth attempt.

"What sort of friend would I be if I did that?"

"We're not friends. You just said we don't trust each other."

"You trusted me enough to tell me about your uncle."

Silence, punctuated by a sniffle.

"Do you have someone there with you?" I asked. "Where's Chase?"

"Out."

"Will he be back soon?"

"Yes."

Okay, we were down to monosyllabic answers, but at least Chase would be able to take care of her.

"I'm sorry I pushed you to a place you didn't want to visit. This might be a personal question, but have you ever seen a therapist?"

Alexa's snort of laughter gave me the answer.

"When my old boss suggested I should seek professional help, I had the same reaction, but it did make a difference. I really struggled after I had my daughter. I was so young, and my own mom abandoned me, plus my dad's in prison, but I expect you already know that."

"Of course I do."

Ah, there was a glimmer of the old Alexa. "Just consider it. And I get that you hate the idea of the cops, but in this case, I think we should call them. How about a compromise? If Meryl doesn't do a sensible amount of jail time, then I'm not going to object if you introduce a little extra difficulty into her life."

"And the Peraltas?"

"Same."

"My name stays out of it."

"Deal. I'll need a recording of my conversation with Meryl, and don't tell me you didn't make one."

"I made one. Do you want the camera footage of her arriving and leaving too?"

"No, because I wouldn't be able to explain how I got it. But I'll tell the cops there's a camera outside, and they can do the legwork."

"They'd better do it quickly. The city only keeps the recordings for twenty-four hours."

"I'll make sure they know that. Now we just have to hope there's thallium in this damn smoothie."

CHAPTER 59
ARI

Three hours later, it was done. Round one, anyway. Under Alexa's instruction, Don Kessler had backed off an inch, and Detectives Metcalfe and Riker had listened with no small amount of incredulity as I laid out the bones of the case I'd been investigating, first on behalf of AnyBet and then for "a concerned friend." They agreed to check into the issue and promised they'd have a thousand more questions later, but I'd cross that bridge when I came to it. For now, we all had to wait for the lab tests on Lila's breakfast to be processed.

As for Rennick, well, he looked kind of green. His chief financial officer had come back with the news that it wasn't just any old corporate account that had been targeted by Troy and Meryl—the account in question was a director's current account. Over twenty years ago, Digby Rennick had used the million bucks he'd received for solving Baxter's Last Theorem to start his gambling empire, and as a consequence, the AnyBet group owed him money that he hadn't yet collected. No, he'd left it in a designated company account in case it was needed to fund future expansion, and with the addition of interest and early salary payments that he'd ploughed back into the business, the amount owed had grown to just over six million bucks. Lila checked the balance during the first week of each month as part of her admin work, and it always matched her expectations. But she wasn't an accountant. She'd never dug into the transactions. If she had, she'd have seen that Meryl had often "borrowed" a hefty sum during the middle of the month to fund her illicit activities.

But Zach's win at Surf 365 meant she hadn't been able to put the money back at the end of September, so she'd taken drastic measures to avoid Lila performing the reconciliation.

Thallium.

As for why Meryl had started stealing from her employer in the first place, that was a question we still had to answer. Alexa was busy digging through her entire life history as I sat with Lila and Rennick, waiting for Zach's quarter-final against Kai to begin. Exhaustion washed over me in waves. My stress levels had been sky-high since the fight with Zach, but now I could finally start to heal, content in the knowledge that the man I loved was safe even if he was no longer by my side.

Alexa assured me that now we'd found the link between Tyler and AnyBet, Tyler would be out of Zach's life by tomorrow. Strangely, I felt a twinge of sadness over that. The end of a long friendship, betrayal by the man Zach thought of as a brother. Why had Tyler gone along with the scheme? To avoid a bank loan?

To me, that was the biggest puzzle of all.

"You look tired," Lila said.

"Isn't that my line? How are you feeling now?"

"A little better. They gave me something for the nausea." She slid up the arm of her hospital gown to reveal a beige patch stuck to her skin. "No needle. It's transdermal. But my hands and feet have gone weird. Kind of tingly."

"Are you still taking the Prussian blue?"

She nodded. "The doctor's hopeful that I'll make a good recovery, but I'm going to lose some of my hair. Maybe all of it." The way her face crumpled, I understood how much that upset her. "But I'll be back at work real soon, I swear."

"Work doesn't matter," Rennick told her. "Take as much time as you need."

"But if Meryl leaves…"

Leaves? How diplomatic of her. Meryl was going to jail or hell, depending on whether Alexa got her way or not.

"I'll hire another assistant to help out. Your health is far more important than picking up my dry-cleaning. Do you need a wig? I can order a wig that looks just like your regular hair. What about someone to clean your apartment? You'll be tired when you get home."

I realised Rennick was only trying to help, but enthusiasm or nerves or guilt—or perhaps a combination of all three— had caused him to blur the lines in their relationship. Right now, he was thinking of himself as her father, not her boss.

"Is there a friend who can water your plants?" he asked. "Or should I do it?"

"Uh, Mr. Rennick…?"

The formality seemed to jar him back to reality. "Or you could just charge some new plants to your expense account."

"Really?"

"Technically, you were injured at work. You shouldn't be left out of pocket."

"I don't know what to say." She managed a sad smile. "My last supervisor questioned whether I needed a whole day off for my mom's funeral."

"You're more than just an employee to me, Lila. I care about you."

Oh, he definitely wasn't thinking before he spoke today. Lila took his words, saw the way he was looking at her, did the math, and came up with completely the wrong answer.

"Mr. Rennick, I care for you too, of course I do, but not in that way. You're so much older than me, and I'm focused on my career at the moment, and...and..."

Horror dawned as he realised what she was saying, and he looked to me for help. Mr. Cool, Calm, and Collected was definitely panicking, and under any other circumstances, I would have laughed.

"Just tell her," I said. "She deserves to know."

"Know what?" Lila's voice held the same anxiety—like father, like daughter. Although they didn't look particularly alike, they shared many of the same mannerisms, and now that I'd spent more time with them, I realised their personalities were uncannily similar. Genetics had a lot to answer for.

"I...I..."

Yes, his discomfort was definitely amusing, but I could see he needed assistance.

"Lila, how much do you know about your father?"

"My father? What does that have to do with anything?"

"Before we got a diagnosis, the hospital staff were asking for details about your family history yesterday."

"Oh? Well, I understand he didn't have any weird genetic diseases if that's what they're concerned about." She gave a nervous giggle. "I guess that sounds like a strange thing to say, but I never knew him. Neither did my mom. Which sounds even stranger, but she mostly hated men." She glanced at Rennick. "Sorry."

"There's nothing to apologise for. Her sexual preferences were hers and hers alone."

"Oh, she wasn't a lesbian. She got married young, and the jackass—that's what she always called him—put her off men for life. But she always wanted children, so she went to one of those fertility clinics and picked a guy out of a book. He was really smart, she said. Smart and healthy."

"Did you ever get curious about his identity?"

"Oh, sure. Who wouldn't? But while Mom was alive, I pretended I didn't care. She got upset if I asked questions. Defensive. Which was silly because she always gave my sister—half-sister, technically—and me enough love for two."

"And after she passed away?"

A tear rolled down Lila's cheek. Rennick passed her a handkerchief, which seemed to embarrass her more than anything. I only hoped a nurse didn't come to check up on her—if the staff thought we were upsetting a patient, they'd throw us out.

"I just wanted to find out who he was, that was all. I guess I had some stupid notion that he'd give me a hug and tell me everything would be okay, which goes to show I wasn't thinking straight at the time, doesn't it? What man would want a random child to show up on his doorstep? He probably has his own family now. A wife. More children. Imagine if he's a famous movie star? Or a world-renowned scientist? Anyhow, I called the clinic, but apparently, they don't give out that information. The only thing I could do was submit my DNA to a bunch of those ancestry websites." She gave us a watery smile. "Who knows, maybe he'll get in touch someday?"

"He already did."

"What are you talking about? I think I'd remember if that had happened."

Finally, Rennick spoke, his voice thick with emotion.

"I'm your father, Lila."

The *beep, beep, beep* of the heart-rate monitor punctuated the stunned silence. Lila's tears turned into full-on weeping, and I wasn't sure whether she was happy or sad. Rennick was no use either. He just stood there. I gave Lila's shoulder a squeeze to reassure her that she wasn't alone, and the sobs subsided into sniffles.

"If this is a joke, it isn't funny."

Rennick shifted from foot to foot. "Have you ever known me to joke?"

"No." She looked up at him through teary eyes. "You're really my father?"

"Yes."

"But...but... Why didn't you tell me before? I've been working for you for almost four years."

"I wasn't certain you'd want to know, and nor did I have any idea how to be a dad. But I didn't want you to be alone after the tragedy."

"So you...what? Gave me a job out of pity?"

"Not at all. It stood to reason that if you shared half my DNA, then you'd be smart, well-organised, and able to cope with a challenging work environment." What about humble? He forgot to mention humble. "My assumption was right. You're the best assistant I've ever had, although..." He sighed. "Although I'll understand if you don't feel able to continue."

"You want me to leave?"

"Absolutely not. If the arrangement doesn't make you feel uncomfortable now that you know we're related, then I very much want you to stay."

"I... I'm scared everything's going to change."

"Nothing needs to change, not unless you want it to. Just know that if you ever need assistance with anything— whether that's ensuring you have the best medical care, or watering your plants, or buying you an apartment—you can come to me."

"I'd never ask you to buy me an apartment."

"That was merely an example. For now, we can simply carry on as normal." He settled back in the high-backed chair beside the bed and changed the subject. If I'd been a gambling woman, which I definitely wasn't after this case, then I'd put money on Lila getting a new apartment for her next birthday. "Look, Zach Torres is about to surf."

Lila settled back against the pillow, eyes focused on the screen but her mind clearly elsewhere. And who could blame her? She'd just found out that the man she'd spent years working for shared half her genes. Which was kind of cool. Although Rennick could be a bit odd with his zen garden and dumb-ass list, they were clearly on the same wavelength. Plus he cared. He cared enough to drop everything to be with her. I felt a pang of jealousy because if someone had asked my father to choose between me and his Porsche, I'd have been left staring at his tail lights as he roared off.

"I hate when Zach and Kai are pitted against each other in the quarter-final," I said, turning my attention to the contest. "It means one of them will be in fifth place overall or lower."

Rennick took a sip of water. "Let's hope Zach wins. If he loses, I'll need to hire a forensic accountant to untangle the financial mess."

"Kai's good, but when Zach's on form, he has an extra…" What had Erin called it? "An extra flair that Kai can't match."

"Is he on form?" Rennick studied the screen critically, head tilted to one side.

"He won his heat by two clear points."

"You know, it's strange. We were still taking excessive bets against him through yesterday morning. Meryl's gang must have been confident he'd lose."

"His sister's been watching everything he eats or drinks like a hawk. There's just no way someone tampered with his food."

But why were Meryl and Troy still placing bets after Maya implemented her new dining regimen? Surely Tyler must have realised he couldn't spike Zach's drink as usual? Why hadn't he told his brother so Troy and Meryl could do damage control? Or were they truly gambling this time, hoping Zach would screw up, just one last desperate attempt to plug the hole in Rennick's bank account?

Or…or had they come up with a different way to hamper Zach's performance?

My gaze drifted across to Lila… The patch on her arm… The gloves the doctors wore… Last night, Tyler had been wearing gloves as he waxed Zach's surfboard…

Dammit. Dammit! Why hadn't I picked up on it at the time? I'd watched him prep boards in the past, and he always wore gloves to apply the wax remover, but then he took them off before he began the new coat of wax. Yesterday, he'd kept them on the whole time.

No…

Oh, no.

"It's on Zach's board," I said, my voice hollow. "Tyler messed with Zach's board. That's how they're going to drug him. It's the only way."

"Won't it simply wash off?" Rennick asked. "He's in the water now."

"It's mixed into the wax, and that's waterproof."

My fingers shook as I grabbed my phone and called Maya, but she didn't answer. I caught a glimpse of her on-screen, bobbing around on a jet ski, oblivious. Either she couldn't hear the phone over the noise, or more likely, she'd left it on the shore. I tried Alexa instead.

"Tyler put something on Zach's surfboard. Some sort of drug that goes through his skin."

"He's in the ocean—won't it just wash away?"

So she was watching the contest too.

"No, I don't think so. They'll have thought of that. It's mixed into the wax. We need to get him off that board right this second."

"I… *Fuck.*" The silence stretched painfully. All I could hear was the *beep, beep, beep* of Lila's monitor and my own heartbeat racing twice as fast. "Give me ten minutes, and I think I can get a message onto the scoreboard."

"We might not have ten minutes. I don't know what substance they've used."

Rennick came to life. "I'll find a doctor and ask which drugs can be transferred transdermally."

"Don't forget to ask about antidotes," Lila called after him as he ran out of the room.

"What if I took down the whole camera network?" Alexa asked. "I could kill the TV feed. They'd have to delay the contest while they fix it."

"What if Zach stays out on the water? He could get into difficulties, and we wouldn't even be able to see."

"Erin's there. Get her to cause a distraction. Fire a gun into the air or whatever."

"Are you crazy? Who would take a gun to a surf contest?"

"Literally everyone I know."

"Well, *I* wouldn't—" Shit, we didn't have time for this. "I'm calling Erin."

She picked up on the second ring, although I could barely hear her over the cheering.

"Tell me you're at Pipeline."

"Right on the beach. There's a guy selling cotton candy, and do you know how long it's been since I had cotton candy? Are you watching on TV? Can you see me? I'm by the podium. Wait, I'll jump up and down."

"I don't have time to go into the details, but there's poison on Zach's surfboard, and we need to get him off it. Can you cause a distraction? Yell 'shark' or something? Anything to make them bring the surfers in."

"Whoa, poison? On his surfboard? What kind of poison?"

"We don't know yet, and there's no time to chat."

"Okay, so I don't think the 'shark' thing will work. They have drones in the air checking for those. But don't worry, you're talking to your number-one investigative assistant right here. I'll come up with a better idea."

"He might not have much time."

The waves had to be fifteen feet tall, and the surf zone was brutal. I knew from personal experience what water could do to a person's body if they slipped beneath the surface.

"Just relax, I've got this."

Relax? I'd never felt so helpless in my life.

CHAPTER 60
ZACH

"You okay, dude?"

Zach focused on Kai, sitting twenty feet away on a surfboard, and considered the question. The whole damn world was waiting on the beach, but out here, it was just the two of them.

"Tired. Should've overruled Maya and had an energy drink."

"She's still paranoid, huh? Baylee really got into her head."

"Yeah, something like that."

Why did he feel so drowsy? Was it hunger? He'd barely eaten, just a bowl of fruit and yogurt that Maya had conjured up from somewhere. There were no snacks in the damn refrigerator. Seriously, this had to stop. Fainting from a lack of food would be as bad as puking his guts up from a bad reaction to lactose. He'd tell his sister that she had to change her ways, but first, he had to get through the forty-five minutes of this quarter-final. One good wave, that was all he needed. Zach scanned the horizon, hoping Neptune was in a benevolent mood this morning.

But Kai was looking the other way.

"What's happening over there?" he asked.

"Over where?"

"On the beach. Aw, hell, it looks like a protester. She's waving a sign in the air."

Had security screwed up again? Zach squinted, and his head began to throb. A girl… In the water… What was the protest about this time? Jet skis disorienting sea turtles? Nelson's spectacle disrupting the local ecosystem? Or was it another more general complaint about plastic in the ocean?

"That's hella strange," Kai said. "The sign just melted. Maybe it wasn't a sign. Maybe it was cotton candy."

"Why would a protester have cotton candy?"

Drugs? Was she on drugs? Whatever, the woman had managed to get pretty far out into the water. Now she was splashing around, arms flailing.

"Who knows?" Kai shrugged, hands out. "Tyler's going to get her."

"You think we should wait? If there's trouble, they might extend the time."

"If I see a good wave, I'm riding it."

Tyler would get the woman out of the way—it wasn't the first time he'd dealt with a protester. In Keramas two years ago, a dozen women had leapt into the water, naked except for bikini bottoms and painted-on clamshells over their breasts. The camera had zoomed in close enough to read the #SaveOurSeas slogans written across their stomachs before the director gave the order to cut away. Anyhow, Tyler had managed to coax two of them onto his sled before the security team got their act together and found a boat.

A wave of nausea came, and Zach gripped the board, willing it to pass. What was wrong with him? Last week, Alexa had emailed a warning to stay on his guard and avoid any food not sourced by Maya, ditto for drinks. He'd kept his word, although he was worried about his sister. She'd become militant about the restrictions, even snapping at Kai when he'd offered Zach a beer the day before yesterday. When the contest was over, he'd have to persuade her to back off. Baylee was clearly to blame for any past contamination.

Zach shifted his position on the board, legs hanging into the water, feeling more tired by the second. When he'd paddled out, his big concern had been whether to catch the first half-decent wave and throw in some air, or wait for the perfect break and hope to get barrelled. But now he was anxious about standing up at all. He gripped the rails harder, willing the exhaustion to pass.

Near the shore, Tyler reached the protester, and after a brief conversation, she reached for his offered hand. But instead of swinging up onto the jet ski behind him, she…no… Did she really just punch him in the face?

"Holy cow." Kai knelt on his board to get a better look. "Zed's gonna shit a brick."

"Nah, think of the ratings."

Then Tyler was in the water, and his assailant was on the jet ski, heading in their direction, yelling something unintelligible.

"What the…?" Zach's brain was turning to sludge. "Is this…some kind of terrorist?"

Where was the security team? If the woman had a gun, they'd be in trouble. There were no rideable waves coming, and even if there were, Zach wasn't sure he'd be able to catch one. Out of the corner of his eye, he saw Maya turn in their direction, and he tried to wave her away, but he couldn't raise his arm. The woman got closer.

"Get off! Get off the board!"

Why? Why should he? He had every right to be here. The WST had a permit. Besides, if Zach got off the board, he wasn't sure he'd ever manage to climb back on it.

"Get lost, lady."

She was close now, an elfin girl with rainbow streaks in

her dark hair and a determined look on her face. No protest sign. Her shirt sported a picture of a mermaid.

"You don't understand. The board is…"

The rest of the words were whipped away by the wind as she turned her head, and thank fuck, several members of the security team were on their way. Then Zach caught a glimpse of Kai's face. His mouth was open, his brow furrowed in total disbelief.

"Joy?"

"Just get Zach off the board. Please? I'll explain later, I swear, but I need you to do this one thing."

"Who…? Who…?" Zach started.

"Get off the board, buddy."

"No…can't…tired…so tired…"

Kai pulled him off the board and towed him over to the woman's jet ski. Why was he doing this? No gun… Contest… Ratings…

"Lift him onto the sled," she ordered. "Hold him there."

Then Maya arrived in a hiss of spray. "What's happening? What are you doing to my brother?"

"Zach's sick," Kai told her.

Was he? Yeah, yeah, maybe he was. Strange sick. He felt tired, but weirdly happy. As if somehow, this was all meant to happen.

"He was fine half an hour ago."

"Well, now he isn't."

"Tyler put poison on his surfboard," the stranger said. "Probably we should keep that for evidence."

"Who the hell are you?"

Kai spoke again. "This is my sister."

"What sister? You don't have a sister."

Even through the fog, Zach saw the girl wince. Kai *did* have a sister. He'd confided in Zach late one night, a night when they'd both drunk too much sitting on the terrace at Haven's Rest. Not all the details, just the bare bones. There'd been a family fight after his dad died, and he'd left home. Wandered for years and learned how to surf. Later, after he settled in Seagrass Point, he'd tried to get in touch with Joy again, but their mom told him that his sister was married now, happy, and she didn't want him in her life. He was a part of the past she tried to forget, not her future.

That was the only time Zach had seen his friend cry.

But this lunatic on the jet ski, this was Joy?

Wait a second… Poison?

"Zach has to get to the hospital. Like, right now. Alexa and Ari are gonna be real mad if he dies."

Alexa? Alexa was involved in this stunt? He should have realised. And Ari? Beautiful, sweet, traitorous Ari… How did she know about Joy?

Tyler poisoned his surfboard?

No, no, Tyler was his friend.

Zach found himself on the sled, held in place by Kai. Someone unfastened the leash from around his ankle, and then the board was gone. *Poison?* And here were the waves, beautiful monsters that left any humans in their path bobbing around like corks before they peeled away left and right. He should be riding those waves, but lying around, watching the sky was cool too. Where was Ari? She should be right here next to him, at his side, where she was meant to be.

"What kind of poison?" Kai asked.

"I don't know. I don't even know if Ari and Alexa know. Ari just told me to get him away from the board. Don't touch it!"

"I'm only touching the leash," Maya said.

"How do you know Ari?" Kai demanded.

"So we were in this strip club…"

Boy, that sounded like a good story, but Zach couldn't keep his eyes open any longer. He gave in to the sirens calling him, and everything went dark.

"He'll be okay." Lila gripped both of my hands in hers, an IV line trailing off to the side. I'd been sitting on the edge of her bed ever since my knees gave way. "Erin got to him fast."

Erin had pulled off a miracle. Not only had she dodged security to get to the water, but she'd also broken Tyler's nose and stolen his jet ski. And while she was convincing Zach that his life was in danger, Rennick had grabbed a doctor from the emergency room and persuaded him to act as a consultant. He'd narrowed the substance in the wax down to three likely culprits—fentanyl, buprenorphine, or scopolamine. All could be administered transdermally, and each would cause the drowsiness we'd seen on TV when the camera zoomed in. By the time Zach reached the shore, he'd been unconscious.

My heart rate hadn't fallen below a hundred since Erin punched Tyler out. No, seriously. The doctor had checked it. Now we were waiting for news, and whatever drugs they were giving Lila, I needed some.

"How far away is the hospital?" I asked nobody in particular. "What if it took too long to get there?"

"Seven point nine miles." That was Alexa on speaker.

While Erin was busy dealing with Tyler, she'd made sure an ambulance was on site, and Rennick had persuaded "our" doctor to call a colleague at Kahuku Medical Center to explain what he might expect. Antidotes were available for all three substances, just as long as they were given in time. I had to believe Zach would recover.

Rennick came back into the room. "I've spoken with the detectives handling Lila's case and alerted them to a possible connection. They'll speak with their colleagues in Hawaii."

"Somebody needs to arrest Tyler."

"That will happen."

"Not fast enough," Alexa muttered. "Someone needs to kick him off a cliff."

Yes, they did. And meanwhile, Erin was the one who'd been led away in handcuffs, accused of assault. I was beginning to think Alexa was right about cops. Couldn't they see that Tyler had tried to kill Zach? Alexa assured me that Erin's new identity would hold up, but her legal jeopardy was one more reason for the sweat trickling down my spine. Alexa had an attorney on the way to represent her, but I'd forever feel guilty if my investigation landed Erin in trouble.

"I'm first in line for the kicking. What if Tyler tries to leave the country?"

"He might be"—Alexa coughed—"on a watch list."

My phone rang, and when I saw the name on the screen, my racing heart stuttered to a halt.

Maya.

"Hey." My throat was so dry I could barely get the words out. Who had given her my new number? Alexa? "Is Zach okay?"

A pause. "He will be. The doctors say he will be." But Maya sounded shaken. "He stopped breathing in the ambulance. They had to resuscitate him. Another few minutes, and…and…" A sob escaped. "I didn't realise what was happening. He was sitting there on the surfboard, and I didn't realise."

"I didn't work it out until it was nearly too late. Everything just fell into place in my mind."

"You saved him."

"Technically, that was Erin."

"Who's Erin?"

"Kai's sister."

"No, he called her Joy."

"She hates that name, so she changed it."

"This is crazy," Maya said, almost to herself. "Where did she come from? I mean, how did you meet her? Kai's never mentioned her, not once, and he's totally freaked. As soon as Zach was stable, Kai took off for the police station."

"Her name came up in the course of the investigation, and we ended up working together."

"What about Alexa? How is she involved?"

"She hired me after my first client fired me."

"A decision I'll forever regret," Rennick said in the background. "You promised me you wouldn't let me down, and you didn't."

He might have regretted the decision, but I couldn't. Without Alexa's help, I'd never have found enough pieces to put the puzzle together. Solving this case had been a team effort.

"Who's that?" Maya asked.

"My first client. He's back in the picture. Tyler's brother's lady friend poisoned his daughter, and she's in the hospital as well."

Maya's gasp told me Erin hadn't mentioned that part.

"Is she all right? Did they give her opioids too?"

Opioids? Fuck. So our consultant doctor had probably been right about the fentanyl.

"No, thallium. It's a heavy metal. She's still being treated here in Vegas, but she's expected to recover in time."

"You're in Las Vegas?"

"Las Vegas is home."

For the moment, at least.

"You should come here."

"To Hawaii?"

"I'm so, so sorry for what I said. That I didn't want to see you again. I was just upset that you'd been sticking your nose into my life, finding out things I wanted to keep hidden." Maya choked out a laugh and lowered her voice. "You have no idea what I needed to promise Zed to get onto the safety team today."

I wanted to tell her to stand up for herself, to knee Nelson so hard that he choked on his own balls, but now wasn't the time. Maya had offered me an olive branch, and I had to grab it with both hands.

"You think Zach would mind if I came? I don't want to upset him, but I should be there for Erin."

"Zach's been asking for you. I mean, he's also been delirious, but a person's subconscious knows what they want, doesn't it?"

For the first time in weeks, the snake of tension that coiled around my chest eased a smidgen.

"Then I'll get the first flight I can."

When I hung up, Lila and Rennick were both smiling. It must have been infectious.

"Are you going to see Zach?" Lila asked.

"I hope so."

"Mr. Rennick has a large air-miles balance. Maybe he could spare a few?"

"Lila, I don't expect you to call me Dad, but for goodness' sake, call me Digby. And forget the air miles..." He fished out his wallet and handed me a black Amex card. "Book yourself a first-class ticket."

But Alexa had to beat that.

"Forget first class. I have a plane lined up. Just drive to Nellis and give your name at the gate."

"Nellis?"

"It's an Air Force base. Do you need me to send directions?"

"No, I know where it is."

But I did have a whole lot of questions… How did Alexa arrange a flight from a military base? Who did the plane belong to? And who was the guy in the Hawaiian shirt who met me at the guard hut beside the gate in a BMW convertible an hour after I ran out of the hospital?

On first impressions, he looked as if he'd be more at home on a surfboard than Zach. His blond hair was windswept and six months past needing a cut, and his square jaw would have garnered him sponsorship deals. How old was he? The hard body said thirty-five, but the weathered skin said forty-five. Or perhaps he just spent a lot of time outdoors? His eyes were Caribbean blue, twinkling as he climbed out of the car and headed in my direction.

"You must be Arizona?"

"Am I in the right place?"

"You are." He held out a hand. "Priest. I'll be your pilot today."

Priest? Was that a surname or a nickname?

"I don't want to put you to any trouble." Now I sounded like Lila.

"Taking a trip to Oahu is no trouble. I like to fly, and I like to surf." He waved toward the BMW. "After you."

Priest held the passenger door open for me, then ambled toward the driver's side, his flip-flops flapping as he walked. Relaxed, not a care in the world. But right before he climbed in, I heard a loud *bang*—a gunshot?—and he spun toward the sound in the blink of an eye, one hand moving toward the bulge in the small of his back. I recalled Alexa's earlier statement: *literally everyone I know carries a gun.*

Okay, this guy was no beach bum.

And the *bang* was no gunshot. A vintage Porsche backfired again as it rolled past with a dark-haired woman at the wheel, and Priest rolled those vivid blue eyes.

"She needs to get that fuckin' thing serviced."

He climbed behind the wheel and we trundled off, no haste, no hurry. Priest donned a pair of sunglasses and tuned the radio to an oldies station. The Beach Boys were singing. Was he honestly not going to say a word about the bizarre situation we found ourselves in? Was I just expected to act as if all this was normal?

"How do you know Alexa?" I blurted, not really expecting an answer.

"We work together on occasion."

"Are you her boss?"

"Alexa doesn't have a boss. She's very clear on that."

"Have you ever met her? I only ask because she seems obsessively secretive."

"Sure I have. She's been a pain in my ass for the past two weeks."

"What do you mean?"

"I mean that my dining room is filled with computer equipment, and my kitchen stinks of garlic."

"She's staying with you?"

"Don't know why she couldn't get a hotel room. I'm not a fuckin' waiter."

But he said it with affection in his voice, and I realised that this man, whoever he might be, was one of the few people Alexa had let into her life. She trusted him. And that meant I trusted him too.

Seeing as we were on a military base, I'd expected to be stuffed into a transport plane, cargo-style, but thirty minutes later, I found myself climbing the steps onto a medium-sized business jet, along with a redhead who introduced herself as Tulsa and two men in fatigues who didn't introduce themselves at all. Boxes were loaded into the hold, Tulsa joined Priest in the cockpit, and the plane taxied toward the runway.

Me. On a private jet.

I barely even recognised my life anymore.

CHAPTER 62
ARI

Alot happened during the flight to Oahu. Not to me —I spent the six-hour trip reclining in a luxurious leather seat, snacking on pretzels—but on the ground. First, I hadn't realised how much work Don Kessler had been doing in the background. When he wasn't busy being obstructive, he'd put together a file on the case, essentially a roadmap to prosecution for the deputy DA to follow.

Second, the test results from Lila's breakfast had come back positive for thallium. The smoothie was full of the stuff, enough to kill her. If I hadn't seen that Lexus in the parking lot, *I* might have accidentally killed her. That thought gave me the chills.

The cops had pulled the video from the traffic camera outside Lila's building, and when a judge viewed the footage alongside Kessler's file and the recording of my conversation with Meryl, he'd agreed there was enough evidence for an arrest warrant. A team was on its way to pick up that duplicitous bitch as we landed at Hickam Air Force Base.

Third, and latest, Tyler had just been marched out of the hospital in handcuffs. That story was still unfolding, but

Alexa had promised to keep me updated from her hideout in Priest's dining room. I kind of wished the cops had waited another hour because I'd have loved to be there to witness his perp walk.

"Will someone be able to give me a ride to the gate when I land?" I asked Tulsa. She'd abandoned the co-pilot's seat in favour of one that reclined, but she assured me Priest could handle the plane alone. "I need to take a cab to Kahuku."

"Alexa asked me to drive you there."

"You've crossed paths with Alexa too?"

"Can't hardly avoid her. She's taken over the whole damn dining room. Even Chase is keeping out of her way right now."

"You live with Priest? I'm so sorry, I didn't realise you were a couple."

Tulsa let fly with a peal of laughter. "Me and Priest? Oh, honey, no. I'm not his type. I just stay with him when I'm in town."

Really? Very generous of him to offer his spare rooms that way, although I'd have done the same if I had more than an inch of unused space in my apartment.

"What is his type?" I asked, curious.

"Dumb." Tulsa checked her watch and rose from her seat. "Welp, guess we'd better land this bird."

Tulsa broke every speed limit on the way to Kahuku, but I wasn't about to ask her to slow down. No, I just checked my seat belt was secure, closed my eyes, and willed her to drive faster.

"If you need another ride, call Alexa," she said as she pulled up outside the entrance to the hospital. "But I think you'll be going home with Zach."

Unlikely, but when Maya greeted me with a tentative hug and shepherded me to his room, I figured I might be able to bum a couch for the night. Or borrow Tyler's bed, seeing as he wouldn't be needing it anymore.

"I'll leave you two to talk," Maya said, then disappeared along the hallway.

Talk? Despite having hours to think, I still had no idea what to say. But I couldn't stand outside Zach's hospital room all evening. *Take a deep breath, Ari.* I pushed the door open, prepared for the worst. When I'd first seen Lila in the hospital, she'd looked terrible, but Zach was much better. Just slightly pale, his head and shoulders propped up on a pile of pillows.

In the end, I decided to keep things simple.

"How are you feeling?"

"Like I got crushed by a sixty-foot giant. Hell, Ari, I don't know what to say. I fucked up."

"No, you didn't. You surfed, and that's exactly what you were supposed to do. Tyler was the one who fucked up."

I still struggled to believe what he'd done. Tyler had plotted and schemed to steal from Rennick with Zach's career —and ultimately his life—as collateral damage. Why? Why would a man do that? Zach had always treated him as a brother.

"I meant I fucked up with you. When I found out you'd lied, I acted on instinct and pushed you out of my life without considering the consequences."

"It was inevitable. I always knew it was coming. Some days, I tried to kid myself that everything would work out, that I'd solve the case, confess everything, and you'd forgive me, but I knew."

Since that day he rescued me on the beach, I'd been on a slow descent to heartache. Hitting rock bottom hurt more than I ever could have imagined. Before I met Zach, love had been a myth, an abstract, but now I understood just how much I'd lost.

"I have one question," he said. "Were your feelings real?"

"Oh, yeah, they were real." The tears began to fall. I couldn't stop them. "There were times when I almost forgot I was there to work, when I enjoyed life a little too much. And now I find myself wondering whether, if I'd just focused more, I could have outed Tyler earlier and prevented all this." I waved a hand at the bank of monitoring equipment beeping away beside Zach. "He was a much better liar than me."

So smooth. So practised. He'd committed the ultimate betrayal.

"And that's the worst part of this—losing a man I considered a friend. I think..." Zach paused for a moment, fishing for the right words. "I think the reason I overreacted when I realised you'd been lying is that I'd already been there once before, only that time, I lost two friends."

"In Blackstone House?"

He nodded. "Levi lied, and Ruby died. And for the sequel, I was cast in the role of Ruby, and I didn't even realise it." Suddenly, he gave a quiet snort. "Can you hear Alexa's voice in your head? 'Minus the rape and the satanic symbols, Zach,'" he mimicked. "'Stop being so melodramatic.'"

"Tact isn't one of her best attributes."

Money might not have bought her happiness, but it had allowed her the freedom to bypass diplomacy whenever she pleased. It was a luxury I'd never be able to afford.

"At least she stays true to herself."

"Ouch."

"That wasn't meant to be a dig. But if I had a dollar for every time I've had to bite my tongue on the WST, I wouldn't have to worry about prize money."

"I'll always be sorry for lying to you. It started out as just a job, a way to feed my daughter. I didn't mean to fall in love with you, but it happened, and then I couldn't undo the story I'd spun from the beginning."

"You have a daughter?"

I froze as I realised what I'd let slip. Of course I'd always known that I'd have to tell Zach about my family, but I'd been warming up to it. Damn my stupid mouth.

"Her name is Haven. She's nine years old."

Now Zach sounded wary. "Where is she at the moment? With her father?"

A snort escaped before I could stop it.

"No, oh no. Her father's never been involved. After our 'discussions' over child support got ugly, Maxwell insisted that all communication went through his lawyer, who's also a dick." *Birds of a feather flock together*, Nana said. "I haven't spoken to Maxwell once in the last eight years." No more lies, right? "He spent three of those years in jail for embezzlement and then got disbarred. After he was released, he began flipping houses in Reno, and then he got elected as a state representative, but somehow, he never makes enough money to give Haven a cent."

"Folks voted him into office?"

I appreciated Zach's incredulity.

"As long as you don't look past the six-thousand-dollar suit to the turd beneath, he can come across as quite charming." I pushed thoughts of Maxwell Suker away. He didn't deserve to live rent-free in my head. "Anyhow, Haven and I both live with my nana. My mom ran out on us too, and my father didn't want to know me."

Zach's expression turned to pity.

"I'm sorry that happened."

"I've had years to accept the situation. And honestly, everything was fine until my old boss died. We had a good life. Then my new boss turned out to be an asshole with wandering hands and an attitude problem."

"The guy Baylee saw you with?"

I nodded. "He bad-mouthed me all over Vegas. I was waiting tables and living on my overdraft when I got hired to investigate betting irregularities with the WST. I hated to leave Haven, but I couldn't afford to turn the job down."

Zach motioned toward the blue visitor chair beside the

bed. "Will you tell me the whole story? From the beginning? The truth this time."

I nodded. If he was willing to listen, then I owed him a full explanation.

"Only the truth," I promised.

CHAPTER 63
ARI

Someone had angled the chair so it faced Zach. Maya? Probably. When I sat down, the seat was still warm. Rennick had agreed to waive the NDA to the extent that I could explain things to Zach, as long as I omitted confidential company information and any financial details. When I left Hillview Hospital, Rennick had been a different man to the uptight, zen-garden-raking CEO I'd met at the start of the case. Whether it was the new bond between him and Lila or just the fact that he'd been through the emotional wringer along with the rest of us, I wasn't sure, but he'd stopped being so aloof. I liked the new version of him much better. So did Lila. When he wasn't looking, she kept sneaking little glances at him, as if she couldn't quite believe the way things had turned out.

I started the tale with my first day at Pleasure Point, the chance meeting with Erin that had turned into so much more. If she hadn't squeezed over to make space for me that morning, who knew how things would have turned out? Then I confessed my difficulties in narrowing down the suspect list while I was staying in Seagrass Point, and the call I'd received from Alexa after I left. Apparently, a crisis of trust had led Zach to turn to his old friends, and he'd been lulled into a false sense of security when nothing unpleasant had happened in Tahiti, assuming that Baylee was to blame for any past incidents. The only part I didn't mention was Maya's issue with Zed Nelson. That wasn't my story to tell.

"How did you find working for Alexa?" Zach asked. He was acting friendly, but so far, he hadn't given much away with regard to his feelings. I'd wanted to come here, to see him again, but it was hard. Hard to be reminded of everything I'd lost. But I owed Zach a full explanation, and if I could somehow salvage a friendship out of the mess I'd created, that would be a win.

"Challenging. On the one hand, she's the smartest person I've ever met. Well, I say 'met,' but she hides behind an avatar, so I have no idea what she looks like, although I'm assuming she's blonde. Is she blonde?"

"A blue-eyed blonde."

"And on the other hand… Do you realise she's a hacker?"

"Grey always used to worry that she'd get caught and the cops would show up at our door, but it never happened."

"When I think of a hacker, I picture a six-hundred-pound guy sitting in his mom's basement, so I guess I'll have to change that view."

"Alexa's tiny. Most of her clothes came from the kids' department. A porcelain doll, Justin called her. Pale, delicate, fragile."

That wasn't how I'd imagined her. She had such a big personality, and I'd just assumed her stature would match. These little snippets I learned about Blackstone House fascinated me, and I knew how I'd be spending those all-too-frequent nights when I couldn't sleep. Studying past investigations was both a bad habit and a necessity.

"I'd go with outspoken, pushy, renegade."

Zach laughed. "That too."

"Did she tell you that she gave me a dose of my own

medicine? Hacked my computer, put my entire life under a microscope, and screwed with my mind?"

"She kept quiet about that, but it doesn't surprise me. I bet she was totally unrepentant too."

"I called her some names."

"She won't take it personally."

"So she has a thick skin, huh?"

"Not quite. Under the tough veneer, she's incredibly sensitive. People have hurt her badly. It's more that if she absolutely believes she's doing the right thing, she'll go right ahead and shrug off the consequences."

"People? Do you mean her uncle?"

"Her uncle? What happened with her uncle?"

Zach wasn't aware of the abuse?

"Forget I said that."

He stared at me for a moment, then shrugged. "She never went into the specifics, but whatever happened, it was bad enough that she picked the streets over her family or foster care."

"I guess that makes sense. Did you know her uncle was a cop?"

"Alexa always hated cops. If he hurt her, I guess that goes some way to explaining why. You think she breaks the law to get back at him?"

"Maybe? I'm not a psychologist. Uh, you might want to upgrade your firewall—I'm almost certain that Alexa has access to your laptop."

"I know she does."

"You do?"

"I worked it out a while ago when she installed new antivirus software. At first, I assumed Maya did it, but then she said she didn't, and Alexa put the same program on Brax's laptop."

"You don't mind?"

A shrug. "What's the point in getting upset about it?

Firstly, I've got nothing to hide, and secondly, I can't stop her anyway. She'll always find a way in."

"Have you tried, I don't know, asking her not to?"

"I refer you back to my earlier point—if Alexa believes she's doing the right thing, she'll carry on doing it."

Nothing to hide... But what about the money Zach had used to buy Haven's Rest? Alexa might not have been concerned, but the source of the funds was still a huge question mark that left me uncomfortable.

"What's wrong?" Zach asked. "You just shrank back six inches."

"It doesn't matter."

"Yeah, it does. If we're gonna have any chance at a future together, we have to be honest with each other."

What?

"A future? You...you want a future together?"

For the first time, Zach looked uncertain. "You don't? I thought... Alexa said..."

"I still love you, of course I do, but everything's different now. I mean, I have a daughter I never told you about."

"I won't pretend to know much about kids, but Maya was nine years old once." He smiled at the memory. "I minded her while our parents were busy, and she's still alive, so I guess I did something right."

This was *huge*. Zach was willing to give things another go? The tears I'd tried so hard to rein in burst free, and I wiped at my face with a sleeve in an attempt not to embarrass myself completely.

"H-H-Haven's usually a dealbreaker."

Zach shrugged. "Just more evidence that you've been with the wrong men until now. You live in Vegas, right? That's gonna be a bigger hurdle because I can't leave the ocean. I've never done the long-distance thing before, but it's only an eight-hour drive."

"You'd do that? You'd really try dating? Even after everything that's happened?"

"Those months with you were the happiest I've ever had. If we weren't together, I'd forever compare every woman to you, and they'd all come up short. I wanted you when you were a travel blogger counting nurdles on the beach, and I sure as hell want you now that you're a genius private investigator who moves heaven and earth to save my life."

"I couldn't have done it alone. Alexa and Erin were a huge part of this." I closed my eyes. "And now Erin's in jail. Alexa sent an attorney, but I need to see if there's anything I can do to help."

"Kai's there. He took off hours ago."

"Did he seem…okay when he left?"

"Okay?"

"Was he upset?"

"Who wouldn't be?" Zach ran a hand through hair still caked with salt. "A guy we've known for seven years nearly killed me. Tyler was involved in every facet of our lives. He has keys to our homes. He makes our boards. We've travelled all over the world together. Why would he betray us like that?"

"I don't know for sure, but my gut tells me Meryl was the instigator." The way she'd acted in Lila's apartment, so kind and concerned before handing me a bag of poisoned food. *Are you hungry?* she'd asked before I offered to take it to the hospital. The woman was a sociopath. "But I meant to ask whether Kai was upset about Erin showing up."

"'Shocked' is a better word. After she got married and cut him out of her life, he never thought he'd see her again."

"What? Erin didn't cut him out of her life, and she was forced to marry a man she hated. She missed Kai so much that she's been low-key stalking him for years. I'm not sure how much you know, but their whole family is horribly messed up."

"He rarely mentions them, but I realised that much. You think wires got crossed somewhere?"

"Yeah, I do." I thought back to the little information I'd gleaned about People's Promise. "Or maybe the two of them got manipulated into thinking that way. I only hope their story has a happy ending."

"Like ours?"

Zach reached for my hand, and my heart skipped as his fingers twined through mine. But the rush of warmth quickly cooled when I remembered my earlier hesitation. The one unanswered question I had about Zach. Wrapped up in passion at Seagrass Point, I'd buried it under the weight of my own lies, but now I realised that any doubts lurking at the back of my mind could derail our future.

"I…I don't know how to say this."

His grip tightened. "Just tell me."

"Alexa wasn't the only one who snooped through your computer. I did too."

"Sweetheart, I gave you the password."

"But I looked at *everything*. Even your tax returns."

"All of them?"

"Yes."

"Things are going better now, huh? If I had a buck from everyone who told me I couldn't make a living by surfing, I'd have almost as much money as I made in sponsorship deals."

"How did you buy Haven's Rest?" I blurted. "On paper, you couldn't afford it."

"Oh. That."

"Yes, that."

CHAPTER 64
ARI

Zach gave a weighty sigh. Would he tell me the truth? I needed him to tell me the truth, no matter how much I might dislike it. If he was honest, I might be able to overlook the money's origins, but if he lied… Better a broken heart now than a year down the line.

"Alexa gave me the cash."

"Alexa? But…but Haven's Rest cost over a million bucks." Property records didn't lie.

"She called it reparations."

"For what?" Then I understood. "For Blackstone House?"

"Exactly. She escaped scrutiny because she was female and technically still a child, but the rest of us had our names dragged through the mud to some degree or another. I know now that she was working in the background, killing every story she could, but she didn't stand a chance against the Sykes family. Levi's parents were wealthy, old money, and they were determined their precious son shouldn't go to prison and drag their name down with him. His mother in particular was a real piece of work. She hired the best lawyers, paid people to write favourable op-eds, got private detectives to follow us…" Zach pulled a face. "Maybe that was another reason I flipped out when I heard you were an investigator."

"I'm so sorry you had to go through that."

"It cost me any chance of getting custody of Maya, Justin's fiancée called off the wedding, Brax lost a scholarship, and Nolan got fired from his job. And then one day, it all stopped. The stories, the PIs, the legal wrangling."

Something about the way he said it…

"That wasn't a good thing?"

"It stopped because Alexa stole their money."

Crickets on a cracker. "She gave you stolen money?"

"She divided up the loot and put each share into an offshore bank account, then arranged for the seven of us—Jerry was a no-show—to meet one last time." Zach closed his eyes, a faint smile on his face as he remembered. "She handed out the account numbers and passcodes in 'Time to Celebrate' greetings cards and told us to burn them afterward. Dawson was furious with her, Justin too. Nolan and I were both freaking out in case the cops managed to trace the cash. Brax said we'd earned every cent, and Grey didn't say much at all." Zach opened an eye. "On a scale of one to ten, how mad are you?"

"At you or at Alexa?"

"Both, I guess. She refused to put the money back. Told us if we didn't want it, we should wait a while and then donate it to charity. I've always felt guilty I didn't do that, but I wanted Maya to have somewhere nice to live when she eventually got released from foster care."

"Did the others keep theirs?"

"Brax invested his share. Dawson paid his sister's medical bills, Nolan rehabbed the vineyard, and Justin started a business. Grey used his to run for office. Got elected too. He's in the state senate and running for congress now."

"What about…" Who was left? "What about Jerry?"

"Who the hell knows? She did a better job of disappearing

than Alexa. If she got a share, she probably spent it all on her rust bucket of a car. The damn thing was a money pit, and it never did run right. Dawson said it was jinxed."

"Wait, wait, wait... Hold up. Jerry's a woman?"

"Oh, yeah. Most of the papers got that wrong. The police ruled her out fast along with Grey, so she didn't get the same scrutiny."

"I always wondered why she didn't get mentioned much."

"Kind of ironic—if I'd had to put money on any one of us being capable of killing, it would've been her."

"Why do you say that?"

"She was ice cold. Detached. Meticulous. Never lost her cool, never raised her voice, never got emotional. But what do I know? My best friend was poisoning me for years, and I never suspected a thing."

Wow.

I had my answer, but how did I feel about the new revelations? Yes, Zach had kept stolen funds, but I'd read some of those op-eds, and they were nasty. Vicious, even. And no amount of money could make up for those lost years with his sister. I was inclined to agree with Brax—they'd earned that cash.

Zach was looking up at me, his gaze hopeful but guarded.

"You did the right thing." His shoulders sagged in relief. "And you've given to charity in other ways. Helping with surf camps for kids, sponsoring first-aid courses, making donations to fundraising auctions, promoting the *Say No to Nurdles!* campaign."

"The nurdles thing was Maya."

"Stop talking and kiss me."

I didn't have to tell him twice. He knifed up with surprising speed and pulled me onto the bed with him, which was probably against hospital protocol, but who cared? When his hungry mouth pressed against mine, it was like coming home. His kiss was soft at first, but then bossy Zach took over, nipping at my lips with his teeth until they parted for him.

This time, the ache in my chest was a good one. Love, happiness, and anticipation for the next chapter of my life. A shudder ran through me as Zach slipped a hand under my shirt and caressed my side, his fingers spidering their way upward to my breasts. His phone pinged, but he ignored it.

"I've missed this," he breathed. "I've missed you."

We'd almost lost everything.

"I don't ever want to let you out of my sight again."

"Guess you'd better move to California, then."

He meant it as a joke, but my answer was serious. "I will."

Gently, he pushed me away so he could study my face. Guess he didn't quite understand.

"I mean it," I said. "I fell in love with the place while I was there. The climate, the people, the ocean." I couldn't keep the grin off my face. "One particular surfer. We were planning to move to Clovis."

"Clovis?"

"It's near Fresno."

"I know that. Why Clovis?"

"I had to balance affordability and the likelihood of finding employment."

"I hear a guy in Seagrass Point is looking to hire a hot girlfriend."

"Think I'll get an interview?"

"The job's yours."

I grew serious again. "Seagrass Point is out of my price range unless I want to live with Ms. Carrington again, and you'd be bailing me out for murder if I did that. But if I can find a job, I might be able to rent an apartment in Santa Cruz."

"Haven's Rest has plenty of space. Just saying."

"If it was only me, nothing would make me happier than

being in your bed every night, but I have a family. That wasn't what you signed up for."

"I have three spare bedrooms and good soundproofing."

"You'd let us *all* stay there? But you haven't even met Nana or Haven."

"The place feels empty now that Maya's moved out. And I've met you, so I already know I'm gonna love your nana and your daughter."

Could that work? Haven would love Zach's place—the huge yard, the pool, the ocean close by—but would Nana be happy somewhere so quiet? We'd always lived in an apartment block. She had neighbours to visit for coffee and pinochle.

"I'd have to discuss it with them."

"Is that a 'maybe'?"

"It's a maybe."

"Better than an outright no."

Zach wrapped me up in strong arms and kissed me again, and if we'd been anywhere but the hospital, I'd have been halfway to naked by now. Zach's libido had recovered remarkably quickly from his earlier near-death experience, and his dick still worked, which was something to celebrate.

But not right now.

"We should take it easy. The faster you recover, the faster you can leave the hospital."

"I feel pretty damn good. Does that door lock?"

"We're not having sex in a hospital, not unless we want spectators. Did you forget you're wearing a heart-rate monitor?"

"Can you bust me out?"

"No."

"But I thought you loved me?"

"I do, which is why I'm offering to take a cab to your rental property to pick up your toothbrush and clean underwear."

"Clean underwear? I don't even have dirty underwear."

He didn't? How tempting. I glanced toward the door, but I couldn't see any kind of lock whatsoever.

"Aw, they took your Speedos?"

"A nurse cut them off me. I'm almost certain I told her not to, but maybe she just wanted to get a look at the whole Zach Torres package?"

"For my next career move, I think I'll become a nurse."

"I'll let you examine me any time."

"Oh, gee, it's time for your colonoscopy, Mr. Torres."

The last tatters of tension fluttered away as we fell back into the easy camaraderie we'd enjoyed before Baylee played her home movie. Zach was giving me a second chance, and I was determined not to squander it. I kissed him again, keeping half an eye on his heart rate because we didn't need an audience.

But we got one.

"OMG! You guys are back together! I knew it. I *knew* it." Erin ran over to the bed, and when Zach didn't let me go, she flung her arms around both of us. "This is the best day ever! Apart from the whole poisoning thing, I mean. That sucked."

"They let you go?" I asked dumbly. Really dumbly, because of course they had.

"Kai sent Zach a message. Didn't he read it?"

Now Zach checked his phone. "No, we were busy."

Her eyes widened. "And you didn't lock the door?"

"Not that busy."

"It doesn't lock anyway," I added. "What happened? Did the lawyer get you out?"

Kai answered for her. "Tyler's refusing to press charges for the damage to his nose. That's what we were told, anyway. I haven't spoken to him."

And what would any of us say? I'd be tempted to greet him with a right hook if Erin hadn't already done the honours. Quite honestly, not pressing charges was the least he could do.

"Where did you learn to punch like that?" I asked her.

"So three years ago, I was staying in this really shitty part of Miami, and one of my roommates was a cage fighter. The Titan of Tampa." Erin giggled. "He taught me the basics. A guy tried to mug me once, and he totally regretted it. I guess I should thank that jerk for the practice."

"I didn't know you could ride a jet ski either."

"Oh, now that's a *real* good story. I was working for this tour place in Fort Lauderdale, and the owner had a bunch of other rental businesses up and down the coast. And he'd make us move the PWCs around—the personal watercraft— depending on where they were needed. That was one of the funnest jobs I ever had. He'd be, like, 'Those two need to go to Hollywood,' and we'd jump on the PWCs and take them there."

"Why'd you quit?"

"Oh, he got arrested."

"What for?"

"Running drugs. You remember the airport parking guy? This was his brother. And it was actually kinda cool. He had these little drone subs that followed us on the PWCs, and we had no idea until the cops came. I wasn't working that day." She crinkled her nose. "I always did wonder how he afforded a Ferrari when he spent most of the time complaining about profit margins."

So she'd basically been employed as a drug mule. Yikes. Zach started laughing while Kai put his head in his hands. *Kai.* He hadn't taken his eyes off his sister since they arrived, and his expression was one of mild disbelief. As if he couldn't quite believe she was really there. At least he hadn't rejected her all over again—she didn't deserve that.

"Kai, can you give Ari a ride to the villa?" Zach asked

when he could speak again. "Looks as if I'll have to stay here tonight."

"Sure."

"And Erin… It's Erin, right?"

She nodded.

"Are you staying with us too?"

"I have a hotel room—" she started, but Kai cut her off.

"She's staying with us," he said firmly, and I took that as a good sign.

This case had torn Zach's surf brotherhood apart, but it had brought three other families together—Lila and Rennick; Kai and Erin; and Zach, Haven, and me. I could see myself spending the rest of my life with this man. Friendships had been broken and new ones created. Despite Alexa's duplicitous nature, I did count her as a friend now, albeit an unconventional one.

The future had changed for every one of us, and I vowed to make the most of mine.

CHAPTER 65
ZACH

"Come on, come on, you can do it. Nearly there."

Haven Danner splashed toward Zach with a stroke that was more doggy paddle than freestyle, got close, closer, and finally swam right into him.

"Easy, tiger. Did you close your eyes again?"

"The goggles leaked."

"We'll get you different ones, okay?"

Ari followed her daughter, swimming smoothly down the pool. She'd mastered backstroke and breaststroke now, but freestyle was proving to be a challenge, mainly because she hated to get her face wet. But she had time to learn. They had all the time in the world.

Haven and Nelva—Ari's Nana—had come to stay right after Zach's return from Hawaii, the two of them moving into spare rooms at Haven's Rest. A trial run, Ari had called it, although it became evident within a week that none of them were going anywhere. Haven loved living by the ocean, and in a heartfelt conversation that had left Ari in tears, confessed that she was being bullied at school again, but she'd kept quiet because she didn't want to ruin her mom's job. Ari was raw afterward, bleeding from her soul, guilt pouring out of her. But she'd been doing her best. Living paycheck to paycheck was a constant struggle, and Ari had been chasing the dream that eluded so many in today's society: financial stability.

Haven was a great kid, still shy but curious as hell and always asking questions. In many ways, she reminded Zach of Maya at that age. Maya had been bullied too, and after much discussion among the whole family—and that was what they were fast becoming, a family—Ari had decided to enrol her daughter in an online private school for the next year at least. That also gave them more scope to travel together, to see the world the way Zach had done. He and Maya had been homeschooled for years. It was only once they'd gone into foster care that they'd attended mainstream school, and he knew which he'd preferred.

At first, Ari had worried about the cost. But Zach promised to pay the fees, an offer she'd turned down when she quickly picked up new clients. Or rather, old clients. There'd been a moment of worry for Zach when Digby Rennick offered her a position as internal auditor at AnyBet, and he feared she might decide to move back to Vegas, but after some back and forth, they'd come to the conclusion that much of the work could be done remotely, and an assistant could handle most of the in-person tasks. So Rennick had created two part-time positions, and Lila had offered Ari her spare room for any trips back to her hometown.

The other client?

Alexa.

Zach wasn't certain how he felt about that. On the one hand, Ari got along with his old roommate and said she relished the challenge of working with the brat. On the other hand, Alexa was a lunatic.

"I did it!" Haven yelled. "Did you see me? I swam the whole way."

Ari found her feet, a siren in a yellow bikini. "I saw you.

But keep your voice down, remember?" She glanced toward the wall. "Ms. Carrington likes her peace and quiet."

"Okay," Haven whispered. "Can we go out for ice cream now? You promised."

All remained silent next door. Ms. Carrington had become more accommodating when she realised Nelva was a fan of pinochle. The pair of them played every afternoon, usually accompanied by a glass of sweet iced tea and a plate of Maya's cookies. There'd been a temporary glitch with the loss of their weed supplier—aka Tyler—but it turned out Erin knew a guy. Erin knew a lot of guys. Not in that way—she just seemed to talk to everyone in the entire world. Except for her family, obviously.

And there was a good reason for that.

The verbal autopsy of Erin and Kai's life in the Promised Land had involved tissues, alcohol, and a pact to take their secrets to the grave. Their father had been a monster, and their mother had lied to both of them in an attempt to keep Erin under the cult's thumb. That they'd found their way back to each other was the true miracle.

"We can go for ice cream," Ari said. "Or do you want pizza?"

"Duh, that's not even a real question."

"Okay, after you've done your homework, we can go for pizza."

"I hate homework."

"But you don't hate pizza."

"That's so unfair."

Haven huffed, but she did splash over to the steps and climb out, then grabbed her towel and flounced into the house.

"Welcome to parenthood," Ari muttered.

"No complaints here."

With Haven inside, Zach took the opportunity to trap Ari against the side of the pool. She didn't complain when he pressed his lips to hers, but she did gasp when he nudged her bikini bottoms aside.

"We can't. What if she comes back?"

He slid one long finger inside her. "Just smile and ask how her homework's going?"

"Zach!"

"Relax, I'm kidding. Seriously, relax. You're too tense. I'll stop if she comes back, I swear, but you deserve an orgasm."

And now that Zach was stepping into the role of father, he had to take the opportunities where they arose. He wouldn't change the new living arrangements for all the gold in Fort Knox, but he did miss fucking Ari on the kitchen counter. Maybe tomorrow, Nelva could take Haven out for lunch?

Ari knew Zach was right, and when he stroked the magic spot, her eyes glazed and she sagged in his arms. He watched them in the mirrored glass—from outside of the pool, it looked as if they were just having a conversation, albeit a cosy one.

"I love you," he said softly. "I love waking up next to you in the mornings. I love that you trust me with your daughter. I love holding you in my arms. I love that you're sweet and smart and kind and courageous. I love that our lives fit together so well." Her eyes closed as she gave in to him completely. "I love seeing you tied spread-eagle on my bed. I love the way you suck my cock. I love how you try to hold in your screams and then gasp them out at the last moment. I love that goofy face you make when you come."

Her eyes flew open.

"I do not—"

But she was too close, as he'd known. She gasped and bit down on her bottom lip, breathing hard.

"There it is."

"Shut up!"

"Did I mention that I love your sense of humour?"

She glanced at the house, checking Haven hadn't

reappeared before she kissed him. "I love everything about you."

"Good. Because someday, you're gonna marry me."

"Oh I am, am I?"

"Yeah. How do you feel about having more kids?"

"With…with you?"

"No, I thought we could ask your ex to take a break from his politics gig. Or maybe Rennick can give you the number for the sperm bank?" Zach snorted. "Of course with me."

"Honestly? I've never given it much thought. Having Haven was hard, so hard, and…"

"You're not on your own anymore."

"Doesn't the thought of siblings freak you out?" Ari shuddered. "After everything that happened?"

"Not every family is like those ones."

The Kealohas and the Peraltas. Both fucked up, but in such different ways.

Tyler had been the first to talk, spilling his guts about everything he'd done while also attempting to absolve himself of any blame. Troy had put him up to tampering with Zach's drinks. Or rather, he'd emotionally blackmailed him into doing it. Claimed he had a gambling problem, that he owed a pile of money to loan sharks, and they'd kill him unless Tyler helped them out with one tiny thing. All he had to do was make Zach lose a contest.

And Tyler claimed that he'd genuinely believed his brother was in danger. One night in Bakersfield, he'd witnessed Troy being held at gunpoint by a man demanding repayment of the debt, and another weekend, Troy had shown up with a knife wound—all staged, of course. Then there was the guilt factor—Troy had lent Tyler part of the money to buy Board Stiff, and Tyler felt as if he owed his brother.

If that was the truth, then Zach felt pity for him.

Ari had told Zach about her old boss, Morty, and his

theory that all motives boiled down to one of four Ls: love, lust, loathing, or loot. Tyler had acted out of love for Troy.

Once Tyler had spiked Zach's drink that first time in Tahiti, Troy and Meryl had him cornered. If he refused to keep doing their dirty work, they'd spill the beans. One contest turned into two, three, four, and then Tyler was in so deep he couldn't kick his way out. The surf wax was never meant to kill Zach—Troy had given it to Tyler and said it contained a mild tranquilliser, that was all. Or so Tyler said. On balance, Zach was inclined to believe him. Two weeks ago, he'd paid his former friend a visit, and Tyler had spent an hour begging for forgiveness. The jury was still out on that part. At the moment, the bad times were still too fresh in Zach's mind, but maybe at some point, it would become easier to remember the good times.

Troy, on the other hand, had acted out of lust and a desire for loot. He'd denied everything until the detectives pointed out the link between the names on the corrupt AnyBet accounts and his list of clients. Then a little more of the story had come out. Unsurprisingly, he'd blamed the entire scheme on Meryl, who hated Lila with a passion—there was another L: loathing. She'd loathed that Lila had been given the job as Rennick's first assistant that Meryl assumed would be hers after the previous incumbent quit. To see a younger, prettier, less qualified candidate parachuted in ahead of her had made her snap. Rennick was probably fucking Lila on the side, she'd told Troy. Ari had nearly choked when she heard that part.

But Lila's appointment would have been justified even if she wasn't a blood relative. She had the qualifications. And Meryl had clearly had too much time on her hands at work because she'd come up with the gambling scheme as a way to fuck with Rennick's precious company and steal his money at the same time. The fact that Lila had nearly died was just the frosting on the cake. Meryl had been the one who mixed up the surf wax, and when the police searched her apartment, they'd found the fentanyl in her spice rack, along with thallium, diazepam, and strychnine.

Meryl, equally predictably, had sworn the entire shitshow was Troy's idea.

Now it would be down to a jury to separate fact from fiction, to unravel the half-truths and lies.

Zach refused to give Meryl any more of his headspace.

She'd taken too much from him already.

The future was still uncertain, but surfing was one constant. Glenn had offered to shape Zach's boards for the moment, and since Glenn had taught Tyler everything he knew, those boards were top notch. The surfing community had begun boycotting Board Stiff out of solidarity with Zach, but he'd asked them to stop. Tyler's livelihood wasn't the only one at risk—he employed two more assistants besides Glenn, and they needed to eat. Maybe Tyler would sell the place? Rennick's lawyer thought there was a fifty-fifty chance that Tyler would do time, so he might not be around to run the business anyway.

"One day," Ari said. "One day, we'll have children together. But let me settle into this new life first. And if Haven ever brings a boy home, I'm gonna run a full background check before he steps over the threshold. No, I'm gonna ask Alexa to run the background check. If he so much as looked at someone funny in kindergarten, we'll find out."

"Speaking of background checks…"

"Uh-oh."

"Don't you think Maya's been acting weird lately?"

"Wait, you want me to background check *your sister*? Because I did that months ago, and she's clean."

"She's just acting cagey about something."

"Did you ask her?"

"Yeah, and she told me I have an overactive imagination." But a week ago, after they'd gotten back from the second big-wave round in Nazaré, Maya had driven into Santa Cruz to meet Pete, one of the guys who worked with Sal's Army. Except while she was out, Pete had called to ask if his girlfriend could borrow Zach's paddleboard, and he said Maya hadn't been there at all. So where had she gone? "Will you talk to her?"

"Me?"

"She likes you. Plus you're female, and I'm her brother."

Ari sighed. "I can try. No promises."

Just then, Maya appeared from the direction of her apartment, and she didn't look happy.

"What's wrong?" Zach asked. Was he about to find out why she'd been acting so mysterious?

Her movements were stiff, her jaw tense. "You're gonna hate this."

Hate what? Hadn't enough shit happened in the past two months already?

"What happened?"

"Zed called. There have been two shark attacks at Todos this week, and nobody can find the shark."

"Let me guess—he wants us to wear chain-mail wetsuits?"

"Worse. He's moving the final round to an alternate venue."

"Which is?"

But Zach didn't need to ask. Maya's face told the story. Zed Nelson planned to hold the third of the big-wave contests and the final instalment of this year's World Surf Tour at Mavericks, Zach's nemesis. Fuck. All the work he'd put in, the horror show at Pipeline, and the difficulties at the last two rounds where he'd been hounded by paparazzi wanting the full story of what had gone down with Tyler, it had been for nothing. He could kiss the championship and the full-season bonus goodbye.

"Mavericks," Maya whispered, confirming Zach's worst nightmare.

"I'd better go congratulate Kai."

At least the trophy would go to a good man.

Ari came to life. "Wait, wait, what's going on?"

"Zed's taking the tour to Half Moon Bay, and I don't surf Mavericks. Ever."

CHAPTER 66
ARI

"This is a nightmare." Maya put her head in her hands and slumped over her dining table. She'd fussed around making coffee for both of us, and hers was sitting by her elbow, untouched. "Zed's such a jerk. I'll freaking kill him. Why can't he just monitor the ocean with drones the way he usually does?"

He'd been blackmailing her into fucking him for over a year, and this was what tipped her over the edge?

"I'm as upset as you are, but safety's important, and those shark attacks were nasty." I'd looked them up on the internet. Shark sightings were rare in Todos Santos, but a great white with a poor sense of timing had decided to move into the area. "One surfer died, and another got his arm torn off. Plus there's another guy missing."

"Any idea how many sharks there are at Mavericks?"

"No?"

"Well, it's a lot."

"Have there been many attacks?"

"Whose side are you on?"

"Zach's, but I need to understand the full picture."

"Sorry, I'm sorry. Maybe the sharks at Mavs don't kill

people so often, but Zed can't claim it's safe, and he knows how Zach feels about surfing there. Why couldn't we go to Waimea? That's gonna be huge too. Or Ghost Trees? Zed got a permit to run an event there two years ago, and he could do it again."

Zach had told me about that contest—Ghost Trees was a tow-in wave, and jet skis were normally banned in the area. Nelson had negotiated with NOAA, who granted an exception on the condition that all PWCs were launched from boats offshore instead of travelling through the neighbouring marine sanctuary. I couldn't imagine those arrangements were made quickly.

"Mavericks is probably the most convenient."

"He's just screwing with Zach, I know it. He wants to push him around for ratings. Trust me—you don't know Zed the way I do."

That much was true. And thank goodness. If I had to put that man's cock in my mouth, I'd puke all over his leather couch.

"There might be another problem."

Maya groaned. "What?"

"Zach knows you weren't with Pete the other evening, and he's worried you're acting distant. He asked me to speak with you about it."

All the colour drained out of Maya's face, and I almost wished we could borrow some of Meryl's spice stash. A little sprinkle, and we could dump Nelson into the ocean and let a great white do its worst. On second thought, would fentanyl harm marine life? I didn't want to kill the poor shark. Having to chow down on Nelson's sorry ass would be punishment enough.

"What did you tell him?" Maya asked.

"Nothing. But he's asking questions, and unless you want to start lying to his face, you need to get out of this arrangement."

"Don't you think I'm trying? I kept telling myself that if I just made it through until the end of the year, Zach would be crowned champion and nobody could take that away from him. And he'd already have won if Meryl hadn't interfered. I *hate* her." Tears welled in Maya's eyes. "I can't do this for another year. I can't do it."

"Tell Zed that. Let the chips fall where they may. Zach will understand."

He'd also join the line to kill Nelson if he found out the truth, but I wasn't going to tell him. Did that count as a lie? Probably. No doubt I'd be joining Alexa in hell someday.

"No way! Zach's the best surfer in the world, and we've been working toward this for a decade. I'm not giving up now."

Maya's unshakeable belief in her brother left a lump in my throat, but the way she was prepared to put his happiness ahead of her misery tugged at my heartstrings. What if there was some way of persuading Zach to surf Mavericks? He had the technical ability. The only thing holding him back was the ghost of his father.

I swallowed hard because I understood what that mental barrier felt like. I could swim in the pool now, but the moment the ocean lapped over my ankles, I hotfooted it back onto the beach. If I was going to convince Zach to take a chance, I'd have to put my own demons to rest first.

And there wasn't much time left. The big-wave contests weren't scheduled like the other rounds; they depended entirely on swell conditions. Everyone was on standby, sometimes for months, and competitors would get forty-eight hours' notice to haul their asses to the venue if the break activated. The swells had come early this year. Mid-November, and the season was already well underway.

"Hang in there," I told Maya. "Everything's gonna be okay, I promise."

Why had I made that dumb promise to Maya?

Zach's initial anger about the schedule switch had passed, and he'd been moping all week. The heartache had only intensified after the others left for Mavericks this morning, the three of them—Kai, Erin, and Maya—driving an hour north of Seagrass Point to Half Moon Bay. Zach had taken off for the beach soon after, and I stared through rain-splattered windows, trying to catch a glimpse of him outside.

"Why are you so sad, Momma?"

The dining table was littered with paper and paint and brushes and glue and glitter as Haven created mermaid masterpieces. Ms. Carrington had taught her the basics of watercolour painting (she's kinda scary, Momma), and I'd had to make Haven promise never to eat the cookies next door.

Was "sad" the right word? I was more disappointed, both in Zach and in yours truly. I'd tried to force myself into the ocean this week, honestly I had, but the water had only made it to my knees when something touched my leg and I bolted up the beach. Zach said it was probably a plastic bottle with an outside chance of a fish, but Nelson was still harping on about sharks, and I freaked out.

And speaking of Zach, he was still refusing to go anywhere near Mavericks. At first, he'd shut down whenever I tried to talk about it, but last night after Haven had gone to bed, he'd begun to open up. He wasn't scared of death itself, he said, but of leaving others behind, the way his dad left Maya and him. I understood his feelings—when I'd stepped into the ocean three days ago, a flash of fear had passed through me at the thought of Haven being left motherless. Sometimes fear could be irrational, but it was still difficult to conquer.

In one small glimmer of hope, Zach had agreed to speak to a therapist, but it was too little, too late. The contest was scheduled to start tomorrow morning, with competitors expected to participate in interviews and meet-and-greets this afternoon.

"I'm sad because Zach's hurting," I told Haven.

"Because he won't win a trophy?"

"That's right."

"Mrs. Bridgman says that it's not the winning that counts, it's the taking part."

Wise words, but being a runner-up still sucked.

Mrs. Bridgman was one of Haven's online teachers. My sweet daughter had taken to online school like a duck to water, and I loved seeing her so excited as she logged on each morning. It was a far cry from the stoic determination she used to project as we walked to the bus in Vegas.

"Zach isn't taking part either."

"Well, that's just dumb."

Oh, to be nine years old again and see the world in black and white, not the many shades of grey that cast shadows on my happiness.

"He has good reasons. We were meant to go to a place called Mavericks, and Zach's daddy died there a long time ago."

"Was that a bad thing?"

A fair question. I'd never had anything good to say about Maxwell. If he popped his clogs, I'd pop the champagne cork.

"Yes, it was a bad thing."

"Then Zach should put flowers there. Olivia put flowers where her pop died."

Olivia was a girl from Haven's class in Vegas, and her father had died high as a kite when he crashed the stolen car he was driving into a signpost. *Seat belts are important, kids.* The cops had been right behind him, but there was nothing they could do for a broken neck.

"Maybe he'll take flowers someday."

"I'm gonna make him a flower."

Haven went back to her crafts while I paced the living area. Was Zach okay? Physically, I knew he would be—Pete had offered to keep him company with his jet ski today—but mentally, I wasn't so sure. Should I bundle Haven up in a slicker and head down there? Or I could take her next door to Nana…

My phone rang, and Cartoon Alexa popped up on the screen. Did she have work for me? I wouldn't mind a distraction today.

"Could you do me a favour next week?" she asked.

"What kind of a favour?"

"There's a guy in San Francisco, and I'm almost sure he's a person I've been hunting for the past three months, but I need to get a good picture of him."

"What did he do?"

"Overheard something he shouldn't, then freaked out and escaped witness protection."

"And you want me to take the picture?"

"Exactly."

"Send me the file?"

"On its way. I take it Zach's still moping?"

"He's moping on a surfboard. I mean, he's not getting eaten by a shark, so I guess that's something, but he should be winning the WST tomorrow."

Kai had done the honourable thing and offered to withdraw in solidarity, but competitors got one point just for competing in the heats. If neither Zach nor Kai showed up and Scottie Stenson won, then he was close enough in the rankings to take the championship by a single point, and nobody wanted that to happen. So Kai had gone to Mavericks. Reluctantly. He was angry too. Yes, he wanted to win the title, but not like this.

"A shark?" Alexa asked. "Are there sharks in Santa Cruz?"

"No, in Mexico. I'm just paranoid. Zed Nelson moved the contest from there last week because a surfer got killed by a shark in Todos."

"That's what he said? Zed Nelson's full of shit. He moved the contest to Mavericks before the shark ate that dude."

"What?"

"Yeah, a month ago. Wait, I'll check the date on the email." A pause. Why didn't it surprise me that Alexa had access to Nelson's communications? "My mistake—it was more like six weeks. I'll forward you the message."

"Are you serious?"

"Nearly always."

That…that *fucker*.

Again, I shouldn't have been surprised, but I'd been wading through the sewer of human nature for months now. Was a little decency too much to ask for?

"I'm gonna wring his freaking neck."

"I don't think that's so easy to do. You want me to check?"

"What?"

"From what I've heard, necks are harder to break than the movies suggest. You're still not carrying a gun?"

"Are you crazy?"

"Hey, I'm only trying to help. Don't forget to set up an alibi. The file I sent should be there now—call me if you have questions."

There was a *ping* as the dossier on the missing witness arrived, but I barely heard it over the steam hissing out of my ears. Maya had been right. Once again, Nelson had been up to his manipulative tricks, and the losers were her and Zach. Why had he done it? Purely for the ratings? If Zach had gone to Mavericks, it would have been a monumental event, a highlight for the surfing world. Or was he trying to force Maya into providing her "services" for another year? If he had half a brain, he must have realised she'd back out of the arrangement if Zach took the crown.

Either way, I wasn't going to let Zed Nelson ruin this family.

"Haven, I need you to sit next door with Nana."

"But I hate pinochle."

"It won't be for long, and if you do this, I'll buy you pizza *and* ice cream tonight."

"Both? At the same time?"

"With whatever toppings you want."

"Where are my sneakers?"

I ran along the beach, wet sand splattering against my legs, squinting into the fog that hung over the water. Where was Zach? I spotted Pete idling on his jet ski and scanned left to the spot where the wave would break. There. A flash of red against the murky sky. Zach sat astride his board, a lonely figure on the horizon, waiting for the swell. For the ocean to take his pain away.

It was almost high tide, the waves foaming over the sand as they broke halfway up the beach. While I lay in bed at night, I found the rhythmical roar almost relaxing, but now my guts churned along with the water. *Face your fears, Ari.* The currents would be stronger now, but at least I'd learned to avoid the rips. Damn, this was the hardest thing I'd ever had to do.

I hit the edge of the surf, and I kept running.

If I'd stopped to think about what I was doing, I'd probably have had a panic attack, so I blocked out the whole drowning part and waded deeper, deeper, yelling Zach's name. I knew right away when he saw me. He paddled once, twice, and rose nimbly to his feet to catch the next small wave instead of waiting for a perfect one. Thirty seconds later, he glided to my side and leapt off the board, then wrapped me up in his arms and squeezed me tight.

I was alive.

I was still a-freaking-live.

"What happened? What's wrong? Is Maya okay? Haven?"

"What *happened*? Zed Nelson is a lying bastard, that's what happened."

"You waded all the way out here to tell me that? Didn't we already know he's a jerk?"

"No, I—"

A wave broke over our heads, and I gagged on seawater. It felt as if soda was being poured into my brain. I kicked frantically, choking, but Zach kept hold of me and then I was being pulled onto his board, safe from Neptune's clutches for now. He sat behind me, arms around my waist like a safety belt. An engine buzzed, and I caught a glimpse of Pete approaching, but Zach waved him away.

"We're okay," he called.

Were we? The board rocked, and I squeaked, but Zach balanced us out.

"I think I'm gonna puke."

His response? He kissed my shoulder and held my hair back.

"Lean forward and support yourself with your hands. I won't let you fall."

I swallowed down bile, and after several shaky breaths, the nausea subsided.

"Do you always feel this way? So...so vulnerable?"

"On a surfboard? Yeah, but that's why it's such a rush. Me against the ocean. Ari, why are you here?"

"Because you have to go to Mavericks. You can still make the contest if we leave right now."

Nelson had a rule—anyone who didn't attend the pre-contest briefing wasn't allowed to surf. No exceptions. I couldn't see Zach's face, but I felt his arms tighten.

"Sweetheart, we spoke about this. I can't."

"You *can*." I'd faced my fears, and now it was time for Zach to face his. "If I can sit out here in this…in this… Shit! Something just bumped my leg."

"That was my foot."

"Oh. Well, if I can sit here in this wetter version of hell, then you can ride a wave the same way you do almost every day."

"Mavericks isn't a normal wave. What if… What if…"

"What if you die?" I made the mistake of looking down and shivered. "We could both get eaten by a shark in the next thirty seconds, and you don't seem worried about that."

"You've been spending too much time with Alexa."

"It's still true."

"I have so much to lose now. Even more than I did before."

"Then maybe you should quit surfing altogether? And driving your truck, and crossing the road, and putting salt on your food, and drinking wine, and using stairs, and—"

"Okay, okay, I get the message. But you know I can't quit surfing. Saltwater runs through my veins."

"Exactly! So get off your ass and go surf Mavericks. If you don't, you'll regret it, and you can't turn back the clock."

For the longest time, he didn't say anything, and only then did I realise how far out to sea we'd drifted. There was a guy walking a dog on the beach, and the pooch was just a tiny black dot bounding among the grassy dunes. Was it Poppy? I thought it was Poppy.

"I can't go. Even if I wanted to, I can't. I told Maya to withdraw me from the contest."

"Well, she didn't. Not yet. She knows you can win, and believe me, she's as invested in your career as you are."

"You really think we could make it?"

"Yes."

I'd gladly take any speeding citations that came my way.

Luggage didn't matter much—we only needed Zach's surfboards, leashes, air vest, and wetsuit—Nelson had graciously agreed that the competitors didn't need to freeze to death this week. I could pack the clothing while Zach selected the boards he—

I shrieked as he got to his feet, lifting me with him.

"What are you doing?"

"Getting us to shore." He waved to Pete. "We're going to Mavericks."

"'Bout fuckin' time."

I tried closing my eyes, then quickly decided I'd rather see death coming. Water rushed beneath us as we hung on the face of the wave, and I felt every twitch as Zach expertly kept us upright. And through my terror, I felt a tiny bit of the rush he must get, the reason he got up at the crack of dawn to do this every day.

"You can get off now," he said. "The water's only knee deep."

"My feet are welded to the board."

"That's good—we'll make a surfer out of you yet."

"Nice try."

Could Pete take this board for us? If we had to carry it back to the house, that would slow us down. And I'd have to throw a spare outfit for Haven in the bag too. We'd missed out on so much time together, and I wasn't leaving her behind again. She'd loved our recent trips to Portugal and Hawaii, adored this new life that I could never have given her alone.

Pete took the board without being asked, then Zach grabbed my hand and set off at a jog. Why had I run to the beach? I'd been so hopped up on adrenaline that it hadn't occurred to me to bring the truck. We could have shaved off two minutes.

A shadow passed overhead, and I glanced up at a giant helicopter, the *whomp-whomp-whomp* of its rotors audible over the wind and rain. Were people allowed to fly that low? Ms. Carrington was gonna lose her mind.

Then it began descending.

"Zach, why is there a helicopter landing next to your house?"

The beach ball Haven had left near the terrace took off rolling, never to be seen again. A potted palm fell over, and water lapped over the edges of the pool. What was happening? A figure jumped out and strolled toward us, and I did a double take when I recognised him.

"Priest?"

Zach stared at me. "You know this man?"

Priest saluted both of us. "Sorry about the plant. Alexa told us to bring a helicopter with a twelve-foot payload."

Of course she did.

"How did she know we'd be going to Mavericks? What did she do, hire a guy with binoculars?"

Priest held his hands up. "Don't ask me; I'm just the baggage handler. There's a car and driver waiting for you at the other end."

And, it turned out, a hotel room, a bottle of champagne, and a basket of craft materials for Haven.

Alexa might cross every boundary and drive me crazy at times, but I was so damn glad she'd come into my life.

CHAPTER 67
ARI

Beside me, Erin was leaping up and down, cheering, even though her brother had come second. Me? All I felt was an overwhelming sense of relief. The day had been brutal on the competitors, but after a tense first heat, Zach had begun to relax, and he'd smashed the final against Kai. Scottie Stenson had wiped out in spectacular style in the semi, only for Maya to pull off a hairy rescue on the inside. My heart had been in my mouth just from watching her, along with the rest of my internal organs.

As for Zach, he was standing on the beach with his board now, still, silent, seemingly oblivious to the noise of the crowd as he stared out at the monster waves he'd just tamed. What was going through his mind? Thoughts of his dad? Kai strode across, the first to congratulate him with a hug and a few words.

"OMG, I'm so stoked!" Erin managed to pick me up in a hug, even though she was several inches shorter. "Zach is the champion, Zach is the champion," she sang to the tune of the well-known Queen song. "Of the waves."

Maya parked her jet ski and ran across to join her brother and Kai, and the three of them stood with their arms around each other, heads bowed. Zach didn't realise just how much of his victory he owed to her, and he never could.

"I thought you'd be sad that Kai lost," I said to Erin.

"This year was Zach's year. Next year, that'll be Kai's time. He said I could go to all the rounds with him. I'm gonna be his official surfboard waxer."

"You two are getting along great, huh?"

"Crazy, right? I thought he'd hate me forever. Anyhow, I offered to get a real job, but he said there was no need, that he has plenty of money and plenty of stuff for me to do, kind of like Maya does for Zach."

Plus Kai had been worried that Erin would end up accidentally running drugs again. I'd been there when he had the conversation with Zach. But most importantly, Kai wanted to make up for missed time with his little sister, and that meant she'd be travelling with us for the next season at least. I couldn't wait.

And now I understood the bond Zach had shared with Tyler and Kai. Being part of a squad, a group of girls I could share my life with and confide in, was something I'd never had before. And I liked it. I liked it a lot. Zach still had Kai, and Pete was hanging around more. Last week, he'd confessed a desire to qualify for the WST, so maybe our group would expand someday?

Next to us, Zach's old roommates were high-fiving too. We were seated at a private table in the VIP area, courtesy of Braxton Vale. Half of the remaining Blackstone House contingent had shown up—Nolan, Brax, Dawson, and Justin. Brax said they'd begun to grow closer again in the past few months, although Greyson didn't talk to them much anymore, apparently, and Jerry was still in the wind. Alexa was probably watching via a spy satellite. All of those present had come alone except for Brax, who'd brought his PA to fetch and carry.

He turned to her. "This calls for champagne. Could you get us a couple of bottles from the bar, my darling?"

The girl put her hands on her hips. "I'm not your darling, and I'm not your slave either."

"No, but I do pay you to assist me. The champagne, please?"

"You drink too much."

Brax took a slow breath. "I only drank two glasses of wine on the flight."

"*Large* glasses. And my contract doesn't say anything about carrying drinks. If I'd wanted to carry drinks, I'd have taken a job as a waitress. At least they get tips."

"You don't have enough cleavage to get tips."

The woman's mouth dropped open. "Screw you."

"That's not an option, I'm afraid."

She grabbed my half-empty glass of water from the table and threw it at him, then stormed off. I figured he'd be upset, but he just picked up a napkin and began wiping his face.

"Reckon that counts as a resignation?" he asked.

Justin grinned. "Yup. Who won the pool?"

Brax checked his phone. "She lasted three weeks and four days, so… Fifteen bucks to Zach."

"He's winning everything today."

"What pool?" I asked. "What's going on?"

Justin did the honours. "Brax always hires assistants he hates, and me, Dawson, and Zach run a pool on how long they'll last."

No, I was still confused.

"This might be a dumb question, but why doesn't he just hire someone he gets along with?"

"Because if he's unfaithful, his prenup says his wife will get most of his money."

I'd been vaguely aware that Brax was married, although I'd never met his wife. They were going through a rough patch?

"So…are you considering a divorce?" I asked Brax.

"If only."

"They're currently playing a game of 'Who blinks first?'" Dawson filled in.

"Every time a woman flirts with me, I have to assume she's being paid by Carissa to do so. Rather than fighting temptation, it's easier to hire female staff I dislike." Brax stared at the departing figure of his former assistant as she fought her way through the crowd. "With hindsight, I should have passed on the one who listed 'organising feminist protests' among her hobbies."

Nolan snorted. "Why would she apply for a job with a man like you? You run a chain of sex clubs, for goodness' sake."

My turn to snort. Sex clubs? Why hadn't Zach ever mentioned that? Sheesh.

"Because I pay well. And who knows, maybe the idea of powerful men getting their asses paddled appealed to her?" Brax must have caught my shocked expression. "Any time you and Zach want to visit, let me know. I'll arrange complimentary passes." He winked. "We have a large selection of rope and plenty of handcuffs."

That Brax knew about Zach's sexual preferences shouldn't have surprised me—they'd lived together, after all—but my cheeks still burned.

"I-I'll think about it," I stammered, and Erin burst out laughing.

"I worked in a sex dungeon once," she said. "Mostly just serving drinks, but one night they were short-staffed and I had to walk over this naked guy in spike heels. But I'm not real good on heels, so I lost my balance and one of the spikes went up his—"

"It's a good thing your brother isn't around to hear this," Dawson told her.

"Oh, yeah. Anyhow, the guy was a great tipper."

Zach was heading in our direction now, one arm around Maya's shoulders, and I shoved the sex-club conversation out of my mind as I hurried to meet him, pausing to collect Haven from the next table on the way. Another of the competitors had a daughter the same age—Shara—and they'd quickly become buddies. When I took her out of in-person school, I'd been worried that she'd end up socially isolated, but the opposite had happened. Away from the bullies, Haven's confidence had grown, and she was making friends wherever we went.

"What a fuckin' rush!"

Zach picked me up and spun me around, my feet narrowly missing Maya as she stumbled back out of the way. Kai caught her, and not for the first time, I saw heat in his eyes as he looked at her for a beat too long. Wouldn't it be perfect if they ended up together? Kai was a good man; Maya just needed to ditch Nelson first. They had a "date" this Saturday night, which gave her five days to rehearse her "It's not me, it's definitely you" speech. I'd promised to take Zach out for dinner that evening so her absence wouldn't be noticed.

"I knew you'd win. You were amazing out there."

"Did my flower help?" Haven asked.

Zach had peeled his wetsuit down to his waist, and now he fished around in the pocket of his swim shorts and pulled out the pink-and-yellow flower that Haven had made out of beads.

"Sure did. This is my lucky flower now."

Something else had fallen out of his pocket, and I bent to pick it up before it got stomped into the ground. Something sparkly. A...ring?

Zach cursed softly under his breath as I stooped, and Haven told him off.

"Momma says you shouldn't say that word."

"What is this?" I asked, even though it was obviously a

diamond. A diamond set in platinum, surrounded by glinting sapphires.

Rather than answering right away, Zach dropped to one knee, and my heart lurched. Was he…? Was he…?

"I was waiting for the right moment, but I guess this is it. Arizona Danner, will you marry me?"

That stupid lump in my throat. I couldn't speak, but Haven answered for me.

"Yes, yes, yes! Can I be a bridesmaid?"

Everyone laughed. I later found out that thousands more people were watching live, so thank the stars I'd combed my hair that morning.

"Ari?"

"Yes. Of course yes."

I never thought I'd cry on TV, but at least they were happy tears. And my little family wasn't so little anymore.

CHAPTER 68
ARI

On Friday evening, I sank into a hot bubble bath with a glass of wine and a good book, relishing my first moment of solitude in weeks. The first time I'd been able to truly gather my thoughts. Nana was next door with Ms. Carrington, planning for the trip to France they were taking next summer; Haven had gone to a sleepover at Shara's house—it turned out her family lived in Santa Cruz; and Zach had driven to San Francisco for a media interview. Oh, and Erin had summoned Maya to discuss their top-secret plans for my bachelorette party. They'd promised to organise an event that Haven could attend too, but beyond that, they were staying tight-lipped about the details.

I was getting married.

Married.

On the beach, obviously. There was no better place, although I'd vetoed Erin's suggestion of matching bikinis for the bridesmaids and a one-piece for Maya as maid of honour. With both of my parents absent, Rennick had offered to walk me down the aisle as well as pay for all the dresses, no budget constraints whatsoever. We'd become close over the past few months, and he was more than just an employer now. Lila—

bridesmaid number three—was busy booking appointments at bridal salons. Turned out she was a closet romantic who'd watched every single episode of *Say Yes to the Dress*.

Haven was over the moon about the wedding, and she'd already started calling Zach "Daddy," which had left both Zach and me emotional the first time she said it. One day, we hoped to make the position official, if Maxwell would sign the adoption papers.

Alexa said he'd definitely sign the papers.

Speak of the devil… I groaned as my phone rang. So much for an evening of R&R.

"This had better be good. I'm busy relaxing."

"Won't take long. I just need you to say that Maya was relaxing with you."

"What? I'm in the tub."

"Okay, then say you were watching a movie together."

"You're gonna have to explain."

"No time for that—I'm busy doing damage control. But everything's in hand, and it was definitely an accident."

"What are you talking about?"

"Trust me."

She hung up, and I swore at the phone. Why did Alexa always have to be so cryptic? And what had Maya done? Fuck. I pulled the plug and watched as the water drained away, taking what was left of my sanity with it. My phone pinged again, and this time it was Zach.

ZACH

Interview's over, went well I think. Everything okay?

Was it? *Was it?* I had no freaking idea anymore. But in situations like this one, I trusted Alexa.

ME

All good. Just watching Aquaman with Maya.

ZACH

Don't get any ideas. I'm not growing my hair long.

ME

Would you get a tattoo?

ZACH

Maybe. Leaving SF now.

I began streaming the movie, just in case anyone could track these things. Alexa would know, but when I tried calling her back, I got the Church Group answering service. Damage control? What the hell did she mean by "damage control"?

I found out ten minutes later when Maya pulled into the driveway, and I didn't need prior warning to realise something was wrong. Very wrong. Tears were streaming down her cheeks, and she was pale, so pale.

"What's wrong?"

"H-h-he's d-d-dead."

Every atom in me froze. "Dead? Who's dead?"

"Zed. I k-k-killed him."

Shit. Shit, shit, shit!

"Are you sure? What happened?"

"He f-f-fell down the stairs."

"Come inside." Holy hell, what was I meant to do? "How did he fall down the stairs?"

"We were fighting, and I pushed him, and then he just... he just lost his balance."

So she hadn't killed him in cold blood, not that I'd have thought for a moment she was capable. And if he'd lost his balance, then perhaps Alexa was right and it had been a simple accident.

Wait.

How did Alexa know it was an accident?

"Are you sure he's dead? What if he's only bruised?"

"His neck was all twisted, and his eyes...his eyes... They were just staring."

"Did you call anyone? An ambulance?"

"N-n-no. I p-p-panicked and got in the car and started driving."

I half carried Maya as far as the couch, and she slumped into a heap, staring blankly at Jason Momoa. Holy shit. Why hadn't Alexa given me a proper warning? I quickly muted the TV and took a seat next to Maya, feeling way, way out of my depth.

"Why were you at Zed's place tonight? I thought you were going to see Erin?"

"I d-d-did go to see Erin. And when I left, Kai followed me out to the car and asked if I'd have dinner with him after his gig on Saturday. And I thought... I thought that maybe he was going to kiss me, so...so..."

"So...?"

"So I freaked out and jumped into the car." Another sniffle. "Do you have any idea how much I wanted him to kiss me?"

"I had an idea that the two of you might have feelings for each other."

"But how could I say yes to a date with Kai when I was meant to be meeting Zed tomorrow?"

This was starting to make more sense now.

"So instead of coming home, you went to tell Zed the session was off."

She nodded. "He was nice at first. Well, as nice as Zed gets. We drank wine—only a small glass—and he said he wouldn't stand in the way if I wanted to date Kai, as long as it didn't affect our arrangement. Our freaking *arrangement*. But when I told him my days of sucking his dick were over, he got nasty. Said that he owned me. *Owned* me, like I was some kind of slave."

"Did you try to leave?"

"Yes, but he dragged me up the stairs, and that was when I pushed him." Maya pulled her knees up to her chest and heaved out great racking sobs. "I'm gonna go to jail, aren't I? Just when I thought everything was okay, I'm gonna go to jail."

I wrapped her up in a hug and stroked her hair. Thank fuck Zach wasn't home tonight—the fewer people who knew about this, the better. And Maya wasn't going to prison, no way. Not for a man who'd been abusing her for months.

A year ago, I'd probably have called the police, explained everything, and trusted the justice system to do its job. But Meryl was still protesting her innocence, and the lawyers predicted the AnyBet case would run for years. Maya didn't need to be entangled in yet another legal fight. No matter what the evidence might say, she was a victim, not a criminal.

What was Alexa doing right now? Erasing camera footage? Sometimes, she frustrated the hell out of me—this wasn't the moment to go incommunicado.

"You're not going to jail, I promise. But you need to compose yourself before Zach gets back. If he sees you crying like this, he'll start asking questions."

"What if the cops come?"

"Did anyone see you there?"

"I d-d-don't know."

Alexa had told me to trust her, and when the chips were down, I did.

"Go and change. Give me those clothes—I have to get rid of them."

I could burn them in the firepit. We often sat on the terrace at night, so if Ms. Carrington or Nana saw the flames, they wouldn't think it was unusual. Or I could bag them up and drop them in someone else's trash, but pickup wasn't until Monday. Burning the evidence would work better.

Alexa had corrupted me.

"Forget everything that happened tonight. Text Kai and say yes to dinner, and we'll never speak of this again."

"Really? You don't think they'll arrest me?"

"No, I don't. You're free. Free from Nelson's fucked-up demands and free to live your own life. I get why you spent so much time supporting Zach, but you need to do something for yourself now. He would want that. Let me and Erin take some of the load."

Maya was still crying as she hugged me. "You're the best sister I could ever have hoped for."

Ditto. From this moment on, nothing and nobody was going to tear our family apart. The ocean had taught me an important lesson: you can't fight the tide because you'll never win, but you *can* ride it.

A FEW WORDS FROM JERRY...

If you're curious about what Jerry has to say, I've written down a few of her thoughts for members of my reader group...

Download the bonus chapter here: www.elise-noble.com/j3rry

WHAT'S NEXT?

My next book will be a novella in the Blackstone House series, *Blurred Lines*...

They say love is blind, and in Lauren Rossi's case, that's certainly true...

Navigating life in LA is always a challenge, but after a series of dating disasters, romance novelist Lauren Rossi has finally met a decent, down-to-earth man in app developer Theo.

But the course of true love never runs smooth, and Lauren soon finds herself being tugged in different directions by A-lister Kane Sanders, brooding gym owner Cristian, and Mario, who's going all-out to prove that he's her biggest fan. Lauren loves to give her characters happily ever afters, but can she find her own?

For more details:
www.elise-noble.com/blurred-lines

If you enjoyed *Hard Tide*, please consider leaving a review.

For an author, every review is incredibly important. Not only do they make us feel warm and fuzzy inside, readers consider them when making their decision whether or not to buy a book. Even a line saying you enjoyed the book or what your favourite part was helps a lot.

WANT TO STALK ME?

For updates on my new releases, giveaways, and other random stuff, you can sign up for my newsletter on my website:
www.elise-noble.com

If you're on Facebook, you might also like to join Team Blackwood for exclusive giveaways, sneak previews, and book-related chat. Be the first to find out about new stories, and you might even see your name or one of your suggestions make it into print!

And if you'd like to read my books for FREE, you can also find details of how to join my advance review team.

Would you like to join Team Blackwood?

www.elise-noble.com/team-blackwood

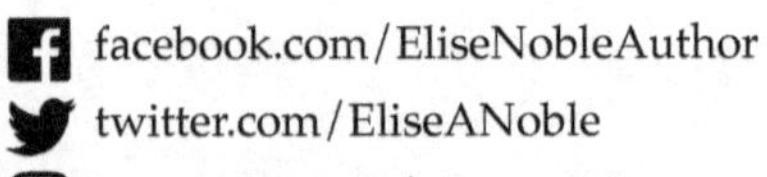

facebook.com/EliseNobleAuthor
twitter.com/EliseANoble
instagram.com/elise_noble

END-OF-BOOK STUFF

I'm writing this at the beginning of December, and winter has finally arrived in the UK. Single-digit temperatures (which isn't as bad as it sounds, US folks, because we use Celsius (which I can never spell, thanks spellchecker)), and snow is forecast for the end of the week. Time to dust off the scarves and snow boots? Lol, no. I'm going hibernating. Wake me up when the sun's shining.

Or take me to Hawaii. The research for this book was fun —I watched pretty much every surfing documentary on Amazon plus a bunch of YouTube videos, all in the name of work. I love my job <3 I even got on a surfboard, although I went wake-surfing rather than surf-surfing because there aren't any big waves in the Gulf of Aqaba.

In truth, this book didn't go quite the way I planned. I always sketch out a rough outline before I start writing, and although I've got a good idea of the beginning and end of a story, the middle is usually quite flexible. When I wrote the little scene with Erin at the beginning (who was originally called Elora), I thought it would be fun to bring her back later in the story, but until I got there, I had no idea she would play such a big part in Kai's life. I blame Netflix. I was watching a documentary on cults at the time.

Another year is nearly over, and these days, it seems that each year is worse than the last. Here's hoping that 2023 reverses that trend. A little peace for all mankind would be nice right about now. I hope that 2023 brings you all that you're hoping for.

I'm almost ready to hit "publish" and head back to my writing cave. I've written four of next year's books already—Blurred Lines and Hard Limits in the Blackstone House series, Phantom in the Blackwood Security series, plus another little Blackwood story I can't say too much about at the moment. Next up on my list are Sara's book in the Baldwin's Shore series and another Blackwood vs. Baldwin's Shore crossover.

Thanks so much for reading!

Until next time…

Elise

ALSO BY ELISE NOBLE

Blackwood Security

For the Love of Animals (Nate & Carmen - Prequel)

Black is My Heart (Diamond & Snow - Prequel)

Pitch Black

Into the Black

Forever Black

Gold Rush

Gray is My Heart

Neon (novella)

Out of the Blue

Ultraviolet

Glitter (novella)

Red Alert

White Hot

Sphere (novella)

The Scarlet Affair

Spirit (novella)

Quicksilver

The Girl with the Emerald Ring

Red After Dark

When the Shadows Fall

Phantom (novella) (2023)

Pretties in Pink

Chimera

Secret Weapon (Crossover with Baldwin's Shore)

The Devil and the Deep Blue Sea (2023)

Blackwood Elements

Oxygen

Lithium

Carbon

Rhodium

Platinum

Lead

Copper

Bronze

Nickel

Hydrogen

Blackwood UK

Joker in the Pack

Cherry on Top

Roses are Dead

Shallow Graves

Indigo Rain

Pass the Parcel (TBA)

Blackwood Casefiles

Stolen Hearts

Burning Love (TBA)

Baldwin's Shore

Dirty Little Secrets

Secrets, Lies, and Family Ties

Buried Secrets

Secret Weapon (Crossover with Blackwood Security)

A Secret to Die For (2023)

Blackstone House

Hard Lines

Blurred Lines (novella) (2023)

Hard Tide (2022)

Hard Limits (2023)

Hard Luck (TBA)

The Electi

Cursed

Spooked

Possessed

Demented

Judged

The Planes

A Vampire in Vegas

A Devil in the Dark (TBA)

The Trouble Series

Trouble in Paradise

Nothing but Trouble

24 Hours of Trouble

Standalone

Life

Coco du Ciel

A Very Happy Christmas (novella)

Twisted (short stories)

Books with clean versions available (no swearing and no on-

the-page sex)

Pitch Black

Into the Black

Forever Black

Gold Rush

Gray is My Heart

Audiobooks

Black is My Heart (Diamond & Snow - Prequel)

Pitch Black

Into the Black

Forever Black

Gold Rush

Gray is My Heart

Neon (novella)